THE CHORISTER AT THE ABBEY

A gripping cozy murder mystery full of twists

LIS HOWELL

Suzy Spencer Book 2

Revised edition 2021
Joffe Books, London
www.joffebooks.com

First published in Great Britain in 2008

ISBN: 978-1-78931-671-1

1

He sitteth lurking in the thievish corners of the streets,
and privily in his lurking dens doth he murder the innocent.
Psalm 10:8

It was five o'clock on the Friday before Christmas when Tom
Firth left the carol service rehearsal. He stood on the Abbey
steps in the misty evening, trying to make up his mind what
to do. Should he go for a drink with some of the singers from
the Abbey Chorus, or go back to Norbridge College where
he was a student?

'Cheerio, Tom.'

'Bye, Tom.'

Frantic brightness buzzed from the shopping mall, cut-
ting through the drizzle. Office parties spilt onto the pavement from the pub, despite the damp. But, set back from
the high street, the biscuit-brown Abbey seemed dunked in
the wintry evening. The only lights were those sprinkled like
sugar on the Christmas tree in the porch. Here, the unique
hiatus of the holiday had already descended. Soon the rest
of the world would press the pause button, and the special
atmosphere of the Abbey would take over.

'Goodnight, Tom!'

The last of the choristers were coming out now, testing the air. Some started wandering towards the Crown and Thistle pub, and others hurried away to the shops. The Chorus members were all enthusiastic amateurs who sang at special concerts as an adjunct to the Abbey choir. Most had taken the afternoon off work for the extra rehearsal. The carol service, traditionally held in the Abbey on Christmas Eve, would be the highlight of their winter schedule.

'Not going for a drink, eh, Tom?' a jeering older male voice called.

Tom shrugged and looked into the distance.

'Got better things to do, eh? Is it a lass? Some girls will fancy anything!' It was Morris Little, leader of the bass singers.

Robert Clark, another middle-aged bass, added quickly, 'See you later, Tom, if you want to get away.'

The boy glanced gratefully at Robert Clark, but still looked indecisively towards the lane that ran round the Abbey to the college.

'Suit yourself then!' Morris Little called crabbily to Tom; then he turned to Robert and said loudly, 'You've got to ask why he sings with us. How old is he? Eighteen or something? He must be up himself, or downright peculiar!'

'No, Morris, you're wrong,' Robert said, aware that Tom was listening, and that Morris knew it. 'Lots of kids have hobbies. My stepson has friends who are into all sorts of obscure things and plays jazz saxophone himself.'

'Sax and drugs and rock and roll, eh?' Morris sniggered. He started to walk away.

Tom Firth was mooching off in the opposite direction. The boy's long legs seemed too thin to hold him up and his hunched shoulders were topped by a squashy hat pulled over his ears. He looked just like all the other gangly youths in the town, Robert Clark thought. But Tom had a remarkably mature tenor voice and he was a gifted sight reader, one of the best singers in the Abbey Chorus. Robert had noticed him in the corridors of Norbridge College. They would both nod briefly at each other, Tom pink with embarrassment in case his mates saw him being greeted by a lecturer.

Robert was waiting for Edwin Armstrong, the Chorus secretary, who was last to leave the rehearsal. Edwin stood on the steps, running his hands through his long dark hair. He decided it wasn't wet enough for his umbrella, and pulled up the collar of his jacket.

'Where's Tom gone?' he asked.

'Back to the college, I think,' Robert said.

'Oh, that's a pity.'

Edwin had been hoping for a word with Tom Firth. The boy had real ability but he wasn't studying music. His parents had insisted he took subjects which they thought more practical. Edwin was Deputy Head of the Music Department at Norbridge College, and he would have liked to persuade Tom to change courses. But he had been slow to approach him. Despite being much younger, Edwin lacked Robert Clark's easy manner with the students.

'And has Morris gone too?' Edwin asked warily.

'He said something about having a drink, but I don't know where.'

Edwin raised his eyebrows; Robert nodded in guilty collusion. They walked towards the lights of the Crown and Thistle, knowing that Morris Little preferred the smarter Norbridge Arms Hotel where the town's business people went. Morris owned a thriving convenience store in Uplands village on the edge of the town, and everybody in Norbridge knew him. But as he had grown older and more successful, Morris had become increasingly intolerant, believing himself to be the greatest living expert on old Norbridge. Nowadays, even during the Christmas rush, he left his long-suffering wife to run their shop while he indulged in his interests — choral singing, local history and baiting people who he said were 'up themselves'. That was one of Morris's favourite phrases. Even poor young Tom Firth was taunted for his talent!

But with luck we've escaped from Morris tonight, Robert thought.

'So you've got time for a pint?' he asked Edwin.

'A quick one.'

Edwin followed Robert through the wooden doors of the pub where the stained glass emblems joined England and Scotland in a rare warm glow. This was Border country. The Crown and Thistle had stood at the edge of the Abbey Close for over two hundred years, protected from invaders by the sandstone tower at the end of the high street. Norbridge Keep was now surrounded by neat civic parkland. But the town had a violent history. It had been built for defence, in a valley where the Tarn River broadened out, before melting into the muddy Solway plain to meet the Eden near Carlisle. There were views over flatlands on three sides, and shelter from the rocky Pennines in the east. The villages of Uplands to the south, Fellside to the west and Tarnfield to the north hung on to Norbridge's skirts. It was the only place for miles with chain stores or a supermarket, but in winter the town centre still attracted a ghostly lingering fog, hardly dispersed by the bright lights.

But in the glow of the Crown and Thistle it was easy to forget the dank weather, or to enjoy the cosy contrast.

Robert sipped his half of bitter. 'So you're off out later?' he asked Edwin.

'Yes, the Cliffords have invited me over for supper. And I'm supposed to be giving someone a lift there. It's a woman called Alex Gibson in the Finance Department at the college. Do you know her?'

'No, never heard of her.'

'She's working late tonight so I'm going back to get her.' Edwin smiled ruefully, hoping this unknown woman wasn't another of his half-sister's attempts at matchmaking. But Alex Gibson sounded more like one of Lynn Clifford's lame ducks than a blind date. Lynn was always taking needy people under her wing. Even so Edwin was looking forward to the evening. He enjoyed the occasional exposure to family life which he got at the Cliffords'. He and Lynn had always been close, even though she was more than ten years older than he was. And a swift pint now was just what was needed after all that singing. Then he would walk back to the college, finish some last-minute work, pick up this Gibson woman and drive her over to Uplands, where Lynn and Neil Clifford lived.

* * *

Outside the pub in the Abbey Close, the mist was thickening. Young Tom Firth shambled out into the busy thoroughfare on the other side, towards the college. He pulled his brown woolly scarf around his throat and scurried between the cars that chugged into the town for last-minute attempts to park at the nearby multi-storey.

Dodging the shoppers, he hurried towards the college entrance, flashed his student ID card at the bored security guard, and tried to swipe his way in at the barrier before he realized it was open. What a plonker folk would think he was!

Not that he met many people. The Frost brothers, in their hooded jackets, were lurking in the stairwell with a couple of their gang, but Tom avoided them. A grumpy woman he recognized from the Finance Office glared at him as she went past, clutching paperwork. He went upstairs to his department and sidled past the office to the smallest of the brightly lit computer labs. He was the only person in the place. Tom sat down and logged on.

Email blossomed on to the screen; he pounded in his password and pressed 'enter'.

And he wasn't a plonker after all! His skin cells tingled as they sang the 'Hallelujah Chorus'. But the screen only told him that Chloe Clifford had replied. She had gone to university in September, while Tom stayed in Norbridge retaking his exams after a disastrous attempt in the summer. But now she was back for Christmas. They had both been singers as kids, in the church choir in Uplands village. Chloe was an all-round high-flyer from a middle-class background whereas Tom's talent was a one-off. He wasn't from a musical home unless you counted his dad's passion for Waylon Jennings, and the posh kids had sometimes intimidated him. But he was getting braver these days.

So he had emailed Chloe Clifford in a moment of madness. Now that she was home for Christmas, maybe she would say yes to seeing him . . . weirder things had happened!

He pressed the button.

Un-stonking-believable!!! She'd agreed. She'd love to meet. His head pounded with a Gloria.

My mum and dad are having a family dinner party tonight with Uncle Edwin and some woman from the college, Chloe had written, *so I'm grounded later, but I'm shopping with Poppy Robinson and we'll be in the Mitre Lounge at about five thirty*.

It was now five twenty. Tom stood up, sat down again, logged out, grabbed his coat, caught his scarf on the keyboard, and felt a familiar churning in his guts. It was the excitement. He left the computer lab, turned down the corridor past the Music Department and into the Gents. It wasn't one he normally used because it was old and shabby; he liked the toilets on the ground floor better. But this was a bit of an emergency.

A few minutes later he was wiping his hands on his trousers, despairing of the stupid hot air dryer, when the lights went out.

He stumbled towards the door, catching his hip on the angle of a basin. He felt the darkness press on him as if someone had wrapped a scarf round his eyes and blindfolded him. He had never before experienced total lack of light and he knew his eyes were working feverishly to find a pinprick.

When he pulled the door open, there was still no light source. Tom felt a need to shout for help, but at the same time he told himself not to be stupid: it was just a power cut. He was unnerved by how disorientated he felt.

To his surprise, as he probed along the wall, he found a doorway he'd either forgotten about or ignored in the past. He had a vague idea it might lead to the Music Department. He'd once thought of applying to study there, but his dad had laughed at him. Perhaps the lights would be on in there.

'Hello?' he called nervously. His voice sounded like a stupid kid's.

Why did this have to happen when he was in a hurry? He stretched out his long thin arm. The door opened, giving him a scary sense of falling into space. Then his foot hit something soft but heavy, like a bag of clothes. As his boot impacted he became aware of a sweetish but unpleasant smell. Perhaps the best thing to do was to bend down and move the bundle out of the way — probably someone had left a backpack. But his hand hit something which he knew at once was warm, wet skin. And he cried out, an involuntary yelp.

The lights burst on in the corridor and he found himself looking down at his hand, covered in bright red blood.

This time Tom yelled as loud as he could.

2

I am clean forgotten, as a dead man out of mind; I
am become like a broken vessel.
Psalm 31.14

At five past six that evening, Lynn Clifford heard the front
door open. But her daughter bounded straight up the stairs
without coming into the kitchen to say hello. Lynn stripped
off her rubber gloves and went into the hall.

'Chloe?' she shouted. Then in the gloom of the hallway
she saw Chloe's best friend lurking in the dark by the front
door. 'Oh, hello, Poppy. Was that Chloe going upstairs?'

'Yes, Mrs Clifford.'

Lynn Clifford sighed. 'I hope she's not thinking of going
out again,' she said, 'because I could do with some help with
the supper.' Lynn usually sang in the Abbey Chorus like her
half-brother Edwin, but she had missed the carol service
rehearsal to make the dinner.

The dumpy girl by the door looked uncomfortable and
shifted from foot to foot. Unlike Chloe, Poppy Robinson
wore sensible shoes, a proper coat and woolly hat. Chloe had
gone out in a tiny little bum-freezer jacket which threatened
to show inches of naked puppy fat even in December.

Lynn felt sorry for her daughter's best mate. They were at different universities now, Chloe in Leeds and Poppy closer to home in Newcastle, but they had kept in touch through email, phone texts and messaging. Although Poppy frequently came back for weekends and was a less flamboyant type, the moment Chloe had flounced in from the station — all tight jeans and chunky jewellery — Poppy had been like a rabbit in headlights.

Lynn checked the time as she peered through the unlit hall at the grey face of the grandfather clock. 'Aren't you back earlier than you thought?' she questioned Poppy.

'Er, yeah, Mrs Clifford. We were going to meet someone but he didn't turn up.'

So that explained Chloe's angry stomping upstairs. Her daughter didn't like to be crossed, and since she had been a tiny child Lynn had been terrified of rowing with her. She wondered who had let them down. Nick or Seth or Sam? She tried to remember the boys who had traipsed through the house behind Chloe the previous summer.

'Who were you supposed to be meeting?' she couldn't resist asking.

'Tom Firth,' Poppy mumbled.

Tom Firth! Well! Chloe had always acted as if Tom was a minor accessory, but Lynn rather liked him. He was just as gauche as the rest of them, but he had a warm smile and chocolate brown eyes. He appreciated classical music, too. Lynn had seen him at the Abbey Chorus rehearsals. And earlier in the summer she had been playing a CD in the kitchen when Chloe's friends had been in the garden lounging about, 'chilling'. Tom had drifted by and had said, 'Mmm, Bach's Magnificat. Very nice,' and then edged away in embarrassment, clutching the ice tray he'd been sent to fetch.

Lynn had been surprised to hear he'd failed his exams. Chloe had said tartly, 'Well, what do you expect when people's *parents* pressure them to study the wrong things!'

A noise of stamping boots on the landing accompanied by the jangle of cosmetic ironmongery meant Chloe was heading for the stairs.

'I've got it, Pops,' she called.

'Got what?' asked Chloe's mother.

There was a slight pause while Chloe rallied. 'My extra money,' she said. She stood on the landing, ready for a confrontation.

'And you're thinking of going out again?' Lynn enquired calmly.

'Yes, I am actually.'

Lynn sighed without showing it. What was she to do now? She genuinely wanted Chloe's help with the meal, and she also wanted to get half an hour alone with her daughter. They'd always had a good relationship in the past — or so she believed — at least before Chloe went to university. But now there was something wrong.

'Look, darling, if you can get back before seven thirty it would be wonderful. You could give me a hand. Then you'll be here when Uncle Edwin arrives.'

'God, must I?' the girl said harshly, and clattered down the stairs, gathering Poppy in her wake, before slamming the front door behind her.

* * *

A couple of hours earlier, the Finance Director at Norbridge College had emerged from his glass bowl office and called to his last remaining clerk.

'I'm off, Alex. D'you know how long you'll be?'

'An hour at least. Probably more. I'm still finishing sorting out all the expenses cheques. I can do some later but I need to rush with these for the Music Department. You know what the new boss is like.'

It was infuriating. This was the first time in ages that Alex Gibson had been invited out for supper. She was almost looking forward to going to the Cliffords' — though it would be too late for her to get home to Fellside to change, especially as she no longer drove. She was getting a lift there, and she had hoped to grab some time before leaving the college to get washed and changed in the Ladies, and even perhaps apply some make-up and look halfway decent. But work had been piled on. With all these last-minute cheques there wasn't much chance of smartening up.

But there wasn't much chance anyway, if Alex was honest. Dressing up was a joke. Living with her mother had hardly been conducive to wearing high fashion. She'd searched out one of her old kaftans and stuffed it into a bag for the evening at the Cliffords'. It was already creased, because her mum's ancient iron had seized up with brown lumpy water and spat it out all over the black cotton before blowing up. And she hadn't bothered to go to the hairdresser's since her mother's funeral. Nowadays she just pulled her grey hair back off her face and put it in a clip on top of her head. It made her face look really round, but did that matter? She pushed up her heavy old-fashioned glasses, another legacy from her mother. They kept slipping and had given her an ugly red weal on the bridge of her nose. She knew she was a mess. She had been struggling to get over the disaster of her sordid divorce, when her mother's death had knocked her back. It was one more awful thing. Had anyone asked, she would have said she was prepared for the death of an eighty-year-old woman with infuriating dementia. But it was the last straw.

Losing a parent was more universal than having a baby, but no one talked about the devastating effect it could have. Particularly if life had already taken a wrong turn. And though she knew it happened to everyone, Alex felt totally alone. Was it worse for her because she was childless? She was becoming increasingly bitter about it all. With her mother's death, she felt as if she had lost the one unconditional support she had ever had. Even in her mental decline, her mum had been full of shrewd good sense. Alex had been drinking too much already — but, without Mum to say 'You'll be the size of a house if you go on guzzling!' the wine and spirits in the evening had taken the place of any social life she might have had. Once, she thought ruefully, she had been vibrant,

successful, happy. The Golden Age is always over, by definition, she had thought in a moment of insight.

When her marriage had broken up in disaster and
humiliation, Alex had slunk away from London, back to
Cumbria, on the edge of a breakdown and desperate to keep a
low profile, after more than twenty years away. She had been
brought up in Workhaven on the coast, but her mother had
retired to Fellside, near Norbridge, a few years earlier. Her
sister and brother-in-law lived locally but they were intent
on maintaining their own lifestyle without a burdensome
relative. Alex knew hardly anyone. The only person she had
recognized in Norbridge was someone she had met at a conference years before, in London, and she had no intention of
remaking his acquaintance.

Apart from her sister's occasional dutiful invitations, the
kindly Cliffords were the first people to ask her to their home
in ages.

Her boss's remarks cut in. 'The Music Department's
probably deserted. I bet they've already left for Christmas.
This place is like the *Marie Celeste*.'

'Well, that's up to them. But if the new music head has
her cheque ready by five thirty, at least she can't blame me.'

'OK. Suit yourself. But I'm going.'

Alex was not gifted as an accounts clerk, but she was
extremely diligent. Her boss occasionally wondered what it
was she had to prove. He'd taken her on as a temp a few
months before, and she had stayed, plodding along, doing
the tedious jobs and rarely speaking. But she was awesomely
thorough.

Alex sighed, and checked all the expenses chits once
again. She was amused to see that Wanda Wisley, the new
Head of Music, had high expenses for the last month,
whereas Edwin Armstrong, her deputy, had hardly recharged
anything. That was interesting. Edwin would be giving Alex a
lift to the supper party that evening. He was Lynn Clifford's
younger half-brother, or something, she thought. He was
good-looking in a morose way. Alex had noticed him around

the college, and someone had told her he was an expert on choral music. Once, that would have intrigued her and she would have looked forward to chatting with him. But now, Alex just had to make sure she looked presentable, said the minimum, and didn't drink too much — until she got home.

She was suddenly aware how silent the office was. A few shiny decorations twirled pointlessly in the draught from under the door. There were some dirty, abandoned coffee cups on another desk and the remnants of a box of cheap mince pies. Although she had already eaten four, Alex got up and helped herself to a slice of greasy pastry. It was supposed to be comfort eating, except it brought no comfort. Nothing did.

She grabbed her old, bulging shoulder bag. There was no way she was leaving it in the empty office while she went on her rounds. It occurred to her that her boss hadn't even said 'Merry Christmas', though he would be off now for the holidays. The thought propelled her into a fugue of self-pity.

I'm a non-person, she thought bitterly, a fat frump who is functional at best. Is this how depression feels? Her doctor had suggested treatment, but she'd been unresponsive. There was nothing anyone could do. It wasn't necessary to try and analyse what was wrong. It was obvious anyway. Her life had ended in two stages: first when her marriage collapsed and she left London, and then again when her mother died. This was just some sort of existence, dragging on from day to day with no one giving a monkey's.

Except the Cliffords, and that was just pity of course.

'I'm still here,' she said to the security clerk at reception. 'I'm just going over to Music, but I'll come back.'

'OK,' said the guard, hardly looking up.

She delivered the signed cheques in their sealed envelopes to the in-tray in the Music Department. The office door had been left open but it was empty, and really rather sinister, with a raucous CD blaring out cheap Christmas schmaltz on someone's computer. The noise was horrible, shrieking and distorted. Half a bottle of red wine and some coagulating fruitcake sat unwanted on a desk. For a moment, Alex was tempted to grab some cake and take a swig, but thought better of it. Then she started to make her way out.

She was just outside the office when the lights went out. She stayed absolutely motionless for what seemed an age, aware of how utterly silent it all was. Just as she was getting accustomed to it and thinking of groping her way out, the lights snapped on and she hurried towards the double doors.

The noise of the boy wailing reached her long before she saw him.

3

Behold, how good and joyful a thing it is, brethren,
to dwell together in unity!
Psalm 133:1

In the town centre, Wanda Wisley, the new and controversial Head of Music at Norbridge College, stood in the middle of the Cloister Centre shopping mall and looked angrily at her watch. Ten to six. She'd escaped from the department to do some shopping and she was furious. Where the hell was Freddie? She had so many bags, she had to put them down. And one was from McCrea's, the dreariest shop in Cumbria. What was she doing, toting carrier bags from Norbridge's dated department store? So much for her image!

Of course it was Freddie's fault. He'd spotted a garish waistcoat in McCrea's that he just had to have. Who would have thought that an ageing German rock star with a ponytail and interesting tattoos would have become such a liability? But Norbridge had brought out an alarming rusticity in him.

'Oh wow!' Freddie would exclaim. 'Little calves!' Or, 'Oh Wanda, look — home-made chutney!'

He'd become addicted to farmers' markets and Women's Institute stalls. He sounded far more German than he ever had before, when they'd lived in London and New York. Well, if she was honest, they hadn't really lived in New York. But a few years ago Freddie had had a couple of gigs playing in the Village and Wanda had gone along for the ride. It had probably been the high point of their relationship.

'Where are you, Freddie?' she murmured through clenched teeth.

She saw the Principal of Norbridge College in the distance, with his wife in a particularly smart coat that looked like Bruno Magli. Bugger. Who'd have thought it! Wanda struggled to wave, while holding her mobile and her classy Fiorentina bag. She refused to put it down anywhere near the grasping mitts of Norbridge's fast-fingered juveniles.

'Hi there!' she warbled, but the Principal had waved and moved on. Wanda felt stupid and looked around guardedly.

Norbridge might be an attractive market town but it had its fair share of hooded louts, all more rodent-like than their larger, bejewelled, exotic London equivalents. She had seen the notorious Frost brothers lurking round the college when she had sneaked away early that afternoon. She had been so anxious to escape that she'd left without her expenses cheque. She'd hurried past the Frosts in reception; with their red hair and white hatchet-shaped faces, they looked subhuman to her. They worried her far more than the gobby louts at home. Not that there were many louts in Notting Hill now it was so smart, thank God.

The Principal had disappeared down one of the lanes. It would have been really useful to have a word with him about the problem of menacing youths hanging round the department. Not to mention the terrible facilities she was supposed to cope with.

'You're an unusual choice for the job,' the Principal had said when he offered her the post. 'I must be honest, the obvious candidate withdrew. It's going to take drive to make it work, but I think you've got it!'

Too right. The sole person who seemed able to fix any-thing in Norbridge was Edwin Armstrong, her deputy. Of course he thought he should have got her job, but there was some story about his pulling out at the last minute. Ambition interruptus, Wanda thought. Edwin probably didn't have the balls. Well, he didn't have the job, either. And it was her role to kick ass. His.

'Wanda!' Freddie leapt up behind her and landed a sharp little bite on the back of her neck.

Wanda turned on him. 'I've told you: don't do things like that, Freddie. Not here.'

'*Ach*, teacher — you've become terrifically conventional all of a sudden! Me too! Look!' he said, and flashed open his full-length leather Barbour-style coat. Inside he was wearing a ghastly yellow waistcoat. 'I just had to go back to McCrea's and pick it up!'

'Freddie, that is truly gross.'

'Not for when I join the huntsmen! I'm a country-man now! We're a celebrity couple. I *looove* it so much here, Wanda!'

'Don't be ridiculous. And keep your voice down. Give me a hand with all the bags. I've been frozen waiting.'

'So, a coffee calls my *Lieblich*.'

Freddie, who was an imposing man, turned around with his huge coat flapping and ploughed a way through the crowds towards Figaro's Coffee House. He had taken to the naughty side of Norbridge like a duck to water, becoming the aged *enfant terrible*, beloved of both students and their parents who saw him as the acceptable face of creativity — especially when compared with his sharp and successful female partner. More than one dad had sidled up to confide about a misspent youth smoking dope, or a brief, heady time in a band. A few had even bought Freddie's album, *Fabrikant's Factory*, in the old days. After fearing he would be on the fringes, Freddie Fabrikant was really enjoying himself.

'Cappuccino, Wanda? With skimmed milk for your waist-line?' Freddie laughed heartily and others smiled with him.

She nodded, trying not to show her irritation. She hated going to Figaro's. Freddie waved cheerily to people, greeting them all expansively as if he was some mad lord of the manor.

Wanda Wisley sank into the sofa. She closed her eyes. They would be in London in twenty-four hours, at her flat. I've got to get out of here, even if only for a fortnight, she thought. It would be awful to be reduced to just getting to Town for the odd concert or, God forbid, a 'show'. Look at pathetic Edwin Armstrong, once a budding composer, now nearly forty and marooned in Norbridge. It was too frightening.

'Wanda!' Freddie's loud voice boomed at her from the counter where he was still waiting for his latte laced with reindeer droppings — or whatever muck she thought he was ordering.

'Wanda, can't you hear? Your phone's ringing.' Freddie had famously acute hearing, honed rather than blunted by the recording studios. Postproduction and synthesizing was his thing. He hadn't been very successful with live gigs. Not enough real energy.

Wanda fumbled in the Fiorentina bag and found her phone. As she listened she felt suddenly sick, the hot steamy smell of coffee and milk making her nauseous. The message was telling her to call North Cumbria police. Urgently. In connection with a problem at the college.

Had there been a break-in? Or was one of the students in serious trouble? Wanda had become aware that Norbridge was a place of undercurrents. The curious smiles she had taken for bucolic friendliness had hardened into blank looks, or even sniggers behind her back. Freddie understood country life much better than she did. But he would be no help in anything where the police were involved.

She scrolled through the numbers on her address list. She had never expected to use this one, but she had no option. She pressed the call button to connect her to Edwin Armstrong's mobile.

Whatever the problem was at the college, she knew it was serious, and she didn't want to go there.

* * *

At seven thirty, Suzy Spencer arrived home in Tarnfield, tired and irritable. She'd driven back from Tyneside after an exacting day in the TV studio working on the Christmas special *I'm a Geordie, Get Me Out of Here*. The title was a bit dated but the show worked well — though it was fraught to produce. It was about people from the north-east of England who'd moved to more exotic locations and still had a hankering for home.

'That bloody director. I've had it up to here with men!' she snapped.

'You must be very athletic then,' said Robert Clark.

Suzy flung her handbag at him, just missing the *Daily Telegraph* he was reading. He'd arrived home himself an hour earlier. She ran her hand through her spiky fair hair and tipped her coat untidily over the end of the banisters.

'Get lost, smart-arse. I'm going into the kitchen. Where's Jake?' Jake was her son, just turned fifteen.

'There was a note to say he's round at Oliver's for, would you believe, a "jam session". He said Ollie's dad would drop him back later.'

'And Molly got away to the Brownies' Christmas party?'

'Yep. There was a note from the childminder saying she went off safely.' Molly was Suzy's eight-year-old daughter. Tarnfield kids were almost all car-dependent, with elaborate rotas for driving them to activities in Norbridge, Carlisle and even Newcastle. Suzy was always on edge about Molly's safety.

'Have you already had a drink?' she asked Robert.

'Yes, I stopped for a quick half with Edwin Armstrong.'

'How is he? All geared up for the carol service? Or still depressed about his new boss?'

'I think he's getting used to her.' Robert got up and followed her into the kitchen where he put his arms round Suzy and kissed her. Usually, these days, the old house was full of kids. But there was peace and quiet in the kitchen for once.

'And how was the Chorus?'

'Morris Little was his usual irritating self.'

'Sounds like you could do with some wine,' Suzy whispered. 'I'm gagging for some.'

She moved a pile of half-finished home-made Christmas cards from the table and picked up a bottle of wine from the wobbly new rack in the corner. When she had moved into Robert's house, The Briars had been dusty but impeccably tidy. Robert, a childless widower whose wife Mary had been a supreme Good Housekeeper, had lived on ready meals, tinned soup, and egg and bacon sandwiches after she died. Now the residue of family life was spread across every surface.

Robert opened the red wine. 'Something funny happened this evening.'

'What?'

'When I was talking to Morris Little, I called Jake my stepson.'

'So?'

'Well, I've never thought of Jake in that way.'

'I shouldn't worry about it. Morris probably didn't notice. Why were you talking about Jake?'

'Oh, Morris was getting at poor Tom Firth for being interested in church music at his age. Tormenting as usual!'

'I thought Morris got obsessed with things himself.'

'Yes, but he's an adult. He seems to think all kids are ignorant louts like the Frost brothers.'

Suzy rolled her eyes. She had only met Morris Little once, at a drinks party after an Abbey Chorus concert. He had pinned her against the wall and lectured her on a derelict nineteenth-century convent in Fellside, which he wanted listed as a Norbridge monument. He had inundated her with information and been childishly crude about nuns.

She remembered him jabbing her in the shoulder when her attention had wandered, before making snide remarks about career women being too tired to concentrate. Sexist bore!

'Anyway, you're right,' Robert was saying. 'Morris has been going on about the choir singing something by John Stainer. He keeps hinting mysteriously that he knows of some local connection. But I haven't heard of one and neither has Edwin.'

'Stainer the Victorian composer? Wrote *The Crucifixion* or something?'

'How did you know?'

'I don't think classical music is Elton John, you know!'

They moved back into the sitting room, where Robert stooped down to light the real log fire in the big, tiled fireplace. Suzy looked round the room and waited for the warm glow to bring it alive.

She had come to love The Briars, though she had moved there as an emergency measure at first. She and Robert had met during a disturbing time in Tarnfield eighteen months earlier, when several people had died and Suzy, a townie, had found herself in the middle of a country life dream which had become a nightmare. She and her husband Nigel had already been splitting up and she had agreed to sell their modern family house on the edge of Tarnfield so Nigel could buy the smart flat he was renting in Newcastle. Suzy had considered moving back home to Manchester, or buying a smaller place in Norbridge. But she had just met Robert — and also landed a lucrative contract at Tynedale TV. So when Robert suggested that she decamp to The Briars, she did — with the kids, the cat, her battered furniture, and no intention of staying.

But a year later they were all still there, including the cat.

'Are you going over to the church tomorrow?' Robert asked her over his shoulder as he messed about with the paper and kindling.

'Yeah,' Suzy nodded. 'Can't escape. It's village life, as you always tell me!'

Most people in Tarnfield had been corralled into help-ing at All Saints Church over Christmas. Suzy had always been a helper at the church, if rather a sceptical one. And she had genuinely warmed to the new female vicar.

'There are preparations to do for the Christingle service,' Suzy explained. 'Oh, and that reminds me, Jake wants to go up to Fellside Fellowship sometime over the holiday. It's that jazz and rock "big band" they're running. He reckons he might be able to play with them.'

Robert groaned.

'Oh, come on, you old fart,' Suzy laughed. 'It sounds quite nice for young people, and I'm pleased Jake is taking an interest. Beats going over to Oliver's to mess about in "jam sessions" in the barn and read dirty magazines. Anyway, if you don't want to go, I'll take him.'

Robert knew Suzy was trying really hard with her teen-age son, and that she was under a lot of pressure from Jake's father. The Newcastle flat hadn't been glamorous enough for Nigel's trendy young girlfriend and they had recently sepa-rated. Hurt and resentful, Nigel was now on the prowl for problems. His ways of dealing with another man's role in his children's life were either to find fault, to ignore Robert's existence or to carp on about his age.

But Robert, stooping to arrange the sticks in the grate, was a fit man, with brownish hair and a warm smile. He seemed younger than his years. He knew Suzy was looking at him; he turned and smiled.

'I do love you, Suzy,' he said, conversationally.

'So you should. Oh, by the way . . .' Suzy said, talking to his back as he went on making the fire, 'I forgot to mention that I saw Lynn Clifford in Tesco's last night. She's having people over tonight, including Edwin and some new woman she's befriended. She asked us too, but I said we had to be in for when Molly gets back.'

For the first year or two after moving to Tarnfield, Suzy had been seriously lonely. But since living with Robert she had slowly met more people, including the Cliffords from

Uplands. Lynn was older than Suzy but she had been a great support. And from Lynn's uncritical kindness a real friendship had grown, though Suzy still found Lynn's marriage to Neil Clifford hard to understand. But then every marriage was a mystery, even when you were in it, Suzy thought. She was glad she was out of hers.

Robert interrupted her thoughts. 'You met Lynn Clifford in Tesco's? I thought you were against big supermarkets?'

'We all have our weaknesses. Mine is their new blueberry yoghurt.'

'So you have no principles!'

'Shut up or you won't either when I get my hands on them!'

Robert laughed. They had made a pact when Suzy moved in, never to take umbrage. Both had been in marriages where tension had ruled.

'Lynn was looking harassed,' Suzy said. 'I think Chloe's been a bit of handful since she came back from university for the holidays.'

'Well, it must be difficult when kids are away all term and then suddenly come home. We've got all that to come.'

Have we? thought Suzy in surprise. They never talked about Robert's relationship with her children, or discussed the next stage of their own relationship. The newspaper under the logs reared as the flames lifted it.

'I hope that's your bloody *Daily Telegraph*,' Suzy said. 'I don't know why we have it in the house.'

'You're right. Your *Guardian* burns better. More hot air, especially the media section.'

He grinned at her. And it was true: they could say anything to each other. But that didn't mean that they said *everything* — there was still a big silence on the subject of what would happen next. The sense that the Spencer family had moved in pro tem still lingered.

Just as well, Suzy thought. When Robert came over to join her on the sofa, she went back to living in the present, which was just about as much as she could deal with after the drama of the last few years. I don't want anything to change, Suzy thought. I have what I need, which is peace and stability. She felt Robert's arms round her, and the warmth of the flickering fire filled the room.

4

After Chloe and Poppy left to walk back into Norbridge, Lynn Clifford glanced again at the grandfather clock. There was no chance her daughter would be back home in Uplands for seven thirty. The dinner was a lot of work and she realized she had been a bit too ambitious with the starters. She sighed, went back into the kitchen and faced the disgusting mass of vegetable peelings on the counter.

'Oh no, not again!' she sighed, feeling suddenly bowed down with despair. She leant against the fridge freezer for coolness, as the heat spread from her collar bones and inflamed her head. Depression came first, then lack of breath, and then the need to rip any clothing away from her neck and face. The sticky sweat glands oozed perspiration which dripped into her eyes.

'Please God, let it stop,' Lynn heard herself begging, meaning it as a genuine prayer.

This time it had been brought on by Chloe's behaviour, but on other occasions Lynn had no idea what started it.

Most people said the hot flush phase 'would pass'. But it wasn't passing. No one understood, not even her husband Neil.

But of course she was lucky to have him. Morris Little, who ran Uplands village store, thought his wife's menopause was a joke for the customers. He would snigger, 'Ooh, look, Norma's blushing. Her toy-boy must've come in!' And Norma, small, spry and ceaselessly grafting, would laugh dutifully, even as her face went on fire to match her wiry red hair. No wonder she encouraged Morris to take up hobbies and get out of the shop!

The flush faded, leaving Lynn feeling grimy and tired, and she started peeling again. This supper party was her last chance to see her half-brother before the holiday. He was leaving the next day to go and spend Christmas with their parents in Yorkshire. Their father was a Norbridge man, but Lynn's stepmother had wanted to move back to Harrogate. Lynn was glad Edwin was taking on the dutiful son thing. She wasn't close to her stepmother. Lynn's own mother had died when she was five, after a long illness, and Lynn had always felt that mother–daughter relationships were a mystery. She had spent most of her childhood motherless and then she had been sidelined by her father's new wife.

Which was why it was astonishing that, from the moment her half-brother had come along, she had adored him. They had a lot in common, including a strong sense of Norbridge heritage, which made her often wonder why Edwin had never put down roots by having children himself. Lynn Clifford loved her daughter with a deep, understated passion for which she had no template.

'Don't you want kids?' she had asked Edwin once, after a few drinks.

'No . . . well, not since Marilyn left,' he said, and she knew better than to pursue it. His one great serious love affair with Marilyn Frost was a subject they never mentioned.

She hoped her brother wouldn't mind that she'd invited someone else to supper that evening. This time she wasn't matchmaking because Alex Gibson was obviously not a candidate. Alex was a quiet, sad middle-aged woman who was alone for the Christmas holiday in her bleak bungalow in Fellside and Lynn had been trying to be kind.

She sighed. Even so, she hoped Edwin wouldn't do his usual trick with single women. It was as if he wanted to put them off, with discouraging small talk on Stamford's anthems or Quaile Woods' settings for the Psalms. But at least there was no need to chat up Alex. And she worked at the college, and enjoyed choral music. Lynn had met her at the parish church in Uplands with its small choir and musical tradition. So perhaps some conversation might flow.

The front door banged. 'Is that you, sweetie?'

'Of course it is, Mum, who else?' her daughter shouted back, taut with irritation.

'Come and help me with the nibbles, Chloe.'

'Oh, for God's sake, Mother! I've got to get changed.' Feet thumped and clattered across the stairwell and Lynn heard the shower going full blast.

The bathroom door slammed angrily.

* * *

Five miles away, where Tarnfield nestled under the sandstone outcrops of the Pennines, the lights in The Briars' front room snapped on, eclipsing the flickering firelight. Suzy started looking for her trousers.

'That was an unexpected pleasure.' Robert Clark heaved himself up from the sofa and laughed. After his wife died he had never expected to resume a sex life, and he certainly hadn't expected to fit it round the Brownies' meeting in Norbridge, or a lads' rock band practice in the local barn. Robert was new to the juggling of child rearing.

Suzy was pulling on her jumper. 'Well, it was certainly a quickie! Would you believe it, we've even got time for a cup of coffee before Molly gets back!'

'That sounds good.'

'And I need it. I drank my wine and yours too! Anything to forget *I'm a Celebrity Bonnie Lad* or *When the Gloat Comes In* or whatever they're going to call the next series. I could do with some gossip about the college as a change from TV navel-gazing. Tell me more about Edwin's new boss.'

Robert followed Suzy into the kitchen. 'She's called Wanda Wisley. She's in her late thirties and she's quite formidable, apparently.'

'Oh yes. Of course.' Suzy raised her eyebrows. 'She's a woman in a position of power so she must be a monster. Been there, got the scars.'

Robert shrugged. 'OK. You don't have to tell me how women bosses get a bad press. Or not again. But this appointment really was rather an odd one.'

'You mean the job should have gone to Edwin?'

'No doubt about it! Seriously. Impeccable credentials, ten years' experience in Norbridge, research on church music. But he withdrew his application.'

'Did he? I didn't know that. Well, if he backed out, he can hardly complain about this new woman, can he?'

'I don't think he's complaining exactly. He's just upset that they've nothing in common.'

'So she's not keen on discussing communion settings over morning coffee?' Suzy had met Edwin a few times: she liked him and could see he was very handsome, but sometimes she thought his 'young fogey' manner rather contrived.

Robert laughed. 'Wanda Wisley made her name running a music trust for teenagers in Birmingham, but her real claim to fame was fronting that radio series on rock music for kids.'

'She sounds great!'

'Maybe — but she's throwing her weight around. She acts as if everyone in Norbridge is a bumpkin and treats Edwin as if he's completely irrelevant.'

'Yeah, well, he is a bit intense. The dark brooding look isn't really for me. Orlando Bloom with a hymn book! So why did he withdraw his application for head of department?'

'I don't really know . . .' Robert cuddled his coffee mug, aware suddenly of how dark and wet it now was outside the kitchen window, and how little he really knew Edwin.

'Perhaps he felt he couldn't compete?' Suzy suggested.

'Unlikely. Edwin is an expert on a lot of things. He's a great jazz pianist, he likes all sorts of choral music, and he's written some amazing stuff on the Psalms of David.'

'But that's hardly twenty-first century!'

'I don't know. Smiting and destroying. Sounds like TV entertainment.'

'Actually you're right — and that's just behind the scenes!'

Their eyes met; Robert smiled and Suzy grinned back. It was amazing that, despite a different attitude to politics, religion and rural life, he and Suzy were so close.

He could tell that her mind was already moving to the clock on the kitchen wall. Molly was due home, and soon Suzy would start to fret. Partly it was the twitch all mothers develop. But for Suzy it was intensified by the real danger which had threatened her children eighteen months earlier. Robert put the mugs in the sink and tried to distract her.

'So, looking forward to Christmas at The Briars?'

'Absolutely! But what about you? I don't know how you cope with us. Your life with Mary was so settled before, and living with us is madness. Thank you for putting up with us . . .'

'It's my pleasure. And equally unexpected.'

He hugged her.

* * *

Lynn Clifford sighed. Chloe was still in the bathroom. It was getting late. Where was everyone else? Neil was always busy at this time of year and might well be delayed, but Edwin was usually on time. Then the doorbell rang and, with relief, Lynn hurried into the hall. The uneven stone floor, with its bright red and orange runner and panelled walls, exuded warmth. The house was welcoming, and Lynn was smiling as she opened the door.

Edwin stood there, and with him was Alex Gibson. Alex's round moon face was white in the darkness, her big glasses like headlights. She was wearing her shapeless anorak, and a red velvet scarf which was tied in a miserable ratty knot round her neck.

Edwin said, 'Can you get us a drink, Lynn? We need to sit down.'

'What on earth is the matter?'

Alex stopped in the hallway. 'There's been a death at the college.'

'Alex found the body,' Edwin said quietly. 'Or rather, she found a boy with the body. Tom Firth.'

Chloe shrieked triumphantly from the landing. 'So that's why he wasn't at the Mitre! I didn't think he'd stand me up!'

'What?' Edwin sounded sharp.

'Tom was supposed to meet me and Poppy. But he didn't come.'

Edwin was fond of Chloe but her self-absorption, even for a teenager, surprised him. He was aware that Alex was becoming increasingly wobbly. She staggered slightly. For a moment they all stood, waiting for her to find her feet. Lynn reached out to put her arm round her.

'But who was it? The dead body?' Chloe was saying in a nagging voice as she bounded down the stairs. Edwin led Alex by the arm into the warmth of the living room.

'It was Morris Little,' he said over his shoulder.

5

The sorrows of death compassed me, and the overflowings
of ungodliness made me afraid.
Psalm 18:3

'Morris Little? Oh no!' Lynn's voice followed Edwin into the
sitting room. 'How dreadful! What happened?'

'He was attacked. The police think they've got the lads
who did it. The Frosts, of course. Who else?'

'Oh, how terrible! Edwin, this is awful. Chloe, call your
father at the church or on his mobile. If she's at home, I
need to go and see his wife straight away.' Lynn grabbed her
coat from the peg in the hall distractedly. 'How absolutely
dreadful. Edwin, can you hold the fort here with Chloe? Get
Alex a drink or something. Poor Norma!'

'But Mum . . .'

'Chloe, I need to get straight to Uplands store, and you
need to get hold of your father for me.'

'Yes, ma'am.'

Cliffords to the rescue as usual, Chloe thought. OK, it
was awful, but Morris Little was a grumpy old sod. And now
he'd got himself attacked and of course her marvellous capable parents were at the centre of everything as usual, while

she was left to do the boring stuff. Everyone else thought the Cliffords were so wonderful, except their daughter.

'Make yourselves at home, everyone,' she said sarcastically. 'I'll phone Dad.'

Teenagers were always last on the list, she thought angrily. Especially when your father was the rector!

* * *

In Tarnfield, the doorbell rang at The Briars. 'That will be Molly,' said Suzy in relief. She leapt to answer the door. Within seconds Robert could hear Molly's squeaks of excitement.

The phone rang at the same time, and Robert answered. It took a moment for him to recognize Edwin Armstrong's agitated voice. There had been an accident at the college. The police were at the scene. But could Robert help by coming to the rectory at Uplands?

Suzy entered the kitchen followed by Molly in her Brownie uniform, still talking, a mass of handmade Christmas decorations in her arms.

'Look, Rob, see what Molly has made!'

'They're great! Suzy, I have to go out.'

'Something serious?'

'I don't know.' Robert was keeping his voice down. 'Some sort of incident at the college. I've just been asked to help hold the fort by looking after someone at Uplands. I'm going over to the rectory to help. I won't be long.'

Molly was still talking, sorting her decorations on the table: '. . . and then, Mummy, we glued this bit to that bit . . .'

'That's lovely, sweetie . . . When will you be back, Robert?'

'I don't know. I'll call you.'

The last thing he saw as he backed out of the kitchen was the colourful pile of decorations littering the table, and Molly's upturned face, focusing on her mother who was giving her all her attention.

That was the dream family Christmas I wanted, thought Robert. But already he suspected it had been spoilt. Hurrying into the rain, through a sobering blast from the icy wind, he opened the car door, sank into his seat, and started the engine.

* * *

For Alex Gibson the first few jumbled minutes after their arrival at Uplands Rectory seemed to be happening to someone else. She was vaguely aware that Lynn Clifford had hurried out into the night. Then Edwin Armstrong's mobile rang. It was his boss, she realized, the dreaded Wanda Wisley, calling again for more information. As soon as he got rid of her, Edwin started phoning someone else, a friend of his, asking him to come over straight away.

I'm a non-person, Alex thought again. Things are being arranged round me. But this time it was worse than the usual self-pity. With a cold frisson that cut through the shock and brought her back to earth, she suddenly realized who Edwin had been calling.

'Listen, Alex.' Edwin was speaking to her slowly and carefully as if she was a child. 'Wanda Wisley wants me to go back to Norbridge to see the Head of Security at the college for her. A friend of mine, Robert Clark, says he'll come over and stay with you and Chloe. I don't feel I can leave you on your own.'

Robert Clark. Could this be happening? 'Oh . . . no. Please, there's no need for this. I'll be OK in a minute. Perhaps if I can have a drink?'

'Of course. I'll get Chloe to pour you one. You will stay the night here, won't you?'

Alex tried to shake her head but it was caught in a paroxysm. 'I'm all right,' she whispered. 'It was a bit grim but nothing I can't cope with. I ought to go home to Fellside.'

'But you've had a shock, and there's been the police questioning too. You ought to stay here. What would you like to drink?'

'Whisky, please.' She could stay for that. She needed it. But then she would escape.

Chloe called loudly from the room next door which served as the parish office, 'I've got Dad on the phone. Where's Tom Firth now, Uncle Edwin?'

'The police let him go. I should think his parents will have called the doctor. He was pretty shattered.'

'So what exactly happened to boring old Morris?' Chloe asked.

6

Break their teeth, O God, in their mouths.
Psalm 58:6

Alex Gibson spoke brusquely. 'There was a lot of blood. The boy had it on his hands.' She shuddered, remembering. Tom had been stunned, white-faced, and had been shrieking at her. It had never occurred to her that he might be the attacker. He seemed too distraught. She had cleaned his hands with some wipes from her bag, taken him by the shoulders and turned him away, into the wide corridor and down the stairs.

Tom had been making a strange noise, half sobbing and half crying out, and the security guard had come towards them from the desk. He had sat Tom down behind the counter and contacted his colleagues. Then the police and ambulance arrived, bringing the cold air with them, and suddenly the atmosphere had become official.

And while all this was going on, Tom had been whining softly and Alex had watched the goings-on distractedly, as if through a thick pane of glass. A half-amused little voice kept saying in her ear: so, this is shock again. You know all about this, Alex.

And then Edwin had arrived, supposedly to pick Alex up and take her to supper at the Cliffords'. By that time, things were becoming clearer.

'There was something about the body and a piece of wood. They were suddenly more interested in that, than in quizzing Tom,' Alex said to Chloe. She added firmly: 'Look, Edwin, I'm OK now. You ought to go.'

'I'll wait till Robert comes.'

'No, really.' Alex sounded more forceful. 'Please.' She mustn't see Robert Clark. As soon as Edwin had gone, she would leave too. She recognized the feeling of consciousness after a crisis, the strange mental tingling, as if blood were trickling back into numbed mental extremities. It hurt a bit but it meant you were returning to life. I don't want to be sitting here, she thought, with these concerned people, being the object of sympathy, waiting to face Robert Clark in this condition. It made her feel nauseous.

Edwin put his hand on her shoulder for a moment, but she felt rigid and determined.

'Do go, Edwin. I'll be fine.'

He decided not to argue. He needed to get back to the college or Wanda Wisley would have hysterics. It seemed the head of department had no intention of getting involved herself, so it was all down to him. Robert would arrive at the house soon. And Chloe was coping. Edwin glanced back at Alex, who had sipped her whisky and had her eyes shut. He slipped quietly away.

But when the front door shut behind him, Alex Gibson forced herself to focus, and stood up decisively. 'Thank you, Chloe,' she said, her voice suddenly authoritative. 'I'll go now. I think I'd be much better at home. I'm going to call Burns' Taxis to come and meet me at the end of your lane. You've all been very kind.'

Chloe nodded vaguely at her. She was already texting her friends.

Alex went out into the night, feeling the sleeting rain which had blown down from the fells, falling like needles on her unprotected hair. It was freezing now. She didn't care about waiting outside. The icy rain was almost cleansing, and when she got home she would be justified in opening a bottle of malt whisky and making very high-class hot toddies. Of course she would look like a drowned rat when the taxi came — but so what?

It was Christmas. She might not see anyone for days. It didn't matter if she caught a cold, and even less what she looked like. She trudged to the junction where the lane met the main road. In the distance she could see Morris Little's convenience store, still garishly lit up. She had often popped in when she changed buses at Uplands, on her long dreary journey home to the much bleaker village of Fellside. She was sorry he was dead, but in her opinion Morris Little had been a thoroughly unpleasant man.

But no one had bothered to ask her what she thought. She had just been the fat woman from Finance who'd found the boy and the body.

She tasted the watered-down rectory whisky on her tongue. Yuk.

Through the needling drizzle she heard the taxi approaching. She recognized the driver, a taciturn man, and she was grateful that she wouldn't have to talk. He knew her too, and where she lived. He grunted something which sounded like 'How do', did a neat three-point turn and took her off to Fellside, her bungalow . . . and a serious drink.

* * *

At midnight Robert Clark crawled into bed beside Suzy, who was immediately awake.

'So what happened?' she asked.

'Morris Little has been murdered. A violent attack.'

'Oh my God!' Suzy sat upright in bed and put the bed-side lamp on. 'Do they know who did it? Where was it?'

'He was found just inside the Music Department. One of the lads from the Chorus had gone over to the college to use the computers, and stumbled on Morris's body during a power cut.'

'How did he die?'

'He was beaten about the head. His teeth were staved in.'

'Good grief!'

When Robert had arrived at the rectory in response to Edwin's phone call, Chloe had told him that the other woman had gone home. His visit wasn't really necessary but he'd stayed there until Lynn and Neil returned from Norma Little's house. Chloe had retreated to her bedroom and her mobile phone.

'So do you know what happened?' Robert had asked Neil Clifford.

'It all seems cut and dried,' Neil had murmured. 'I've been to see Tom Firth, and Norma Little too. Norma won't accept it but the police think Morris had some sort of contretemps with a gang. The Frosts are being mentioned.'

The Frosts came from Chapterhouse, a sink estate on Norbridge's murky west side where the marshes crept up towards the town. It had always been the haunt of the tinkers and nomadic workers who had drifted between England and Scotland for centuries. It had been built up during the making of the canals which cut through the soggy coastal plain. And later the Victorian railway navvies turned the area into one of the roughest in Britain. In the 1960s, new jerry-built council housing had made it worse.

Now, back in the warmth of his own bedroom, Robert gave Suzy the gist of what he'd heard.

'Well, whaddaya know!' she said. 'Everything evil in Norbridge boils down to the Frosts, doesn't it? The local bad lads. What would we do without them?'

'Well, in this case, at least it means Tom Firth is off the hook. Neil heard that the police found half a plank flung outside the college. The Frost brothers had been seen messing about near the side door with the wood earlier. The police are hoping they'll get Frost fingerprints or DNA on the piece of wood.'

'But why would the Frosts kill Morris by hitting him with a plank?'

'There's building work at the college. There was timber lying about. And Morris apparently had a run-in with the Frost brothers more than once at his shop. They went in for a lot of petty thieving.'

Hardly surprising. Trying to do anything for the kids on the Chapterhouse estate was doomed to failure, and it was obvious, Robert supposed, that they would commit some sort of terrible crime sooner or later. But it seemed to him to be doubly sad. What made children turn out like that? They were hardly poor compared with kids in the Third World. Was it drugs? Or neglect? Drink? Or broken homes? Absent fathers? No role models?

Robert felt wound up. Ten minutes later he said suddenly, in the dark, 'I can't help thinking about how I was talking to Morris only this evening. I told him Jake was my stepson.'

'Oh yeah,' Suzy yawned sleepily. 'Just a form of words.' She wanted to drift into sleep.

'Maybe,' Robert said. 'But then again, maybe it would be better if Jake really was my stepson?'

'What?' Suzy snapped on the lamp again.

'I think we should get married.'

There was a long silence. Suzy looked at the wall in front of her. 'Robert, Jake is fine. Death makes everything seem all out of proportion. Anyway, the next few days are going to be really busy. We won't get a moment on our own to discuss it. Let's talk after Christmas.'

'OK,' he said softly.

His words hung over them both, heavier than the duvet. Suzy lay awake for a while. Then she whispered, 'I do love you, Robert Clark. But I can look after my children myself!'

But he had fallen asleep, shattered, and was too far away to hear her.

7

Leave off from wrath, and let go displeasure; fret not thyself,
else shalt thou be moved to do evil.
Psalm 37:8

In the last few days before Christmas, Tom Firth found himself the centre of attention. 'Oh Tom, how are you?' everyone said in the same solicitous voice. But they were saying it, not asking it. He had the feeling no one really cared. It was just a form of words.

'Oh, fine,' he would answer. And after a while, he *was* fine. But he felt different.

He had been hysterical at finding Morris Little's body, but very quickly the memory became familiar. He often found himself re-examining what he had seen, like probing a tooth socket, which wasn't surprising seeing that Morris's mouth had taken the brunt of the attack. One side of his jaw had been smashed, though Tom's counsellor had told him that death had come from the blow to Morris's temple.

Mrs Firth, a quiet woman who was a machinist in the last Norbridge textile mill, was off work for the Christmas closure, and followed her son around the house. They lived on the town side of Uplands.

'Are you sure you're OK?' she kept asking him. He wanted to say, 'I'd feel better if you got me a laptop,' but he knew that would be out of order.

The one person who hadn't made a huge fuss was Alex, the grumpy woman from Finance who had found him. She'd said hardly anything, but used loads of tissues from her big bag to wipe the blood off his hands. Then the police had come, and talked to him for what seemed like ages, and at last he'd gone home. Then the doctor had come out in person, and the rector had been to see him, and Tom had taken his first ever sleeping pill which had knocked him out and made him dopey all the next day. Despite the fact it was the weekend before Christmas, a student counsellor had come to see him at home, and that had made him feel better. Afterwards he watched non-stop DVDs. Making it into a story had lessened it somehow. Everyone had been really interested, except of course his dad.

Tom's father already found his son embarrassing. Mick Firth thought there was nothing wrong with being into bands and going to gigs — but the church business was creepy. At least Tom wasn't a shirt-lifter, if the magazines under his bed were anything to go by. That was a relief. Still, the way people were coming round and cosseting him would be enough to turn any lad into a sissy. Mick Firth, who was a truck driver, had no time for counsellors and women police officers and vicars!

'You'll get over it, lad,' he said to Tom the next day. 'Pull yourself together. I've seen some nasty road accidents in my time. What you need is to get back to college and get yourself some practical qualifications.'

Typical! But then after a second chat with the counsellor woman, who came specially to see him on the morning of Christmas Eve, Tom had felt all right. A few mates had emailed or texted him. But he had been annoyed that there had been nothing from Chloe Clifford. He wondered whether she had turned up at the Mitre Lounge that night. If he hadn't been such a dickhead, running back to college to see if she'd emailed, then he wouldn't have got involved.

Her dad, their local rector, had come to see him again, which was nice, but a bit pointless really, as Tom told him he wasn't depressed or anything, just a bit shocked.

'I'm OK now, thank you, Mr Clifford. How's Chloe?'

'Chloe? Oh, in great form. Talking non-stop about life at university.'

Oh, was she? Nice of her to completely ignore me, Tom thought.

Neil Clifford had no idea that his daughter was supposed to be meeting Tom Firth on the night of the attack. He wondered if the boy had any inkling that he might have been in a cell now if it hadn't been for the piece of wood found outside. And of course there was the drugged malice of the Frosts, who'd played into police hands by ranting about how they hated Morris, 'that fucking bastard with his crap shop'. Not to mention showing off about how they'd broken into the college plant room and tripped the circuits.

By the afternoon of Christmas Eve, Tom was already sick of being treated like an invalid. The Abbey Chorus members had accepted the Dean's judgement that they should perform as planned at the carol service. The biggest congregation of the year from the whole Norbridge area could not be disappointed, and to cancel would be to give in to thuggery.

So the carol service went ahead with Tom in the choir. The Dean mentioned the tragic events in his sermon, and talked about the endemic violence in society today. There was a short silence and a prayer for Morris's family. The choir sang the rehearsed anthems. And Tom was there with the rest of them, though his fellow choristers treated him as if he were a fragile musical instrument in constant need of tuning.

After the service, Tom was surrounded by concerned adults. It was quite heady for him. His parents had come along, but his father was irritable, hating to see his son being fussed over.

'Come on, lad, we haven't got all night,' Mick Firth called gruffly, making for the territorial security of his car, his wife scurrying behind him.

Tom loped after his parents, till he felt a tap on his arm. It was Chloe Clifford and, behind her, Poppy Robinson. He thought Chloe looked rather rough.

'Hello, Tom. Are you — ?'

'Don't ask me if I'm all right. Anyway, you could've been in touch.'

Chloe jumped. Her eyes widened. 'OK, no need to go over the top.'

'If you'd emailed me sooner none of this would've happened!'

He could hardly believe he was talking like this to the girl he had fancied for months, but so what? Everything was different now. He was in the limelight. He felt braver, more attractive. And he was less than impressed with Chloe's newly tinted jet black Gothic hair, which he could see had tarnished her high forehead, so that it looked slightly green round the edges. The heavy earrings were like something cut-price from an ironmonger's and the tiny skirt made her bum look huge. She'd put on weight at university. He'd never noticed before that her legs were quite chunky.

Chloe shrugged elaborately. 'Suit yourself then, but wait till you get headline deprivation. Come on, Pops.' She strode off, jangling.

Poppy lingered for a minute, fiddling with her woolly scarf and chewing a stray bit of hair from under her pulled-down hat. She crossed her eyes, making him laugh.

'I'm sorry it was you that found him, Tom.' She looked straight into his face. 'I understand how sick you must be of people going on about it. But they only ask how you are all the time because they like you.'

'Oh yeah? Well, not my dad. He's a complete pain.'

'Oh, parents!' sighed Poppy. 'What can you expect?'

'Yeah, correct.' It seemed like the first really *personal* sympathy he had received.

'Tom!' his father bellowed.

In the car on the way home, Tom watched the Christmas lights go by, and thought that Poppy Robinson had been quite decent. He would have liked to talk to her, because underneath all this fuss there was something on his mind. But she wouldn't have understood because she wasn't a chorister.

It was a pity Chloe had turned out to be such a cow, because at least she had sung in a choir. Tom was still baffled by something which no one else had even noticed. The dead Morris Little had been holding something in his right hand. Tom had only thought about it afterwards. You'd have to be a chorister to realize what it was, but any church choir member would have recognized the long narrow book, with the words of the Psalms printed underneath the few bars of each chant. But it was an odd thing to be carrying round.

Why on earth had Morris Little been clutching a psalter?

* * *

Robert Clark had no experience of a child-orientated family Christmas, twenty-first century style. He had known it would be different, fraught even, but he'd mentally fast-forwarded to the day, imagining Jake and Molly sitting round the tree opening presents with delight.

He had to admit he hadn't considered the intensity of last-minute arrangements, the literal weight of shopping, the crazy round of kids' activities, which meant constantly chauffeuring children about, and the exhaustion of trying to get The Briars to look like a Christmas card for Suzy's mother's visit.

And on top of it all there was the awful business of Morris Little. Robert had offered on behalf of the Chorus to go and see his wife Norma. The funeral was to be sometime after Christmas when the initial legal formalities were over. This left the Little family in a sort of limbo where receiving visitors was all they could do, in shocked silence punctuated by platitudes.

'Does it have to be you?' Suzy had said irritably when he said he was going to Uplands store again on Christmas Eve.

'I offered to. Norma is very low . . .'

'But what about coming to Norbridge? You said you'd drop me there and pick me up. I need to get Molly that game she wants for her stocking.'

'Can't you take your own car?'

'But parking's a nightmare. You said you'd wait for me. A job that should take me half an hour will take hours now.'

'I'm sorry, love.'

'Oh, forget it. I'll manage.'

Robert went from Uplands into Norbridge to buy Suzy a present. He had wondered about getting her a ring, but then thought a bracelet might be more appropriate. Earrings were out as Suzy always lost them. And she'd recently ruined her watch by wearing it in the bath, and declared that cheap watches were all she wanted.

He took a while to choose the bangle, relishing the calm of the jeweller's shop.

When he came home, a little later than planned, he could hear Suzy yelling at Molly upstairs.

'I had to leave you on your own for five minutes because I needed to go to Lo-cost Supermarket and Robert let me down by being late. And now look what you've done!'

'I'm sorry, Mummy.'

'Sorry! How could you, you disgusting little beast. It will take me hours to clean this up. You should be ashamed of yourself. How inconsiderate can you get? It's Christmas Eve and I'm run off my feet. And this isn't our house, you know. You can't just wreck it . . .'

'But Mummy, it just came out . . .'

'Don't lie to me!' Suzy was shouting now. 'How could a whole tube of glue get all over the carpet like that? You sloshed it about and then you trod in it and you just didn't care. Get into the bathroom and try to scrape it off your hands. And your jeans. I'm not letting you make any more decorations.'

Molly was starting to scream. Robert went up the stairs two at a time and was shocked to see Suzy standing over her daughter who was cowering on her bed.

'Suzy! It's all right. Really. I don't mind about the carpet. Don't shout at her. You're just upsetting her.'

Suzy rounded on him. 'I beg your pardon? What do you think you're doing, telling me how to deal with my daughter? Molly, do as I say. Shut up, and go and clean up. Now.' The little girl scuttled out of the bedroom.

'Don't ever do that, Robert. Don't ever tell me how to bring up my children.' Suzy walked away from him, down the stairs.

Robert went and changed into his jeans and a sweatshirt. When he went down to the kitchen, Molly was sitting at the table with milk and a biscuit, showing Suzy something in a book. The crisis was over.

Suzy came over to him and put her hand on his arm. 'Listen, Rob, Molly and I have big rows every so often. It's how we cope. All parents get angry at some point, you know.'

'Of course I know,' he said more sharply than usual. I'm not naive because I'm not a parent, he thought.

'And it really was wrong of Molly to get glue all over Mary's rug.'

'It's not Mary's rug,' Robert said. 'Mary's dead.' It sounded brusquer than he meant it to. He had been trying to say that he understood how difficult it must be for her, here in Mary's house at Christmas. But Suzy jumped away from him as if he had hit her.

'Mummy!' called Molly imperiously, and the chance to talk was gone.

8

I am become a monster unto many, but my sure trust is in thee.
Psalm 71:6

Christmas Day dawned dark and dreary. Alex Gibson got
up and pulled the thin, cheap brown curtains aside to reveal
the view from the picture window of her mother's bungalow
bedroom. She looked down at the rolling scene of beige-
green fell. Fellside was not a cute village, and today in the
grey dawn it looked especially dreary. A stunted leafless bush
framed the panorama. The hillside dropped away to a disused
slate quarry which was about as pretty as an inverted slag
heap. In the other direction, the crazy turret of the deserted
red-brick convent, once home to a dying group of Anglican
nuns, punctured the skyline. Alex could see their deserted
overgrown garden and the depressing, lurching stone cross.

The window was cold, single-glazed; slimy rivulets of
condensation ran down the pane to collect in fat drops on the
chipped and warped window frame. The bungalow had been
built in the 1970s and the minimum had been done to it
since. Her mother's empty recliner chair cluttered the room,
still with the plaid blanket on top of it. To get to the heap of
clothes she had dumped there, Alex had to manoeuvre her

47

way between a big, old-fashioned oak veneer wardrobe and a hideous kidney-shaped dressing table with some tatty pink frilled pleats curtaining its spindly legs. Alex had loved her mother, but she'd had no illusions about her taste.

And she missed her terribly this morning. Even last year, when things had been so wretched and Mum was declining, Alex had made a pretence of Christmas being special, trying to be patient.

'What day is it?'

'It's Christmas Day, Mam.'

'Christmas Day? But you didn't tell me! What am I going to do for dinner?'

'It's all right, Mam. Christine and Reginald are coming. Your other daughter and her husband, you remember? I've done the veg already and we'll put the turkey in soon.'

'Oh, taking over, are you? You've always been bossy.'

'Have some toast, Mam.'

'I don't mind if I do. Put jam on it. What day is it?'

'It's Christmas Day, Mam.'

Tears came to Alex's eyes, but she shook her head. It was all very well to try and pretend she'd been a dutiful daughter, but she'd only come back to Fellside when her own life had fallen apart and she had nowhere else to go. Her mother had already started to deteriorate; it was fitting that the disgraced daughter and demented mother moved in together.

Her sister Christine and brother-in-law Reg had of course been delighted, though there had been an unspoken nervousness on their part that perhaps this would mean losing out on their share of the bungalow. But Alex had been scrupulous about that. In the fallout of her divorce she had been left with half the money for her marital home, and nothing to spend it on, so, of all the horrors Alex had had to face, poverty wasn't one of them. Not that you would know, looking at the dilapidated bungalow with its leaky gutters, gas-scented kitchen, charcoal-edged carpets and drooping curtains. Her mother had been dead eight months. Since then, Alex had become even more inert.

But how different things had been once! For a second a memory of Christmas before the fall came back to her, like the scene from a film. Buck's fizz on Christmas morning, carol singing in their fashionable church with her own voice rising high in the descants, and then the kisses and hugs of all their friends in the church porch before drinks at a neighbour's house where Alex wore her new designer jacket and the jewellery her husband had given her. All very South-West London. All very over.

The dressing-table mirror was smeared but it still reflected back to Alex her bulging waist in one of her mother's bright blue nylon nighties. Not helped by another bottle of white wine the night before. And a whisky nightcap. Now, after the usual deep drugged sleep, and restless awakening from about five thirty, it was eight o'clock. Only four hours — well, three hours, seeing it was Christmas — before she could start the next bottle of wine.

There was no point having a shower or washing her hair. She wasn't going to see anyone who mattered. She had told Chris and Reg she was going to the Cliffords' for Christmas lunch. She suspected they knew she was lying, but were relieved to leave her alone.

She would go to church to fill in the hours before the corkscrew came out. She would attend Fellside Fellowship, with the trendy young vicar Rev Paul, his clever wife, and their wide-eyed, happy young congregation. She would sing choruses and torture herself — and them — with her dumpy, off-message presence. There was no point in actually trying to enjoy anything, and religion wasn't there to make you feel good. It was there to make you feel bad, like everything else.

Except the white wine. And of course there was the sort of dull relief that Morris Little was dead. A few weeks earlier Alex had made the mistake of visiting Uplands off-licence for two days running. 'Putting the sauce away a bit, aren't you, Miss Gibson?' he had leered. What did he know? Had he guessed? Did she look like an alcoholic? Was that what she was? Usually it was only a bottle in the evening with supper, though of course lately it had perhaps been a bit more . . .

For a minute she was tempted to get a bath, clean up and go down to sing lovely traditional carols at Uplands — maybe the Cliffords would invite her to lunch after all, on the spur of the moment. But she couldn't stand the thought of Lynn Clifford's kindness — the confiding remarks about the menopause or pension problems. I'm probably at least ten years younger than you think, Alex wanted to shout. I've taken to wearing my mother's clothes because I've got so fat. I'm even wearing her old glasses because I cried so much I gave up on my contact lenses, and my face is grey because I can't be bothered with make-up or moisturizer, and even smiling seems a waste of muscle power. I only use my mouth to stuff it with food or to gulp drink or to snarl at people. But what was the point? Alex looked and felt like an old bag. And that was what she was.

So she would go and embarrass the scrubbed, cheery kids who came to the Fellside Fellowship. And to the backing of the hackneyed guitar she would try and pray for the soul of the departed Morris Little. But it would be hard.

* * *

'Good to see you. God bless.'

'Fab talk, Paul. Happy Christmas.'

'Praise the Lord!'

Rev Paul, as he liked to be called, was an Anglican priest and one of Neil Clifford's team ministry. He stood with his right-hand man Mark Wilson outside their ugly red-brick church and said goodbye to their communicants. There had been sixty people at the Fellside Fellowship Christmas Morning All Age Worship, which was an all-time record, and most of them were under thirty — as the roar of a dozen high-tuned engines testified.

The Fellside Fellowship was based in a drab chapel, built in the 1850s for the terraced village that had grown up around the Cumbrian slate industry. It had been called St Luke's, but everyone knew it as Fellside Fellowship now.

'Great service, Paul. Really cool.'

Rev Paul had revived the place. He had seen that the prettier village churches, like St Mary's in Uplands and All Saints over in Tarnfield, already had established congregations. So he had set about making the chapel at Fellside something different.

Paul was a good operator and had been careful to work gradually towards something contemporary, without distressing the old guard. After a while there had been no objection from the parochial church council to his idea of a pop-based evensong for local teenagers, and the development of a 'big band' of teenage rock musicians on any instruments they could muster, plugged into massive amplifiers. Paul himself played the guitar.

Slowly, more and more local kids came to Fellside. Paul retained a basic communion service every Sunday morning for a sprinkling of older people, but for Christmas Day it had been the beat service.

'Nice one, Paul. I like a tune to get me going.' It was one of the pensioners who made no secret of enjoying seeing the girls dancing in the aisles. ''Appy Christmas, lad.'

'Happy Christmas to you too.'

He and Mark stood talking to people leaving the church, and Paul glanced at his most dedicated parishioner. It was brilliant that help, in the shape of Mark, had come along. In the last year Mark had taken on much of the church administration. He was now secretary to the parochial church council, and an assistant at communion. The older people were happy to let him take over the work. And the young ones liked him because he was handsome in a blond, surfing sort of way, and they took for granted that he would do boring stuff like running meetings and taking minutes. Surprisingly, for one so cool-looking, Mark was an accountant, in his early thirties, but with a real common touch. A godsend, Paul thought sincerely.

Not that they were joined-at-the-hip in liturgical matters. Tentatively, almost apologetically, Mark had developed a different sort of approach since first coming to the Fellowship a year earlier. Paul had expected him to become one of the evangelical types who predominated at Fellside, but Mark had started to change. He was becoming much more interested in High Church stuff — crossing himself and kneeling to pray. Which was fine. Two people couldn't have identical views, and Paul already had his wife's support. He and Jenny really did think as one.

'Mark's such an asset, isn't he?' Paul had said to her after Mark had been with them a few weeks.

'Marvellous,' Jenny had said, a touch curtly. 'I must go and see to Joseph.'

Joseph was a joy but he was hard work too, especially as Jenny had insisted on feeding him herself for ten months. Jenny was a brilliant mother, a fantastic sounding-board and a great helpmate, even if these days she was abrupt at times. Paul had to be patient and remember that she had, literally, borne the brunt of the new baby. They had waited until their mid-thirties to have children, and Jenny had been such a capable, clever woman that it had never occurred to either of them that having a baby would be more than they could take in their stride. But for Jenny, former secondary school teacher, potential deputy head, now full-time mother and mere parish sidekick, it was tough.

But there was no need to think about that today. After all, it was Christmas, and so far so good. Joseph, exhausted, had let them sleep till six thirty, his stocking had gone down well, the untidiness in the tiny vicarage was under control and the morning service had been a triumph. And now Jenny was coming out of church at last after tidying up behind the little kids who'd been drawing pictures at the back. Joseph was on her hip and she was laughing for once.

She called to them both: 'I'm running off to see that the turkey's cooking. I hope you're hungry, Mark.'

Paul said, 'It'll be a bunfight. I could scran a gadgee off a scabby hoss!'

Mark's face beamed. 'What does that mean?'

'It means I could eat a man on a scab-covered horse. Cumbrian dialect.' Paul grinned.

His grandfather's family had come from Cumbria. Paul had been born in Bristol, but he'd been delighted to come back. Since his father's death just a few months earlier Paul had become hooked on genealogy, sneaking off to the computer when he was supposedly writing his sermons. He had not been close to his dad, who'd been nonplussed by Paul's vocation, but Paul was sure that somewhere in his genetic make-up there was an ancestor who, like him, had faith. His heritage meant a lot to him and he felt it showed God at work through the generations. He wanted to know what he was passing on to his son. He had told Mark all about it — and his parishioner and friend thought it all rather exciting. Not like his wife, who was a little bit dismissive.

'Yum! Dinner sounds deee-licious. Can't wait, Jenny,' Mark said good-humouredly, with his warm smile.

Thank God, Paul thought, sincerely. He was suddenly filled with a sense of peace. He was brought down to earth by his last parishioner lumbering towards him. Alex Gibson had been left behind in the rush. He wondered for a minute why she was here at the Fellowship. It clearly wasn't her thing. But he tried to be a good priest and he advanced towards her, extending his hand.

'Happy Christmas, Alex. God bless.'

'If you say so,' she mumbled, shaking his hand with the enthusiasm of a wet dishcloth. She hardly paused in her heavy stride, and walked past him up the hill.

Perhaps I should have been more supportive of Alex Gibson, Paul thought. Wasn't it Alex who had found Morris Little's body? The thought made Paul shiver involuntarily and he put the local murder out of his mind. But, watching Alex walk slowly up the hill, past the boarded-up convent and on towards her featureless bungalow, he thought that if he had said anything, she probably would have been her usual ungracious self anyway.

He could hear Jenny and Mark laughing as they walked down to the cramped council house which served as his headquarters. Thank you for friendship, Lord, he thought.

Merry Christmas.

9

Blessed are they that dwell in thy house:
they will be always praising thee.
Psalm 84:4

Three hundred miles away, Wanda Wisley peered over the top of her duvet. The view of the white room was broken only by the slight swaying of an orchid on its thin stem, bobbing almost unnoticeably to the waves of heat rising from the radiator cover. Her head ached in a dull, general sort of way, and she felt nauseous, but, lying there stretching her neck muscles, she willed the mild pain to go. The hum of traffic, always minimal in this Notting Hill cul-de-sac, was almost non-existent today, and the world seemed silent except for the occasional shout from the street below.

'Freddie,' she whispered, but he was still out of it. A snore rippled between his rubbery lips. He turned away from her into the pillow, flicking her with his swatch of grey-black hair, still tied back in an elastic band, even in bed.

She had a vague, disturbing memory from the night before. 'Wanda, I would like to go back up to Norbridge for New Year,' Freddie had announced.

'Why on earth do you want to do that?'

'Oh, you know, it sounds fun. First footing and all that. I would like to try that.'

'Oh, don't be ridiculous.'

'Seriously, Wanda, I miss the cottage in Norbridge. We always go to your friends' New Year party in Bayswater. Let's have a change this year.'

'I can't believe you mean this, Freddie.'

Is that what had happened? The conversation was the last but one thing before they crashed, muffled by drink and dope. But I wouldn't be bothered if Freddie took off over New Year, Wanda thought. He wasn't quite the accessory he had once been.

'Well, you do what you like,' she had said. 'But you're not getting me back to Norbridge till I have to go!'

'*Lieblich*, let's see.' Freddie had started playing with her, pulling her towards him. 'Come here . . .' Wanda had sighed theatrically but had fallen into his arms, thinking, why not? He was different in London . . . less Germanic, less manic even. In Norbridge he was a caricature, which meant sex with him just couldn't be taken seriously. But here, in the flat, for a few minutes, it had been like old times.

But not for long. In the cold light of Christmas Day, looking at the blubbery mass beside her, Wanda thought that Freddie was welcome to go back to the north for New Year's Eve, alone. But she would stay put. She lay relishing the idea of being at home in the flat. Then, perhaps because of the contrast, her thoughts rambled back to the grisly cottage.

They had rented what they'd assumed was a vintage gem on the outskirts of Norbridge. But what Wanda had mistaken for cosy charm was a fake. It was a drab nineteenth-century labourer's home, extended and 'prettified' in the 1930s. It was wrinkled with beams and open stonework, inglenooks and fitted shelves. The windows were small, with leaded-light sections of frosted glass. The walls were panelled, and the ceilings were alarmingly low. When the previous tenant had moved out, taking the china animals and costume dolls, the built-in shelves looked stained, ringed and shabby.

To replace the ornaments Wanda had bought some small modern sculptures, which looked as if a collection of unidentified garden tools had been left on the mantelpiece. She had to admit that the cottage just didn't work.

Freddie liked it, of course. 'It's really cute! I think we need to grow some herbs, here at the back where it's warm near the kitchen. And in the summer there will be tomatoes and beans.'

So far, Freddie was all talk where the garden was concerned. The square of grass at the back was now coated with rotting leaves and the kitchen was a continual swamp. There was a cleaner once a week, but often she didn't come, leaving an incoherent phone message. And there was no back-up, unlike in London where a proper agency did the job.

Wanda became restless, throwing the duvet about. She hadn't wanted to think about the north. She just couldn't relax in Norbridge. And that stupid man getting himself killed in her department was just typical. Everyone would be yakking about it, of course, and there would be some sort of scare about security. What had Edwin Armstrong said? The bloke had been beaten over the head by some local ASBO yob? It was just hard luck it had been in the Music Department. Wanda had gone to Newcastle to take the plane south as arranged, leaving Edwin Armstrong in charge. If he were so at home with the local community, he could take care of this!

Edwin had said on the phone, 'The police are now pretty sure it was the Frost brothers. They're well-known trouble-makers.'

'So they weren't enrolled at the college?'

'Not really. They've been seen hanging around, though. Years ago one of their older sisters was a student for a time, but she didn't finish the course. And lots of people use the college. People can go anywhere.'

'So why did they choose to beat this man to a pulp in my department?'

'A lot of kids hang about the Music Department, Wanda. You know that. Security's a huge issue because of that separate exit. The guys in the admin office say they thought they'd seen them earlier that day. Maybe they just spotted Morris and went for him.'

'So these people walk around with planks of wood at the ready?'

'It's the building work. Things like that are available.'

Edwin thought it odd himself, but the police appeared to be satisfied. Wayne and Jason Frost had both been remanded in custody and carted off to Carlisle. At least two people had seen Morris arguing with them in his shop. One witness said he had seen Morris throwing out Jason, who was a little runt. The general view seemed to be that Morris had caught the Frosts shoplifting, and that they'd recognized him in the college and gone for him. There had been a spate of unprovoked attacks all over Britain that winter, with drugged-up hooded youths attacking anyone who tried to argue with them.

The idea of the Frosts killing someone didn't surprise Edwin. But no one was asking why Morris was in the college. Of course he could have gone there for a number of reasons: to meet someone, or pick up some music, or just to spend time in the library. It was the 'Community College', after all. And Robert Clark had only assumed Morris was going to the pub after the rehearsal. Morris must have changed his mind.

But Edwin felt uncomfortable about it all. Morris was an inverted snob who would taunt anyone he thought was intellectually pretentious, yet like many similar people he would show off all the time himself. It seemed odd that he would have business with the Music Department which he hadn't trumpeted to everyone.

Edwin had mentioned this to Wanda Wisley.

But all she wanted was for the issue to go away so she could have a sophisticated London Christmas.

* * *

At The Briars, Christmas Day suddenly fell into place after Suzy's manic planning. When the last preparation was over, a sense of calm descended and Robert realized that the Christmas he had hoped for was going to happen.

Even so, he had no idea how complex the day's arrangements would be. With his late wife, Christmas had been centred on the church and on the two of them: midnight mass, late breakfast, matins at eleven, a quiet sherry with Phyllis Drysdale who was Mary's oldest friend and had since died herself, an exchange of thoughtful gifts and a pleasant evening watching TV.

With the Spencers it was a different world. Midnight mass was followed by racing home to set out drinks and mince pies for Father Christmas, not to mention a carrot for Rudolph the reindeer. Then they were up at six thirty to see Molly open her stocking and throw paper everywhere, her messiness forgiven. Then it was Jake's turn and, despite his grown-up attitude, he was still thrilled. Then Grandma had to open her stocking.

And finally, to Robert's surprise and embarrassment, there was a stocking for him, all wrapped and organized by Suzy, but with little presents which either Molly had made or Jake had chosen — who else would have bought him the classic *Little Britain* episodes? Next was a big breakfast with Buck's fizz, then a walk to give the kids some fresh air, and a drink at the neighbours'. Then back for a late lunch which was a huge, jolly, messy affair culminating in a flaming pudding which set fire to the paper napkins. They damped it down by chucking mineral water everywhere amid hysterical laughter, and then followed the crisis by pulling really vulgar crackers.

And after lunch there were presents from round the tree. When it came to the bracelet for Suzy, her eyes filled up.

'Thank you, Rob. It is lovely.'

'Well, it's safe anyway. You can wear it in the bath.'

Later on, the early evening quietened down, but there were still party games with Grandma and a drink with Jake's friend Oliver and his family who were 'just passing'. No one had ever 'popped in' on Robert and Mary — especially not on Christmas Day!

It was great, but it was completely exhausting. When everyone had gone to bed, Robert and Suzy slumped on the couch.

'Fancy a nightcap?' he murmured.

'I thought you'd never ask!'

'It's been great, Suzy. I know how hard you worked.' He smiled and got up to pour the drinks.

'Well, we're very lucky. When you think about what it must be like for people like the Little family . . .' It was an olive branch from Suzy.

Robert leant on the mantelpiece and looked reflective. The fire was dying down now, a cosy glow. 'Norma Little refuses to believe it was the Frosts who attacked Morris. She says they had no reason to kill him because he would never have had the guts to report them to the police for shoplifting. She says he let them take drinks and magazines all the time. He was a bit of a wimp in some ways. People who tease and torment usually are.'

'Interesting . . .' Suzy tried to sound engaged, but Robert could see that she was tired out. For all the success of the day, there was a drawn look on Suzy's face.

'What's up?'

'Oh, it's just poor Nigel. Without his kids or his family while we're here . . .'

Robert frowned. Suzy was planning to take her mother and the children over to her husband's before New Year. Then they would all travel to the north-west for a get-to-gether. She had relatives to see, and friends in Manchester to catch up with. Nigel was still staking his claim to his family, and demanding holiday time with them, so it had seemed a good compromise to spend Christmas with Robert and New Year with Nigel. But it wasn't the best arrangement in the world.

Since the evening when Robert had suggested marriage, he and Suzy had discussed nothing more personal than who should carve the turkey. There was an amnesty on emotions. Nothing was really resolved. But Robert was painfully aware that he wanted it to be. He pulled Suzy to her feet and held her for a minute, feeling her warmth.

Then he kissed her on the nose. 'We've had a great day. You're seeing Nigel in forty-eight hours. Put him on hold and come to bed with me.'

'OK,' she whispered softly.

* * *

In Notting Hill on Christmas night, Wanda whispered 'Freddie' again, to no response. She wiggled her toes and wondered why she felt irritated. It could be because of Freddie's comatose sleep, but over the years she'd grown used to his inert body beside her. Strange how something so still and heavy could emit funny noises — little piping snores or great rumbles, booming farts or whimpering sighs.

So what was on her mind? They had had a marvellous dinner party with two local gay friends of hers from the BBC, who were experts on all the latest TV chefs' recipes, and she and Freddie had been able to walk back to the flat which was so clean and white and chic after the bric-a-brac horror of the Norbridge cottage.

But during the conversation one of the guests had mentioned going to midnight mass, much to the amusement of the others, and it had jogged Wanda's memory. Whatever her failings, Wanda Wisley was conscientious. She had a nagging feeling that she ought to check her emails. She swung herself out of bed and, naked, padded over to the real beechwood desk where her computer sat waiting.

What had Edwin asked? Why had that man Morris Little been in the Music Department? With a horrible sense that she might know the answer, she logged on.

Here it was, the correspondence between herself and a man called . . . shit. Wanda had been so busy and preoccupied, she really hadn't put two and two together. When Morris Little had started to email her she had just written him off as the church music nutter.

I'd like to talk to someone really knowledgeable about music in Norbridge, he had written, flattering her. He had some pet theory about 'church music with a local connection'. He had emailed her every day until she had given in and agreed to a meeting.

Wanda glanced quickly through the correspondence. Now she knew why Morris Little had been in the Music Department. It was because she had invited him — and completely forgotten about him. The Friday before Christmas, she had suddenly decided she couldn't bear another minute at work and had left without even picking up her expenses. But would anyone believe her? What a pain! Wanda logged out and padded back to bed.

There was no way she was going to mention this to anyone.

10

Thou shalt not be afraid of any terror by night,
nor for the arrow that flieth by day.
Psalm 91:5

Six days later, the only spot of nightlife in Norbridge which
was still rocking in the New Year at two in the morning was
Strumpets on Fletchergate. Chloe Clifford pulled a reluctant
Poppy Robinson after her and they sidled down the alley
beside the club.

'Go on, Poppy, try it.' Chloe was giggling and trying
to light up a badly made joint. She succeeded in starting
a small fire at the end of the paper but after a minute
the shreds which had flared up calmed down. Chloe had
already spilt bits of grass and tobacco down her new black
silk-effect jacket. She'd dropped the grinder and Rizla
papers a few times because she'd already drunk six shots of
vodka in an hour after meeting Poppy in the Crown and
Thistle.

'I don't think it's for me,' Poppy said nervously.

'Oh, go on, twit. Everyone does it in Leeds.' Chloe took
a huge drag and then poked the mangled bit of paper and
vegetation towards her.

'All right.' Poppy put the soggy end in her mouth and inhaled. But nothing happened except that a badly ground bit of hot grass detached itself and stuck at the back of her throat. She coughed and spluttered so much, the joint fell out of her mouth, hit her ample bosom in its lurid top, and dropped into the muck around their stiletto heels.

'Oh, fuck you!' shouted Chloe angrily.

'I'm sorry, Chloe. I couldn't help it,' Poppy whined.

'You should have watched what you were doing with your fat fingers.'

'That's not fair!'

'Not fair, not fair. Christ, Pops, what a baby you are!' Chloe put out her own plump fingers and jabbed Poppy in the chest.

Poppy squawked. 'Stop it,' she said weakly.

'Well, you've cost me good money wasting that spliff. You deserve a bit of a slap.' Chloe advanced on her friend, her eyes narrowing and her bright varnished fingernails at Poppy's eye level. Poppy's eyes crossed dramatically.

'Well, fuck off yourself!' Poppy suddenly yelled. 'I'm sick of the way you're behaving. You've been foul since Christmas. You're a slag, Chloe Clifford.'

Chloe was taken aback for a second. Poppy had never dared to speak back to her. What was happening? She felt a tight band round her head and was unsure whether it was anger or shock. She opted for anger, but for once she couldn't find what she wanted to say.

'Who d'you fuckin' fink you is . . . ?' she heard herself screaming, all the words coming out wrongly.

But Poppy had backed away and slid past her out of the alleyway and into the street. Chloe realized she had been left. She called after her: 'Sowwy, Pops. Reeely sowwy now . . .' But Poppy's silhouette hardly paused before, plump legs wobbling, she disappeared.

Fuck, thought Chloe. The ground was swaying a lot and her head felt as if it would burst. All she wanted to do was sit down, but the ground was filthy, she knew that. She leant back against the wall and felt a huge lump of sick rising in her stomach. Then it went down again, which was worse than coming up. The weed was making her really nauseous. She had tried a few pills before now and the effect had been great — dreamy, weird, and maybe headachy in the morning — but not this awful tidal sickness.

I have to get back into the club, she thought. Suddenly she felt cold and then scared, out there in the dark alley by herself. How could Poppy do this? Chloe tried to walk, but her high heels stuck in the cobbles. She was concentrating on her feet, so at first she didn't see another figure at the end of the alley. When she looked up, she noticed the outline of a man. She couldn't go back because the alley was blocked off at the far end. She could only go forward and even then very slowly.

'It's Chloe Clifford, isn't it?' said the man, who spoke very softly and seemed to be all dressed in black, and very big. 'I've just seen Poppy running away. Let me help you walk.'

Chloe wanted to ask him how he knew her, but she couldn't look at him and concentrate on her feet at the same time. She felt his strong arm under her shoulders, but no other part of his body touched her, which was all right, really. She realized he smelt of masculine sweat, overlaid with deodorant. It was a nice smell but at the same time it seemed to attack the pit of her stomach like a punch in the gut. She was going to say, 'I'm OK, leave me alone,' when the vomit really did come up. It shot out in a stream of white liquid, catching the light from a street lamp on the main road. It looked like slime and it was all down his coat. She retched even more and caught the acrid smell of sick in her nostrils. The shame was as bad as the smell. She had to shut her eyes.

'Oh dear,' he said. 'I think it's time someone got you home. Come with me to the car.'

No, she wanted to shout, I don't know you . . . where's Poppy? But the strong arm was propelling her into the main street, and then she felt her legs give way and all she could do was keep her eyes shut and pray that her feet kept moving.

* * *

At the rectory Lynn Clifford couldn't sleep because of the night sweat from hell. She grabbed her dressing gown. She couldn't get back into the bed: it was soaking. She could see the outline of her own body in the dark damp blotches on the sheet. Like the Turin shroud, she thought.

Neil rolled away from the wet patches and pulled the double duvet round himself. There was an easy chair in the bedroom, with Lynn's clothes on it ready for New Year's Day. She perched on the edge of it.

They were going to Edwin's for New Year's lunch, with her father and stepmother. Lynn was dreading it. She found her father's constant digs about religion very trying. Once an easy-going, soft-hearted man, he had become bitchy in old age, as if being over eighty gave him a licence to be rude. Lynn was no fan of her stepmother, but she found herself sympathizing. The old man was very hard work. Marriage! You never knew how it would end up.

Was that why Edwin had never married? It was something Lynn had asked herself a hundred times. But she had never asked *him*. Although they were close, Edwin rarely talked about his emotions, and after the disastrous relationship with Marilyn Frost he had become much more reserved. Even now, with the Frost brothers in custody, Edwin had never referred to his intense affair with their older sister. His involvement with the Frost family was never mentioned.

'You really loved Marilyn, didn't you?' she had said to him once, years before. Edwin had looked back at her blankly.

'Loved her?' he had said, astonished at the question. And Lynn had thought — no, it was almost worship. Marilyn had been a strange girl, not like the other Frosts. Her mother and uncles were local ne'er-do-wells, and one cousin was a notorious drunk. Her younger brothers probably had different fathers and she was the eldest by a long way, born when her mother was in her early teens. Jason and Wayne had come along a few years later and maintained the family tradition, but Marilyn was quiet and very pretty, with the most beautiful long auburn hair like something out of Burne-Jones.

Edwin had been older than her but she had always seemed mature. They had been inseparable — and then Marilyn had left him, just like that.

Afterwards, a little bit of the light had gone from Edwin's eyes.

New Year's Eve always makes me morose, Lynn thought. She padded out across the landing to the bathroom. After the Watch Night service at the church, she and Neil had been out 'first footing'. It could go on for hours, with people visiting houses, byres and barns, having a dram at every one. There was something quite pagan about it. The hooded figures mooching down the dark lanes often had a medieval look as they skulked past, mumbling 'How do, Rector?'

So when they'd come home, much later than planned, she and Neil had hurried upstairs, shattered. She had presumed that Chloe was in bed, as she'd been under strict instructions to get a taxi home before it was too late. But Lynn hadn't wished her only child 'Happy New Year'.

Lynn tiptoed to her daughter's room, knocked softly on the door and then pushed it. It swung open. Chloe's bed was empty. Lynn Clifford screamed.

* * *

Suzy Spencer had a miserable New Year. Her mum had stayed with them at The Briars until they left to go to Nigel's in Newcastle. It felt odd leaving Robert. And it was a tight squeeze in Nigel's flat, with Suzy and her mum and Molly in one bedroom and Nigel and Jake in the other. Nigel had spent his Christmas drinking Armagnac, and now he was concentrating on his family with manic intensity.

He was in denial. He looked on Suzy's stay at The Briars as if it was a sort of lodgers' arrangement that had no emotional significance. He ignored Robert's existence, treated Suzy like a naughty girl, fussed over her mother and arranged a breakneck schedule of fun for the kids that left Molly sobbing and overtired in the Metro Centre, and Jake wildly bright-eyed, clutching more new gadgets than he could possibly deal with.

Suzy felt destabilized. She had tried really hard to help her son acclimatize to a new home, but now Jake was being seduced by his own father.

'Come on, Jakey, try this crazy ride.'

'Look, Jake, more e-games!'

'Want to try extreme skate-boarding, Jake?'

The worst of it was that Suzy felt desperately sorry for Nigel. She no longer loved him, but she had loved him once and she was ashamed to admit that his bravado had been part of the attraction. But to feed it, he had needed the admiration of women. So Suzy had turned a blind eye to his affairs. It was a vicious circle and she had been a link in it, reinforcing Nigel's image as a ladies' man. She had assumed that even if his current girlfriend didn't last, Nigel would find a more glamorous bet and disappear from her emotional life for good. Didn't men always want younger, more beautiful women? But now, astonishingly, Nigel's supply had dried up.

Her mother had enjoyed Christmas at The Briars but had been unable to conceal her delight at seeing Suzy and Nigel together again as a family. Suzy had driven them all down to her mum's house for New Year's Day with Nigel beside her, advising her when to use the windscreen wipers. His dominating behaviour had infuriated her in the past, but this time she accepted it. She was beginning to think all men wanted control. Surely Robert's sudden misguided marriage proposal was about establishing himself as head of the household? But if she was going to gratify any paterfamilias, shouldn't it be Nigel?

Suzy felt parcelled up, unable to talk to anyone, except when she called her longstanding London friend Rachel Cohen on the phone.

'Jesus, Rachel, this is awful.'

'Jesus who? Shalom to you too.'

'Oh, stop joking! I feel so muddled up. Robert's been acting like a moral force and Nigel is mooning round wanting to be a family man again.'

'So you've got a new guy who wants to marry you and a husband already. You should be so lucky!'

'You're joking. I mean, Nigel is so pathetic that I feel really sorry for him.'

'Well, it's classic. When Nigel was behaving like a bastard it was easy to move on. But now he's suffering, you treat him like your third child.'

'But it makes me so sad. I don't know what to do. Look, I'd better go. Mum's making cocoa for everyone and Molly will probably chuck it up, the way Nigel throws her around. Come to Tarnfield and stay with us soon.'

'Will do. But who is us?'

The thought stayed with Suzy as she crept into the narrow bed in the room she'd had as a child. As always, Rachel had put her finger on the problem. Just who was 'us'?

11

Thou hast shewed the people heavy things;
thou hast given us a drink of deadly wine.
Psalm 60:3

On the evening of New Year's Day, Edwin Armstrong waved goodbye to his parents. His mother was still talking at him through the driver's window of their ancient car as she manoeuvred out of the tiny driveway in front of his cottage. The car groaned and took a rasping breath before finally moving. Thank goodness they're off, Edwin thought. He was desperate for some time to himself.

It had been a very odd New Year's Day. He had been expecting the Clifford family to join him and his parents for lunch, but when they arrived Lynn had looked absolutely exhausted. Even Neil had seemed distracted. And Chloe had been pale and quiet, dressed in a long dark skirt, flat boots and a baggy jumper discarded by Lynn. He had hardly recognized her.

They had arrived early, and after one gin and tonic his sister had followed him into the kitchen. 'We've had a really weird night,' she said to Edwin's back as he basted the roast potatoes. 'Chloe didn't come home till six o'clock in the morning!'

'Really? Was she having fun?'

'Fun? Well, it's hard to say. I was absolutely terrified. She hadn't phoned although we bought her that state-of-the-art mobile, and she hadn't said anything about staying out all night.'

'So how did she get back home?' he asked.

'Well, that's just it! I was nearly hysterical when I realized she wasn't in bed, and I shouted for Neil and we tried the mobile but there was no answer. We were just wondering about ringing the Robinsons or even the police and then . . .' Lynn paused, her eyes round and pink at the rims with her sleepless night. '. . . the phone went and Chloe called us! She said she was fine, but she'd been sick and that someone had rescued her. She said she'd be back at six o'clock in the morning. And rang off. We sat there for two hours, scared witless. Then, bang on the dot, we heard her key in the lock.'

'You must have been relieved. But you know at that age a lot of them stay out all night.'

'But transport is such a nightmare! The kids with cars drive like madmen on New Year's Eve. We'd given her money for a cab and told her to be home by three.'

'So how did she get back?'

'She said she'd been very silly but that someone had looked after her, then given her a lift home!'

'Who? One of her mates?'

'No, Edwin, that's what was odd. She wouldn't say who it was.'

'That's strange. Were you annoyed?'

Lynn looked shocked. 'No! I hate even the thought of rowing with Chloe; you know that, Edwin . . .'

Her eyeline drifted away as she remembered the early hours of the morning, sitting there in the kitchen waiting for dawn, with her daughter slumped in front of her, drinking hot chocolate.

'I've been really stupid, Mum,' Chloe had said. 'And I'm sorry. If I hadn't been rescued I don't know what would have happened to me. I was really sick in the lane by Strumpets club.'

71

But when Lynn had asked her who had taken care of her, she had shaken her head.

'Just some bloke I know. He was really kind.'

Then, suddenly, Chloe had begun to cry, huge gasping sobs of relief. And it had all come out. How uni was scary and lonely and how the only boy she had fancied there just ignored her, and how the other girls in her hall were all so much prettier, and how people who'd done gap years all seemed so much more sophisticated. Chloe had been wretched.

So she'd come home, to find that her mum was absorbed in Christmas preparations or hot flushes — and her dad was always out. She'd been so homesick. But home had just gone on without her.

'Edwin, she isn't even doing very well with the academic work. She was always such a star at Norbridge High. Since she came home, she's just been showing off — to pretend it was all fine at university.' Lynn's tired eyes filled with tears and self-reproach.

Edwin looked past Lynn to the living room where Chloe was leaning forward, smiling with enormous concentration at her grandfather.

'Well,' he said softly, 'whatever happened certainly seems to have had an effect. She's behaving angelically now!'

'I know! She's been totally different this morning. Look how good she's being with Dad.'

Even so, the dinner had gone on to be the usual stressful affair, dominated by the old man making heavy-handed jokes about priests, rabbis and vicars with endings he couldn't remember. Edwin almost longed for Chloe's old-style comments like, 'Oh, belt up, Gramps,' or, 'I wish I'd hidden your dentures.'

When at last he shut the door behind them all, Edwin went up the stairs two at a time to the tiny spare room at the front of the cottage where he did his work. He'd had enough reality for one day. He was studying the Psalms. One of the local clergy in Victorian times, who rejoiced in the name of

Cecil Quaile Woods, had reportedly written some interesting psalm settings, but most of them had been lost. While Edwin was not particularly interested in the man, he was fascinated by the idea of renewing the interest in psalmody — if only locally at first. It wasn't a project which would get much support from his new boss. But on New Year's Day, now his family had all gone, he would give himself a treat and settle down to some work.

He needed to find out where the Quaile Woods psalter editions might be. It was the sort of totally absorbing activity which would keep Edwin busy for hours. And then there would be no time to think about Marilyn Frost.

Or Morris Little.

* * *

Alex Gibson had succumbed to her sister's invitation to go for dinner on New Year's Day, although the cold she had incubated since before Christmas was threatening to explode into her head, and she felt dazed and fuzzy. During the day she had managed to stick to just half a bottle of wine, but it had made her feel unusually dizzy. Her brother-in-law had offered to pick her up.

Reg held her arm as she walked to the car. 'There's no need for that, Reg; I can manage.' But she felt even more breathless than usual, getting her scarf tangled around her knees, and stumbling.

'All right, all right, I was only trying to help.' He sighed with great patience. 'You know David and Pat Johnstone from Uplands Golf Club, don't you?'

Reg cheerily signalled a couple in the back of the car. Alex twisted round to say 'Hi', but suddenly thought that her breath might smell of alcohol so instead she just grimaced at them. The man was in his sixties, with thick grey hair and a smooth, padded look. His wife was stringy and tired-looking, with thin crispy curls. She gave a sort of cackling laugh.

Yet another black mark, Alex thought. Well, if I'm being flaunted as the dysfunctional female of the family, I might as well enjoy it.

Reg said, 'David is the very successful estate agent. You'll have seen his boards: "Johnstone — sign of success".'

'Not just real estate, Reg,' Johnstone boomed. 'I've got thumbs in lots of pies!'

Reg laughed uncomfortably. 'But you'll have seen David's posters, Alex.'

'Oh, yes . . .' The Johnstone logo, in orange and fuchsia, littered local villages. But in Fellside, the signs were up for so long they faded to the same brownish-grey colour as everything else in the village.

'I might be able to help you with the bungalow . . .' David Johnstone leant forward; Alex could smell the toothpaste on his breath.

'Oh?' she snapped. 'Good at hoovering, are you?'

Reg squirmed, and Alex turned to stare angrily out of the window. Reg and Christine frequently made remarks about 'capitalizing' on the bungalow, which she resented. She didn't like the house and had no intention of staying in Fellside, but this was all too soon.

The wrinkly Pat Johnstone, who looked older than her well-upholstered husband, laughed in her irritating, cackling way. 'Dave means he could help you sell it.'

'She knows what I mean, thank you very much,' David Johnstone snapped at his wife. Alex felt guilty for giving him the opportunity.

'Oh, don't mind me!' Pat Johnstone laughed her coarse laugh. Then she started to sneeze. 'It's your scarf,' she said wheezily to Alex. 'I've got an allergy to cheap man-made fibres.'

'I'll take it off.' Alex stuffed it in her bag, but when she leant forward to do it she felt suddenly nauseous. I'm really not very well, she thought.

The rest of the journey passed in silence.

Reg and Christine Prout lived in a smart detached house on the main road between Fellside and Uplands. Reginald

Prout was in his early fifties and worked for the council, counting the days until retirement and endless afternoons on the golf course. He had been handsome as a young man, but he had gone bald in middle age; his face, without his dated chestnut bob, was pale and weak. He had a nervous habit of stroking his head as if hoping to find more hair to cover his pate. Alex's sister Christine was plump and motherly, missing her two daughters, who had both left home for London. Her house was too neat and tidy without them.

There was no chat until they were all installed in Reg and Chris's front room, each with a very small whisky. Alex had said nothing to her sister and brother-in-law about Morris Little's murder, but it was inevitable the conversation would turn to it.

Eventually Reg said with his usual lack of originality, 'Well, let's hope we have a better year next year!'

'Oh yes,' cackled Pat Johnstone.

'Spot on, Reg, old son.' David Johnstone had warmed up over his whisky.

'It couldn't get much worse where we live!' Pat said. 'You'll have heard about the chap from the off-licence? Murdered!'

The conversation galloped to the next stage. Alex listened, and drank another whisky — it took some flaunting of her glass to get Reg to fill it. She heard how it was disgusting the way teenagers were out of control, the Chapterhouse estate was a sewer that should be cleaned out, they should bring back corporal punishment . . .

'I was just saying, the way these girls behave,' David Johnstone ranted, 'I mean, well, with boys you expect it, but girls! Yelling their mouths off, skirts up round their bottoms, boobs hanging out . . . I wouldn't be surprised if girls egged these Frost lads on! Everyone knows they did it, little bastards.'

Alex swallowed any response she might have made. She said brusquely, 'I found your shopkeeper. I found his body in the college. I'd like another whisky, please. Fill it right up.'

12

I became a reproof among all mine enemies,
but especially among my neighbours.
Psalm 31:13

Edwin Armstrong was settled behind his desk. He had given
up on Quaile Woods for another evening. It really wasn't
coming and he worried that creatively he was at a standstill.
He turned to another project.

He was struggling to write a modern setting of Psalm
110, the *Dixit Dominus* made famous by Handel. It would be
impossible to improve on that, but after singing it with the
Abbey Chorus Edwin had been fascinated by the words. Like
many psalms they were brutal, he thought, yet humanistic in
a way that transcended the centuries.

Years ago, on one wet night, feeling grotesquely alone
after Marilyn had left him, he had forgotten to eat yet again.
Consumed by the indulgence of misery, he had found himself at evensong in the Abbey. He was following the words as
well as the music of the intermingled voices.

It had been Psalm 102, and suddenly he had heard, *my*
heart is smitten down and withered like grass so that I forget to eat
my bread . . . Yes! At last, someone who wasn't trying to jolly

76

him out of his gloom. His 'emotionally induced eating disorder', as his patronizing doctor called it, was a real response to misery in the heart. It was almost comforting to know he was going through the same despondency as another man in despair, thousands of years ago.

And how about the next bit? — *thou hast taken me up and cast me down* . . . That was exactly how he felt. What sort of God could give him Marilyn, just to take her away? He had loved Marilyn so much that it had transformed his life, and when she had gone he had felt both black rage and a sense that something so wonderful couldn't possibly have lasted. The psalmist too had hated God for what had happened. But he had found relief in being just one tiny bleeding bit of a huge creation. *They all shall wax old as doth a garment, and as a vesture shalt thou change them and they shall be changed, but thou art the same and thy years shall not fail.*

Hardly Wanda Wisley's cup of tea! But he loved it. There was something about the psalmist's grumpy, egotistical, almost teenage belly-aching — 'It's not fair'; 'It's their fault'; 'Stuff you, God!' — which seemed profoundly normal to Edwin.

Take Psalm 41: *if he come to see me, he speaketh vanity . . . Yea, even mine own familiar friend, whom I trusted, who did also eat of my bread, hath laid great wait for me* . . . My best friend hates me! It was adolescent petulance, and the final *world without end. Amen* was almost a throwaway reminder of the greatness of God and the smallness of man.

And even now, it fitted the way Edwin felt about his own fate at Norbridge College. He had wanted to be head of department, but someone had ensured that it didn't happen, and his own resentment made him feel small. It was so good to know the psalmist was huffy too.

Edwin looked up from the keyboard and faced an unwelcome thought. There was another line in Psalm 41 which made him ponder: *and now that he lieth, let him rise up no more.* Of course it didn't mean what Edwin wanted it to mean, but there was a finality about the cadence which made him smile grimly.

Morris Little! He just wouldn't lie down, would he! Edwin put the thought aside, and bent over his computer screen.

* * *

At the Prouts' house, Reg poured Alex Gibson yet another drink. She'd never known him so generous. It was strange to be suddenly listened to with respect again. She managed to get the glass of whisky down, while dragging out the story of the body.

'It was quite appalling; you know, he was still warm . . .'

'Oh, how ghastly!' breathed Pat Johnstone.

'Of course it was ghastly, woman.' David Johnstone looked as fascinated as his wife. 'But you didn't see the Frost kids? Or anyone else?'

'Nobody. The place was deserted. There was only me.' Alex was aware she was showing off slightly. 'And the boy, of course.'

'How awful for you, Alex.' Christine sounded genuinely concerned.

She basked in their sympathy. After all, she'd seen more of the gore than that poor lad who had stumbled over the body. He was on the other side of it, further away from Morris's crushed lips and smashed teeth. Alex had started by hamming it up for her audience, but after a while the memory made her feel sick. Best to get some food down . . .

After this, dinner was a fairly blurred affair. Alex was beginning to feel really ill. Her head had started to pound and her nose was totally blocked up. She lurched into her sister's neat little downstairs loo and tried not to make huge retching noises. When she came out, Reg was waiting with her anorak. She was being bundled out as an embarrassment.

Chris had moved on down the tidy garden path as if to encourage her to leave while Reg had hurried forward to the car. Alex felt herself weaving slightly, and halted abruptly in the porch to get her balance.

'Fancy meeting someone who found that body!' she heard Pat whisper behind her to her husband. 'No wonder she's drunk so much. Can you imagine what it must have been like?'

David Johnstone muttered harshly, 'Reg says she drinks all the time.'

Oh, he does, does he, she thought. But when Reg came hurrying back to support her on the walk down the path, Alex needed his arm. As he drove her home, the dark fells seemed to whizz past the window at double speed.

Reg said, 'David Johnstone's all right, you know. Bit of an eye for the girls but a good businessman. There's nothing going on in Norbridge he doesn't know about. Some of it a bit under-the-counter, but Johnstone's a wheeler-dealer.' Reg was patting his naked head. 'This body business must have shaken you up. You could do worse if you were thinking of selling . . .'

'I'm not.' The words sounded slurred. And if I was going to sell, she thought, it wouldn't be through a bastard like David Johnstone, smart operator and complete creep. She felt the world wheeling around.

'Would you like me to stop?' Reg asked in a particularly patronizing voice. All she could do was shake her head. She knew her body was going to collapse in a spectacular way, but she would not let it happen in front of her brother-in-law. He pulled up beside the bungalow.

'Shall I come in with you?'

'No. I'm fine.'

'Can you manage your keys?'

"Course. G'night.'

She stood and waited on the dark doorstep until he pulled out of the drive. When she was sure the car had gone, she fumbled for the lock. She knew she was crying.

Oh God, she thought, I used to be the one person you could always rely on at parties. I said all the right things, everyone wanted to talk to me, and I made sure everyone was happy. I was an ideal guest. Now, I'm pissed out of my skull with the strain of talking to a horrible couple from Reg's bloody golf club! And how disgusting, to make a 'turn' out of talking about Morris's death like that! I'm gross.

Her front door swung open and bounced madly against the wall. Alex tumbled into the hallway. She kicked it closed behind her, and fell headlong on her hall carpet. Her big glasses toppled off. With her face in the pile, she smelt mud and earth and long-dead cat pee. It was vile and her nose was right in it. She groaned, and then crawled into the cloakroom. She lay down on the cracked linoleum floor, head on the skirting board.

Morris Little must have fallen against the wall, just like this, she thought.

And in drunken clarity she recalled something else. Morris had been holding a book, but she hadn't been able to see the title. Reliving the scene for Reg's friends had made her remember the odd shape of the slim volume. But what was it?

Oh God, she thought, my head feels as if all my ears and eyes are falling out. There's a band of pain from my neck right over my skull and down my nose. I haven't got the strength to move. I'm going to die too, she thought. So what? In the past, she had wanted to die through self-pity. Now she wanted to die through self-loathing. And good riddance to life, she thought.

13

Keep thy tongue from evil, and thy lips, that they speak no guile.
Psalm 34:13

Robert looked greyer when Suzy arrived back from Manchester, the evening before school resumed. It was hectic getting the kids' stuff unpacked, and sorting things out for the morning. At half past nine when Jake disappeared up to his room and Molly was asleep, Suzy and Robert sat down in the living room.

Suzy closed her eyes. She was exhausted. Seeing old friends and relatives with Nigel over the last few days had been tiring and dislocating, and the drive back up north in the fading light had been shattering, with rain and sleet sweeping down off the fells onto the windscreen as if to repel her. Robert handed her a cup of coffee.

She was dreading the stress of going back to work and felt that while Christmas had been good, New Year had been awful and she was more confused than ever.

'I've missed you,' Robert said.

'I've missed you too . . . well, actually life has been non-stop and most of my time has been taken up with arrangements.'

'How was Nigel?' He leant forward slightly. 'How did he get on with Jake?'

There was something about his instant questioning which made her angry. She wanted to relax, not to be interrogated.

'Do you have to start talking about Jake and Nigel the moment I get to sit down? Is it that stepfather business again?'

Suzy could feel her voice rising. How was this happening? She was no sooner home than a row was brewing, with Robert of all people, the calmest person she'd ever met. But why had he brought up the question of Nigel and fatherhood and who was best for Jake the moment she had walked in the door?

Robert was aware he had mistimed things. But Suzy had been racing round with the children, seeing old friends and relations, spending time with Nigel, while he had been sequestered in Tarnfield, trying to write again, getting nowhere, and worrying about the future.

'I never mentioned the stepfather issue, Suzy!'

'But that's what you're thinking about, isn't it? How you should marry me in order to provide a role model for my son. The perfect husband strikes again!'

Robert was not easily provoked but he heard himself saying angrily: 'Well, at least I never walked out on my wife like Nigel did!'

'So if Mary wasn't dead, you'd still be married to her. In love with her, even . . .'

'Yes, of course I would. I would never have left Mary.'

'So where does that leave me? Am I the default option?'

'No! That's not it. It's you, Suzy. I love you. And I want to live with you.'

'So what's wrong with this?'

'Nothing,' Robert said miserably. He felt rebuffed, and it hurt more than he could ever have imagined. Suzy was independent financially and emotionally, and all he knew of marriage was the symbiosis he had had with Mary for two decades. Maybe Suzy was right and he was craving that old insularity. It was important not to be controlling, he could see that. That's what Nigel was. Robert wanted to be cool and not clinging.

'OK, Suzy. Maybe you're right and I'm forcing the issue. If it hadn't been for all the drama in the village bringing us together . . .'

'We might never have been here? Yes!'

So had Robert become involved just because she and the children were in a mess? The suggestion that he had fallen for her because she was vulnerable hurt Suzy deeply. She knew that what she was going to say next was cruel but she still said it.

'Well, you're not the only person who has sensitivities about marriage. Technically I'm still married to Nigel and he's the kids' real father. And he loves them. He's not all bad.'

Robert stared into the empty fireplace. Suddenly The Briars seemed dreary, and the Christmas decorations dusty and forsaken.

'OK, Suzy. Perhaps we both need to cool it.'

Suzy felt the pit of her stomach lurch. They had been so compatible, the odd couple on the outside, but, to their own secret joy, best friends and lovers inside the warmth of The Briars. The thought of losing him made her feel sick, but she was too proud to say so.

Oh bugger, thought Robert. How has this happened? Even though he had suspected it, he had been knocked sideways by the thought that Nigel might really be back in Suzy's emotional life. It made him feel somehow immobilized, incapable of doing anything.

That night lying beside her, not touching, Robert thought, what a pain pride is! Why do I always come over as so smug? '*I would never have left Mary.*' How sanctimonious that sounded. Robert Clark, a template for reliability. Suddenly he had a shaming memory which made him blush in the dark.

Mr Perfect. What a joke — and what a mess.

* * *

83

'Mr Armstrong?'

It was the first day of the so-called spring semester, but winter was in total control. Edwin hated the time between Christmas and Easter. He had been hurrying along the corridor to a meeting of the Inter-Department Committee on Module Changes, one of the many jobs delegated to him by Wanda Wisley. He half recognized the voice, but was surprised when he turned round to see Tom Firth following him, looking agonized but determined.

'Tom! Do you want to see me?'

'Yeah.' Tom rolled his eyes. He would hardly be lurking, calling 'Mr Armstrong,' if he didn't want to see him, would he? Adults were idiots.

'Would you like a cup of coffee?' Edwin asked. Pastoral care was much more important than Module Changes. And this might be a chance to talk to Tom about transferring to Music.

Tom looked even more appalled. 'No, I'm not thirsty. And anyway . . .' He glanced over his shoulder.

'You don't want to be seen with me?'

'Too right!' Tom muttered.

'You'd better come to my room.' Edwin turned back towards the Music Department. Tom followed him warily, a few yards behind.

The office Edwin shared with two visiting lecturers was tiny but dominated by a carved Victorian bookcase stuffed with volumes of church music, his colleagues' tribute to Edwin's full-time status. Tom slumped into the battered easy chair under the window. His body language said that this wasn't to be a teacher-pupil type meeting and Edwin felt disappointed.

'So what can I do for you, Tom?'

Tom twisted and looked out of the window. It was starting to snow in sleety wet streaks on the glass. The weather had suddenly turned very cold after New Year's Day. It was the first day back after the holiday and the building slowly steamed to combat the icy conditions. Tom wrenched his face back to stare at Edwin. His eyes looked huge. He seemed to have become even thinner.

'Did you have a nice break . . . ?' Edwin suddenly stopped. What a stupid question to ask a boy who had found a body, days before Christmas.

But Tom said enthusiastically, 'Yeah, brill. Mam got me a laptop.'

'Very nice!' And very pricey. Mrs Firth must have been working hard on her son's behalf.

There was a long pause.

'So why did you want to see me? Is it about the choir? Or the Music Department?' Edwin asked hopefully.

'Nah. Neither. Look, it's about, you know . . .' The boy drew his hand across his throat in an unmistakable sign.

'Ah, yes. The murder. Very sad. As I said to you at the time, if there's anything I can do . . .'

Tom stared at him. Edwin shifted in his seat. He felt that the balance of power was moving away from him to the strange intense youth. But then, Tom's harsh adolescent voice and staccato manner, not so very different from the Frost brothers' grunts, broke the spell.

'There was summat weird-like about him. Mr Little, that is.'

'Well, yes, Tom . . . he was dead!'

'You can say that again!'

'So what was weird? Apart from the hole in his head?'

Suddenly, they both started to laugh, each horrified at his own reaction. Edwin felt his whole body rock with a release which spread to Tom, whose laughter rippled through the office and set them both off, until tears filled Edwin's eyes and Tom was reduced to wiping his nose on the sleeve of his tatty sweatshirt.

When the laughter faded away they looked at each other in embarrassment.

'Look, Mr Armstrong . . .'

'Call me Edwin.'

'OK, Edwin.' Tom coughed awkwardly. But his accent softened and his eyebrows came together in concentration. 'I've gone over and over this in my head, but I'm sure that Mr Little was carrying a psalm book. You know, verses and chants. A psalter.'

He hardly paused to register Edwin's look of surprise, and then the words came flooding out. 'I was sure that was what it was. But then I thought, why would he want to bring a psalter across from the Abbey? But it wasn't one of theirs, honest. It was different. It was flopped open and the first page was missing. Why would the Frosts want to do that?'

'Why do vandals want to destroy anything?'

'No, Edwin, you don't get it. The first page was torn out properly, not in the way the Frosts would have done it. I knew it was missing because the book opened straight on to a psalm. No introduction.'

'So it wasn't just torn and wrecked. You mean the page was deliberately taken out?'

'That's it exactly. And you could tell it was a special book. Not just the Parish Psalter that we use. I wondered if maybe it was from the college library, or something?'

'We don't have that sort of book in the library here. In fact the only books on the Psalms are here, in my book-case.' Edwin jumped up and unlocked his glass-panelled bookcase. All his books were there, beautifully sorted and in order. Among them were a few nineteenth-century books of music.

'Was it like this?' he asked, taking out a psalter from about 1890.

'A bit . . . I don't know why. I don't know anything about books.'

'But you know about music.'

'Yes, I do. It's my hobby.'

Edwin stroked his chin. 'Why did you want to tell me?'

'I told you, because it was weird. And what happened to the book? If anyone should have it, it should be you and not the police. What would they want with a psalter?'

Edwin felt a sudden protective urge, which shocked him. Teenage church music enthusiasts were few and far between. In Tom's gauche and guarded isolation, he recognized something of himself twenty years earlier.

He said earnestly, 'Look, Tom, I'll find out about the book. It was probably taken away with Morris's body.'

'And you'll let me know what happened to it?'

'Of course I will.'

Tom shrugged, and edged toward the door. 'And summat else . . .'

'Yes?'

'That woman who found me, no one has said owt about her. I asked in the Finance Office yesterday. She's not been back to work.'

Edwin was taken aback by the boy's concern. He hadn't given Alex Gibson a second thought since the night Morris was killed.

'I'll call her,' he said lamely. 'And Tom . . .' Edwin wasn't sure why he was saying this or what good it would do. '. . . don't tell anyone else about the psalter, will you?'

'Are you doolally? Like who?' Tom said, curling his lip up. Then he left the office, banging the door behind him.

A few minutes later, the telephone rang and rang in Alex Gibson's bungalow in Fellside. There was no reply.

14

Such as are blessed of God shall possess the land,
and they that are cursed of Him shall be rooted out.
Psalm 37:22

David Johnstone, estate agent and local developer, poured himself a generous gin and tonic, and took some paperwork into the lounge. The large new house had been built for him and Pat only two years earlier. It was on the edge of one of the prettiest views in the area and the planning permission had taken some getting. Fortunately there had been a barn on the site and the house was technically a conversion. There were still some remnants of the thick boulders which had made up the walls and there were two beams in the kitchen which were original.

But the lounge was David's pride and joy, a vast space with beautiful smooth modern plasterwork, a huge glass sliding door at the end, and a small fireplace with a gas coal-effect fire.

'D'you want this gin or not?' he called to Pat, who was in the kitchen across the large, parquet hallway with its massive mahogany staircase plundered from one of David's developments. 'The ice is melting.'

It was the Saturday after New Year and one of the rare weekends when the Johnstones were not involved in the busy social life which David needed to keep up with his 'contacts'. Some of these people were leading lights in local business organizations. Others were murkier characters he met in bars in Newcastle or Manchester or in remote pubs in the country. But they all needed schmoozing. Drinking was a big part of his life.

David sighed. He loved to sit with a drink by the fire, but he was damned if he was going to have dirty coal or flaky logs in his front room. Yet it wasn't quite the same. He remembered his mother shouting, 'David, you little bastard, you've let the fire go out!' and clouting him on the side of his head. Keeping the fire in had been a religion when David had been a lad.

His mother's hands had been like leather, ingrained with coal dust. His father, a much older man, had once been a miner, when there had been busy pits near the coast. They had always had coal. But his dad wasn't very reliable, in and out of work depending on his drinking and his women. The pits had all been closing anyway, and his dad had been left with one hobby — the local male voice choir. David had been dragged along to it, until he found girls more appealing.

'Come on, Pat,' he called, his bad temper growing. 'Let's have a cuddle.'

His wife was a bit past it, he thought. She'd never been very interested, but he'd persisted and then got her into trouble. That was it, in a family like Pat's — they were Catholics, and marriage was the only option. He had been a bit wet behind the ears then. But it hadn't been too bad, although Pat wasn't the world's greatest brain, as he frequently told her.

The Johnstones had two boys, both in good jobs in the south, and Pat's favourite, the younger, was about to present them with a grandchild. She was really looking forward to being a grandma. Not that David was going to let her bugger off down south every other weekend. She had already started angling to get away. Well, sod that. Her job was here. She was a wife first and a grandma second.

David grimaced. Married to a grandma! He had inherited his father's tendency to womanize, though he could afford higher class totty! And for a bit of rough, there was a woman in Fellside he visited from time to time. But she was unlikely to blab. Safe as houses.

Houses. Now, there was his real passion. He had made a mint in property. He stretched his legs. It was funny how he'd been thinking of his mam and dad. It must be because Fellside, where he was born, was on his mind. Sixty years ago it had been a grim village of terraced houses, homes once for miners and before that for the slate quarrymen, a blot on the local landscape. It wasn't much better now. It was ugly.

But maybe not for long.

On the edge of the village there was a dilapidated Victorian house, boarded up for years, which had housed a group of Anglican nuns when David had been a boy. But there was land around it, and at the back it sloped to the quarry. He'd had his eye on it for some time. The problem was that there was some wrangle about who owned it and no one really cared because Fellside was such an uninviting spot. If he could get over the ownership issue and if he could manoeuvre the council into thinking big, then the quarry could become a lake and leisure area and there would be huge potential for holiday flats in the convent itself.

The problem was the chapel inside the old house. Johnstone could remember it from going there once as a boy for choral evensong with his nan, who was religious and made him sing church music. It was a Victorian monstrosity, he thought, but the sort of thing Little loved. Now he was dead, only a handful of people could remember it in its prime, and if a developer moved fast, it could be stripped before anyone thought about all that listed building crap.

As far as he was aware, the quarry was still owned by the ancient Lord Cleaverthorpe. And Cleaverthorpe had some sort of claim on the convent too. Johnstone's posh mate Brian Dixon was connected to the Cleaverthorpes. The Dixons sang in the Abbey Chorus. Maybe joining this choir might be a good idea?

David pondered a strategy. He needed to get his hands on that bungalow where baldy-bonce Prout's drunken sister-in-law lived, too. He'd checked. The bungalow's squalid little garden bordered the convent's grounds.

But his imagination was running away with him . . .

'Come here, woman!' he yelled, more aggressively this time, and scrawny Pat came running in from the kitchen at his command. David pulled her onto his lap, pinny and all, and stuck his hand down her jumper in a proprietorial way. She still had tits, he thought, though only just.

'You'd better forget any ideas about going down south for a while,' he said.

Pat's eyes narrowed. She looked out of the french window at the dusk lengthening like fat dark fingers in the garden, and waited for him to get bored.

These days it didn't take long, thank goodness.

* * *

Alex Gibson shifted in the lumpy, dented bed that had been her mother's. She had wanted to die but she hadn't had the energy to do anything about it, and so here she was, alive. She knew, deep down, that she wasn't the suicidal type. It required too much organization. She had got to the point where she just didn't care enough about herself even to negate herself. Her pain had been too low-level, the miserable discomfort of the hangover from hell meeting a rotten cold. She had been ill for days and had fed her condition with painkillers, washed down with whisky and hot water, till she had no memory of exactly when she had collapsed in bed.

But on the evening of the fifth night, she had run out of sleeping tablets to scrabble for on the tatty old bedside table. She started dreaming, all the usual old horrors. Except that this time they ended with her racing down the corridors of

Norbridge College, away from Robert Clark. She woke in a sweat. It had been luridly realistic except that she knew she was too fat and breathless now to run anywhere.

She had put Robert Clark out of her mind over Christmas and New Year, but now in the cold light of day she looked back to the night she had found Morris Little's body. Even in her shock and distress, the one thing she had wanted to avoid at all costs was meeting Robert again. She had gone out in icy rain and waited in the lane for a taxi rather than risk bumping into him at the Cliffords'.

But eventually he would come face to face with her, at short range. She mustn't let that happen. If necessary, she would resign from the college. She hadn't been to work for days anyway, and no one had so much as phoned her. She could sell the bungalow and go away. Chris and Reg would be pleased. She'd bugger off and leave them to it, with their ghastly friend David Johnstone. They could have the cash and get rid of the embarrassment.

The next morning she would give in her notice.

Her night was sweaty, restless and wretched. When she woke, in the soggy light of the winter morning, she dragged herself into the smelly kitchen to drink some scalding coffee. This is it, she thought. Goodbye Norbridge.

And then her phone shrieked out. Astonished, she picked it up, her hand looking surprisingly small and bony, shaking in the greasy grey light of morning.

'Alex, how are you?'

'Fine. I'm OK. Who's speaking? What time is it?'

'It's five past nine. I tried yesterday but there was no reply.'

'I've been rather poorly. A fluey cold. Did you say your name?'

'It's Edwin. Edwin Armstrong. You know, from the Music Department. We met the night of Morris Little's murder.'

Alex sat up on the rickety kitchen chair, and listened.

'Young Tom Firth asked me to call you. We were worried about how you were. Are you OK? You sound a bit shaky.'

'I'm fine. Just a fluey cold like I said. There's no problem. I'm coming into work later today.' Was she? Well, she would have to, now.

'I'm glad to hear it. Look, there's something I'd like to ask you about. It's a bit complicated. If you're feeling better, could we meet today? Just for a few minutes? I need your help.'

Alex stared at the phone. What could Edwin Armstrong possibly want from her? She didn't know what to say.

'Look, Alex, I'm in a hurry now. Should we have lunch? In the staff restaurant? Twelve fifteen?'

'Uh . . .'

'Good, see you there.'

'Oh, OK then. And Edwin, thanks.'

The word sounded rusty on her lips. But she had said it. And she knew she would have to turn up in what they called the 'staff caff'. It was literally years since anyone had asked her for help other than in settling an invoice. What could it be about?

At the other end of the line, Edwin wondered if he had done the right thing. Alex was hardly his lunch companion of choice. But she had seen Morris Little's body within seconds of Tom finding it. If there had been a psalter knocking about, she would perhaps have recognized it. What was it Lynn had said about her before the abandoned dinner party? '*Alex Gibson likes church music so you'll have something to talk about.*'

Maybe Alex would be able to clarify things. It was worth a try. There was something rather odd about the whole business and Edwin was beginning to wonder what exactly had happened in the corridor outside his office.

15

And He hath put a new song in my mouth,
even a thanksgiving unto our God.
Psalm 40:3

'It's great to have a minute to ourselves,' Rev Paul said to his wife.

He had been rather surprised when Mark Wilson had turned down the usual invitation to supper that evening. Mark was their neighbour on the estate, in a short-term council let. He made no secret of the fact that he had taken a lower grade job for a while, so he could think about his future in the Church. Even so, his maisonette flat had more space than Paul and Jenny's house. They needed an office for Paul on the ground floor, but despite the squash Mark liked the warmth and busyness of the vicarage.

But tonight Mark wasn't here. The baby was asleep. So for once Paul and Jenny were alone. Paul approached his wife rather gingerly. She seemed to tense whenever he came near her.

'I mean,' he went on, trying to hit the right note, 'I really like Mark, but he's been here every night since New Year and I suppose that must be a bit awkward for you.'

'For me?' Jenny stared into the sink where the potato peelings curled like fat tropical vegetation. 'No, he's all right.'

'But I can see it from your point of view. I mean, you're the one who has to look after him — making the meals, chatting, and things . . .'

'You can't see anything from my point of view, Paul.'

'What do you mean? What have I said?'

'Well, implying that I can't cope with Mark, for a start.' She talked angrily to the wall. 'I'm your equal and your partner, spiritually and practically. So everything I do, I do because I want to. If Mark wasn't welcome here, I'd tell him.' Jenny peeled with a new intensity.

'So how do you think Mark is doing?' Paul asked his wife in an attempt to build a bridge. It was the sort of excluding, couple-affirming question that they had asked of each other throughout their relationship.

'Mark's very certain about things. And you know, Paul, his interest in the liturgy is different. I find it quite exciting.'

'You do?' Paul looked at his wife's back with new interest. Jenny wheeled round, peeler in hand.

'Yes. I know we come from the evangelical wing of the Church. But I've been thinking about what Mark has said . . .'

'Like what?'

'Well, here at Fellside the church is ugly, isn't it? But we should think about aesthetics too, for the poor souls that live here. I know you're going to say that it's fine, somewhere like Oxford, say, to have choral evensong, and fabulous music, and that we can't do that properly in Fellside. But Mark has made me think about another form of spirituality. The beauty of holiness. We maybe should be guardians of beauty too. You know, I'm sick of rap and grime beat and harshness.'

'But that's what people want . . .'

'Is it? What about the Victorian Church in darkest Liverpool? Or London? It was those self-denying priests in inner cities who reinstated beauty. I've been thinking about those old East End priests. The first priests to be called

95

"Father" were Anglicans, you know, not Catholics. Fathers to their people. Gerard Manley Hopkins, Cecil Quaile Woods up here. You know all about him, don't you?'

'So what are you suggesting? That I flap around in a lacy surplice and ask people to call me Father Whinfell?'

'Don't mock me. And what would be wrong with being Father Paul? People need to look up to their priest. I've been reading this pamphlet Mark lent me — it's called "The New Puseyites". There's a movement, just the beginning of one . . .'

'But that's the exact opposite of everything we've stood for!'

'No, it isn't, really. Life with unemployment, drugs and dreariness isn't so different from the Victorian post-industrial revolution with its laudanum and drink and dark terraced housing. Only with us it's post-computerization. Mark has been talking to me about it . . .'

This was all totally new. Despite his genuine interest, Paul was feeling little stabs of shock and hurt. When had she been having these long conversations with Mark? Why hadn't he been included?

'So do you know where Mark is tonight?' He tried to make it sound casual.

'He's gone into Norbridge. He's thinking of joining a choral society at the Abbey.'

'What? You mean the Abbey Chorus? But that's just a load of sad oldies.'

But Paul felt strangely undermined. He left her peeling, and crept away back to the computer to log on to ancestry. co.uk. The past seemed reassuring. He was searching for his great-great-grandfather, and it was proving truly absorbing. But whenever he had mentioned it to Jenny, she hadn't wanted to know.

So it was funny that she had mentioned Cecil Quaile Woods.

* * *

96

Alex Gibson met Edwin Armstrong for lunch in the college canteen as planned. Her face looked like waxy old cheese, her nose jutting out like a bright pink plastic beak with her big heavy bifocals perched on top. Her hair was more scraped back than ever and she was wearing an enormous androgynous cardigan.

Edwin felt sorry for her. Lynn had told him that she had gone to pieces after her mother died and there had been some sort of crisis prior to that. Alex was fumbling with files and bags and papers, and looking huntedly around the room. She was sitting at the only table which had been available when she arrived — an island in the middle of a fast-food motorway.

For her part, Alex had been horrified. She had only been in the canteen once or twice before, and had hoped to sit in the darkest alcove. But everyone was back for the busiest period of the year, and the place was packed. Edwin joined her and said hello, aware of her discomfort. He put down his tray at the table and went straight to the point. She clearly wanted to escape.

'Alex, I'm sorry if this seems insensitive, but when you found Tom with Morris's body, did you notice a book?'

'Yes, I did as a matter of fact. I only remembered it on New Year's Day.' She winced.

'Look, what sort of book was it?'

'How would I know? Look, I can't be sure, but it was an unusual shape. My impression was that it was old. With respect to speaking ill of the dead . . . was it something Morris had pinched from the college?'

Edwin was surprised at her directness. 'I don't think so,' he said, 'but I've been wondering why Morris was in the college at all.'

'Me too. Was the book something to do with music? I thought it might be because of the shape of it. It was landscape. Longways. My first thought was that it was an antique children's book of some sort.'

'What did it look like? Just say whatever comes into your head.'

'If you push me I suppose it looked like a . . . well . . . a psalter.'

'You thought so too! So did Tom. How did you know?'

'I sang in a church choir for years. In London. With my husband.'

'Really? What sort of choir was it?'

'Oh, High end. Actually it was bloody precious, to be honest. The sort of choir where people wear Prada under the surplices. And that's just the men!'

Edwin laughed. Alex looked startled and then laughed herself.

'I just wondered, because the police haven't said anything about a book,' Edwin said. 'I'm going to ask them what happened to it.'

'Could the Frosts have come back and stolen it?'

'Maybe, though I doubt they'd have known a psalter from a copy of *Nuts*.'

'Well, I did, though I'm more into *Loaded*.'

Edwin laughed again, surprised at her sense of humour. 'Seriously, how much do you know about this? What have you sung in the past?'

'The last thing I did was Handel's *Dixit Dominus*. But I've done just about everything from Mozart to Mahler.'

Dixit Dominus! What a coincidence, when he was working on that himself. And the Handel version wasn't exactly easy. If Alex Gibson really knew her stuff then she might well recognize a psalter.

He needed more strong women singers. On the spur of the moment he said, 'Look, Alex, if you're an experienced chorister, why not join the Abbey Chorus? We need people like you.'

'What, ageing sopranos?'

'Rubbish. A good singer with proper intonation can keep going into her fifties, or even her sixties and beyond.'

Alex squirmed. Did she look that old? She would have described herself as forty-something. And anyway, there was no way she wanted to start singing again, getting involved.

What was she doing, gassing on like this? It was the intoxication of being listened to, and light-headedness after hardly eating for days. But she had to go back to the office. She was behind with her work.

'Hey!' Edwin was signalling at someone. 'Look, there's Robert Clark. He started singing with the Chorus a couple of years ago.'

A look of wild panic seemed to pummel Alex's podgy features from the inside. 'I'll think about it. I've got to go.' She stood up, turning her back on Edwin, but as she bent down to grab her belongings, Robert strolled over, clutching a baguette.

'Hi,' he said, his eyes floating past her to Edwin. And that was that. There wasn't even a flicker of acknowledgement.

Had she really altered so much? Alex thought. In real horror, she looked down at her bulging waist and fat thighs. She'd given up on them. But her face? Had that really changed beyond recognition? The two men were talking about the choir practice that night, and how they might do Stainer's *Crucifixion*. Alex loved that piece.

'Why not join us?' Robert said to her. But his eyes had a faraway look.

There's something wrong with Robert, Edwin thought. He's completely distracted. He's hardly acknowledged us. It's not like Robert to be rude.

'I must go,' Alex mumbled, head down. 'Excuse me.' She turned away from them, and started pushing between the crowded tables to get out of the cafeteria.

'Who was that?' Robert asked, without much interest.

'Alex Gibson. She's the woman who was coming to supper at Lynn's before Christmas. The one who found Tom with Morris's body. You remember. I asked you to come and look after her, but she went home. She's one of Lynn's sad cases.' He paused. 'But actually, she's not like that really. She kept her head and dealt with Tom very well. I quite like her. I was trying to get her to join the Chorus, but she didn't seem keen.'

'Pity.' Robert had moved away, towards the queue to pay. Edwin was mildly surprised. Usually, Robert would stop for a chat, especially about something so interesting.

But this time his friend strode ahead, lost in his own thoughts.

16

The singers also and trumpeters shall he rehearse . . .
Psalm 87:7

That evening, Edwin looked in astonishment at the heaving
group of people in the chancel of the Abbey. It was the first
meeting of the New Year. Usually after Christmas it was hard
to herd everyone back because of the weather and the dark.
But this time, everyone was there. And there were three . . .
no, four new people milling round in the group. He thought
he'd better take some names.

'Hi, I'm Edwin Armstrong, the secretary. And you are?'

'David Johnstone. The estate agent. You must have
heard of us. New member. I'm here with my lady wife. Pat?'
the man called. 'Get over here and meet this chap.'

'Well, David, it's nice to see you. We do usually have a very
simple audition, but I don't think we'll have time to do that
now . . .' Edwin looked around wildly for the musical director,
Robin, a small fussy man who was also the Abbey choirmaster.
He would not be impressed by the sudden invasion of hopefuls.

'Which part do you sing?' Edwin asked David Johnstone.

'Oh, bass of course,' the man boomed at him. Edwin
knew the choirmaster was keen on younger voices and David

Johnstone looked to be in his sixties, but his spoken voice was clear and confident enough. And men were at a premium.

'Used to be a boy chorister, y'know,' Johnstone was saying, though he knew hanging about at the edge of the Fellside Male Voice Choir while his father drunkenly bawled was hardly the same as singing 'Oh for the Wings of a Dove' in Westminster Abbey. But he went on gamely: 'And we do know some other people here — the Dixons.'

Edwin's heart sank. The Dixons both had thin voices. Brian Dixon had a posh accent and a ferrety face; his wife was inclined to sing flat. They contributed far more fuss and angst than volume to the Chorus.

'And you?' Edwin asked Pat Johnstone. 'Which part do you sing?'

'Oh, you know, I like to sing the tune.'

Edwin's heart sank further. He needed good sopranos desperately but Pat sounded like another wavering Millie Dixon.

'Thanks,' he added courteously. 'Do take a seat in the stalls.' Pat looked rather shocked and her eyes widened. Then she cackled.

'The choir stalls,' Edwin said. 'Not the loos.'

'Ooh, silly me! By the way, do we wear robes?'

'Only occasionally for some big services.'

'They're not man-made velvet, are they? I've got an allergy.'

'No, they're not.'

This was going to be a fun practice. There were two other newcomers. The next was a handsome fair-haired younger man who smiled warmly at Edwin.

'Hi. I'm Mark Wilson. I heard about the Chorus because I'm involved with the Church. I go to Fellside Fellowship.'

'Really? I wouldn't have thought this sort of thing was for you.'

'Well, I'm new to it, I must admit. But I can read music and play guitar. I think I'm probably a tenor.'

'You are? That's good news. If you sit in the choir stalls, I'll make sure you get a place next to Tom Firth. He's our rising star in the tenor line.'

Mark beamed back. 'Thank you so much.'

'And there's me!' A very large man with a long grey ponytail moved out of the crowd, leaving a wake behind him. Oh no, Edwin thought. Freddie, Wanda Wisley's partner. What on earth could he be doing here?

'Hello, Edwin,' Freddie was roaring. 'I read about the choir after that man was killed and thought, *ja*, it sounds interesting and I would like to sing. Different style, but what the hell, eh?'

He nudged Edwin heartily. At least Freddie was honest about his motives.

A minute later he called everyone to order. There was the usual interminable shuffling into the stalls, with people saving places for their friends or clambering into the front row.

'Everyone, shall we start with a minute's silence for Morris?' There was some nudging and shushing and everyone looked suitably reflective.

'Thank you, everyone.' Edwin broke the silence sixty seconds later. 'Welcome back to our weekly practices. Robin and I' — he indicated the choirmaster, who smiled icily at the group — 'have been discussing our next concert. The suggestions this time are from Robin, who'd like to nominate Duruflé's Requiem, which is a beautiful and unusual piece, and of course Stainer's *Crucifixion* which is much simpler and more congregational and was suggested by poor Morris, before he died. Any thoughts?'

There was always a huge hubbub at this stage and Edwin often had to work very hard to keep the members happy. The more ambitious singers had been voluble before Christmas in wanting the Duruflé and a row with Morris Little had seemed inevitable. But, for the first time Edwin could remember, all the choristers seemed to be saying the same thing with more or less dutiful enthusiasm.

David Johnstone coughed noisily. 'Look,' he boomed in his deep voice, 'I know I'm a newcomer, first time here tonight and all that. But that's why I'd like to speak. It seems to be everyone's view that we should do what poor Mr Little wanted. I had the greatest respect for him. It would make sense, wouldn't it, to sing the music of his choice? And perhaps to even dedicate the concert to him?'

'And wasn't Morris talking about a local connection? With the Stainer?' Brian Dixon piped up.

'Well, I'm not entirely sure about that,' Edwin said tactfully, 'but Morris was certainly very keen on doing the piece.'

'And surely we should take account of his wishes,' Johnstone boomed again.

'Well, that settles it,' Edwin said. 'I've brought my CD player. Let's familiarize ourselves with Stainer's *Crucifixion*.'

He was reassured when the music started. He had forgotten how evocative it was and felt guilty for thinking snobbishly that it was too simple for the Chorus. He listened as the opening bars of the organ music soared under the tenor voice. *And they came to a place named Gethsemane.* The beauty of the piece asserted itself, and Edwin found himself concentrating.

Then there was a sudden shuffling movement at the back of the stalls and Edwin looked up. Yet another new member was coming to join the Chorus, but this one was very tentative. She stood unnoticed by most of the choir, who were intent on the rousing melody of 'Fling wide the gates'. Then she saw Edwin and smiled. He was amazed at how that smile transformed Alex Gibson's face.

* * *

The following week, Wanda Wisley made it public that she was having a prestigious lunch party and inviting everyone to bring partners.

'You must bring someone, Edwin,' she said with a touch of malice. 'I don't want spare people hanging about.'

Her invitation caused Edwin problems. He was wary of asking any of the single women in the choir. As a group the sopranos were rather weak. One had a boyfriend in Glasgow;

one was having a painful affair with a married bass; one was rather butch; and the fourth was very pretty, in her early twenties and very giggly. She was already being targeted by David Johnstone who stared at her breasts, and bought her bottles of Bacardi Breezer in the pub while Pat either watched indifferently or let rip with her horrible cackling laugh.

After the third practice of the term Edwin had found himself on the Abbey steps with Alex Gibson. He had asked her a few times how she had enjoyed the choir and she had mentioned how rusty she felt. She had bought a new red coat and seemed to have lost weight; that evening he had heard her quite clearly, a beautiful, rich mezzo-soprano which sounded surprisingly young.

'You seem to be fitting in well,' he said. 'Are you coming to the Crown and Thistle?'

'Oh . . . No, I don't think so. I'm trying to cut down on drink.'

'Post-Christmas is always a problem, isn't it?'

'With me its post anytime, I'm afraid. I was drinking far too much.'

'I went through a patch like that,' said Edwin. 'It crept up on me. I wasn't eating and I hardly noticed how much drink I was putting away.'

'I always eat! But it hit me a few weeks ago when I went to church, saw the chalice coming and thought, hair of the dog.'

Edwin laughed. 'So I guess I can't persuade you?'

'No, but thanks anyway. I'd better get back.'

For Alex, the confession had been simple but saying it made her shake. She had intended to open a bottle of wine at home, alone, as usual. Her drinking was a private affair, and she realized she had refused his invitation because she was scared of going to the pub and getting drunk with other people. The insight shocked her.

When she got home, she went to the fridge and then paused. On Chorus practice nights she came home much later than usual. If she could do without a drink at half past six, why start at half past nine? But without the wine, how

105

would she relax? What was the point of the day? Her hand twitched towards the fridge handle. And then she remembered Edwin's face. She had refused his invitation on the grounds she was drinking too much. She felt uncomfortable about deceiving him even though he would never know. She didn't have to give up drink forever. But how about . . . well, just not having one tonight?

She would need something to do, to keep her mind off it. In the dark living room, which still held her mother's frayed three-piece suite, there was a chest of drawers. Alex had stuffed some of her own papers there when she had moved in. She had always kept meticulously researched notes for her work. They were cramming the drawers now, her notebooks discarded, rammed away where she couldn't see them.

In the third drawer down, she found the *Dixit Dominus* score. Just opening it reminded her of the best days of her marriage. But instead of letting anger choke her, she tried to think about the music.

Under the score, an old tape cassette fell out. On it was a Post-It note, with her husband's writing: *S. McFay: Bass*. Alex waited for the friendly pain, but it didn't come. She took the cassette and inserted it in the ancient radio cassette player in the kitchen, wincing at the amount of grease that was clogging up the buttons. The music sounded alien, thin and strange at first, but she realized it wasn't the Handel which was at fault, but the unfamiliarity of any music in her kitchen.

Then she found herself scrabbling to find the place in the score. It really was so beautiful and very challenging. She sang along with the recording, listening to her own voice filling the drab kitchen. An hour later she made some tea, drank it, and went to bed with her head full of music. The next morning she woke after sleeping for six hours, her first continuous natural rest for months. It was another grey, dreary, winter's day, but this time Alex was looking forward to it.

It was later the next evening, when she was practising the Stainer, that Edwin Armstrong rang. 'Are you busy a week on Sunday?'

'I'll just look in my handheld organizer, also known as a pocket diary. Yes, that's free.'

Edwin laughed. 'I'm not sure you'll be interested, but my boss in the Music Department, Wanda Wisley, is having a drinks party. I'm invited and she's asked me to bring a guest. She's made quite a fuss about the fact that no one is supposed to go alone.'

There was a long pause. Alex felt surprised and then suspicious.

'So you want me to go with you?' Her voice was cynical, more sophisticated than he remembered.

'Yes, I do.' Edwin felt uncomfortable. Perhaps this was a misguided move. He had thought that Alex Gibson was the last person anyone would take as a serious partner. By inviting her he would be proclaiming his singleness more effectively than by going alone. And like many men he had assumed she would be grateful. But suddenly, he felt that Alex had rumbled him.

'So you think that by taking a fat old frump like me you'll call Wanda's bluff, do you?'

He said, 'I'm sorry. Please forget about it.'

'I don't want to forget about it. I want to know why you asked me.'

He felt the prickly blush of embarrassment creeping over him. It had been totally wrong of him, cruel even, to use Alex in this way. He was being arrogant, insensitive, having a private joke at someone else's expense.

'Because . . .' He swallowed. 'Because I like you and I know that with you, there'd be no fuss.' He paused. She said nothing, so he went on: 'I think Wanda insisted on me taking a partner to embarrass me. Everyone knows I've been on my own for quite a while. I'm always awkward at these things.'

Suddenly Alex's voice sounded light and amused. He wanted to mumble some further explanation but it wouldn't come. And then he realized she was laughing.

'You're in a hole, so stop digging! Actually, Edwin, I'd love to come! I can't wait to see Wanda Wisley's face when you turn up with the drudge from the Finance Department. I might have to put my knickers on my head and give you all a rendition of "I will survive". This could be fun.'

Fun was not an Edwin Armstrong word, but suddenly he suspected that it might be an Alex Gibson one. And for the first time in a long time, he wanted to do something with no catch, alongside a woman who was old enough and worldly enough to take Wanda Wisley in her stride.

'So you'll come?'

'Yes, knickers or not.'

Alex knew that when Edwin rang off he was both relieved and embarrassed, and it amused her. Later, the inevitable worry about the dress code at the party nearly sent her fridge-wards. And then she thought, what the hell does it matter what I wear? He's taking me as a piss-take, so even in Mum's Crimplene tracksuit and carpet slippers I'd be fulfilling my role.

But she was enjoying the idea of turning up at Wanda's party and surprising them all. Including Edwin Armstrong.

17

They talk of vanity every one with his neighbour;
they do but flatter with their lips and dissemble in their double heart.
Psalm 12:2

On the morning of the party, Wanda Wisley stood in her small kitchen feeling mildly hysterical. In front of her were trays of Marks and Spencer's party food, piles of mismatched plates, and cutlery and napkins jostling for space. Her cleaner, a lumpy woman from the Chapterhouse estate, stood next to her.

'Well, I don't know how you expect me to deal with this,' the woman said with a malicious air. 'We'll never get all them into the oven!'

'I had no idea they needed heating,' Wanda said. 'But if they do, you'll have to try and use your initiative.'

The woman gawped at her, standing with her arms folded while waiting for instructions. Having to give paint-by-numbers instructions to a grumpy 'daily' was not what Wanda had anticipated when she planned her party. Freddie of course was still upstairs, having snored his Saturday night excesses away, and finally risen to lock himself in the bathroom.

Wanda had made a big decision after Christmas to change the focus of her Norbridge social life. When she'd arrived in the autumn she'd tried to target what she thought of as the artistic community, but it had slowly dawned on her that the motley crew of painters, sculptors and writers she had latched onto were not the district's movers and shakers. Artists in the Norbridge area tended to be New Age bohemians living in squalid crofts, or well-heeled business people with their own shops and galleries. They were not generally thought of as local celebrities.

One arena she was woefully ignorant about was the Abbey, which she had written off as impossible to penetrate. And then Freddie had joined this ridiculous choir and come home bleating about the important people there — the Johnstones who were filthy rich in property and talking about sponsoring concerts; the Dean who could open up the place to a college performance; the Dixons who seemed to be related to one of the major local landowners; the Cliffords and Clarks who seemed to know everyone; and of course that boring pain Edwin Armstrong.

So she had invited them, along with the college Principal of course, to a Sunday lunch party. This was to be high-powered. No flirting, no sex, no dope. They would all go to church, she assumed, so there was no way they'd arrive till well after one o'clock, would they? It was eleven forty-five, so surely she'd have enough time.

'I don't think we'll get this done. They could be here any moment,' said the cleaner with satisfaction.

'What? I'm not expecting anyone before one.'

'You said one o'clock on the invites. I saw,' said the cleaner accusingly. 'If you said one o'clock, they'll be here at one! Or before one, mebbe.'

'What? On time? Holy shit! Hicksville! So we've got about an hour to get it all done. Not being ready is not an option,' snapped Wanda. 'Just get your finger out, will you? The oven trays are there. I'm going to sort out the ice and the champagne.'

'Ooh, very a-la-posh,' mumbled the cleaner, and she started to open the packets, painfully slowly. Wanda switched on the oven with an angry flick of her wrist. The bloody thing had better heat up fast!

When she'd finished racing round, the living room of the cottage did look rather nice, Wanda thought, because she had bought dozens of hothouse flowers which she arranged, Mediterranean-style, in kitchenware, with buckets and jugs all round the place. A giant modern oil painting was propped on the mantelpiece and all the tatty chairs and needlepoint cushions had been relegated to the spare bedroom. Coats could go on the pegs in the porch — she had dumped Freddie's huge fake Barbour and massive new cycling cape in the blanket box, where a fabulous arrangement of lilies and peonies balanced scarily on the top in an asparagus steamer.

'Well, hello! Here we are!' announced a booming voice.

The Johnstones were the first to arrive, fifteen minutes early, bringing a tired-looking box of Belgian chocolates which Wanda imagined they'd received for Christmas. But as far as she was concerned this confirmed that they were filthy rich. Everyone knew the rich were mean. She gushed over them, pouring champagne into flimsy flutes.

'Cheers! Such a pretty . . . er . . . lounge,' gushed Pat.

But the Johnstones didn't want to talk to Wanda. They were clearly waiting to pounce on the college Principal. David Johnstone was involved in putting forward some sort of tender to sell college land. He really was a mover and shaker, Wanda thought. And he was donating money to ensure that proper programmes were printed for the Stainer concert with the names of benefactors in full, along with the Johnstone logo.

The cottage slowly filled up with couples. It had amused her to embarrass Edwin Armstrong by demanding loudly, in front of the Principal, that he brought a guest. One of the few bits of local gossip Wanda had picked up was that Edwin was alone after being dumped a few years ago. Strange! He wasn't Jude Law but he wasn't bad-looking — in fact she might have quite fancied him herself with his thick dark hair, square jaw and quiet manner — but there was a withdrawn, slightly superior quality about him which irritated her.

So who would he bring to the party? She could hardly wait to find out.

* * *

The day after receiving Edwin's invitation, Alex had left work early, come home, called a contract cleaning company in Carlisle and arranged for them to blitz the bungalow. It was easy if pricey, but the one thing she had was money in the bank — booze was relatively cheap and she hadn't bought much in the way of Christmas presents this year. She'd had an orgasmic time in Yellow Pages, calling window cleaners, gardeners, a plumber to sort out the drains in the bathroom and a gas installer to come and sort out, once and for all, why the kitchen always smelt as if fifteen big cats had peed in the sink.

Then she'd taken a deep breath and called a hairdresser. The effort of making the appointment had made her long for a whisky, but she'd told herself; no drink till she had lost a stone. The scales in the bathroom were grey with fluff and dust, so she had to take her glasses off and stoop to peer at the result — which was an unbelievable one hundred and eighty pounds. She had never been more than ten stone before. She started taking her clothes off, throwing shoes, socks, trousers, a fleece, a blouse and a hideous vest to the four winds till she was naked and had lost four pounds. She was going to get this down. She had never been slender but she had always been curvy. Now the curves had amalgamated into one large round ball. But the skin tone wasn't bad and the boobs could be heaved up into place. She had good basic bones, and she suddenly caught sight of herself in the greasy mirror on her mother's bathroom cabinet. She was smiling. For a moment Alex saw herself as she had been twenty-five years ago, in this same bathroom, before she had gone to London, to university and marriage.

I had a life before I met my husband, she suddenly thought. My mum loved me and told me I was beautiful, and my older sister said I had talent. She was right. I earned a living through my talent which is more than most people do. I was a happy person, in my own right.

She remembered her mother saying: 'You get away from here, girl. You go to university. We'll always be here if you need us.' So she had gone to London to study, and then slowly and carefully worked away at her hobby until it had become a real job, and she had been successful. She had never looked back — till now.

Her mum had already been in decline when Alex had returned to Norbridge. That was what made Alzheimer's so strange and cruel. It wasn't just holes in the brain. The person changed. Everything became cruder and narrower. Her lovely mum, who had been so optimistic, so adventurous without ever living anywhere but Cumbria, had been reduced. And of course Alex had been reduced with her. Living with her mother, in what should have been the warm womb of the bungalow, she had really been in a box with her, buried alive.

The idea made her shudder. Being trapped was one of her greatest fears. Then she thought, I may have claustrophobia but I haven't got dementia. I'm going to survive, like I told Edwin.

So here she was now, in Wanda Wisley's cramped little sitting room, trying not to sneeze because of all the pollen from Wanda's absurd flowers, flicking back her new shiny auburn hair from her plump but less flabby features. She was wearing a long black slinky skirt retrieved from the suitcase full of London clothes. The zip didn't quite do up but it was covered by a deep red shirt with beads all over it, which she had bought in one of those wonderful cottage-industry craft shops you could find only in Cumbria. She had even bought a matching lipstick.

And Edwin had said, 'Oh! You look rather exotic. But where are the knickers for your head?'

'Darling, don't tell anyone but I'm not wearing them!' To her relief, Edwin had thrown his head back and laughed. It was a good sign.

'I thought you were a good churchgoer,' he said.

'Actually,' she said, more seriously, 'I'm an agnostic really. I go to church through habit. Any faith I had, I lost when I was divorced. Does that bother you?'

'Not at all,' Edwin said. 'It's interesting.'

I *am* interesting, Alex thought for the first time in years. So here she was, orange juice in hand, making conversation with the great and good of Norbridge. And only once had she caught herself straining to see her husband who wasn't there.

But someone else was. Across the room Alex saw Robert Clark. It hadn't occurred to Alex he would be here at a Music Department party. But Norbridge was a small place and she should have realized everyone socialized with everyone.

Bugger. She had to behave normally. She smiled at him, and he smiled back, uncertainly.

'Who's that?' Robert said to Lynn Clifford.

'Oh, that's Alex. You know her — she found Tom Firth with Morris's body. Now she's joined the Chorus. I think she usually wears her hair tied back and sits at the dark end of the stalls.'

'Oh, I know who you mean. I just didn't recognize her. Big woman. Grey!'

'Well, she was!' Lynn laughed. 'She's certainly made an effort today. I used to think she was rather negative but she's got quite a sense of humour. It always helps.'

It certainly does, Robert thought. He felt rather low. At the last minute Suzy had been commandeered to take Jake to the Fellside Fellowship so he had come on his own, much to Wanda's irritation. He was missing Suzy's commentary on the guests. But that wasn't all. In this awful, dreary month, with such a formal coolness between them, he longed for her jokes and the old cheeriness of their unlikely love affair. But he had been the one who suggested cooling it. And he had to stick with that.

He looked across the room again, as Alex moved to talk to the Johnstones. For a minute he thought . . . It was ridiculous. But he felt as if someone had walked across his grave. Or Mary's.

* * *

The Cliffords left the party early. Neil had a christening at three o'clock and Lynn was busy. She would be working all the next week, helping out at Uplands School. Sometimes she ran the church office, sometimes she helped at the Deanery, and once she had done a few weeks in the Abbey shop. It wasn't the career she had expected but being a rector's wife satisfied her in a way she had never thought possible.

The phone rang and she put down the laundry basket.

'Mum.' Chloe's voice sounded tight. Lynn felt a frisson of alarm.

'What is it, darling?'

'Mummy, I want to come home.' Chloe was crying — ugly, snuffling noises.

'What on earth is wrong?'

Since her New Year's Eve trauma, Chloe had changed. She had been quiet and unassuming, staying in and working on her revision, until she went back to university in January. Poppy had called once, but Chloe had told her she had too much work to go out.

Mother and daughter had talked more, though not with the intimacy that Lynn craved. She was aware that Chloe was holding back, and it worried her. Lynn was painfully conscious that she had had no mother of her own, and felt hampered and awkward in her reactions to her daughter. Her relationship with Chloe was so vital that she felt she ought to play it down to keep it in proportion. It would have been good to discuss this with another mum, but there was no one she felt she could talk to without somehow betraying Chloe or even Neil.

She had seen Jenny Whinfell in the shopping centre in Norbridge, and had toyed with the idea of asking her for a coffee and having a heart-to-heart. Chloe had babysat for the Whinfells and had said how 'cool' Jenny was. And she was a vicar's wife. But Jenny had been in a hurry, with the baby in a buggy, and her manner had been rather distant. So Lynn had been left, adrift, wondering how to deal with the new Chloe.

Then her daughter had gone back to Leeds, and Lynn had genuinely thought Chloe was feeling much better. But this was a new crisis.

'You're in the middle of exams, darling.'

'No, I'm not! Don't you listen to anything? The exams finished on Friday.'

'So did you go out? To celebrate?'

'I've got nothing to celebrate. I hate it here!'

The sound of sobbing came bursting down the landline. Oh dear, Lynn thought. Chloe had always been a bit of a party animal in the past.

'Darling, if you really feel bad, you can come home just for a week. Get the train tomorrow.'

The sobbing lessened enough for Chloe to say miserably, 'But what about the train fare?'

'Oh, I suppose you'd better use your card and I'll give you the cash.'

The little voice was instantly brighter. 'OK, Mum, I'll be on the eleven twenty-five tomorrow morning.' She's all organized, thought Lynn. She's planned this. But why is she so desperate to come home? And what will Neil say?

18

O be joyful in the Lord all ye lands; serve the Lord with gladness,
and come before His presence with a song.
Psalm 100:1

At the same time, Suzy Spencer was still waiting at the back
of the Fellside Fellowship Chapel for Jake. She was missing
Wanda's party but the kids had to come first. Jake was one of
a group of boys with a mixture of instruments, playing from
messy sheets of music on a variety of tatty stands. Above them
a huge screen hung, with words on it which Suzy couldn't
quite read.

She was getting more used to Jake's musical ventures.
There were usually hours of messing around when nothing much happened, except for self-important men in tight
T-shirts bustling about doing technical things. The boys
would suddenly burst into life with a few seconds of very
loud noise and then sink back into sloping around the stage
sipping cans of something.

She had brought a book to read, partly because she was
genuinely bored and partly because she didn't want Jake to
think she was watching him.

'Hi?'

She turned to the end of the row, where a good-looking blond man was standing. She realized he was one of the older musicians from the stage.

'Can I get you a coffee or something?' he asked.

'Oh, that would be very nice. I'm one of the mums.'

'I guessed so. I'm Mark Wilson, secretary of the PCC and chief dogsbody round here. Most of the other parents just drop them off and come back.'

'But it was my son's first time actually playing . . .'

'And he thought he might not like it? So you were on standby for a quick getaway?'

She smiled, slightly embarrassed. But he just laughed. 'We make the coffee in the kitchen area round at the side. It's a bit more comfortable and you're out of the way of the racket.'

'Thanks, I'd be much happier there.'

And Jake won't be able to see me and feel awkward, she thought. She followed Mark down the chapel and through a side door into a surprisingly large, bright kitchen area with a few tables, café style.

Suzy looked round her appreciatively. She'd had her ups and downs with the Church of England. But there were times when she still found it comforting. To have discovered a church which Jake might enjoy made her feel better. As did the coffee Mark Wilson brought over. He'd put a home-made biscuit on the saucer.

'I see you can read minds. As well as fetch coffee.' She smiled.

'If only!' Mark had a pleasant smile and a trendy haircut. Suzy guessed he was in his early thirties.

'D'you live in Fellside?' she asked, to keep him talking. It was more fun that sitting by herself.

'I certainly do. It's not the National Park but it's near enough. I used to work in the Midlands but I took a job with Norbridge Borough Council. I liked the idea of the place, but I didn't expect to be in the Fellside branch office!'

'Well, Fellside is a bit drab but the Fellowship is a local asset.'

'It certainly is. I came for the music. I play guitar, but not that well. To tell you the truth I've not had much formal musical education.'

'Me neither. You have to have the right sort of background.'

Mark laughed. 'My family weren't into music at all. Do you think it matters? Our vicar, Paul, is bonkers about genealogy.'

'It's the new craze, isn't it? Trying to find out what might make you what you are. I don't know where Jake gets it from. I'm not musical and his dad's completely tone deaf.'

Mark Wilson looked surprised. 'But doesn't he sing in the Abbey Chorus? I'm a tenor there. Haven't I seen you with him? Robert?'

Suzy said quickly, 'Oh, that's not Jake's father. We're separated. The children and I are living with Robert at the moment. We're having a bit of a housing crisis.' She felt momentarily disloyal. She was playing down her relationship. But then again, that was surely fair? After all, Robert was the one who had wanted to cool it.

'Well, don't move away, now that you've found us! It's good to see you at the Fellowship. Paul and Jenny Whinfell are wonderful people.'

They must be the famous Rev Paul and his wife. Suzy had seen Paul Whinfell on the stage with the band — a tall, very thin man in his early thirties with an anxious manner despite his trendy baggy jeans and sweatshirt.

'It's nice to talk to you,' Mark said. 'Will we see you next week?'

'Yes,' said Suzy with more enthusiasm than she expected. She had been cross at missing Wanda Wisley's party, and worried about the increasing distance between her and Robert. But for once, childcare had had its compensations. Mark Wilson really was rather nice!

* * *

On the way home from Wanda's, Edwin pulled into a pleasant country pub on the outskirts of Norbridge and suggested
that he and Alex had a drink.

'It must be a real bore not driving, when you live somewhere like Fellside,' he said.

'Yes. I spend a fortune on Burns' Taxis or I struggle on
the bus. That's how I came across Morris Little. I used to
change buses outside his store and sometimes popped in for
a bottle of wine or three.'

Edwin laughed.

'Seriously,' she said, 'Morris Little was rather a nasty
piece of work. He mocked me a few times in front of people.
But I didn't care. Then.'

But now things had changed. She felt better. She wanted
to stay in her new outfit as long as possible and she'd been
really pleased with the way the hairdresser in Carlisle had
styled her hair. It had been months since she'd had it cut, and
years since she'd had it coloured. The auburn was new, but
it suited her better than the raven streaks she'd had for many
years before she went so grey. Her skin was a good colour
and could take the brighter look, and she'd bought a pair
of new, trendier glasses. She might even go back to contact
lenses before too long. It had all worked very well, except for
seeing Robert Clark. But he hadn't stayed long at Wanda's
and, after he'd gone, Alex had felt light-headed with relief.

It had made her more outspoken, and when David
Johnstone had said nastily, 'Oh, on the orange juice, are we?'
she had replied: 'Absolutely. Have you found anyone else
with a drink problem to exploit?'

He had mumbled something about prices stalling and
people losing opportunities, and turned rudely away, using
his big shoulders to force her out of the conversation. Alex
didn't care. She'd found sweet Lynn Clifford next to her,
asking in a soft voice how she was.

'I thought you managed so well after finding Morris like
that,' Lynn had said quietly.

'Oh, well . . .'

'*Mein Gott!*' Freddie Fabrikant had appeared at their side, dwarfing even Alex. 'You know, I hear you! I have very sharp ears!' His loud voice had attracted the attention of most of the people in the room. 'So you found poor Morris, you and the boy. Tell me, do you really think those terrible Frostie youths did the deed?'

'Well, the police seem to think so—'

'The police! What do they know about anything? They certainly don't know all about me!' Freddie had started to laugh in his infectious but strangely high-pitched way.

'Freddie, sweetie.' Wanda had zoomed like a squirt of air-freshener on a nasty smell. 'I ought to remind you of the time.' She turned to the group. 'Freddie has offered to help with some young people's music, at a church in one of those grim villages over towards the coast.'

'I was born in Fellside,' David Johnstone had said crabbily.

'That's it, Fellside. Such potential!' Wanda pushed her cleavage at him.

'Fellside!' Freddie had trumpeted. 'A terrible village. But you know, with some modern development . . . I have tried to persuade Wanda to look at buying a house up there. There are some very big unused places. With money, what could be done! As long as you bribe the council, of course!' He nudged David Johnstone in a grotesque stage gesture. Everyone joked about Johnstone's methods behind his back, but only Freddie would have dreamt of doing so to his face.

'I really think it's time you went, darling,' Wanda had said, slightly hysterically. 'We're becoming very green, aren't we, Freddie! Freddie's going on his bicycle!' The idea of Freddie driving the car after the amount of toxic substances he consumed had encouraged Wanda to buy him a super speed-bike. He had taken to riding it in all weathers, wearing an enormous cape.

'*Ja*, I must be going . . . See you at the Chorus!'

* * *

121

Edwin and Alex had been amongst the last to leave. Edwin had actually enjoyed himself. He'd had a really good chat with the Principal for the first time since withdrawing his candidature for Head of Music. The Principal had been furious at the time, but now seemed keen to build bridges.

'Tell me, Edwin, why you withdrew?' he had asked. 'Was it really personal reasons?'

'Yes, I'm afraid so. I'm sorry. But things have worked out all right, I think.'

The Principal had followed his eyes to where Wanda was gushing over the Dean.

'I hope so,' the Principal had said. 'Excuse me. I need to speak to David Johnstone. He's been advising me on the sale of some sports playing fields.'

Now, on the way home, Alex and Edwin were talking animatedly about the Stainer concert and the problem of the soloists.

Edwin said, 'If locals don't sing the solos, they get resentful. It's already bad enough with the Stainer because there are no women's parts, just a tenor and a bass. At least we've got some little bits of recitative for the other men. But we need two really strong people'

'So who's the best tenor?'

'You know, I'm beginning to think it really might be Tom Firth. But he's very young . . .'

'Well, that would be good box office, wouldn't it? I mean, Tom's got a lovely voice, you've said so before, and he's still the object of a lot of local attention because of Morris. And it might be good for his self-confidence.'

'Yes, but he's still a teenager. He might screw up through nerves. The bass soloist would have to be really special to support him. And it would need to be someone who wouldn't mind sharing the limelight with a kid.'

'Edwin! What about Freddie?'

'Freddie Fabrikant? Norbridge's answer to Meatloaf? You must be joking.'

'No, I'm not. He's joined the choir in good faith — OK, he's missed a few practices. But he can sing. You can help him. And it would be such fun!'

It was then that Edwin had driven into the pub car park. A few minutes later he and Alex sat in the bar, with their heads together, discussing the possibilities.

'You know,' Edwin said as they got back into his car, 'it could work. Tom would have to develop a bit, though. I won't commit to him for a while. I want to see how he comes on. But we could approach Freddie straight away. If he's interested I'd like to try the idea out on a few sensible people before putting it to the committee.'

The committee was at least ten strong, in an attempt to be democratic, with the result that it only ever discussed things that were faits accomplis.

'Alex, why don't you come round to my place one night this week? We could talk it over. I owe you big-time for coming today anyway; I can hardly pretend lunch at Wanda's is a pleasure. And I tell you what. I'll ask Robert Clark to come too! He's very sound on Chorus matters.'

Alex sat in the front of the car and shut her eyes. She had known that if she stayed around, becoming more sociable, then at some point she would have to face up to this. But she had dreaded it happening so soon.

Edwin saw her face set, and her mouth pulled down, as it had been when he first met her. Her large dark eyes had narrowed behind her new glasses.

'No, I don't think so, Edwin. Chorus matters aren't really anything to do with me. I think you'd better get me home. Thanks for everything.' Her voice was final.

'OK.' Edwin did a neat three-point turn out of the car park and set off for Fellside without speaking. He felt absurdly disappointed.

* * *

At Fellside Fellowship, as Mark Wilson stood up to go, Suzy followed his gaze. A huge man in a flapping cape was coming towards them, in danger of overbalancing the flimsy tables.

'Mark! Hello. Are you well? *Sooo* good to see you. So, I am here, and will advise the boys.'

'Freddie!' Mark Wilson leapt up. 'It's wonderful of you to come.' He turned to Suzy. 'Do excuse me, Mrs . . . ?'

'Ms,' Suzy said firmly. 'Ms Spencer. But please, call me Suzy.'

'Enjoy the rest of your coffee, Suzy. Freddie and I have got some serious gigs to discuss.'

Freddie Fabrikant burst into loud, exuberant laughter, and swept all before him on his way out through the doors, towards the stage. In his wake, Mark moved lankily after him with the gait of a younger man. In the doorway he turned back to Suzy and winked.

To her surprise she found herself blushing. Then she caught the eye of a severe young woman behind the counter, with a toddler on her hip, and she went hastily back to her book.

19

As soon as they hear of me, they shall obey me;
but the strange children shall dissemble with me.
Psalm 18:45

A week later, Lynn Clifford sat in the coffee shop in Norbridge's oldest department store and stared into her cappuccino. She had worked at the Abbey shop for three days that week, but on Wednesday she had the morning off. She was becoming increasingly worried about her daughter and in desperation she had called Suzy Spencer. She needed to talk to someone — which was a dangerous weakness for a priest's wife — but when she assessed her friends she was surprised to find that she thought Suzy would be the most sympathetic. And the most discreet.

'Chloe's still at home and she's very on edge,' Lynn said. 'Sort of jumpy. She's back from university, with post-exam stress. I've no idea when she's going to Leeds again. She's really uptight. She won't have a glass of wine with us in the evenings. She doesn't wear make-up anymore and her clothes are just downright shapeless.'

'Do you think it's just reaction? It sounds like she had a pretty rough New Year's Eve? And Christmas wasn't so easy either. If your friend finds a body it could make you a bit shaky.'

'But I don't think it's that.' Lynn shook her head. 'I realize my daughter is turning out to be a mystery to me, but I doubt she'd let the Little murder get to her.'

'You don't think it could be the Moonies or anything?' Suzy was thinking of the frumpy clothes.

'Good heavens!' Lynn wrinkled her brow. 'I hadn't thought of that. But Chloe can't be into a cult,' she said after a pause, with some relief. 'She asked to come to the Chorus with us last night to hear the Stainer. And she says she wants to go to Fellside Fellowship next Sunday.'

'Well, the Fellside Fellowship is fun. Jake goes there. All that seems positive. Perhaps you're worrying for nothing. Remember how when they were babies, phase followed phase so fast, you scarcely had time to face up to how scary it was?'

'True.' But Lynn still looked worried.

'Listen . . .' Suzy leant forward. 'Ask Chloe to come over on Friday and babysit for me when Molly gets back from Brownies. Rob and I can find somewhere to go to.' Though we do very little together at the moment, Suzy thought. But Lynn didn't need to know about someone else's problems. 'I'll try chatting to Chloe. Maybe she'll let something slip to me that she wouldn't tell her own mum. We all did that, don't you remember?'

But Lynn didn't. She'd had no mother to snub. The thought of Chloe confiding in someone else cut her like a knife, but at least it was a plan. For the first time in twenty-four hours, Lynn felt better.

'That's a good idea. I'll ask her.'

Lynn finished her cappuccino and put down her share of the bill. Then she doused a hot flush by putting ice cubes from her glass of water on her wrists, smiling as Suzy watched her with surprise.

'You wait,' she said. 'It'll be here sooner than you think!'

Then she grabbed her carrier bags and made for the car park. She needed to be back at the shop. Maybe I've helped, maybe not, Suzy wondered, watching her friend hurry away. So what's really wrong with Chloe? It all sounded extremely odd. Perhaps I can get something out of her, she mused. Then Suzy let her thoughts go back to Robert.

He had said he would be away soon on a writing course in London. Suzy had been astonished, then alarmed. He had missed the Chorus rehearsal the week before because he said he wanted to try writing, and had shut himself in his study. It was unlike Robert to be withdrawn, or to take any time off.

The thought made her feel slightly sick and she noticed her hand was shaking as she paid the bill. But in their new, cool relationship she couldn't ask Robert what was going on.

It was ironic that Lynn Clifford had asked for her help at a time she felt so inadequate. Suzy put the money down on the table, picked up her bags, and tried to focus her mind on work, and that evening's recording of the newly entitled *Geordies in Space*.

* * *

'You look different!'

'Do I? I've been on a diet.' Poppy Robinson dumped her backpack at Tom Firth's feet. Figaro's was crowded because it was Friday. Poppy had just got off the bus from Newcastle so she could have a weekend at home. She had arranged to meet Tom and Chloe.

'No, it's your hair.' Tom Firth looked at her critically.

'Oh, I've had it cut. D'you like it?' Her stringy long brown hair had been cut into a neat and shiny bob, with blond stripes. It was much fuller.

'It's not bad,' said Tom.

Actually he was pleased by how good Poppy looked. It was quite nice to be seen with her. She still had her woolly scarf and gloves, but she was wearing tight jeans and a military-style jacket which had enough buckles and pockets to look fashionable. But it was warm and squashy too, and Tom liked that. There was something cuddly about Poppy.

'Is Chloe coming?' he asked. He wasn't sure how he felt about that. Perhaps he had been a bit rude to her at Christmas, but he wasn't going to apologize. Chloe had always been high-handed in the past, which was part of her attraction of course, but he'd had enough of being patronized.

'Yeah — like I told you, she's at home from uni at the moment. Says she's not been well.'

'I know. I saw her sitting at the back of our Chorus rehearsal on Tuesday but I didn't get a chance to speak to her. What's she got?'

'Not sure. Flu probably. I texted her when I was on the train. She must be getting better because she says she'll be here at five. It's nearly that now. D'you want a coffee?'

'OK.'

Tom was surprised to be asked, but he quite liked it. It was annoying the way most Norbridge girls expected you to pay first. Perhaps Poppy wasn't as conventional as she looked. Her dad was something to do with the National Health and her mum was a craft teacher, given to wearing long flowing skirts and layers of crocheted tops. Mrs Robinson's hair was long and stringy, usually put up in a wispy bun.

'Does your mam like your hair?' he asked as Poppy stood up.

'She hasn't seen it yet. But she won't,' Poppy said with some satisfaction. 'She likes the natural look.'

'Parents!'

'Too right. Chloe can't stand hers, you know. I thought wild horses wouldn't drag her back to Norbridge in term-time.'

'She must have been pretty sick.'

But Chloe didn't look sick when she came into the coffee shop. The Goth make-up and the jewellery were gone and her face was a plump wholesome pink. She was wearing Lynn's Gortex anorak and a red velvet scarf tied around her head.

'You look like one of them terrorists. What's up with your hair? Still that funny black colour?' said the new, braver Poppy.

'Yes. I hate it.' Chloe unwound the scarf to reveal jet black flaps of unkempt hair, already topped by a pale brown, softer stripe on her scalp. 'I'm growing it out.'

'What, back to brown? I thought you said you couldn't understand why anyone would want to be a mouse!' Poppy tossed her new shiny bob with its blond highlights.

Chloe shrugged. 'It's the way it's supposed to be.'

Poppy shrugged back. 'Well, you've changed your tune. Want a coffee?'

'Just a peppermint tea, please.'

'Detoxing?'

'Yeah, sort of.'

Poppy had moved towards the counter, and Tom was alone with Chloe — once his dream. But suddenly he found he had nothing to say to her. He searched for something to talk about. She might be able to cast some light on the psalter mystery. Chloe had sung in a choir, too, and Edwin Armstrong was her uncle, so he wouldn't be speaking out of turn. There was a silence between them he wanted to fill, so he said: 'You know Morris Little?' He leant forward confidentially.

'Yes. Well, I did.'

'When he got beaten up by the Frosts, I reckon he was carrying a psalm book. A psalter. You know what I mean.'

'Well, why shouldn't he have been? He was into singing, wasn't he?'

'Yeah, but . . .' Tom didn't know what to say. How could he explain that the book had looked like some sort of antique, not the usual sort of thing you'd have at choir practice? But Chloe wasn't helping him. In fact she looked a bit preoccupied and her eyes kept wandering around Figaro's as if she was looking for someone else. Poppy came back with the drink, and Tom was relieved to see her.

'How about coming up to Newcastle to stay one weekend?' Poppy suggested, not very optimistically. The previous term Chloe had refused her invitation on the grounds that she was just too busy with her new friends. On the spur of the moment she added: 'You as well, Tom. Both of you?'

Chloe shook her head. 'No, I don't think I can, Pops. I'm staying in Norbridge for a while.'

'You're *what?*' Poppy looked at her friend in amazement.

'It's not that strange,' Chloe said with a hint of her old sharpness. 'There are lots of good things about Norbridge. You can get carried away by these big cities, you know.'

'I've not been carried away,' said Poppy.

'No, well you wouldn't.' Chloe put her cup down. 'I'd better go now. I'm babysitting tonight.'

'So you don't want to meet up in the Crown and Thistle?'

'No, sorry.'

'I do,' said Tom suddenly. Poppy stared at him and crossed her eyes. He laughed.

Chloe Clifford had already stood up. 'See ya,' she said vaguely. 'I'll text.' And she drifted out, the long scarf trailing.

'She's gone weird,' said Tom, in a matter-of-fact voice. 'Too weird. Poppy, are you interested in music?'

'A bit. Bands and that.'

'I mean classical music.'

'Classical music?' Poppy bit back her initial response. 'Well, I could be,' she said carefully. She thought of her parents with their embarrassing Bob Dylan fixation. 'I wouldn't mind classical, actually.'

* * *

Later that night, Molly Spencer was sleeping soundly after a riotous game of hide-and-seek with her babysitter. Jake Spencer was rehearsing the new rock and jazz band sound at his mate Oliver's. Suzy Spencer and Robert Clark were still out.

Chloe was the only person awake in The Briars in Tarnfield. She had a long conversation with someone on her mobile phone. Then she crept along the landing with a pair of scissors she'd found in the kitchen drawer. Slowly and thoughtfully she started to chop off her black dyed hair till all that was left was short brown fuzz all over her scalp and a pile of inky tresses on the tiled bathroom floor.

Suzy and Robert returned after a couple of hours in the pub at Tarnfield. Suzy had hoped that having some time on their own would have helped her and Robert to talk things through, but there had been a live country band playing and half the village had been there, so there had hardly been room to move, never mind have a private chat.

'What have you done to your hair?' Suzy gasped at Chloe, who had been waiting for them in the hall and was standing there, by the open front door.

'The dye was ridiculous.' Chloe smiled. 'Look, one of my friends is picking me up straight away. There's no need to give me a lift home. I must run . . .' She sprinted past Suzy, cropped head forwards into the wind, waving cheerily, hurrying out of the door and into the garden.

'Chloe, don't you want a quick chat?' Suzy called after her.

She moved to follow her, but paused. She felt slightly ridiculous at the thought of running down the path, calling to Chloe to come back. She heard a car on the main road starting up.

Suzy phoned Lynn a few minutes later. 'Chloe's left here,' she said. 'She's gone with a friend in a car. I'm sorry I didn't see who it was. She hardly stayed long enough to say goodnight. I feel I shouldn't have let her go. Will you phone me to let me know she's got home safely?'

Then she waited, anxiously. For some reason she felt disturbed. But why? If Chloe wanted to dash off, surely that was OK, even if it hadn't been the plan? Suzy stayed up after Robert went to bed, mooching in the kitchen, drinking hot milk and worrying. As a mum, she felt she had let Lynn down by not getting Chloe to talk as she'd promised. Half an hour later, the phone rang and Suzy jumped to answer it. It was Lynn. Yes, Chloe was safely home. But her friend sounded distraught.

Chloe had walked into the rectory looking perfectly composed and unusually calm. First, she had unwound her scarf to reveal a new, uncharacteristically shorn haircut. And then she had announced with complete conviction that she wasn't going back to university — ever!

20

Like as the hart desireth the water-brooks,
so longeth my soul after thee, O God.
Psalm 42:1

David Johnstone hurriedly pushed his papers to one side as his wife came clattering into the room.

'Do you have to frighten the living daylights out of me?'

'Oh, sorry, I'm sure. What do you want me to do? Knock in my own house?'

'It wouldn't do you any harm, busy-bodying around.'

Must be this new grandchild — it had given her an exaggerated sense of her own importance.

'David, I need some money. I've been invited down to Croydon to help do up the nursery. They say I can go as soon as the weather improves. I'd like to go.' Her tone fluctuated between aggressive and wheedling. David Johnstone was unsure which annoyed him more.

'I've told you, your place is here. I'm up to my neck in one of the most important deals of my career. I need clean shirts and meals made. I haven't got time to look after myself while you gad about.'

Thank goodness, he thought, that he held the purse strings. For a while, when they were first married, Pat had talked nonsense about joint accounts. But he ran the house like his father did. The breadwinner controlled the income and the wife was given the housekeeping money. And he made damn sure that there was no surplus for her to squirrel away.

Recently though, he had made a smart move. Years ago he had made Pat open a little savings account. It wasn't to be touched, he had said. They had left a few thousand quid in it. But a couple of weeks earlier he had dumped a very large sum of cash in there. Pat never checked on it or read the statements. He always opened her post. A man like himself, who wasn't afraid of taking risks, had to make sure there was tidy sum put aside just in case, in someone else's name. As long as Pat didn't know about it, it was safe, and he would still be able to keep his hands on it. Even if she found out about it, he had too much of a hold over her for her to run off with the cash.

His eyes went back to the photocopy he had in front of him. He wasn't so sure now whether the original was all that important: the main thing was that it hadn't turned up. If he could move fast, then he could get what he wanted. In the usual Johnstone style, fast footwork was what was needed, that and contacts. Reg Prout was going to come in handy, and of course the Dixons. It had been a wise move, jollying up to them at the Chorus.

Pat shouted: 'There's something at the door for you, David. Parcel. You've got to sign for it.'

Bloody hell. He pushed his chair to one side and stomped through the hall.

'Where?'

'A delivery man. He must have gone down the drive . . .'

Johnstone strode off, increasingly furious. His wife sidled into his office, duster in hand, and tried to make out what the document was that David had been reading. It looked like some flowery dedication from a sort of Gothic name all intertwined with flowers. The only letter she could make out was a giant Q because it reminded her of James Bond. On a piece of paper underneath it was an interesting valuation for the bungalow on the hill at Fellside. She wasn't sure what to make of the information, but before she could dust the computer she heard him coming back into the house.

'I couldn't find any bloody delivery man. What are you talking about?'

'Oh, that's funny. He didn't mention you by name. He just said, "It's for your husband." Maybe he really wanted the people next door!'

'Oh, for God's sake. Thick old bat! You should have asked the man who he really wanted! Idiot!'

Pat went on polishing the mirror in the hall, smiling to herself. There had been no parcel, of course, but she now had a little package of knowledge for herself!

* * *

Winter lingered miserably in the Norbridge area. The searing cold of January soon melted into continual dreary rain. Alex Gibson thought she could scarcely remember a more monochrome season — grey day followed grey day. She was keeping her head down, scurrying into the fug of her office and hurrying out to the car park, making sure other people delivered cheques and expenses around the college. Always a perfectionist and hard worker, asking people to do this made her more communicative. She seemed nicer. Those of her colleagues who noticed the change in her put it down to the drama of finding a dead man in the corridor. Alex seemed to be someone who rose to the occasion.

They also thought the shock perhaps explained her weight loss. Alex was aware her clothes were looser, but she was concentrating on stopping drinking and repairing the bungalow, rather than on her figure. The Chorus rehearsal, and the orange juice in the pub afterwards with Edwin, was a highlight of each week.

Then one morning she received a business letter which astonished her. It would probably come to nothing, she thought, putting it in her dressing-gown pocket. But you never knew . . .

It encouraged her to maintain her new hair colour with some tint she bought at Uplands store. While she was there, she noticed Norma Little was back behind the till. But she said nothing to her. The Frost boys were remanded in custody, and Morris's body had been released for burial. Alex hadn't gone to the funeral, but everyone had talked about it at the Chorus practice. It had been a very quiet affair, not what Morris Little would have wanted at all. But Norma now went through life grim-lipped and silent, serving at the shop with manic intensity as if she might pull a gun on anyone who argued, and the funeral reflected her anger with the world.

Edwin Armstrong called Alex once or twice each week, as well as enjoying their regular drinks after the Chorus practice. He seemed to value her thoughts.

'Freddie says he'll have a go at those bass solos,' he had said on the phone one Monday night.

'That's great!' Alex loved the Chorus practices, but she made sure she arrived at the last minute, staying at the back next to the warbling Pat Johnstone. There was no way she was making eye contact with Robert Clark again. But in any event, he was missing at most rehearsals.

Freddie Fabrikant was over the moon at being asked to be the bass soloist. He started playing Stainer's *Crucifixion* very loudly in the tiny cottage, and singing along.

'For God's sake stop that noise,' Wanda would shriek at him. She found the congregational hymn music embarrassing. She longed for the days when he played Ozzie Osborne at maximum decibels. 'I thought you had famously good hearing. Why do you need to play this droning crap so loud? It's just ordinary people, for God's sake!'

'What was that? I can't hear you!' Freddie would guffaw at his own joke. It was a relief to her when he donned his huge cycle cape and rode off in the dark for a practice at the Abbey or a jam session at Fellside Fellowship. Wanda was glad to see the back of him. She was trying to write a piece for *Music Today* on Messiaen's relationship to rap. All this amateur church music-making was so provincial. She couldn't believe she had actually socialized with vicars' wives!

In Uplands, the Cliffords were coming to terms with the fact that Chloe had refused to return to Leeds University. They had driven over to Yorkshire without her to talk to her tutor, who seemed to have some difficulty recollecting her. Her room in the hall of residence was pathetically normal. Lynn was moved to tears by the tawdry bits of jewellery and tatty posters, and could hardly bear to collect the few belongings which Chloe had demanded they brought home. Yes, Chloe was going through a difficult patch, her tutor nodded sagely, but it wasn't unusual. Many undergraduates panicked. It was possible she might be able to catch up on the work she had missed thanks to e-learning and email, and if the worst came to the worst she could retake the year, no problem.

But it *is* a problem, Lynn heard herself shouting at this smug man in his jeans and earring. My daughter is suffering.

'Counselling?' he suggested.

'Get stuffed!' Chloe said to them when they got home, with a hint of her old spark. 'I'm all right. I've got plenty of people to talk to. Just give me a bit of space.' Later she was on the phone for over an hour, in her bedroom. To Poppy? Lynn wondered. Or maybe Tom Firth?

The next day, Lynn noticed that Chloe was calm again. It was quieter in the house as a result, but she felt her real daughter was hiding somewhere. Chloe wouldn't be drawn — she just smiled remotely. Then Lynn was distracted by a sudden row on the parochial church council about the 'Lenten array' which would be used in a few weeks' time. Some people objected to the altar cloth, which showed a brutal hammer, nails and whip, appliquéd in red and black on the ivory background. It was traditionally used at Uplands Parish Church. It frightened the kids, some said. But crucifixion *is* frightening, Lynn thought. Sorting out a compromise was absorbing a lot of Neil's attention, and hers too.

Ash Wednesday was less than a month away.

David Johnstone was enjoying the winter. Darker evenings meant his trips to his woman friend in Fellside were more likely to be unnoticed. This time of year was always a quiet time in property, when he would work out his strategies. He chatted to the weasel-like Brian Dixon one night after the Chorus about his plans for Fellside Leisure. It meant a big investment in the area, but Brian had been all for it and had offered to get the Johnstones an invite to Lord Cleaverthorpe's place — just on a social level.

He needed to get the bungalow too, of course. That was crucial. It was a pity baldy Reg's drunken sister-in-law had turned out to be tougher than he'd expected. But joining the Chorus had been a good move, he thought happily. He could keep tabs on her there, and the other contacts were worth having. He quite fancied one of the sopranos. And he liked eyeing up plump little Chloe Clifford who'd been trailing along after her mother. Young ones were much more fun than some of these older, so-called sophisticated types. He felt sorry for Robert Clark, with that TV producer.

Suzy and Robert rubbed along domestically, but that was about all. The closeness was gone. Robert was evasive, and she found that she was nervous of discussing things. Anyway, there wasn't much time for talking. Every Saturday there was a new reason to drive to Nigel's, who found his wife and children much more interesting now his girlfriend was off the scene. And on Sundays she took Molly to Sunday School in Tarnfield, and later drove Jake to Fellside Fellowship to rehearse and play at the rock service. His mate Ollie went with them to play drums. At least she got to chat to Mark Wilson. In the week, her work was hectic. *Geordies in Space* was doing surprisingly well and they needed to record a few 'specials' with north-east celebrities. On one of the rare occasions she and Robert found themselves at home on their own, a row had flared from nowhere.

'I've taken that rug Molly spilt glue on to the cleaners.'

'Oh, you shouldn't have bothered, Suzy. It hardly showed.'

'But it was one which Mary made herself. It's beautiful.'

'I know. She was really good at that sort of thing. But we can't expect a child to keep it pristine. And it's not Mary's house anymore.'

'You sound like you regret it, Robert. Was that what you meant before Christmas when you said, "Mary's dead," in that tone of voice?'

'No! It was just a point of fact.'

'But if Mary were alive then we wouldn't be together.'

'She's not alive, Suzy. She died. I can't say I would have left her for you, because I wouldn't.'

I stayed with Mary and it wasn't always easy, he was thinking. These days his conscience was pricking him more and more. I did some wrong things — but I stayed, he told himself. I really did do my best.

'Oh, and because now I'm abandoning Nigel I'm not as good as you. Mr Perfect stayed the course! You're so flaming sanctimonious!'

'No, Suzy, that's not what I meant . . .'

But she had gone and slammed the door.

21

Let it be unto him as the cloke that he hath upon him . . .
Psalm 109:18

Suzy had arranged to meet Lynn Clifford for coffee again. The part-time contract at Tynedale TV gave her some time during the day while the children were at school, though the erratic shift pattern meant she felt unsettled. But it was good to talk to Lynn. They were in the coffee shop at McCrae's, which was tucked in a corner of the lingerie section, cordoned off and furnished with tiny metal tables.

'Chloe's rather better, I think.' Lynn leant forward confidingly. 'She stays in a lot but she's been out once or twice this week to meet a friend. She's still very quiet and dresses very sloppily, but maybe that's no bad thing.' Lynn was smiling, but Suzy could pick up a hint of concern. People don't change so dramatically, she thought, but there was no way she would puncture Lynn's fragile happiness.

'I'm glad. Will Chloe be going back to university?'

'I hope so. I think the real problem was that it was all too much too soon after living in a little place like Norbridge.'

'Maybe she should defer for a year. She could try travelling, or maybe working somewhere.'

Lynn shook her head. 'Neil thinks she should get over this and get back to normal as soon as possible.'

'Men want things "back to normal" as soon as possible because that means that they're in control.'

Lynn looked at Suzy sharply. What was wrong there?

'Oh, Neil's not like that,' she said vaguely.

But later, when she got home, it made Lynn wonder if her husband was perhaps being a little intolerant. Neil had been tired lately. The Lenten altar cloth argument had drained him. It seemed trivial but was brewing into a local schism. And Paul and Jenny Whinfell at Fellside seemed to be going through a difficult phase, which had meant long phone conversations for several evenings running. It was lucky that Paul had Mark Wilson as such a steadfast supporter, Lynn thought. According to Neil, Mark was doing more and more of the routine parish chores.

Paul had confided to Neil, who was his boss in the hierarchy, that Jenny seemed unhappy and uncommunicative.

'I think she's angry, Neil. But I don't know why. Everything's fine.'

To Neil, most personal issues boiled down to a crisis of faith.

'Why not start a Bible study course?' he said. 'You could relate it to Lent, but you don't have to wait for Ash Wednesday. Get cracking now. Jenny could be a leader; it would do her good. And why not try looking at the Psalms? They would be interesting to Mark with his High Church leanings, but equally interesting to you and Jenny with your evangelical approach.'

'But who would come to a Bible study course at Fellside? It's not really what kids do. Would we get enough interested people at a mid-week session?'

'You would if I didn't do a Lent course at Uplands. I could encourage my parishioners to come to you. I'll help you with the extra work, though with Jenny and Mark you've got a good team.'

'That's a thought. Thanks, Neil.'

In fact it was a great idea, thought Paul. It would be meaty enough for all three of them to get their teeth into. He would publicize the course to everyone in the whole area. And he had his own reasons for feeling it would be particularly helpful. How significant that Neil should mention the Psalms! Then he put the phone down and guiltily tapped into ancestry.co.uk.

* * *

The following Monday, Edwin Armstrong arrived home at about six o'clock. The phone was already ringing as he got out of the car, which he parked outside his small cottage on the road between Uplands and Fellside.

'Hello?' He expected it to be someone selling him financial services, but the rasping voice at the other end was distinctly local.

'Is that Edwin? From the Abbey Chorus?'

'Yes, that's me.'

'It's Norma Little here. Morris's wife.'

'How are you, Norma?'

'How d'you think?' Her smoker's voice rattled irritably. 'Never mind all that. There's stuff here I want you to look at. Music stuff. You know. Morris wanted to talk to you about it.'

Edwin's heart sank. He imagined piles of dusty scores and sticky old-fashioned cassette covers. Morris had been the sort of person to keep everything. 'What sort of things do you have?' he asked guardedly.

'All sorts. But that's not the point. I want you to have a look at the stuff on his computer. I'm not good at technology and my children just keep trying to stop me. They think it will upset me.'

'What are you getting at, Norma?' Edwin knew his own voice was sharpening. This wasn't a routine call by the bereaved.

'My husband was doing some research. I know you all thought Morris was a pain, but he knew what he was talking about. He wanted to talk to you about it.'

'Me?'

'Yes, you. You should look at his work.'

Edwin suddenly felt guilty. No one from the Chorus except Robert had really bothered to talk to Norma. The funeral, once the body had been released, had been a very utilitarian affair and Edwin had wondered at the time why Norma was so tense and fierce. Perhaps she felt there was unfinished business.

'I'm sorry,' he said. 'You're right. Morris was a first-class researcher.'

She sniffed, happier. 'I think you should come over to the shop sometime this week. What about Thursday night? I'm finishing at six that night, and my daughter's taking over.'

It wouldn't harm him to be sympathetic. And there was still a lot about Morris's death that seemed peculiar.

'Maybe I can have a look at Morris's psalter at the same time?' he suggested.

'Salter? What do you mean, salter? Is it something to do with the grocery side?'

'No, no, not at all. It's a sort of music book for singing psalms. Apparently Morris had rather a nice copy. It was with him when . . . when he died.'

'A music book? No, you're wrong there. Morris had nothing with him but the clothes he stood up in. And his wallet and mobile. Funny that, don't you think? You'd think the Frost boys would have taken his money.'

'Maybe they didn't get a chance in the dark.'

'Hmmph. We're all in the dark, if you ask me. But one thing's for certain. There was no music book of any sort with him.'

Were both Tom and Alex wrong? Surely not, Edwin thought. If the police had found a book in Morris's hand, or even near his body, they would have given it to his widow — unless it was evidence. But what sort of evidence could it be?

'I'll be there on Thursday,' Edwin said. 'Definitely.'

Norma grunted, 'Right. We'll see you then,' and put the phone down sharply as if she was worried he might change his mind.

142

Edwin's next move, almost as a reflex, was to push the button he had pre-programmed with Alex's number.

'You're sure you saw a book in Morris's hand, aren't you?'

'Of course I'm sure. A psalter.'

A few minutes later, as he was pouring himself a drink, Edwin's phone rang again. He jumped to answer it, hoping the unexpected caller might be Marilyn. She would call him soon — he knew that.

But it was the husky voice of Norma Little again. 'I've called the policewoman who's on Morris's case. She says there was no book anywhere near him.'

So someone had removed the psalter from Morris's hand. It had been there when Tom and Alex found the body and gone when the police got there, and it wasn't the Frosts because witnesses had seen them disposing of the piece of wood outside at the time. Alex had said that the admin offices in the Music Department had been playing bad schmaltzy carols at top volume. The loud, crass music was still going full blast so she had heard nothing. Then the lights had gone out and the music had stopped. She had waited about five long minutes, hoping the power would come back on, before deciding to grope her way out. Then suddenly light had flooded the corridor where she had been standing; she had picked up her bag and gone out of the door, planning to turn left to the Music Department's separate entrance. But the sound of Tom crying out had changed her mind; she had turned right and found him and the body.

And Morris had been clutching a psalter. She had taken Tom by the shoulders, pushed him into the main corridor and guided him down the stairs to the reception desk. The guard had radioed his colleague, who had gone straight to Morris's body. The dead man had been left alone for about five minutes. And in that time the book must have gone.

But would other people come to the same conclusion that Edwin was rapidly reaching? — that the murderer wasn't necessarily one of the Frosts, but could be someone who stole the book, having attacked Morris in the first place? Someone who expected the Music Department to be deserted, not realizing Tom might be in the toilets, or Alex in the vicinity, with any sound masked by the raucous carol singing?

Edwin knew of no one in the Music Department who would play music like that. They had been playing Bach's *Christmas Oratorio* earlier. Had the murderer put on the blaring music to mask all sound of an attack? But then, in turn, not heard Alex? Had the same person lurked at the scene in the dark, and then watched Tom crying, and Alex leading him away?

Was that possible? If it was, the consequences were crazy. It meant there was a murderer on the loose in Norbridge. Someone with an interest in the Psalms, or why else would they remove a psalter?

Ridiculous, Edwin said to himself. He was being over-imaginative. He would heat up a pizza and then do some work. And tonight, he thought firmly, he would concentrate on modern jazz.

* * *

Freddie Fabrikant grunted as he pushed his bicycle up the hill on the outskirts of Fellside. But he chuckled too. He could still hear Wanda's ringing outrage in his ears.

'What? You're going where?'

'To a religious group meeting, Wanda. It's very interesting. A study for the Lenten season which is coming soon. We're starting early.'

'You're off your head, Freddie. What is happening to you?'

'Well, I am taking a new interest. Religion is the rock and roll of the twenty-first century. *The Da Vinci Code* and Cabbalism and Islam and Scientology, it's all there.'

'But this is some silly little group at a church hall in bloody Fellside of all places. It's hardly Holy Trinity Brompton Road, is it?'

'I don't know of this Holy Trinity. But I'm interested. After all, if I'm going to be singing the main part in Stainer's *Crucifixion*—'

'Oh, is that what it's all about! For God's sake!'

'*Genau!*' Freddie had harrumphed triumphantly, and lifted his giant bicycle cape from the peg in the hallway. 'I'm leaving now, Wanda. It won't be a long gig. I'll be home at ten o'clock for my hot milk drink . . .' He winked and guffawed.

She had still been huffing and blowing as he left. He was very fond of Wanda, whom he found deeply sexy in her driven way, but it was his ability to wind her up which gave him the greatest pleasure. She was a woman of limited sensitivity, he thought seriously as he mounted his bike and weaved unsteadily out of Uplands. She was strangely two-dimensional, wrapped up in herself like a small dark animal that occasionally emerged from a burrow blinking at the world, uttering sharp cries of outrage, and then disappearing again. Of course she had all the outward trappings of a sophisticate. But the real Wanda was really rather solipsistic, like a teenager herself. That was why she didn't want children of her own, he thought. It had begun to trouble him. The idea of family life in the country was appealing more and more. But if Wanda was getting older and wasn't interested then perhaps some younger woman might fit the bill. After all, he had always got on well with young people. And there had been a few escapades since he had come up to the north . . .

His bicycle wobbled. I've been a naughty boy, he said to himself, but not always. Once or twice he had been kindly, avuncular even. He laughed, liking the sound of his own voice booming in the dark.

The back roads to Fellside had been deserted, and he bowled along, singing bass arias from *The Crucifixion* at the top of his voice, through the damp but chilly night. It was that which made him remember the Chorus practice the previous Tuesday. They had had a break in the rehearsal. Everyone had set off for the pub, and he had gone with them, but at the door of the Crown and Thistle he had remembered that his wallet was still in the cape's voluminous pockets. He had returned to the dark recess of the Lady Chapel where he had left his cape draped over a pew.

It hadn't really been dark in there, just misty, with the winter night's damp air swirling in the spotlights over the altar. Robin, the musical director, was playing the organ softly and Edwin Armstrong had been talking to Alex Gibson by the door. Freddie had made his way into the Lady Chapel, which was very dimly lit, and as he'd picked up his cape he'd heard two people talking.

A man's voice had said, 'But it's the only way. It's meant to be. Think about it. Think about the way society's going.'

And an answering female voice had said, 'But it seems so extreme.'

'No.' The male voice had an air of great authority. 'Think about what the psalm says: *The virgins that be her fellows shall bear her company, and shall be brought unto thee.* You have this unique chance to be part of something wonderful which only women can do.'

Freddie had been tempted to say in his loud, cheery voice: 'I could do with some of that!' but then he had heard the man say sharply, 'We must split up now. I'll call you . . .' The voice had been strangely urgent. But by then Freddie had his cape over his head so, despite his excellent hearing, he had caught no more of the conversation.

It had intrigued him, though. And given him the seed of an idea.

And now Freddie was on his way to a Bible study meeting. How strange life was! He liked the feel of the pull in his leg muscles as he cycled up towards the ridge. He was getting a lot fitter and life in the Norbridge area really suited him. Despite his days as a rock star he had always liked being a big fish in a small pool. The image of a bad guy who was really a big softie suited him very well.

And he was immensely flattered by being asked to sing solo for the Chorus. Freddie had a deep vein of country-boy

146

conservatism running through him. He had been brought up as a Lutheran, going to a rural church in a small town on the flat potato plains of middle Germany. That's where he'd first heard his own voice surmounting those around him and realized that music was going to be a big part of his life.

And now it had come full circle. Here he was, going to a church meeting on his bicycle as he had done when he was a boy!

He grunted and pushed on the pedals to lever himself past the bulk of the boarded-up convent, a strange neo-Gothic building in red brick with turrets and gables. From the corner of his eye he saw the dark outline of a large stone cross, chipped and lurching crazily to one side in the overgrown garden.

'Wowwww!' Freddie called out loud as he pedalled, feeling the pressure lift as he reached the brow of the hill and the bicycle wheels spin of their own accord. Freewheeling! This was Freddie Fabrikant, caped crusader.

'Hello, hello!' He careered round the corner into the gravelly car park outside the Fellside Fellowship Chapel where his bike literally ground to a halt. To his amazement, there was quite a crowd.

So many people interested in the Psalms. Freddie chuckled.

22

Let us come before His presence with thanksgiving,
and shew ourselves glad in Him with psalms.
Psalm 95:2

At the former St Luke's, Pat Johnstone was making for the lighted doorway, looking at Mark Wilson in a hungry way as he and Paul Whinfell welcomed people on the doorstep. Lynn Clifford had brought Chloe, who was wearing a strange headscarf like something from post-war Eastern Europe, and Suzy Spencer lingered behind them, looking a bit bemused.

Freddie flung his bike to one side and advanced on her in his usual expansive way. 'Hello! It's me!' he called, totally assured of his own fame. 'You are Robert's wife, yes?'

'No. Just the girlfriend,' Suzy said firmly, but with less mischief in her voice than usual. Lynn Clifford glanced anxiously at her, but was distracted by Chloe who was marching purposefully into the hall.

To Freddie's surprise, someone else from the Chorus moved towards them out of the shadows. It was the big mezzo woman, Alex Gibson, looking brighter than usual in a red coat, and a red velvet scarf like the one he'd bought

Wanda for Christmas. She had rarely spoken to him, but this evening she seemed animated.

'Hello, Freddie,' she said. 'I thought I'd give this a go. You too?'

'*Absolut!* Why not?' Freddie laughed infectiously.

Alex turned to the woman next to her. 'Hi — I'm Alex Gibson.'

'I'm Suzy Spencer.'

'Shall we go in? I don't know what to expect.'

'Me neither. But at least Mark Wilson has got nice shoulders!'

Alex laughed. Suzy Spencer seemed like fun. Alex had been intrigued by the Bible study course — but primarily because it was being held in Fellside, within walking distance. And she was keen to meet people now she was feeling so much better. She could take a risk because Robert Clark was definitely away during half-term week. Or so Edwin had told her at the Chorus practice. There was no danger of meeting him over stewed tea and biscuits in the brightly lit church hall.

Listening to the discussion getting under way, Suzy Spencer had to admit it was interesting but she wasn't sure if she would stick it for the whole course.

She had come partly out of pique. It had hit her like a blow when Robert had said he was going to London on a creative writing course. That night was the first time in eighteen months that she'd got a casual babysitter for Molly; just because Robert was away, she wasn't going to sit at home and mope. She had done Bible study before in Tarnfield and not enjoyed it much, but when Lynn had suggested it, she thought she might give it another try. And Mark Wilson did have an appeal, there was no doubt about it. But getting out on weekday evenings was a pretty tough call, just to hear the painfully serious Jenny Whinfell give a learned analysis of the psalms of lament!

But then Mark followed with some really funny allusions, pointing out the more entertaining episodes. 'The Psalms would make quite a good computer game,' he said.

'How God might defeat thine enemies in over a hundred ways, most of them pretty bloody!'

Suzy laughed, thinking of Jake. Mark made her feel up to date, one of the people who knew the score in the big wide world. At the tea break, Suzy had the feeling that he had singled her out. She told herself not to be stupid. But catching sight of herself in the mirror in the Ladies, she could see that the cold air had brought colour to her face and her blond spiky hair had withstood the rain and damp better than the blow-dry styles of the other women. She was surprised to see that she looked quite trim, too. Obviously having Robert away from home or working in the evenings wasn't doing her figure any harm — the only things she ate these days were Molly's leftovers.

And how old was Mark Wilson? He wasn't a toy-boy himself. Early thirties, and if roles were reversed and she were the bloke, no one would think anything of the age gap. What age gap, anyway? Robert was years older than she was. No one but Nigel ever mentioned that.

Mark bent confidentially to talk to her, and Suzy felt herself twinkling back at him. Get a grip, she told herself sharply.

'No Robert with you?'

'He's away actually.'

I'm flirting, she thought. How bloody stupid. I ought to move off. But Mark said quietly, 'You know, perhaps we ought to have a chat. Maybe we could talk when you bring Jake up to the band.'

'Yes . . . yes, that would be good . . .'

Mark smiled at her, and then went over to speak to Pat Johnstone. He was probably the only person who approached her voluntarily. Pat was all over him like a rash. They'll have to peel her off him when the talk starts again, Suzy thought. Then she realized she was standing dumbly in the middle of the room, holding her cup and saucer at a dangerous angle.

Alex Gibson came and stood next to her. 'He *is* rather gorgeous, isn't he? With the monstrous regiment of single women lusting after him!'

'Actually that's a myth, you know!'

'Really? About the single women or the lusting after Mark?'

'The single women. There are usually fifty-one per cent women and forty-nine per cent men in the population. It's always been like that, except after the First World War. The idea of surplus women is rubbish.'

'So what about all these middle-aged harpies supposedly looking for partners?'

'There are loads of men looking for partners too. It's just that women like to trade up. It's a class thing, not a numbers thing. If you want to meet a man, try the snug bar. He'll be wearing Crimplene trousers and have his teeth in, if you're lucky.'

'I'll pass on that, I think. How do you know all this?'

'I'm a freelance producer for daytime TV. You'd be amazed what we know. That's another myth for you. Look, we'd better get back into our seats. I don't want to miss a word Mark says!'

But the second half of the talk seemed to drag more. Suzy found her eyes closing and had to chew her fingers to keep awake. Paul Whinfell was earnestly looking at similes and metaphors in the Psalms and relating them to the New Testament.

'And there's Psalm 19,' he was saying. 'This is an interesting one. The bridegroom analogy . . .'

'Ah yes!' Freddie Fabrikant had grown tired of listening. 'I find this so weird, Paul. You know, we have all these bride and bridegroom ideas in the Bible. But also there is this big thing about virgins, I mean staying a virgin. You know, virgins keeping each other company. I heard someone say that just recently . . .' He stopped, aware that suddenly the room had gone quiet.

'What is this about?' Jenny Whinfell spoke sharply, annoyed at the interruption.

'I expect Freddie means Psalm 45,' Mark said gently, defusing things. 'You know, there are so many mixed references in the Bible. Perhaps we should move on to our final words. Does anyone have a favourite psalm? And not Psalm 23 please . . .'

'I do!' Everyone turned to Chloe Clifford, who stood up.

Without reference to a book she said, 'It's Psalm 131. It's one of the shortest . . .

Lord I am not high minded; I have no proud looks.
I do not exercise myself in great matters which are too high for me.
But I refrain my soul and keep it low, like as a child that is weaned from his mother; yea my soul is even as a weaned child.
O Israel, trust in the Lord from this time forth for evermore.'

'Thank you, Chloe,' said Paul Whinfell, obviously moved. 'After that there's nothing more to say but the closing prayer.'

* * *

Alex and Suzy found themselves together in the car park. Alex had found Suzy's remarks about single women intriguing. Suzy was an interesting person, Alex thought. Suzy had liked Alex, too.

'It was novel to hear Freddie Fabrikant on theology,' Suzy said.

'Like Bluebeard on domestic violence.' Alex laughed. 'Not to mention Chloe Clifford and that astounding rendition!'

'Yes, I think Lynn's got her hands full with that one at the moment. Have you got any kids?'

'Sadly not. I'm one of your single statistics though I'm not trading up or down at the moment! I'm divorced. And you? Are you local? I haven't seen you in Fellside before?'

'No, I live in Tarnfield.'

'Tarnfield. Isn't that where Robert Clark lives? I know him from the college where I work.' Alex couldn't help asking, like pushing on a painful tooth.

Suzy laughed. 'Funny you should ask. Actually, I'm living with Robert Clark. At least, for the time being.'

In the dark Suzy couldn't see the way Alex's jaw dropped. What on earth was going on? Robert Clark was married to Mary, wasn't he? The love of his life? Who was this bright, spiky blonde woman?

'Well, I'm off,' Suzy said. 'It's been nice to meet you. There aren't many laughs at Fellside Fellowship. I bring my son here most Sundays and get glared at by the vicar's wife!'

Alex felt as if she had been punched in the chest. She smiled vacantly, turned sharply away from Suzy and narrowly missed being hit by Freddie on his bike, as he wheeled in a magnificent uncontrolled arc out of the Fellside Fellowship car park.

* * *

Robert Clark couldn't sleep. He was staying at the Traveller's Hotel in Islington for his creative writing course, and the noise of the heating plus the fact that his room was next to the lift shaft kept him awake. He told himself it was those things, but he really suspected it was his mental state. He had been wretched ever since the coolness with Suzy started, and found it really difficult to try and write anything. Using his imagination was certainly out, so he'd tried 'faction' but that wasn't working either.

'Ouch!' He had rolled over and hit his head on the book he had been reading, which crashed off the bed. It was no good. He switched the bedside light on and got up, ostensibly to go to the loo, but really because he was restless. He stood by the window and drew the curtains back. Below him the city lights peppered the night. He felt guilty because he was literally around the corner from Suzy's best friend Rachel Cohen, but he hadn't called her. Rachel was too perceptive and would have known at once that something was wrong. But he had felt obliged to have dinner that evening with his sister who lived in Hendon.

'So are how are things with Suzy?' his sister had asked.

'I don't know,' he had said.

'I thought it was serious.'

'It is serious. But I don't know what to do next.'

His sister had raised her eyebrows. 'That's not like you,' she said archly. 'You always have things under control.'

He had squirmed a little. There was a sort of conceit about believing that you could act as a counterbalance to people in turmoil. Now he was in turmoil himself. Suzy had destabilized him. It was as if she had seen through his vaunting of marriage and exposed it to a searchlight. Did she suspect that he was a hypocrite? Did she guess that his commitment to Mary had really been less than a hundred per cent? He could hardly bear to acknowledge it even to himself.

Instead, he thought about Edwin Armstrong. Edwin was a calm type as well, but unlike Robert his even-temperedness seemed the product of detachment. Robert remembered when Edwin had been seeing Marilyn Frost, the stunning sister of the Frost brothers. She was the eldest child in the rambling Frost family, the scourge of the neighbourhood. She had enrolled to do music at the college, and was one of those students whom everyone knew, because of her looks and her family's notoriety. She must have been about twenty, Robert thought, and Edwin in his early thirties.

Edwin's quiet joy at being with Marilyn stifled any scruples people might have had about the age gap. It was as if he couldn't believe his own luck. Robert remembered seeing them at Norbridge Abbey once, and Marilyn's face had been shining with delight, her hand holding Edwin's tightly. Edwin hadn't been able to take his eyes off her.

And then Robert had heard that she had gone away. It was when Mary was terminally ill and he hadn't given anyone else much thought. No one had known why the split had happened and there was something about Edwin's despair that stopped gossip in its tracks.

Robert went to the bathroom and then back to the window. London. He loved it, but Tarnfield was his home. How long would Suzy stick it? he wondered. She had been living in the country for four years now, but it wasn't her natural habitat. Much of her work was in Newcastle and Manchester, and she spent hours on the road. He knew she always rushed home to him, giving up the after-work drinks and the occasional parties. They did silly things together which he hadn't done for decades and until recently the bad temper never lasted. There had never been that sense of walking on eggshells which Robert had mistaken, with Mary, for the empathy of love.

He had really tried hard to make his wife happy, that was for sure. But Robert knew that the version of his married life which he had given Suzy had one or two factual gaps in it. For Mary's wonderful husband had not been so wonderful, really. Robert had been unfaithful to her more than once. Five times actually. And though they were usually one-night stands between consenting adults, on one occasion he knew he had behaved badly. He had tried to forget it. But his rows with Suzy had exposed the double standards of his own position. He knew that if things were ever going to be right with her, he had to sort them out for himself first. Then he would need to face the music or the mockery at home. He wasn't sure which would be worse.

Either way, it wouldn't be pleasant, and Suzy would have every right to tell him to take his sanctimonious sentiments about marriage — and stuff 'em.

23

Many oxen are come about me: fat bulls of
Basan close me in on every side.
Psalm 22:12

The same evening, Edwin sat in the box room which Morris Little had used as a study. Morris's hobbies were scattered arbitrarily around. Local history, family history, genealogy, choral singing. He had a bank of folders and about a dozen books all dealing with local families and heritage.

There was a newish computer but there was a lot of redundant equipment which Edwin thought must have been junked from the shop. He had one of those old fax machines that photocopied on a roll of thin paper.

There were racks of files and a small sample of fiction from an author who wrote robust stuff about Victorian rogues. Edwin picked out a paperback called *The West Coast Pirate*, and flicked through it while waiting for Norma to come upstairs with the coffee she had promised. *Adventure stories for all ages. Sandy McFay, originally from Cumbria, writes well-researched rattling good yarns*, he read on the inside sleeve. Very Boy's Own stuff, the sort of thing that was coming back into fashion. The North Country was good at claiming its own, but he had never heard of this chap. Presumably he never came back these days or he'd be roped into readings and signings and talks. But it explained Morris's interest.

Norma came in with the coffee.

'What was Morris's password?' Edwin asked.

'Norbridge — that was his real love.' Norma smiled a little grimly.

Edwin felt uncomfortable as he went through the process of logging on as if he was Morris. The desktop icons littered the screen.

'The stuff he was working on is in My Documents. I'll leave you to look at them.'

'That's fine, Norma. I'll print out all his research stuff and then I'll tell you what I think.'

He didn't know where to start, but, trawling through the document files, he soon found a pattern. Morris had written an enormous amount on old Norbridge, but when Edwin keyed in *Norbridge* with *music* a whole new tranche of material appeared. Most of it looked like pretty accessible local information. Norbridge Clogdancers, Norbridge and Area Silver Bands, the History of Norbridge Abbey Chorus, and so on.

There was nothing to confirm Norma's belief that Morris's latest research was special. But Edwin remembered Morris's assertion that there was a local connection with Sir John Stainer, composer of *The Crucifixion*. He typed *Norbridge, Stainer* and *music* into the search engine, and instantly it scrolled onto the screen: *Norbridge and the Stainer Connection*.

Edwin read it with increasing fascination. Morris quoted at length from the letters of John Stainer to Cecil Quaile Woods, vicar of Fellside from 1860 to 1881. Edwin had never heard of these letters, which astonished him because he knew all about Quaile Woods from a musical point of view. He'd been a pioneering Anglican clergyman and fringe member of the Oxford Movement who'd come up to Cumbria. He'd started like the early Puseyites as an ascetic, and been Father to the depressed ports of the coast which were already past their peak in Irish trade. He set up various missions and charities for the poor. Then at the age of fifty in 1881, he'd suddenly made the odd downward move to the village of Uplands as curate. The church there was much more part of the related — but aesthetic — even indulgent, High Church fashion. There Quaile Woods had started to write his psalm chants. He had been praised for them in newspaper and church articles of the time, but most of them were missing, though others had become quite famous.

So if Stainer and Quaile Woods had written to each other regularly that certainly could be the connection which Morris had been going on about so mysteriously. But like a lot of amateurs Morris had failed to annotate his work. Where were the actual documents? The real letters? And the rest of his source material? It was infuriating. Typical Morris!

Edwin jumped up and started to look at all the hard copy Morris had accumulated. While Morris's computer filing system was predictable, his documents were filed in a totally idiosyncratic way. But the letters between Quaile Woods and Stainer had to exist somewhere unless Morris had invented them. It occurred to Edwin that they might have already been referred to by one of the many other local historians in the area, and that Morris might have been quoting another writer. He remembered that during his own research he had discovered that the Norbridge Local History Society had referred to Quaile Woods in a pamphlet in 1976. They had a website. Edwin Googled them, accessed it and reread the excerpts on the site. There was nothing about Stainer. So where had Morris come across the Stainer connection? Was there more about it in the 1976 pamphlet if you read the whole thing? Did Morris have a copy filed somewhere in this mess?

There was a pile of old material on the top shelf of the bookcase. Morris's idiosyncratic system nearly eluded Edwin, but at last he found the pamphlet filed not under Q or under N but under P — presumably for pamphlet. And here was the answer. The 1976 pamphlet was based on a much older book which was quoted lavishly, all about Quaile Woods' sterling character and great achievements, compiled in complex Edwardian style by someone called Henry Whinfell and published just after the First World War.

But Edwin had never heard of this biography. It would have been of limited interest even when it was published, and any copies had long since disappeared.

He was aware that Norma was standing by the door.

'You've been here hours! I knew he was on to something!' Norma said with satisfaction. 'That's why he wanted to meet you and talk to you about it. That's what I told you!'

'Me? I thought he just wanted to talk generally.'

'Oh no, he was planning to meet up with you. He told me the day before he died that he was writing it all for a document to take to the Music Department at the college along with some old papers. He must have meant you. You're the only person he knows from the Music Department. Didn't he email you?'

'If he did, I didn't get it.'

Norma was looking expectantly at him.

'Go into his emails. I'm sure he said he'd emailed the college.'

With some reluctance, Edwin reopened Morris's email account. But Morris had not been planning to meet *him*. To Edwin's astonishment, he saw that the last email Morris Little had ever written had been sent to Wanda Wisley. And with it was a hefty attachment. It was the same document that Edwin had already accessed: *Norbridge and the Stainer Connection*. But the covering note, written in Morris's unmistakable style, read:

Dear Miss Wisley,

I'll be able to pop over to the college as arranged this evening. I'd rather keep our meeting confidential as there are certain people who are rather up themselves and think they know everything about our music-making in Norbridge. Quite frankly they tend to take all the credit.

It just so happens that I've come across something which proves my point that our own Cecil Quaile Woods was a very intriguing man who wasn't all he seemed. I'd like to show it to you.

Morris Little

'Can I print all this stuff out?' Edwin asked Norma. She nodded. He highlighted the whole of Morris's correspondence file and pressed the print key. 'Look,' he went on, as the printer whirred into action, 'there's far more here than I can sort out now. Can I take it with me?'

'All right.' But Norma was pleased. Her smile had lost some of its bitter edge. 'I told you!' she said, her voice now mellow.

Edwin got away from Norma as quickly as he decently could and drove to the nearest pub. In the car park he sat for a minute to go over his thoughts. His boss Wanda Wisley had a lot of questions to answer, he thought. But had he the nerve to put them to her?

Then his mobile rang. When he saw the number on the screen his heart leapt up and down. It was a number he knew but rarely saw. Yet he had been expecting this call.

'Hello, Marilyn,' he said. 'At last!'

* * *

At the same time, Freddie Frabrikant was whistling in the dark as he cycled down from the Bible study course. The thought made him stop in mid-rendition of Van Morrison's 'Moondance' in honour of the silver light coming out from behind the black sooty night clouds. He laughed out loud. These weird English phrases! But he wasn't 'whistling in the dark' in the metaphorical sense. Far from it! His life had suddenly come together in this remote rural part of a grey and windswept island.

He'd come to Britain after his own album had done well, but not that well, in Germany. It had been mainly heavy rock but had nodded in the direction of melody with some old-type numbers with an all-female backing group humorously called *Die Jungfrauen*, The Virgins. Maybe that was why, in the Abbey, Freddie had noted that quotation from Psalm 45.

He laughed, remembering the past. A bit of misguided philandering with two of *Die Jungfrauen* who weren't, had sent

Freddie scurrying to Britain. He'd joined an old friend on the British music scene in a band called The Cut. He'd done all the usual things, including working and playing hard, and he met Wanda when he was recording with the band one Saturday night. The takes had gone on and on all afternoon, with the other members of The Cut making endless changes. Freddie had great hearing, and was a technical artist in the studio himself, so he had little patience with the musical fumbling that was going on. Bored, he had started to talk to the attractive but crabby woman in a very short skirt and crazy trainers waiting hunched at the back of the control room.

'I'm pissed off,' she'd said suddenly. 'Shall we leave these dope-heads, and go and find some hard liquor?'

Wanda had been waiting for her boyfriend who was the producer. Swaddled in his headphones and the chords of The Cut, he hadn't noticed when she and Freddie sneaked out.

Ten minutes later the drummer had asked, 'Where the fuck's Freddie?'

They'd realized that Wanda had gone too, and that neither of them was coming back. The two of them got completely 'arseholed' in a nearby Soho bar. It was the beginning of Freddie's relationship with Wanda and the end of his relationship with The Cut.

And they'd rubbed along ever since, especially as at that stage Wanda was hard-nosed, determined to hang on to her new man, and she was earning good money. There were trips to the US for Freddie as he did sessions for various named bands with her encouragement. Wanda worked at the BBC as a studio manager and studied at Birkbeck College part-time, landing an MA and eventually a PhD on how percussion music was therapy for some disturbed young people. Conferences, papers, occasional media interviews followed. They both did well, with Wanda eventually becoming the presenter of a radio show herself.

But nothing lasts forever. When Wanda told him that her radio series had failed to be recommissioned and that she was applying for a teaching job in some remote province he had never heard of, Freddie secretly thought it would be the end. He'd accompanied her to Norbridge just to mark time, until he decided what to do.

But he loved it! He loved the smattering of New Age culture, the therapists and craftsmen in crumbly old cottages, plus the close-knit — almost defensive — middle class of a small town. The professionals quietly admired him and were rather proud that he'd come to live among them. Their kids were at the college, and the parents would stop him in the town to confide about their own long-lost ambitions to be rock stars.

And the countryside too! He had meant it when he'd said to Wanda one day that he would be interested in moving further out into the country, maybe buying one of these big old farm buildings or failed hotels or abandoned factories, and doing something with it. Of course he wasn't going to be a farmer or anything like that. This wasn't a character transplant. He needed a place that was a bit crazy, Gothic maybe, with room for his own studio.

In fact, the derelict convent was just the sort of thing. He stopped his bike and looked over the wall at the drunken stone cross which lurched at an angle in the overgrown garden.

'Let's have a look-see,' Freddie said aloud.

He ignored the big wooden gates, which were jammed shut though they looked as if they would break up at his touch, and vaulted over the disintegrating brick wall, hearing the gravelly sound of dried masonry fragmenting under his big hand as the weight of his body swung across it. He landed with a squelching bump, to the crushing sound of thick vegetation being squashed underfoot. The weeds in the garden were higher and damper than he'd expected. He crept slowly through the wet tangled leaves and stems towards the broken windows. He tried to get high enough to peer in for a few minutes.

And then he listened. For a minute, he thought that his leap had caused the whole of the wall to crumble in a delayed action, slowly and almost rhythmically. He stood stock still, and strained to make out what he was hearing. The sound was like water bumping out of an old faucet, or the consistent thump of falling rocks.

Then he realized that he was hearing something bigger than the collapsing of the brick wall. It was certainly falling, cracking and tumbling in a cascade of drumbeats, but on top of that was a sort of rasping, whooshing noise, inhuman but somehow organic, punctuated by deep groans. He turned around.

The gate was open, but the animals were making for it in such numbers that they were breaking down the wall on either side. He saw monstrous heads rearing and hooves pounding. A herd of panicking bullocks was bearing down towards him, crazed and out of control. They were pounding towards him, eyes rolling.

With an agility which seemed impossible for such a hefty man, Freddie leapt sideways and grabbed the big stone cross, pulling himself up with all his strength. It wasn't quite enough. His head was level with the hot breath of the terrified herd. The combination of heat and smell was an assault. And then the pain came. The hooves as they rose and fell caught his shins time after time. The agony was unbearable though it was his aching arms which hurt as much as his crushed legs.

They're going to kill me, he thought. I'm totally conscious but I know I'm going to die. He could hold on no longer. As he slipped between the terrified animals, crushed till he could hardly gasp, he saw a stray skidding hoof raised higher than the others as a bullock lost its footing and went skittering at the side of his head. He felt the impact, heard the crunch and, as he went down, he knew with total clarity that the breath was being kicked out of him.

Then his brain went to black.

24

But it was even thou, my companion, my guide,
and mine own familiar friend.
Psalm 55:14

'He's lucky to be alive! If he hadn't had such good hearing, they'd have been on top of him before he could turn round!' Lynn said.

It was the following Wednesday, a typical cold, wet, dreary February day. Lynn Clifford and Suzy Spencer were having lunch in McCrea's. This time the meeting was at Suzy's instigation. She was the one who needed to talk now. But discussion of Freddie Fabrikant's terrible accident had to come first.

She asked, 'Has Neil been visiting Freddie?'

'Yes. He's broken both his legs and is very badly bruised, but Neil says he's almost perky!'

'What about Stainer's *Crucifixion*? Will he still be able to sing in that?'

'It's not until April and he reckons he'll be able to do it, with his legs in plaster. Neil says Wanda's been in to see him every day and taken him the score and his CDs, and he's threatening to practise in the Infirmary.'

'That'll go down well with the other patients!'

They laughed. Then Suzy's face fell again. She went on to ask about Chloe, but Lynn knew it was just routine politeness, and that Suzy's mind was on something else. And anyway, there was little to report. Chloe was just the same — working on her academic books most days, with a view to studying at the Open University, refusing to discuss going back to Leeds. She spent most evenings with friends whom she never brought back, and she was generally hard to reach. But Lynn was terrified of disturbing the status quo. At least Chloe was safe at home.

'So what's wrong, Suzy? You look pale. Is it Jake? Or Molly?'

'Neither, actually. I'm worried about Robert.'

'Robert?'

Suzy took a deep breath. 'Yes. Before Christmas, Robert asked me to marry him.' She forestalled her friend's delighted smile. 'No, Lynn. I know you're by definition a fan of marriage. But I'm not. I felt that Robert was indicating that something was missing — security, discipline perhaps — in my relationship with the children. I thought he was trying to compensate by becoming a stepfather. I was hurt. I felt put down.'

Lynn looked thoughtful. She knew how hard it could be for women who believed they were in a partnership only to find the man assuming control. Fleetingly she thought about the Whinfells, remembering Jenny Whinfell's tight lips and the way she avoided eye contact. Jenny only blossomed when she was given the floor, like at the Bible study course. And then she seemed aggressive, overheated by the sudden exposure.

But that wasn't Suzy's problem. Robert Clark wasn't the assertive type and Suzy had a good job and financial independence. The cause of their rift lay deeper than gender politics.

'Go on,' she said.

'I don't know if you'll understand, Lynn, because it sounds awful, but I don't just want to be the second wife. As things are, I could never be compared to Mary because Mary was the wife and I'm well . . . the mistress? The girlfriend? The live-in lover? But if we got married . . .'

'You'd be in a competition with a dead person?'

'Yes! I know it sounds stupid. But I would feel that I had to be like her — Mrs Perfect.'

Lynn thought for a moment. Then she laughed. 'Suzy, you could never be a Mrs Perfect, and you know it. There's something else going on here.'

'I guess you're right.' Suzy smiled sadly.

'So what's the real problem?'

Suzy paused to think. 'I'm not really sure. I worry that Robert only cares for me and the children because he rescued us from a terrible situation. There's a protective streak in him which was really brought out when he was married to Mary. But I don't need protecting.'

'No. But you need loving. We all do.'

'Yes, but love is best between equals. If someone thinks they're doing all the supporting then either they become dominating or they feel stifled by the very role they think they enjoy. I think that with Mary he was stifled without admitting it. So he went off to conferences and things like that, to escape. I flattered myself that he didn't need that with me. But since we rowed, he's been away — oh, only overnight, I know, in London. But I feel . . .'

'You feel he's reconstructing the past?'

'Yes! The fun and the honesty have all gone. We can't talk. He's terribly nice, but cold and distant. And with the kids there's so little time for us to be together.'

'Then you'll have to wait till he comes back to you, metaphorically speaking. Just be yourself. It's a dynamic. He can't be the same with you as he was with Mary. It's not possible.'

'That's true.' Suzy smiled wanly. Lynn picked up her bags, leant across the table and pecked her on the cheek.

'Give it time.'

But time was what Suzy did not have. Nigel was snapping at her heels. On the other hand Robert seemed more and more distant. And on top of everything, Suzy was getting increasingly exhausted. Caring for the children and their endless social arrangements — while making sure she kept Robert out of the schedule and asked him for nothing — was absorbing all her spare energy and wearing her out. Even taking Jake to Fellside Fellowship was losing its attraction. Flirting with Mark Wilson didn't fill the hole in her life.

She waved goodbye to Lynn, who was rushing back to Uplands School, and called for the bill. She was working a late shift that evening and had the drive to Tynedale ahead of her. It would be a demanding day. And when she came home late at night, it would be to a man who talked in clichés, then disappeared into his study to his writing. To her own horror she felt tears filling her eyes and she started to sniff loudly. Then she gave in and sobbed quietly and discreetly into one of Robert's large white handkerchiefs.

* * *

Mark Wilson was leaning against the counter in Jenny Whinfell's small but neat kitchen-diner. Jenny was sitting at the table feeding the baby in the high chair. She'd already breast-fed him for starters before Mark knocked on the door, and felt dishevelled and messy.

'Just hang on a minute,' she said, harassed. 'I can't stop in mid-meal. He'll scream the place down if he doesn't get enough.'

'That's blokes for you,' Mark quipped, but Jenny did not respond.

He could see that she was stressed. Her face was pale, and her mouth was set in a thin bloodless line. Her hair, usually a pale brown feathery pageboy around her face, was scraped back into a small tufty pony tail. He hadn't meant to barge in on her, but it would be nice to get a word with her alone.

'I'm sorry, Jenny. I didn't mean to be in the way. I'd forgotten Paul was at a Deanery meeting. I called in to see how Freddie was getting on. I was thinking of going to see him in the hospital this afternoon as I've got the day off and I'll be in Carlisle.'

'Neil Clifford went yesterday but I haven't heard any more news.'

Jenny focused fiercely on wiping a smear of baby food off her little boy's chin. Never chatty at the best of times, she felt uncomfortable now she was alone with Mark again. Since their amazing conversation just after Christmas when he had given her the New Puseyite leaflet, she had been in a state of acute nervousness where he was concerned. He had treated her like someone with a brain, whose views on the Church mattered. It had been months since Paul had talked to her like that. Gossip, yes, chit-chat about parish matters, fine — but major discussions about their mission, about their strategy, about their faith, these had all been subsumed under the daily weight of domesticity.

'When will Paul be back?'

'I don't know.'

And when he was back he would be scurrying to the computer to mess about with that wretched family tree stuff, trying to confirm a local connection. Jenny didn't care whether Paul was a Cumbrian or a Martian as long as he treated her with respect. That had been the deal. But since the baby had been born she had felt pushed out more and more. It was hard to take a suckling baby along to parish meetings; having a newborn inevitably meant withdrawal from the world. But Joseph was ten months old now and she felt as if Paul had never really welcomed her back.

Mark sighed. He had watched the Whinfells' relationship deteriorate from a distance. He liked women but he had never met anyone he felt could be a partner for him in the way Jenny had been to Paul. It wasn't for lack of trying and he could certainly attract intelligent and interesting females, but none of them was quite right. With his blond good looks, lots of younger girls had crushes on him too. That was always an embarrassment and he tried as much as he could to keep them at a distance and help them through the minefield of growing up, rather than encourage them. But the time was coming when the matter of mature marriage would have to be addressed. What Mark liked was spark, but sparky women had this awful dilemma about their position these days. Perhaps that was one of Jenny's problems.

Mark had gone from wanting a wife just like her, to wondering how you could make any marriage really work. He had started to wonder more about the High Church; the idea of becoming a celibate Anglican priest had started to take root. Until recently he hadn't thought that celibacy as an act of faith was suitable to the Church of England, where most priests seemed to be family men. Then he had read about John Henry Newman and the Oxford Movement. Newman had become a Catholic but his colleague Edward Bouverie Pusey had stayed an Anglican. Notwithstanding that, Pusey had valued the celibate life, especially after the death of his wife. Mark had thought about a few ways of serving St Luke's and had already taken some significant steps, including an appointment with the director of ordinands, the person responsible for interviewing would-be priests. He already had a huge dream. But his one big idea, the vision he was nurturing, meant making even bigger moves.

He wondered if he could say something about all this to Jenny now. She seemed to need desperately to talk. He tried to think of something to say which would help. Her tense misery made him feel sad for her and women like her in the confusing modern world.

'Your talk at the Psalms course was really good, Jenny,' he said kindly.

For a minute her back seemed to quiver before she stiffened and turned to him. 'Do you really think so? The only thing Paul said was that it was a bit unfortunate that I mentioned Psalm 22 — you know, the fat bulls of Basan closing in on every side!'

Mark spluttered into his coffee. 'But it was hardly your fault that poor old Freddie got caught in a stampede on the way home!'

169

'Tell that to Paul.' She turned testily back to the baby.

Oh no, Mark thought, don't be angry. During her pregnancy Jenny had looked like the Madonna and he had felt her impending motherhood draw him in, as if her growing belly was a metaphor for the world. It had been so easy to pop over or turn up for meals almost every day, especially as the Fellowship meant there was always so much to talk about. And for months, even after Joseph was born, she and Paul had seemed the perfect couple. He'd been happy to be the outsider, the gooseberry, the third person singular. He didn't mind at all, worshipping at the shrine of their perfect marriage and beautiful baby. It had been a state to aim for.

But something had soured all that, something coming from Jenny. He wanted to think about it, to try and understand why this marriage, like so many, was going wrong. It seemed as if every woman he met these days was unhappy.

He put the mug down. 'I'll be off then. It sounds as if a visit to Freddie might be a bit unnecessary if Neil Clifford's doing the business on behalf of the church. I'll wait till Freddie's a bit better. Maybe next week.'

'Will you be off every Wednesday?' Jenny asked bluntly.

'No. Not every Wednesday. Just today. I wanted to go over to talk to the director of ordinands. I'm really serious about becoming a priest, Jenny. You've been an inspiration to me.'

Jenny blushed, clearly delighted. 'Well, I hope it goes well,' she said rather stiffly.

'I hope so too.' He smiled at her. His face lit up the kitchen. Then he waved his hand and let himself out of the back door.

Jenny Whinfell's heart was thumping. She put her hands up to her face and felt her hot cheeks. She needed to pull herself together and calm down. She would get the buggy out and go to the Co-op. The chill wind off the fells would cool down any inappropriate thoughts she had. But Mark was the first man who had noticed her in more than two years. And from day one she had felt attracted to his warm eyes and bright smile. She grabbed the scarf Paul had given her for Christmas, a stupid red velvety thing, and turned it twice round her neck like a noose. What a nightmare, she thought, as she belted the screeching toddler firmly into place and pushed him out into the street. She kept her head down to avoid eye contact with any passing parishioner and marched to the Co-op where she wielded the buggy in front of her to fend off anyone who might dare to speak to her.

25

For the ungodly hath made boast of his own heart's desire,
and speaketh good of the covetous, whom God abhorreth.
Psalm 10:3

Edwin had suggested to Alex that they meet at lunchtime on Wednesday to talk about his visit to Norma Little. It had taken him several days to wade through all the paperwork he had printed out from Morris's computer. Alex had said, 'Great! But not in the canteen, please.' Edwin had been mildly surprised, but quite pleased, when she had suggested the Crown and Thistle.

'I can get out for about an hour and a half,' she said, 'and if it's Wednesday afternoon you won't be teaching, will you?'

And if we're in the pub there's no chance of running into Robert Clark for a friendly chat, Alex had thought. She had thought about him constantly since the Bible study meeting a week before. What a bastard he was! He must have left his wife for Suzy Spencer. And Suzy had seemed such a nice woman, good fun and just a bit different. How ironic that the first woman — besides the kindly Lynn — that Alex had taken a liking to in years was living with a horrible hypocrite like Robert Clark.

Did Suzy know the truth about him? Alex wondered. Anger had fired her up. She had spent some time the previous weekend shopping in Carlisle. She had already lost a lot of weight and had ordered contact lenses. She had her hair done again — still auburn but darker, more like the old days. And she had bought some smart outfits in warm glowing colours which suited her.

As a test, she had invited herself to Christine and Reg Prout's for the first time since New Year's Day. She had gone by taxi. When Reg opened the door his mouth fell open in his pale round face.

'Yes, it's me. Proof that there's life after death. How are you, Reg?' She brushed past him into the hall. 'Here I am, Chris. I've brought a bottle of Chablis. Make sure I only drink one glass. I'm dieting.'

'You look wonderful! Like your old self.'

'Well, thank you, big sister.'

Chris was smiling, her plump face genuinely delighted. They had never been close but they had never quarrelled either. That was good enough, Alex thought.

They had a good but healthy lunch, and the chat had been uncontroversial. Chris had talked about her daughters and about decorating, which led Reg to talk about property prices — although he was very careful not to mention the bungalow straight away. He did mention David Johnstone, though, patting his bald head with that nervous gesture he had.

'I know this is highly confidential, Alex, but Johnstone has hinted that he's got plans for development at Fellside. He's interested in a scheme for turning the old quarry into a lake — leisure pursuits and all that. Of course the bungalow would be in prime position. He's on the way to getting planning permission and it could be marvellous news for us.'

'If I wanted to sell,' Alex had said evenly.

'Johnstone would make it worth your while.'

'Worth all our whiles, don't you mean, Reg?'

'Alex, I don't want to fall out with you. But bear in mind that Johnstone doesn't mess about. He always gets what he wants. There are a few people around here who've regretted standing in David Johnstone's way.'

'What does he do? Advance on them with thumbscrews? Set Pat to cackling them to death?'

'You may well be flippant. But you should think about it.'

But this development is light years away, Alex had wanted to say. Instead she just smiled at Reg, and for once the meal passed without too much friction.

And she had found out what she wanted to know. She was recognizable again, which meant that either she had to leave town or sort things out with Robert Clark. But not yet, she found herself thinking. If the truth came out it might just prejudice things with Edwin. And her friendship with him was starting to matter more and more.

So the following Wednesday she and Edwin had met as arranged in the lounge of the Crown and Thistle. Alex could tell by Edwin's wider eyes and the way he bent to talk to her that he too had noticed the difference in her. I wonder how many years younger than me he really is, Alex thought.

But Edwin had too much to say to be stunned by her new looks for long. He told her about the contents of Morris Little's emails, and how Morris had been going to meet Wanda Wisley on the night he had died.

'Good heavens! And she never mentioned it?'

'Not a word. Rather strange, don't you think?'

'Yes and no. Dr Wisley's got a reputation amongst administrators for disappearing when anything tedious needs to be done. Maybe she forgot about him.'

'It's possible,' Edwin said. 'But there's this crazy business of the psalter. You saw a psalter. Tom Firth saw a psalter. But there was no psalter when the police came back.'

'I've been thinking about that. It must have been the Frosts or one of their gang who came back and took it.'

'We've discussed this before.' Edwin sounded edgy. 'The Frosts wouldn't know one end of a book from another.'

'That's a bit sweeping? How do you know?'

Edwin looked at her. Then he looked down at his half pint of real ale and Alex realized the conversation had ground to a halt. No, worse — it had crashed into some invisible barrier she hadn't seen. What on earth was the problem?

Why was Edwin Armstrong so sensitive about the Frost brothers?

* * *

At the same moment, only half a mile away in the middle of Norbridge, David Johnstone looked at Reg Prout over his gin and tonic. He saw a middle-aged man slurping greedily, and that pleased him. Prout was a respectable local functionary who worked for the council in the Environmental Health Department. But it seemed as if he might like his little luxuries.

Johnstone had met him through the golf club, but until now their contact had been purely social and Prout had been rather in awe of him. Good. That could be very helpful, Johnstone thought with satisfaction. They were in the Norbridge Arms, the town's best hotel with a plush bar. It was used by the Rotary Club and the Lions, and was a well-known meeting place for Norbridge businessmen. David Johnstone had organized quite a few liaisons there over the years — one or two of them taking place upstairs in the bedrooms.

'Dixon will be along in a minute,' he said brusquely. David Johnstone had scant respect for most of his associates, including the ferrety Brian Dixon, but both Dixon and Reg Prout were going to be useful. And in addition, Dixon was under obligation to him, which always helped.

On cue, Brian Dixon came sidling into the bar, wrapped in a huge sheepskin coat, his tweed cap in his hand. A small man with stringy brown hair that was too long, he looked like a superior rodent.

'Greetings, David and Reg.' He smiled weakly at them. His thin, upper-class voice contrasted with the well-upholstered David Johnstone's rich confident local twang.

"Ow do, Brian my lad. A Jameson's as ever?'

Dixon nodded nervously, and Johnstone turned to the bar. It was useful, in one phrase, to remind Brian Dixon of their several encounters at the Norbridge Arms. They had been joined on occasion by two ladies, whose services had been paid for on Johnstone's account. This had always been preceded by Dixon glugging down a fair amount of Irish whiskey.

Dixon was typical of a class of older local gent — landed family, various sources of income, minor public school — but of the generation and class where, if you were not academic enough for Oxford, you were sent home to manage a business of some sort. In Dixon's case, he had become general manager of one of the smaller textile mills in Norbridge, which had closed down. He and his wife lived in a nice Georgian gem of a farmhouse on the road between Norbridge and Tarnfield. They still had money, but much of it was spent on a son who'd been to an even more minor public school and been equally undistinguished. The boy was now working in Manchester and borrowing from his father to finance his own family. Money was tightish for the Dixons.

Good, David Johnstone thought again.

'Now then,' he said, 'let's sit down, over in the corner.'

He led his two cronies to a dark booth fitted with a rounded banquette and a low heavy coffee table. It was divided off from the bar with dark wood and etched glass screens. There was an air of conspiracy about it. Johnstone thought that the atmosphere would help.

'As you know, I've got my eye on a neat little development idea. I suspect no one's come up with it before, because it's in Fellside, and with all due respect to your wife's family seat, Reg, Fellside isn't exactly Windermere, is it?'

'Actually,' said Reg ponderously, patting his bald head nervously, 'my wife's family is from Workhaven. They only moved to Fellside when my father-in-law fell ill and needed a bungalow, after he retired. My mother-in-law lived there for a few years, that's all.'

'Well, it mebbe helps that there's no great sentimental affection for the place on your wife's part. But your sister-in-law lives there now, right?'

'Yes.' Reg tried to sound decisive but he shifted uncomfortably.

'The point is, Reggie lad, that the disused quarry would make a great site for a leisure pool and the old convent site would be perfect for holiday flats. Use the facade but have it completely ripped out and modernized behind. No one seems to know why the convent's just been left to go to rack and ruin. What's the story on that, Brian?'

'Well . . .' Brian Dixon squirmed too. He was pleased to be included, but there was something about David Johnstone which put a chap on the spot. At least he knew all about this and could answer as required. 'As you know, my wife Millie is second cousin to Jimmy Cleaverthorpe. It was one of Jimmy's great-great-aunts or something who wanted to start a convent.'

'I didn't know the Cleaverthorpes were left-footers?' said Reg Prout in surprise.

'No, no.' Brian Dixon shook his head. 'Not RCs. These were Church of England nuns.'

Reg looked surprised and patted his bald head again, but Johnstone burped and said deeply, 'Go on, man.'

'So when the old man, the first great Lord Cleaverthorpe, realized his cherished eldest daughter wanted to take the veil — and not the seven veils, I assure you . . .' Dixon squirmed in a ratty way and waited for a laugh, but there was none. 'Sorry. Anyway, the old man bought land for her and built a house for her and her companions. He'd been a bit of a dirty old sod in his time and local gossip still says there are bastard Cleaverthorpes in Fellside. But his eldest girl was a bit of a saint and he respected that. She said she would pray for a building, and her father answered her prayers. But he never gave her any title deeds. Of course he didn't need to if it was on his own land. The story goes that despite his love for his daughter, old Cleaverthorpe didn't agree with

177

women owning property, and sorted it out with some sort of male representative when he was on his deathbed. Then the Cleaverthorpe nun died suddenly of something she caught in Chapterhouse . . .'

'What was she doing there?' asked Reg.

'Saving fallen women or so the story goes.' Brian took a deep sip of his whiskey. 'Anyway, the nuns just stayed on there for another century on the assumption it was theirs. No one challenged them and now no one seems sure who the place belongs to. They all died out about fifteen years ago. So it's been boarded up since.'

'And Jimmy Cleaverthorpe can't sell it?'

'Not till the ownership is sorted out. I think the last Mother Superior believed it was theirs and tried to leave it to the Church. But they can't sell it either,' Dixon said.

'But of course it's supposed to be a local historic monument,' Reg Prout butted in, trying to be helpful. 'The chapel is supposed to be beautiful. That chap Morris Little had a meeting with the council about it. He wanted it listed. Of course, then he died.'

Johnstone sipped his drink reflectively. 'But what would happen, Reg, if there was, say, a problem with the septic tank? Or if the fabric was going to collapse? After all, that fool Freddie from the Chorus managed to demolish half the wall being chased by a herd of cattle!'

'But that was just an accident, David, it could have happened anywhere.'

David looked at Reg Prout and laughed evilly. 'Accidents do happen, Reg. Say the place was a health and safety hazard? Especially to the bungalow next door. Do you follow me?'

Reg gulped. 'Well, the Environmental Health Department would have something to say about it, I suppose.'

'So they would, Reg, so they would!' Johnstone patted him on the back. 'I think a visit to the convent might be called for. Who knows what alarming structural or drainage problems we might find! And then the council might have to be brought in, don't you think? And they might have to act quickly and get it sold off, for the sake of public health!'

Reg Prout was looking very uncomfortable. 'I don't know, David.'

'Oh yes, you do!' Johnstone leant forward and tapped him gently on the knee. 'Oh yes, you do, Reg. I think I might take a trip up to the convent and see just how much prayer it needs to keep it standing. Or to have it knocked down!'

* * *

In the Crown and Thistle at the same moment, Edwin looked up slowly and then looked away, but Alex refused to be embarrassed. If she had said something wrong it was inadvertent.

'Edwin, what have I said? It's unfair of you to pull up the conversational drawbridge.'

He shifted on his bar stool. But she didn't give up. She waited.

'Don't you know?' he said eventually.

'Know what? Something about the Frosts?' She moved her eyeline until Edwin was forced to return her gaze.

He saw in front of him a big but surprisingly pretty dark-haired woman with intelligent features, head slightly on one side, and a questioning look.

In a small town all news was high octane. But maybe his story had run out of gas. He wasn't the only person in the world — or in Norbridge, for that matter — to have been dumped. Maybe Alex genuinely didn't know all about it. It was only his pride which made him reticent to tell her.

But Alex had swallowed hers, and occasionally mentioned her past with rueful humour. Perhaps he could do the same. Or at least he could just tell her the basics. No details or emotional trappings, no melodrama.

'I was involved with the Frosts' elder sister for a while.'

'Oh, really? So did she share the family's interesting reputation?'

179

Alex smiled at him. She was surprised but not shocked. She waited for him to continue.

'No, Marilyn was lovely,' Edwin said after a pause. 'Not like the rest. She was the eldest by a long way, with a different father. Her education was non-existent but she had brains. And the sisters helped her. So she enrolled at the college to do music.'

'And you were her teacher?'

'Yes. Dangerous of course. She was nineteen and I was thirty. When we realized how things were going, she left the college. She was over eighteen. It was unwise perhaps, but there was never a scandal.'

'Did everyone know?'

'Oh yes!' He remembered how impossible it had been to hide their happiness. 'There was some talk, and some nastiness. But we planned to get married.'

'And what happened?'

He paused for longer. 'She discovered life outside Norbridge, so we split up. She's in Derby now. We're still friends.'

'That's good.'

Alex could tell there was more to the story, but Edwin looked drained.

She shrugged. 'Well, as I've told you before, I was ditched too. But in my case we weren't friends afterwards. I hated my husband and still do. I could kill him, I really could. He left me for a woman in his office. Someone he didn't have anything in common with, except . . .'

'Except?' he prompted, genuinely intrigued.

'We were childless. He couldn't have kids. It was okay because I loved him so much. I assumed he adored me too. But then he came home and told me . . .'

She found it hard to say. Edwin waited. 'He'd had a one-night stand with her at a Christmas party. She got pregnant. It was a fluke but the child was definitely his. I went off the rails with jealousy. I'd been *sooo* understanding about his low sperm count. And now bingo! Hole in one, as they say. He was leaving me. And he was so bloody thrilled! That was almost the worst of it. He thought that because I loved him, I should be delighted about the baby too. The selfishness of men! I went mad, literally I think. I behaved desperately badly.'

'What did you do?'

'I followed him to her house more than once, and ranted at both of them. I lashed out at him and scratched him on his face. I screamed whole nights away. At first I tried sex with someone else, but that didn't work, so I got madder and madder and eventually I got pissed and crashed the car and ended up in hospital and lost my licence. I was out of my mind for over a year. It's only through good luck that I didn't murder McFay and his girlfriend. Both of them. And I just couldn't be near them and our so-called friends when the baby was born.'

'So you came back to Norbridge.'

'Yes, I did. But not before I'd fallen out with everyone we'd known. You see, they all seemed to be on his side. People are so sentimental about babies. But I behaved appallingly.'

'You were in shock. I sympathize.'

'You do?' Alex's eyes widened.

'I wish I'd done something like that. I withdrew and went cold to everyone, even Lynn, who was out of her mind with worry about me. I stopped eating. You took your anger out, I bottled mine up. But it was the same thing. Jealousy — which is evil, but so very understandable. I know exactly what you mean.' It took the Psalms to tell me that justified anger should be expressed, he thought. You let the sun go down on it as much by repressing it as by feeding it.

Alex tried to laugh. 'We're a right pair, aren't we! Fire and ice.'

Edwin looked at her steadily. 'Maybe we are,' he said seriously.

Alex grabbed her empty glass and stood up. 'I'm going to have another cranberry juice, though I'd love a scotch,' she said to hide her embarrassment. 'Now our confession session is over, we should go back to discussing Morris Little, because you still haven't explained why being in love with their big sister means that you think the Frosts are innocent.'

'I'm not in love with her,' Edwin said to Alex's back. 'Not now.'

She came back with a pint for him and juice for herself. Edwin started talking straight away. 'Marilyn knows what the boys are like. It's been one petty crime after another. They both had ASBOs and Jason had been charged with a drugs offence, though it was dropped. To be honest, I didn't contact her about it because . . . well, because contacting her is difficult. But a few days ago she called me. All she said was that she would be allowed to visit them. And that she didn't believe that they'd done it.'

'And allied with the mystery of the psalter, the assignation with Wanda, and the power cut, it made you wonder?'

'Yes! Say someone else met Morris, beat him on the head, then waited during the power cut, and came back when you and Tom were off the scene?'

'But the Frosts' fingerprints are on the wood, aren't they?'

'Does that mean anything?'

'And they've boasted about causing the power cut, haven't they?'

'But maybe that was a coincidence?'

'So who else would have wanted to kill Morris Little?'

'That,' said Edwin slowly, 'is the easiest question to answer. Almost everyone in Norbridge hated Morris. Including me.' He paused. 'Look at this. I only found it yesterday when I went through Morris's emails.' Edwin fished in his pocket and Alex looked down at the printout he produced.

A moment later, lifting her eyes from the page, she said, 'My God! I'll get both of us a scotch after all.'

26

All mine enemies whisper together against me;
even against me do they imagine this evil.
Psalm 41:7

'This is an all right spot!'

Poppy Strickland eased her large round firm bottom a little closer to Tom Firth's agonizingly thin thighs. They were sitting together in the Mitre Lounge, a dark offshoot of the Norbridge Arms, where the town's youth gathered, faces illuminated by the glowing stained glass window effect of bright beeping game machines. Tom couldn't help jigging his shoulders softly along to the rap. He looked a particularly livid yellow while Poppy flashed scarlet and blue alternately. Both sucked a commercial cocktail of chemicals through plastic straws with the look of suckling babies, lulled by the thudding beat of the music.

Poppy's lush lips parted to reveal very white teeth and, just before she spoke, Tom had congratulated himself, yet again, on getting off with her — if that was what had happened. He wasn't quite sure. Poppy was not a great talker. After a fumbling clinch outside the cinema complex in Newcastle when he visited her, she had just said 'All right' when he suggested meeting the next time she was home from university.

Then he'd had a brainwave. His mum's birthday was coming up. If Poppy was coming home for half-term, he could ask her to help him choose something for his mother. The scheme was a winner. It was safe, cosy, and made him look like a nice guy. And he would have time to think up their next outing, and maybe take things a little further. Predictably, when he'd asked her, Poppy had just said 'All right.'

They'd met at eleven o'clock that morning, and trawled Marks and Spencer, H. Samuel and Waterstone's before choosing a set of Cumbrian Heather Bath Accessories from McCrea's. The gift safely out of the way, Tom had made for the trendy atmosphere of the Mitre Lounge and was now wondering what to suggest next.

'Yes, it's all right here,' Poppy repeated. Then she said brusquely: 'Have you seen Chloe?'

Was this an innocent question, or was she becoming a bit proprietorial? Tom was rather chuffed at the thought.

'No,' he said emphatically, but then he wondered if the truth might be a better option. After all, he had no idea whether the two girls were in touch. 'Well, actually, she's been coming to Chorus practices with her mum. Have you seen her yourself?' he added, suddenly suspicious. He was a bit nervous about where Poppy's loyalties lay.

'Nah.' She shook her head. 'But I've tried texting her. She hardly ever replies and when she does, it's weird.'

'Like?'

'She says she's busy 'cos she's seeing someone.'

'Yer what?'

'You sound surprised.'

'I am. She looks really frumpy and grim. Wears scarves, long skirts, Timberlands.'

'So?'

'Well, it's not exactly sexy.' Tom paused before his next killer sentence. 'You look sexier than her these days.'

Poppy sucked audibly at her straw, which Tom found uncomfortably erotic. I like big girls, he said to himself. And Poppy was less big than she used to be, and shapely with it. He relaxed into her and conversation stopped for a minute.

Then Poppy said, 'I bet he's an old guy. Or married.'

'Who?'

'Chloe's squeeze.'

'What makes you say that?'

'Because then he wouldn't care what she looked like, would he? He'd just get off on the fact she was young. And she's so secretive. Before she couldn't keep her mouth shut about how popular she was and who she'd had sex with. Or nearly had sex with. But now, nada.'

There was a long but not empty silence while they both drank.

'Actually,' said Poppy, pausing to suck voluptuously on her straw, 'I'm a bit worried about Chloe. She was my best friend, after all.'

'So?'

'Well, it's not right somehow. There's summat going on. I think you should keep a lookout.'

'Me?'

Tom cast his mind back to his last conversation with Chloe, when he had told her about the psalter in Morris Little's hand. For a minute he felt uncomfortable. Edwin Armstrong, whom he respected in an obscure sort of way, had told him not to tell anyone. But he had gone and told Chloe. Though surely that didn't matter; they were family, after all. Edwin would probably have told Chloe himself. But the suspicion that he had been indiscreet would not go away. To make amends, he found himself agreeing with Poppy.

'OK, I'll keep an eye on her.' He wasn't sure why, but he felt that this way he would at least be able to check on what Chloe did. 'Maybe she'll have a coffee with me — you know, just as friends.'

'It had better be just as friends,' said Poppy, to his satisfaction.

Spurred on, he said, 'And how about the weekend? Should we go to the Chinese on Fletchergate on Friday?'

'All right.' Poppy sank her plump leg even further into his bony thigh. This is wonderful, Tom thought. My strategy is working. With luck, if I play my cards right and take things slowly, then, with a bit of girly-style romance, we might be able to go a bit further this weekend.

'And in the meantime,' Poppy said in a sudden rush, 'why not come back to my place and watch a movie in my bedroom this afternoon?'

Tom's mouth gaped open and his big brown eyes shone like chocolate drops.

'Great!' he yelped, rather shrilly.

'All right.'

* * *

At that moment, Alex Gibson came out of the Crown and Thistle, blinking in the sudden burst of watery sunlight. The pub had been dark and cosy, which was just as well. She had not wanted Edwin to see how appalled she was by the letter he had shown her. It had been in the mass of paper he had printed out from Morris Little's computer.

'I always wondered who had sent it to me,' he'd said quietly. 'But in a small town like Norbridge there are so many possibilities. Especially if you work somewhere like the college. But I would never have thought Morris hated me enough.'

Alex had been transfixed by the words. *You think you're the most musical man in Norbridge don't you? Up yourself aren't you? And now they say you'll be head of the college's Music Department. But don't they remember what you did to Marilyn Frost? I bet she's not the only one either. Isn't it wrong to shag your pupils? But I'll tell you something — I know where Marilyn is and if you don't withdraw from this head of department thing I'll make sure everyone else knows too . . .*

It had been so spiteful. 'I wasn't sure whether or not to show it to you,' Edwin had said softly. 'But once we

186

started talking about Marilyn, it seemed a lot easier to tell you everything. Anyway . . .' He pulled his battered brown leather briefcase on to his knee. '. . . I'm not the only one. And I'm glad now that I know where it came from.'

He'd pulled out a sheaf of paper. 'There are about ten others. They were all sent from a separate account called Norbridge Man. I printed out everything on his hard drive entitled Norbridge and got these too. I didn't want to show you them because some of them are horrible. And cruel and untrue, I suspect. But Morris was writing to a lot of people.'

'Was there any pattern?' Alex had asked.

'They're all to people he thought were too big for their boots. People who had maybe snubbed him or people he felt were "up themselves". That's a phrase he uses a lot.'

Edwin had seemed saddened rather than angry. He seemed to feel that perhaps he should have listened to Morris, rather than swatting him away. 'Maybe I *was* a bit up myself. At one time I thought I had the world at my feet.'

'When you were with Marilyn?'

'You've been there too, haven't you?'

'The Golden Age.' Alex nodded and they had both smiled.

Then Edwin had looked at his watch. 'Bugger. I'm needed at a meeting of the new Credits Resource Audit Practice committee. CRAP for short.'

'It may be crap but it won't be short if I know the college! You'd better dash . . .'

'Listen, Alex, they're doing *Dream of Gerontius* in Newcastle the week after next. Do you fancy going over, and having supper afterwards?'

'Yes, great.'

'I'll call you.' He grabbed his papers and left suddenly.

Alex gathered her bag and gloves thoughtfully and pushed her way outside, blinking in the glare.

It might have been the whisky, a novelty these days, but her head was spinning. She breathed in the clammy air, aware of a sense of warmth — or at least of less raw chill. Maybe winter was ebbing. It would be the anniversary of her mother's death just after Easter, and for the first time she sensed the seasons coming round again. For most of the year she had stood still or even gone backwards, but now the world was spinning on at a faster rate.

The low bright winter sun went behind a high cloud and suddenly she could see clearly along Market Street. It had the grey quietness of a provincial town where lunchtime was still recognized. Most shoppers were munching, many in the dated snugness of McCrea's. But then Alex saw Suzy Spencer pushing her way out of the heavy old-fashioned glass-plated doors opposite. She was snuffling into a large white handkerchief. Her eyes were red and her head was pulled down into her collar. She's crying, Alex thought.

And suddenly, she thought, I need to sort all this out. I want to go over and ask Suzy what's the matter, but because of the past I can't. I like Suzy. I'd like to be her friend but if I go on evading things like this, at some point we'll both be compromised. And there are other people to think of too. Like Edwin.

Alex walked back to the college, keyed up and agitated. There was to be no more of this stupidity. She went straight to her computer, found Robert's address on the internal address list, and emailed asking if they could meet. And she signed it with her real name.

* * *

Suzy dried her eyes and started driving savagely out of Norbridge. She felt angry with everyone. On the way to the north-east, without thinking she took the old Military Road, not the main A69. The car bounced down the straight switchback which cut the bleak landscape with Roman brutality. Occasionally Hadrian's Wall reared to her left, and on her right the iron grey hills stretched for miles under pearly skies. It was the top of the world.

She had been going far too fast, and forced herself to slow down and pull in at a lay-by. She was ahead of schedule now. She got out of the car and walked over to a stile which led up to the Wall, and looked around her. To the east she thought she could sense the change of light over the big city thirty miles ahead. To the west, hills and bogs and no man's land stretched till it all dropped down to Norbridge in its isolation, and the soft coastal plain. Which way did she want to go?

I'm tearing myself apart, she thought. I don't want Nigel any more, but I don't want Robert as he is now. Yet guilt pulls me to both of them. Nigel was my husband for years and we were a duo, responsible for shaping each other. And I clung to Robert when things went wrong. But which one do I love? And who loves me? And what do my children need? Her head ached with thinking.

She climbed back in the car. The wind was freezing up here on the ridge, but even so the light was brighter and the sensation bracing rather than chilling. The year was moving on and spring was in the wings.

She punched into her mobile phone book and chose a number. Three hundred miles away a mobile rang in response.

'Is that you, Suzy?'

'Oh Rachel, thank goodness you're there. I couldn't have coped with your voicemail.'

'What's wrong with "Leave a message already"?'

'Stop taking the piss. I want to come down to London and see you this weekend. I was supposed to be going to Nigel's with the kids but I'm sick of playing Happy Families.'

'And you'd feel bad having a romantic time with Mr Perfect while poor Nigel does the Daddy thing?'

'It's Mr Perfect who's giving me bother.'

'Wow. This is news.'

'Old news really . . . you *know* it hasn't been right since New Year. I just want time to think without the pressure of places. Everywhere I look relates to one man or the other. I want to be somewhere unconnected with them, where I can go to pieces.'

'Welcome to my world. Car or train?'

'Train. On Saturday morning. I'll let you know what time.'

27

Hear me, O Lord, and that soon, for my spirit waxeth faint.
Hide not thy face from me, lest I be like unto them
that go down into the pit.
Psalm 143:7

On Friday lunchtime, effectively the end of the working week, David Johnstone eased himself into his new Volvo. He'd had a few shorts but he was fit enough to drive — anyway, he knew all the roads around Norbridge and fancied he had a few of the local police in his pocket, so it was worth the risk. The conversation with baldy Prout and weasel-faced Dixon had made him think it was about time he took a closer look at the old convent again. Pity the nights were getting a bit lighter and the Volvo was quite conspicuous. But then there was nothing to stop him or anyone else walking through the huge gap in the rotten wall caused by the stampede, and having a look at the property.

Johnstone farted noisily and then opened the window as he drove through the outskirts of Norbridge. He liked the feeling of control and comfort his big car gave him. Whenever he broke wind in front of Pat she would comment in a silly shrill voice, so to celebrate her absence he did it again, a real trump.

Laughing to himself, he took the road to Fellside. It always gave him a thrill to ease a large, shiny car up the narrow main street where the only lights shone from the Co-op sign, and where the plain terraced houses opened straight onto the pavement. He had been brought up in Scafell Street, then a particularly miserable side road at the top of the hill. It had been a straggling row of cottages, looking over the waste land opposite, littered with old iron implements, post-war rubbish and bits of engines. Often he drove down there just to see the place, which had been done up now and was lived in by a pair of gay teachers, a far cry from housing seven kids in two bedrooms in the 1950s!

He parked carefully next to the convent wall. There was no one else on the road and it was easy to amble into the overgrown garden. He remembered climbing over the wall when he was a kid, wanting to see salacious acts, nuns sunbathing nude or snogging or something. It seemed much smaller inside, though he was pleased to see from a distance that the house brickwork was in good nick. It even looked as if someone had repointed around the window facing away from the road, with the bleak view over the quarry and only the drunk woman's bungalow in sight. Despite the damp grass round his trousers, he kept on going right around the house. With luck he might be able to see in through the windows, which were broken glass on the outside, but boarded up haphazardly inside.

He moved forward and felt the ground give a little under his feet. He pressed his shoes down. This was good news. If the drains were collapsing, then it would just take a little bit of help to render the place a hazard. If he owned the property next door, he'd have every right to demand that something be done, which would mean a quick sale. There'd be no arguing about who owned it then — they would all want rid of it PDQ! He'd get it for a song — and then go ahead with the holiday development.

Then he felt the ground give way under him. As he collapsed into the earth, he had the sense of falling into a deep, square hole. He hit his head as he twisted and fell, and the window ledge came up to smack him in the face.

* * *

Early on Saturday morning, Robert dropped Suzy off at Carlisle station for her trip to Rachel's in London. She was distracted, thinking about the evening before. Nigel had picked the children up on one of his rare trips back to Tarnfield. He had refused to come into The Briars and had been unpleasant about having to manoeuvre the car up the dirt lane which led to the house.

The children had been sulky and uncommunicative. They loved their father — but Suzy thought they sensed that Nigel was bored by childcare when there was no female audience. And Jake would miss his big band practice at Fellside Fellowship on the Sunday evening. Nigel, who was an atheist, had refused point-blank to drive back earlier to Cumbria for what he described as lot of superstitious nonsense with third-rate musicians.

In the station car park Robert said, 'Don't worry. The kids will be fine. Give Rachel my love.' He kissed Suzy on the cheek.

'I will. Thanks.'

There had been no suggestion that he should go to London with her. Suzy had made it clear this was a girls' weekend.

Robert watched her walk through the glass doors to the trains. Then he got out of the car, locked it, and walked into the town centre. Feeling very tense and awkward, he went into Bookends bookshop. There was a section for local writers and another for children's books, and he wasn't sure where to look. He probed the shelves until he found what he wanted.

Seeing it made his heart pound. *The West Coast Pirate* by Sandy McFay. A local promotion. The other eight McFay books, making up the West Cumbrian Chronicles, were there. As always, there was very little on Sandy McFay, just a blurb about how the old-fashioned boys' adventure stories had come back to life.

'Robert!'

He started, looking up guiltily. 'Edwin! What are you doing here?'

'Well, it is the biggest bookshop in the area. Or do you mean here in the local interest section? Did you read in the *Cumberland News* about the Sandy McFay promotion?'

'Yes, I did.'

'I was intrigued. I'd never heard of Sandy McFay's books, but Morris Little had them all, you know. I think I'll buy this one, *The Wizard of Workhaven*. Sounds good.'

'They are.'

'Oh, well, you'd know, I suppose. Listen to what it says on the cover — *meticulously researched and authentic tales which bring the north of England to life in adventures to appeal to readers of all ages*. Sounds excellent!'

Edwin was rather jaunty, Robert thought. He had seemed more cheerful lately, though they had met less frequently than before. The two men moved towards the checkout holding their books. Robert looked at his watch.

'Can't stop, Edwin, I'm meeting someone in the Cumberland Hotel. We should catch up . . .'

'Yes. In fact why don't the four of us have supper?'

'Four?'

'Er, yes. You, Suzy, me and . . . well, maybe it's early days . . .'

Robert raised his eyebrows, but before he could say anything he was summoned to the till. Edwin moved to the one next to him. He was in an uncharacteristically chatty mood.

'These books must make a mint for the bloke who writes them. You should ask Sandy MacFay to give you some help with your writing efforts.'

'Yes.' Robert nodded ruefully. If only you knew, he thought. A fat lot of good it would do me.

* * *

Pat Johnstone didn't report her husband missing because she never really knew when to expect him home. But in the early hours of Saturday morning when the doorbell rang with its cocky three notes chiming throughout the house, she expected that it would be about him. She scuttled downstairs, forgetting her slippers, feeling the thick stair carpet between her toes and trying not to think about anything. There were two men on the doorstep and she didn't need to see the identification which they proffered as soon as the door opened.

'Mrs Johnstone?'

'Yes, that's me. Oh no, it must be about David. Is he all right?'

'I'm afraid he's in the West Cumberland. Fractured skull and internal injuries, but he'll be OK. May we come in?'

'Yes . . .' She shuffled backwards. 'What happened?'

'It's a write-off. His car hit a tree.'

'What? His car? A tree? What do you mean? Where was this?'

'On a side road near Fellside. Pretty remote. It happened last night, we think, but no one saw it till this morning. We can take you over there now, to the hospital. I'm sorry but we do need to ask you a few questions first. Do sit down, or do you need to go and get something warmer on?'

'No, I'm all right.' She was breathing puffily and pulled her dressing gown around her. 'What do you need me to tell you?'

'Was your husband alone in the car?'

'How would I know? I haven't spoken to him since yesterday morning.'

'It's just that we found a couple of things on the passenger seat and we have to be sure there isn't someone wandering out there with concussion. The glove compartment had sprung open with the impact, so we don't know what was inside and fell out or what was left by a passenger. Do you recognize this by any chance?' The police officer held out a scarf in deep red.

Pat looked at it suddenly very calmly and said, 'Oh yes, a velvet man-made polyester scarf.' She sneezed at the thought, but then said firmly, 'Yes. It's definitely mine.'

* * *

'Hello.'

Robert was sitting in the Cumberland Hotel looking at his new book purchase, a half-drunk pint of Old Peculier beside him. The voice was the one he was expecting, but when he looked up he had a strange, giddying sensation.

'Sandy!' he said.

'That's me.' Alex Gibson slipped into the settle opposite him. She laughed. 'Look, I know I've gone to seed a bit — but there's no need to be quite so shocked!'

'I . . . well . . . I don't know what to say!'

'Try "How about a drink?" In the circumstances I'll have a malt whisky, please.'

Robert got up and walked slowly to the bar. Then he turned round and looked back at the woman sitting opposite his seat. It was eight years since he had walked out of the hotel room and left her crying. Now he could see clearly that it was the same person. Sandy McFay. The successful woman author, who wrote well-crafted historical yarns for kids. Like Richmal Crompton and J. K. Rowling, taking refuge in an ambiguous name so no red-blooded little reader would think he was a sissy. They had laughed a lot about that. The hair was no longer raven, and she was certainly bigger, but the smile was the same, the wonderful skin tone and large dark eyes.

And yet now he could also see that it was the same fat, grey woman from the Finance Department. But why should he have known? Context was so important. He thought back to Wanda Wisley's party. He'd suspected then, hadn't he? But why would Sandy McFay be at a party in Norbridge, incognito? He just hadn't wanted to ask the question.

He put two large whiskies in front of them.

'Thanks for contacting me. Why did you wait so long?'

'Oh Robert, think about it.'

'I have thought about it. When you came back to Norbridge why didn't you get in touch?'

'Because I was so angry with you! I had thought you might deliver me from that bastard Sam McFay. When we met at that writers' conference, we had two nights of passion and a wonderful day in London. And then you told me you loved Mary and she needed you, and you were off back up north. Why would I want to contact you after that?'

'But now you have. Why?'

'Because I met your latest girlfriend at a church meeting, of all things.'

'Suzy?' He was astonished.

'Yes. And I wanted to know how you finally summoned up the courage to leave your wonderful wife. Congrats to you and Suzy, and yet another bucket of cold sick for me!'

Robert waited before he spoke. 'No, Sandy. I never left Mary. She left me. She died from cancer four years ago. She was diagnosed a year after we met and died two years later.'

'Oh my God! Robert, I'm so sorry.'

'I'm sorry too,' he said. 'When I asked you why you hadn't contacted me, it was because I *did* contact you. I wrote to you after Mary died. Via the publisher who sent it on to your agent.'

'But I never got it!'

They looked at each other across the table. Alex felt weak with relief. Robert had hurt her — but he had been true to his word. He had gone back to his wife who needed him. Eight years ago Alex had been the opposite of needy — at least on the surface. The star of the show, she was successful and independent, as well as tall, dark and curvy, with a growing reputation as a writer. She had made the key-note introduction at the conference where they met: a witty, intelligent speech. She had been attracted to Robert's quiet, good-natured easiness — but it was just weeks after discovering her husband's duplicity. She was still functioning but the shock was dormant. The nightmare had only just started to close in on her.

'I bet my agent never sent your letter on. He gave up on me because I went to pieces, slowly at first, but when Sam finally asked me for a divorce, after his baby was born, I cracked. I fought it, but then I went completely bonkers. I was in a desperate state for about a year before coming to Fellside. Drink driving, jealous rages, hysteria. I was a nightmare.'

'But you were doing so well with your books!'

'Not after that! I tried writing after coming back north, but I'd lost it. I just vegetated and looked after Mum for a few years. Actually the truth is that she looked after me at first, but she was already going downhill. When she died I got a job at Norbridge College, in the Finance Department, just to do something. Anything. I remembered that you worked there, but I didn't think we would ever meet. And we didn't.'

'But what if we had?'

'Nothing would have happened. I thought you had ditched me so I didn't want to know you. And to be honest, I realize now we'd have been wrong for each other, anyway. I've seen you around at the college since. You're too comfortable for me. Too settled. I thought that was Mary who made you like that. But it's Suzy, isn't it?'

'Yes, I think it is.' Robert smiled. 'Have another drink, Alexandra McFay? Or Sandy Gibson? So you're all of those people, are you?'

'It helps to have a name which you can adapt. Alex and Sandy are both diminutives for Alexandra, and I was known by both as a child. After the divorce I ditched the McFay and went back to Gibson and switched from Sandy to Alex. My new agent knows all this of course — that's why I'm here. She traced me, and wrote asking if she could take me on in January, out of the blue.'

'Was that a turning point?'

'That, among other things. Her letter said they wanted to promote the books in Carlisle so I thought I'd come and see what was going on. Anonymously, of course. And that gave me the idea for contacting you, on neutral ground.'

'Not that neutral actually. I met Edwin Armstrong at Bookends buying *The Wizard of Workhaven*.'

'Good grief! Did you?' Robert watched Sandy's face as she blushed.

'Aha!' he said, realization dawning. 'I wondered why Edwin was more cheerful. Have you got over Sam now?'

She bent her head. 'Who knows? Stranger things have happened.'

'We can all change. I used to be a hypocritical old fart till I met Suzy.'

Alex laughed loudly. 'Hypocritical maybe! Fart certainly. But not old! Suzy is very lucky. But then so are you. She's great and I'm happy for you. Are you in love?'

'Yes, I am.'

That's true, Robert thought. The Sandy he had met eight years ago had attracted him deeply, but along with the dark good looks she'd had an intensity which reminded him of his wife. Suzy was very different, much easier going. She has a lighter touch and a more gregarious nature, he thought, and I do love her very much. She's right for me and I mustn't lose her.

There would be someone else who was right for Alex, maybe someone not so far away.

'Let's drink to falling in love!' he said.

Alex looked at him archly. 'But not with each other!' she said, and they both laughed out loud.

28

My lovers and friends hast thou put away from me,
and hid mine acquaintance out of my sight.
Psalm 88:18

Rachel Cohen swung the car round the corner yet again in a vain attempt to find a parking space in the middle of Islington. Suzy said breathlessly, 'I told you not to come and meet me from Euston. I could have got a cab.'

'I was trying to be a good friend, actually. Look, I think that woman is going. If we wait here a minute I can have her space and it's only five minutes' walk from the flat.'

'So maybe we can get a cab from here?'

'Very funny.'

'Rachel, you'll have to move because there's a big white-van-man right up your exhaust pipe.'

'I should be so lucky.' The van behind started hooting. 'Shit!' Rachel gunned the accelerator and her little car shot forward.

'Watch out, Rache! This is madness. You must be bonkers to bring the car out in traffic like this. On a Saturday afternoon as well. I've seen more cars in five minutes here than you get in Tarnfield in a week.'

199

With a snort of anger mixed with contempt, Rachel seemed physically to hurl the little car into a tiny space. 'Touch parking,' she snarled as they crunched into the car behind. 'Suzy, you sound like those awful people from the provinces who blag invitations to London and then spend the whole time telling you how much nicer it is in Netherbuttock or Brigadoon!'

'I'm not like that.' But Suzy started to laugh. 'Or maybe I am. I need to get away to know that I'm missing it already!'

Rachel had recently moved from a smaller two-bedroom flat to a wonderful attic 'space' with a huge through dining room and living area. It was all very contemporary and minimalist; Suzy gasped in genuine admiration. She was glad, too, that it was a different flat from the one where she and Robert had stayed with Rachel for a traumatic weekend eighteen months earlier. It really was easy, she thought ten minutes later, drinking cappuccino from Rachel's all-singing-all-dancing coffee machine, to put Tarnfield in another place in her head.

'We're staying in tonight and I'm cooking,' Rachel said decisively. 'No negotiation on that one. I'm going to start preparing artichokes and washing the mung beans just in case you forget where you are! Have a look at the roof garden. And when you've filled your lungs with top quality toxins, come back in and tell me everything from the beginning.'

Suzy went out through the new sheer french windows, onto the decking that flanked Rachel's apartment. Rachel had put pots of various evergreen shrubs in the corners, and along the top of the grey metal parapet were shallow boxes with tiny daffodils bobbing in the wind. It was bright and dry, much warmer than in the north. Suzy caught the scent of a tub of fat blue and pink hyacinths placed by the door. She looked over the edge, down to the rows of Georgian houses, the gastro-pub on the corner and in the distance the tower of University College Hospital and the ever-present cranes at building sites in the city.

It didn't help. Her mind seemed to be in constant transit, ricocheting from the past to the present, Newcastle to Tarnfield, Tynedale TV to Norbridge College, Nigel to Robert. And now London.

She went and sat down on the slimline sofa with little wooden legs which Rachel had positioned tastefully in front of the kitchen area where she was chopping crazily.

'That's enough of that,' Rachel announced. 'It's packet opening from here on. So now tell.'

And Suzy did so, recounting everything that had happened since the week before Christmas. As she talked, she surprised herself by how often Morris Little's murder featured. It was the murder which had upset Robert in the first place, making him think about the Frosts and worry that Jake needed a stepfather. And then Robert's solicitous visits to the Little family had wrecked all her Christmas shopping plans and led to so much tension. Since Morris's murder Robert had been less keen on the Chorus, and he'd been so preoccupied, writing away in his study. I wonder, Suzy thought . . .

'You've stopped talking.'

'Yes. I just thought that maybe one of the things on Robert's mind is this murder. Maybe that's what he's writing about!'

'But I thought you said two local lads had been charged with that.'

'They have. But Robert seems to think there's more to it. He's spent a lot of time talking to Norma, Morris's wife. She says there's no way the lads are responsible. Morris would have run a mile rather than confront them. It was quite an elaborate murder, really. The Frosts have confessed but they were so drugged up, who could know what they thought they were doing?'

'Aren't you being melodramatic? Aren't they the obvious suspects?'

'But the timing doesn't fit! First, Morris was killed. Then there was a power cut caused by the Frosts in the plant room. Then the murderer or murderers escaped. Then the light came on and the next person along the corridor found the body.'

'Couldn't it just have been an opportunist killing? Kids can be pretty vicious these days.'

'But why was Morris Little in the college anyway? I can't help feeling there's more to it and I'm not the only one. It makes everyone more uncomfortable. Everyone seems destabilized. My friend Lynn the rector's wife is having awful trouble with her daughter, whose friend found the body. It's as if everything has been a bit off key since. And it certainly hasn't helped me and Robert.'

'Maybe it brought things to a head. Have some wine . . .'

While Rachel fussed in the kitchen area, Suzy got up and walked onto the roof garden again. Below her, Islington went about its business. It was just getting dark. People were hurrying back from Sainsbury's or unpacking cars. Out of the corner of her eye she saw a flock of nuns, three or four or them, hurrying down the road, habits billowing. Then she refocused. They weren't nuns at all, but Muslim women. Of course. There were so few nuns now. She thought suddenly of the only conversation she'd had with Morris Little, about the derelict convent.

'Rachel,' she said, going into the flat, 'I really do think there was something weird about Morris Little's murder. He was a spiteful man. He upset everyone. He even said something offensive to me about that derelict convent and the old nuns. Lots of people must have been relieved when he died. And now those boys are being blamed.'

'So if you think that, why don't you do something? Like you did before?'

'But look what happened last time. My children were in danger!'

'Yes, and as a result you've been frozen ever since!'

'What do you mean?'

'Suzy, you're stuck in time! You're not yourself. You had a terrible experience and as a result you can't move on.'

Suzy thought about it. After the deaths in Tarnfield which had brought her and Robert together two years earlier, she had been unnerved by any hint of violence. It was like being post-natal, when your sensitivities are raw, as if your organs were on the outside. Nature's way of making you care for your tiny child. Since the murders, there had been some aspects of the 'chat show' side of her TV job which she had only been able to do after shutting herself in the ladies' loo, and forcing herself to face whoever was 'victim du jour'. Was she in any fit state to take on more horror?

'So you think I should get involved in this murder? But I hardly knew the man.' Yet as she said it, the nuns drifted through her mind, habits flowing. Morris had been a misogynist.

'Yes! Go for it! Toughen up again! You've not been yourself, Suzy. You've been living in another woman's house with another woman's husband, scared to put your head above the parapet, living on hold. But Jake and Molly are fine. Get on with your own life now.'

Suzy remembered the stupid row she and Robert had had about Mary's rug. It was true. Another woman's home. The subtext was that Robert saved me, and then gave me a place to live, she thought. As always, Rachel's sharp mind had got down to the root of the trouble. And hadn't Lynn hinted at something similar? It was a sense of inequality — a suspicion that Robert cared for her because he had rescued her and her children.

'You're right. That's why I prickled so much when Robert talked about Jake needing a stepfather. I thought he loved me because I was a flake and he was Mr Perfect.'

'But when you first met, there was nothing needy about you, was there? You were little Miss Dynamite, at least by Tarnfield standards. You need to get beyond this idea that you've been rescued, Suzy. You haven't. Have you ever thought that it might be Robert who's really the needy one?'

It was an odd idea. Suzy glanced outside at the everlasting glow of London. It was beautiful and it had made her see more clearly — but the bright lights were not for her. She suddenly wanted to go back to Tarnfield to try and sort this out.

'So would things be better if Robert were Mr Imperfect?' Rachel prompted. 'And you were Miss Dynamite again?'

If only, Suzy sighed. But what had Rachel said? '*In another woman's house, with another woman's husband.*' Was that what was holding her back? She shook her head fitfully. That was ridiculous. Mary was then. This was now.

'Rache,' she said slowly, 'you've put your finger on it. I need to get my confidence back. And to accept that perhaps Robert isn't quite as sanctimonious as he seems!'

'It isn't easy for him either,' Rachel said gently. 'How can he know where he stands with the kids?'

'You're right.' Suzy looked out over the rooftops. 'I hadn't thought of it from that angle. Maybe he needs Jake as much as Jake needs him! Thanks, Rachel.'

'Don't mention it. Just eat your kalamati olives with ariago shavings! Bet you don't get much of that in Netherbuttock. Or Brigadoon.'

* * *

Alex Gibson, alias Sandy McFay, had been invited out again. Not as exciting as her date to hear *The Dream of Gerontius* coming up the next week with Edwin, but not bad. Until recently she had spent every evening comatose in front of the telly, or painstakingly sorting out her mother's possessions. Even at her lowest, Alex's ability to be thorough had not deserted her. Much of her mum's stuff was boxed up now — there were cartons and black bags all over the bungalow marked with labels like *Nighties* — *winceyette* or *Rufflette tape and summer curtains*. It was mostly useless, she knew, but it seemed to bring Mum back for a while and to pay respect to a generation that saved silver paper.

In the past, Christine and Reg Prout had invited her round to their house, but it had always been at the last minute and out of a sense of family solidarity. This time, her sister's invitation to a local gathering had been genuinely enthusiastic.

'Do come. It's a wives' do.'

'But I'm not anyone's wife, Chris.'

'Well, I know you're not, not anymore, but what I mean is — it's the girls! Me, Pat Johnstone, Millie Dixon and a few more people. I know Millie's rather posh but she can be good fun. We do it every so often and we're getting together because poor Pat needs a break.'

'Pat Johnstone? Why?'

'Oh, come on, Alex, you must have heard. Or has your head been in the clouds because of that Bookends promotion?'

'You promised me you wouldn't mention it.'

'Don't worry, little sister, your secret is safe with me. Anyway, didn't you know about David Johnstone? He had a terrible car accident not far from where you live! Wrapped himself round a tree.'

'Oh, that's awful! Will he be all right?'

'Oh yes. But he's hospitalized for quite a while. Pat needs taking out of herself.'

'Well, in the circumstances I don't see how I can refuse. Where are you meeting?'

'At the Workhaven Motel, on the road from Fellside. They do a lovely weekday pasta night with two for the price of one.'

So here Alex was in a Burns' taxi, going for a good old-fashioned female night out. It took her mind off Edwin. The Workhaven Motel was a long, low building converted from a 1940s airbase, now painted bright pink and resplendent with fairy lights. Pat Johnstone and Millie Dixon seemed already quite plastered and had their arms round each other. Alex and her sister joined them at the bar, and then they all weaved their way onto what could only be described as a dance floor though it was crowded with tables. They plonked themselves at a long, thin trestle affair covered with a thin pink cloth and alive with jangling cutlery.

'Poor Pat,' Christine whispered.

'She doesn't look poor to me. She looks pissed!'

Christine sipped her gin and tonic genteelly. 'Oh no, Alex, that's unkind. Pat's had a terrible few days. She's been over to the hospital every day. David is quite out of it. Saying all sorts of things.'

'How do you know?'

'Reg told me. He went to see him straight away after the accident. I don't know why, but anyway he felt he had to go. David was rambling. He seems to have been completely confused and to think the accident happened at the convent!'

'Another one?'

'Yes. Strange, isn't it?'

Pat Johnstone came tottering towards them. She was wearing very high heels and a low-cut silky dress which revealed a pancake-flat chest.

'Chris and her sister. The odd one. How luvverly to see you. Have you heard about poor David? Bet this'll put a stop to his shenanigans in Fellside.' She laughed her trademark cackling laugh. 'He'll have plenty of time to look at old books now!'

'Sorry?' Alex felt her ears twitch. 'What do you mean, old books?'

'Oh, it's garbage, you know. He was looking at some old book he'd come across. A photocopy, anyway. But that's over now. And I'll tell you what . . .' She leant across to Alex, who could smell the drink on her breath. '. . . I'll be paying that other woman a visit. I'll soon find out who she is! I've got her scarf!'

29

Be still then, and know that I am God. I will be exalted
among the heathen, and I will be exalted in the earth.
Psalm 46:10

Wanda Wisley sat at the end of Freddie's bed and wondered why hospitals always made her feel so nauseous. A volunteer went past with a cup of coffee and she thought she might gag there and then. Well, at least that would punctuate the boredom. Freddie was as restless as it was possible for a big man in a small bed to be.

'I want to go hoooome,' he whined like an irritable child. 'Let me oooout!'

'They say you can go home tomorrow. The consultant wants one last look at you this afternoon.'

'*Ach*, Wanda, you're so strict. Discipline! It would be nice if you could be like that at home sometimes! In black leather!' He leered and made as much of a lunge at her as he could.

'Gerroff! This is a hospital, for God's sake, not a bear garden.'

'A bare garden. What a sexy idea, Wanda! I can see you now, like a little gnome with no knickers on. How cute. But we need a bigger garden.'

'Oh yes? Like at that stupid convent place where you nearly got killed? If you think that after this whole business I'm going to live anywhere other than the middle of town you're mad. I want to get rid of that cottage, Freddie, and move to one of those new refurbished lofts above the shopping mall. Or if they're too boring we'll go to Carlisle or Newcastle and commute. No more rural idyll crap!'

'But Wanda, I love the country!'

'Well, it doesn't love you. Look at the state you're in!'

'You don't understand, *Liebchen*. What happened to me was nothing to do with the country. Real country people don't let their cattle out to roam over the mountains in the winter! The animals are snug inside.'

'So what do you think happened, Mr Lonely Goatherd?'

'Don't mock, Wanda. What happened to me was deliberate and whoever did it did not care whether or I lived or died. I think they made a hole in the wall for the animals to go through.'

'What are you talking about?'

'I've had time to read the Psalms since I was here. Listen to this, Psalm 22 verse 12 — *Many oxen are come about me; fat bulls of Basan close me in on every side. They gape upon me with their mouths, as it were a ramping and roaring lion. I am poured out like water and all my bones are out of joint.* And Wanda, it goes on to talk about dogs being set on me! I guess that would have been next!'

'But you managed to survive . . .'

'It was a guardian angel, Wanda, or at least the herdsman who found me! But I tell you there are some strange things happening around here. But I won't let it put me off. That house of the sisters is a lovely place. Someone wants to stop us having it, but it's a special place that needs special people. Psalm 147 verse 13: *For He hath made fast the bars of thy gates and hath made blessed thy children within thee.*'

'Yeah, right. All your children are down the loo with the Durex.'

'That may be. But there's another psalm which says: *I will sing a new song unto thee O God. And sing praises unto thee upon a ten stringed lute*. The bass guitar, Wanda! Maybe that is what we are here to do!'

'Oh, for God's sake! It must be years of drug abuse. You're over the top. You make me want to vomit!' And Wanda lurched towards the nurses' station, calling for something to be sick in.

* * *

Poppy and Tom stood some distance away from the bus station in the middle of Norbridge.

'I don't really like doing this,' said Tom.

'Well, you've no choice.'

'But it's spying on her, isn't it? I mean she's got a right to go wherever she wants to go, hasn't she? It's not our business.'

He was cold. He'd left his squashy hat at home in recognition of a burst of soft sunlight, and also because of Poppy's disgust as he'd reached for it, but now the wind was coming down from the fells, where it was still winter, and his ears hurt. It wasn't helped by the fact that Poppy had made him get his hair cut. 'God tempers the wind to the shorn lamb,' the barber had said, laughing at the old saying. It was bollocks, Tom thought; his neck was bloody freezing.

'There she is,' whispered Poppy. They were looking intently into the window of a games shop and the plate glass gave them a clear reflection of the scene opposite. 'God, what does she look like!'

'Yukky.'

Chloe was wearing an old tweed coat of Lynn's, thick stockings and flat heavy trainers. This time she didn't have the red velvet scarf round her head, but a handkerchief was tied behind her ears. Her hair was tucked back.

'Which bus is she getting, Tom?'

'The one back to Uplands. That's a bit weird, isn't it? After getting her mum to drop her off in Norbridge, now she looks as if she's going straight back home.'

It was the Saturday morning of the most momentous week of Tom's life. Poppy was now officially his girlfriend in every possible way and he was still reeling from the effect of her awesome persuasive powers. Here he was, scrubbed up, hair like some sort of smoothie, on a mission impossible which would have seemed madness only a fortnight earlier.

The day before, Poppy had suddenly announced: 'Chloe needs to know about this!'

'Does she?' They had been lying in Poppy's bed again, watching old episodes of the *Torchwood* series.

'Yes, she does. She might have ideas about you herself. Anyway it's my time for showing off!'

'Don't tell her everything.'

'I'm not some sort of perv! I just want her to know that we're an item. And anyway we used to text every day.' Poppy frowned; Tom watched as her thumbs tap-danced over the mobile keys. Then they had watched more TV, but there had been no response from Chloe. Poppy tried again and a few minutes later the noise of a message arriving pinged through the sound of video gunfire.

'Yes, it's her,' Poppy had said, and concentrated deeply on the message. 'But she doesn't want to meet. I'm not important enough for her, it seems. Well, I'm not going to let her get away with just saying *No, I've got plans*. What about tomorrow then?' Poppy's thumbs had clacked like lobster claws.

'Look, this is better,' she'd said when the replying message pinged back. *No. Going t Nbridge w mum. Busy after.*

Poppy texted, *C u Figs? 1030?*

The message replied, *Can't. Mum at hairdrs 10. Then have plans.*

'Cow!' Poppy had said angrily. 'I've been back all this week and she hasn't wanted to see me once. She's either jealous or stuck up worse than ever. Or . . .' She'd chewed her hair and crossed her eyes reflectively. The eye-crossing was her favourite trick.

'Or what?'

'Or there's something going on that she doesn't want me in on.'

That was when Poppy had formulated her plan. There was one multi-storey car park in Norbridge, serving the shopping mall. They would wait there between nine twenty and ten to see where Chloe went. 'I know which hairdresser her mum goes to. It's Sessions in the mall. They wouldn't park anywhere else but the multi-storey. Anyway it's worth a try. Something to do.'

Tom had acquiesced without saying anything. He was completely uninterested in Chloe's secret lover and he suspected there wasn't anyone at all. But he liked Poppy's style. She was becoming quite forceful; he thought that coming out from under Chloe's shadow was the best thing that had happened to her. He'd completely recovered from his crush on Chloe and thought she had lost the plot since Christmas, but he liked the way Poppy still cared about her, even if she had a funny way of showing it!

So here they were, following her. That made him uncomfortable, of course; but there was no way he was going to argue with Poppy over it.

'Shit,' Poppy whispered. 'What shall we do? The bus will be leaving in a minute. And if we get on she'll see us.'

'Her bus is going to Uplands, isn't it? It's not far. We can get a taxi.'

'Can we? Where from?'

'The rank by the shopping precinct main entrance. Come on, Poppy. I've got some money.' He was starting to enjoy this. He felt like a secret agent and Poppy was clearly impressed. She followed the newly authoritative Tom to the taxi rank and was bowled over when she heard him say, in rather a deep and decisive voice to the driver: 'Follow that bus!'

* * *

In Tarnfield, Robert held the telephone away from his ear as Edwin Armstrong shouted at him.

'So you're telling me that Sandy McFay is Alex Gibson. But why didn't she tell me?'

Yet even as Edwin said it, he thought of Marilyn and his own mystery. We're older, he thought. Life is full of baggage. I haven't exactly come clean. The thought calmed him.

It was later on Saturday afternoon. Robert had made his call straight after arriving home from his meeting with Sandy, before he could bottle out.

'Yes, that's right. Alex Gibson is Sandy McFay,' he said again.

Robert understood why his friend sounded outraged and confused. But he had promised Alex that he would tell Edwin what had happened. It seemed a fair exchange for leaving her sobbing in their bed in London all those years ago. She had insisted that he told Edwin everything, however embarrassing. Edwin would either accept it or not. So Robert took a deep breath and went on . . .

'There's something more. Sandy and I know each other because we met eight years ago at a conference and fell for each other. I never followed it up because Mary . . . well, we were married and there was no way I would leave her. And soon afterwards Mary became very ill. But you should know that Sandy — sorry, I mean Alex — and I were very close. Just for a few days.'

Robert listened to the other man's breathing. He had given Edwin a lot to take in. Finally Edwin said, 'And now?'

'What do you mean, "and now"?'

'So is there anything between you and Alex now?'

'She's a very attractive woman, Edwin. But I've met Suzy. And Suzy is the one for me.' Even if she doesn't think so herself, Robert thought.

Edwin took a long time breathing in and out. 'Does Suzy know about Alex?'

'Not yet. Suzy's away in London. She's back tomorrow night. I'll tell her as soon as she gets off the train.'

And that might be the end of everything, Robert thought. So much for the Perfect Husband. Once Suzy finds out how good a husband I really was, she'll either laugh and never take me seriously again, or send me packing as a charlatan. But that isn't Edwin's problem. Edwin was obviously thinking of something else.

'So there's absolutely no chance of you taking up with Alex again?'

How odd, and how significant, that that should be his first concern.

'Absolutely none. In fact, when Suzy comes home we'll invite you both round to dinner.'

If we're still together, he thought dourly. But it was a good idea, strange and impetuous though it seemed. In a small place like Norbridge so many people had been involved with each other that if dinner parties excluded former lovers, there would be no entertaining. The great thing about social life in a small country town was that there was no escape — you were one society, and once the gossip died down, all you could do was face the facts and get on with it. Life went on with the same people. There was no alternative.

Edwin said, 'I'm seeing Alex next week. We're going to *The Dream of Gerontius* in Newcastle.'

'Rather you than me. It's not my favourite piece.'

'But the point is, it will give me a chance to talk to her about all this. It's a lot to take in. Unbelievable.'

'Oh, come on, Edwin. Surely you sensed there was more to Alex than a deeply depressed and bad-tempered finance clerk? Alex is a formidable woman who even managed to make her mental breakdown very thorough. But at Wanda Wisley's party she was starting to look her old self again. You could tell she had something about her.'

'I suppose you're right. I did sense there was more to her than met the eye.'

'And you're similar people, Edwin. Both creative.'

That was a point, Edwin thought, surprised at Robert's remark. Maybe that was one of the many things that appealed to him, intuitively, about Alex Gibson. He had been pottering around looking at the Psalms again, but nothing had yet inspired him. Maybe talking to Alex would help.

'Thanks for telling me, Robert. It can't have been easy.'

'And it won't make any difference?'

'Of course it will! But it might be for the better! The truth's always best, you know.'

Robert winced, and thought: We'll see about that. And at the same time Edwin was thinking: Yes. But I'm not telling the truth myself. Not yet. At least Alex had made sure he knew everything now. Could he do the same?

In The Briars, Robert put the phone down with relief. Now the only thing left was to tell Suzy. How would she react? Jealousy? Contempt? Disgust? Fury at his hypocrisy?

The one reaction he did not expect was the one he got on Sunday night.

30

Norbridge bus station was not a pleasant sight on a Sunday evening. The passengers were largely grey-faced pensioners and students, the latter exhausted by a weekend of partying and the former just exhausted. The prospect of a long bus journey in the dark was not the warmest and most welcoming thought at this time of year. There was a smattering of tourists, some in walking gear and some in smart bulky coats or macs. But most people were dressed in dreary layers, trailing all sorts of mismatched luggage and occasionally strewing sweet papers, magazine pages and flyers to be mashed on the dirty concrete floor by hundreds of feet. The platforms had a down-at-heel feel. And it was cold.

Poppy and Tom sat close together on a bench waiting for the bus to Newcastle. You could see their breath in the air.

'It's been a good week,' Tom said again. The best thing was, he was absolutely sure that Poppy agreed. And she was reliable. The knowledge that there would be no more pounding hearts over emails, or terrifying insecurity, like the sort that had taken him to the Gents during that power cut at the college, made him feel more truly grown up than their sexual initiation. Manly, even.

'Yeah. Good. Really good,' said Poppy, and then she did her now familiar cross-eyed frown. 'What did you make of that business with Chloe yesterday?'

'Dunno. Weird.'

'You can't just keep saying "weird" as if that explains it.'

'Well, it does explain it. Weird behaviour.'

'But why, thickhead?'

'Dunno.'

They both sat thinking about their spying activities the day before. The taxi ride had been hairy, partly because the bus driver knew his route like the back of his hand and rode his suspension with a panache which the minicab couldn't emulate, and partly because it was just such a crazy thing to be doing.

The local bus to Uplands had pulled up to a screeching halt outside Little's store. There were cars parked outside and Saturday shoppers milling round. Tom asked the taxi to pull up behind it. While Tom paid the fare, Poppy had watched Chloe get off the bus, cross the road and walk up the hill for a few yards to get another bus.

'Shit. She's changing buses. Quick, look in Little's window so she doesn't see us.' Poppy fixed her frown on a fascinating box of satsumas.

'Which bus will that be?' Tom asked.

'It's the bus to Fellside, I think.'

'She must be going to Fellside Fellowship.'

'On a Saturday morning? Don't be a plonker: even I know that they don't do anything on Saturday mornings and I never go to church.'

Tom thought back to his days in the choir at Uplands Parish Church. 'Maybe it's a coffee morning?'

'Chloe at a coffee morning? She may be going nuts but she's not that nuts. Dream on, Tom.'

Nettled, Tom had to think of a new idea. 'OK, so if we walk in the other direction we can pick up the Fellside bus at its previous stop. And if you get a paper, something big like er . . . the *Daily Telegraph*, and we sit at the back reading it, she won't notice us. And if she does, well, we just say "Hi!" We don't owe her an explanation.'

'Yeah, you're right. Good thinking, Tom.'

Poppy had gone into Little's to buy the paper, and they walked quickly down to the previous bus stop. The Fellside bus, half full of early shoppers coming back from Workhaven, pulled in and they got seats at the back on the lurching bit which no one liked, perched over the engine. Poppy unfolded the *Telegraph*.

Chloe boarded the bus and didn't see them. Poppy had thought she looked as if she was in a dream anyway, and for a moment she wondered whether Chloe had taken her experiments with drugs a bit further. But that wouldn't square with the self-consciously dowdy clothes.

'C'mon,' she'd said when Chloe got off the bus at the Co-op in Fellside. They had hurried to catch up with her, but it was a busy stopping point and they were at the back of the bus. The strategy which had helped them follow her unseen now let them down. By the time they were off the bus, Chloe had disappeared.

'Where's she gone?' Poppy had looked down the road to the low brick building that was St Luke's, now Fellside Fellowship. Chloe was nowhere in sight, so she certainly wasn't going there. But there was no sign of her up the road either.

'She's gone,' Tom had said. They stood there, waiting for something to happen, but nothing did. 'We'd better give up.'

'All right. I'm getting cold anyway.' They'd gone into the Co-op to buy some fizzy drinks, but they never reached the checkout because of some mad woman ranting on about a missing scarf, and taking up all the attention of the girl on the till.

'Might as well go home,' Tom had said.

So they had taken the bus back to Poppy's house between Uplands and Norbridge, and watched DVDs. Occasionally

Poppy frowned and crossed her eyes, but in an unspoken pact they didn't mention her former friend again. The rest of the weekend had been OK. Well, great really.

Now it was over. The bus to Newcastle rocked into the bus station. 'Time to go,' Poppy said resolutely.

Tom felt an awful lurch in his stomach. 'Can I come and see you?'

'Yeah. All right.' She looked at him intently and he wondered what she was going to say.

'Keep an eye on Chloe for me?' she said surprisingly. 'There's something really weird going on.'

'That's what I said,' yelped Tom. 'Weird!'

'Yes.' Poppy was on the bus now. 'I know you did. You're right. See you.'

'See you.' Then in a moment of madness he added: 'Love ya!'

'Love you too,' Poppy said, chewing a bit of hair and crossing her eyes. Then she disappeared to make way for a noisy family seeing off their tearful grandma.

Love you, love you, love you, Tom sang all the way home.

* * *

At the same time, Suzy Spencer was getting out of the train at Carlisle station. She travelled to Tarnfield in a cab and let herself in at The Briars. She took her overnight bag upstairs and then came running down, face flushed.

'Robert, we have to talk.'

'Too true. Let me get you a drink. I want you to sit down, Suzy, and listen to me. No, this can't be a discussion. I've got things that have to be said and you need to listen.'

He had rehearsed this moment but he still found it hard to speak. Since his confident conversation with Edwin the day before, he had thought constantly about what he was going to say to Suzy. He needed to apologize for being so pompous about marriage when he had made a mess of it himself. He needed to explain that he didn't think she needed a stepfather for Jake but that he would be privileged to take on that role. And most importantly he had to make her see that she would never be another Mary and that he would never be that sort of husband again. Every marriage was different. And if one day, perhaps, she would marry him, then it would be for his good and not necessarily for hers. He would never again presume to tell her what she needed.

He blushed and stumbled through his confession. 'So, you see I wasn't a good husband. I did my best but I was tempted more than once.'

'So you were unfaithful! You hypocrite! Mr Perfect with his trousers down.'

'If you put it like that. I loved Mary, but it was tough. And though I wasn't faithful, she never knew.'

'Well, that's one for the village to enjoy!'

'If you want to put an ad in Lo-cost's window then I'll have to grin and bear it.'

'You should, literally! But seriously, how much damage did you cause?'

'I think that Sandy — that is, Alex Gibson — was the only woman I really hurt. I'm deeply sorry about that. I know you must think I'm a self-righteous old fart and you're right. But I needed to escape from Mary sometimes, and I will never need to escape from you. You've saved me from all that mess.'

'You mean *I've* rescued *you*?'

'Absolutely! Saved me from myself! Thank you!'

And to his astonishment Suzy leapt off the sofa, did a pole-dance round the door jamb and kissed him with a warmth and passion he hadn't felt for months.

'I love you, Robert Clark. It's so much better now!'

'What, now you've found out I was unfaithful? After all I said?'

'Of course! What do you think it's been like for me living in the shadow of your unimpeachable behaviour? And thinking that you only loved me because I was the local flake in need of care and protection?'

'But Suzy, I was a bad husband.'

'Yes, you were.' She paused. 'But maybe you'll get another chance . . .'

* * *

Pat Johnstone looked at the velvet scarf and sneezed. 'Horrible thing,' she said, and pushed it away.

'Oh, I don't know,' Christine Prout said, sipping her coffee and looking as if the scarf on the coffee table in Pat's lounge was a snake about to strike. 'It's all right in itself. It's just the implications. You say they found this in the car with David?'

'Yes, the police brought it over. I said it was mine straight away but of course it's not! I wanted to get my hands on it. Ugh. It's already brought me out in a rash.' Pat scratched her skinny arm under her lambswool sweater.

'So you think it must belong to, er, David's other woman?'

'Well, who else could it belong to? That was my theory anyway. I thought he was up to something in Fellside. I followed him once, you know, last year. He parked the car on the edge of the council estate and walked in there. I couldn't go any further or he'd have seen me. But I'm pretty sure it was some woman he was meeting. So now I thought I'd go into the Co-op and ask if I could leave the scarf there for someone to pick it up. I wanted to leave my name and address so the owner could let me know she'd got it back.'

'And what happened?'

'The stupid girl on the till said these scarves were ten a penny. McCrea's in Norbridge had job lots of them. Everybody's got one.'

'I think you're right. I think my sister's got one like this.'

'Exactly! So I brought it home. I must say right up until Saturday night I felt pretty good about having it. But now, I don't think it's going to help me at all.'

'Do you really want to find out who David might be . . . seeing?'

'I don't know . . .' Pat paused. 'I'm not sure any more. You see, it's not the fact that he's got another woman which bothers me.' She stood up and walked to the big plate glass windows looking over the hills. The house was almost too warm, but she shivered. And she suddenly changed the subject. 'You can see the old convent from your sister's bungalow, can't you?'

'Yes, you can. It's the only good view of the grounds.'

Pat paused. 'I can trust you, Chris, can't I? We've been friends for years, haven't we? And you know what David's like?'

'Oh, Pat . . .'

'You know what I mean, Chris. The reason I'm asking you is that I want you to ask your sister if she's seen anyone in the grounds of the convent. Digging.'

'Digging? Why on earth would you want to know about that?' Chris wrinkled her brow. When Pat had asked her to come over on Monday morning for a heart-to-heart she had imagined all sorts of things, but not this.

Pat scowled and walked up and down in front of the window. 'You know I said I followed David last year? Well, I followed him on Friday as well. When he left Norbridge, I followed him to Fellside and I saw him park the car by the convent. He strolled through the hole in the wall. He walked through the garden and then he fell.'

'Fell? Where?'

'Into a bloody big hole in the ground, that's where. From what I could see it looked like someone had dug a great big grave. I just turned round and ran back to my car. I thought David would start yelling and people would come running, so I drove away like the clappers. But then I went round the block and came back; the car was still there so I guessed that David was knocked out.'

'And you didn't do anything to help? I mean, like go and find him or get an ambulance?'

'You must be joking. If David had seen me he'd have known I'd followed him and my life wouldn't be worth living! No, the convent's right on the main road. Someone would have come for him sooner or later.'

Chris Prout swallowed. She would never describe her relationship with Reg as particularly warm, but she couldn't imagine leaving him in a hole in the ground!

'Anyway,' Pat was saying, unfazed, 'someone must have got David out of the pit and into the car.'

'But what makes you think it was a properly dug pit?' Chris was confused. Something slipped into her mind that Reg had said worriedly a few days earlier. 'Couldn't it have been subsidence? Or collapsed drains?'

'Nah! I had my driving specs on and I could see the edges. Clean as a whistle. Believe me, it was dug really deep, and then covered over. Like an animal trap.'

'Well, maybe someone was doing the garden. Or putting in a new septic tank!' Chris reasoned. 'And then maybe poor David was concussed and climbed out himself — and then drove when he was only half conscious which is why he hit the tree?' Chris was trying to be helpful, but Pat looked at her with contempt.

'No one's officially working up there. And no one could climb out of that hole unaided. No, I think the person who got David out of that trap was the same person who dug it.'

'But that means someone deliberately tried to injure him!'

'Oh, clever girl! Go to the top of the class and give the pencils out!'

'But Pat, shouldn't you go to the police? And anyway, why do you want to know?'

'Because the person who dug the pit must be onto something too! There's something big going on and that convent is right in the middle of it, literally. And your sister's place is too. David wouldn't usually go to such trouble over a jerry-built bungalow. If there's any money to be made, I want to know about it. The bastard has tucked it all away and I haven't a penny. But things are changing here!' Pat gave a cackle. 'The only reason I need to find out about his tart is to make sure she hasn't got her nose in the trough. It's his money I'm after. Not his willy! I've had enough of that!'

31

And yet they think that their houses shall continue for ever,
and that their dwelling-places shall endure from one generation
to another, and call the lands after their own names.
Psalm 49:11

Paul Whinfell met the postman coming down Fellside High
Street.

'How do, Vicar?'

'Very well, thanks. Got anything for me?' He wanted
to get to the post before Jenny did. If she found out how
much he'd been spending on replica birth and marriage certificates she would go mad. He felt some guilt about it but
underneath he knew it was justified. His religious faith must
have come from somewhere. His parents were agnostics of
the most annoying 'you-don't-have-to-go-to-church-to-be-
Christian' types; he was sure there was something in his God-
given genes that made him different.

'Here's another of these for you, Rev.' The postman
handed him a large envelope with the TNT logo on the front
and the initials of the Office of National Statistics on the
back. Paul's hand trembled with excitement as he took it,
trying not to grab.

He hurried home and into his office. Jenny was doing the washing and would assume he was hard at work on his talks for Sunday. In the past he had asked her advice about his sermons, but at the moment he pretended he was working alone so she wouldn't guess how much time he spent at the computer. Genealogy had come to feel like some secret vice, like porn or violence. But he couldn't help it.

The door was shut. Then, everything ready, he opened the big white envelope.

He had seen the details on the web but it was wonderful to hold the facsimile in his hand. There it was. The birth certificate of Henry Quaile Whinfell. Author of the only definitive biography on Cecil Quaile Woods. Paul had first been given the book on Cecil Quaile Woods by an elderly parishioner who was intrigued that his new vicar shared a name with a long-dead local biographer.

'I reckon this copy must be the only one left,' the old man had said. 'It was written in the twenties and belonged to my grandmother. Funny that the author's got the same name as you. There aren't any Whinfells left up here now but they used to be a well-known local family.'

So Paul had started his search to try and find a link between his family in Bristol and this nineteenth-century Cumbrian branch the old man referred to. And he'd got back to what must be the very same Henry Whinfell. But why had Henry Whinfell written a biography of Cecil Quaile Woods? Paul thought he was onto the answer.

Just as he'd seen on the screen, no father was named on Henry Quaile Whinfell's birth certificate. Whinfell was Henry's mother's name — Harriet Whinfell, housemaid. The date was 1880 and the place of registration was Workhaven.

It was the Quaile which gave it away. That and Harriet's address. She had put it down as The Vicarage, Fellside. Paul looked through his great-grandfather's book again. *A Memoir of The Reverend Cecil Quaile Woods, Vicar of St Luke's, Fellside, by Henry Whinfell.* Quaile Woods had been a saintly priest in the High Church tradition, celibate, dedicated to his flock of wretched miners who had called him Father Cecil and who had depended on him to get them through the dark days of accidents, illness and deprivation. He had been a padre to the miners, and also priest in charge of the convent, which did so much work with the underclass of the whole county. But in 1882 he had left Fellside for the parish of Uplands as curate. A downwards move. And he had withdrawn from pastoral work, dedicating himself to writing church music.

Why? Could it have been shame? Was that because he had sired a son? A son who forty years later wrote his father's biography as a secret acknowledgement? Did the boy's birth explain why Father Cecil had given up being a parish priest and had retreated from Fellside to Uplands as curate — only taking over the full parish role on the death of his rector ten years later? It seemed that he had needed to retract, to withdraw and come to terms with something. And could that something be his own illegitimate son?

Quaile Woods. Jenny's new inspiration. And now it seemed he might be Paul's own great-grandfather on the wrong side of the blanket. Someone local surely had to be the father of Harriet's baby. And why else was that mysterious name Quaile on the birth certificate? Quaile was a common enough Manx surname, but there were no other Quailes in Cumbria in 1881, according to the census results on ancestry.co.uk. So was this name an acknowledgement of sorts without going public on the illegitimate child? Paul had read that such ploys weren't uncommon. Lots of working-class Victorians had two surnames. This use of Quaile *had* to refer to the vicar of Fellside, and maybe the inclusion of the name meant that he had taken some responsibility for his child? Henry's later writing indicated a superior education to any the Whinfells could provide. Although there was no Harriet Whinfell in the census of 1891, Henry was there as a ten-year-old boy, the grandson of a retired dockworker called Matthew Whinfell and his wife. There was only one Henry Whinfell in the whole of England.

And then thirty-one years later, in 1922, someone called Henry Whinfell had written the biography of Cecil Quaile Woods which Paul now had in his hands. It had been published in Bristol. Was it possible that Henry Quaile Whinfell had moved south? And settled in Bristol, siring a whole line of Whinfells of which he, Paul was the next to last, culminating in Joseph — Paul and Jenny's baby son?

Starting from the other end, Paul had retrieved his own father's birth certificate three months earlier. His father's death had set him off on the trail. Paul's father had been called straight Paul Whinfell too. But his father, Paul's grandfather, had been listed on the birth certificate as Leslie Quaile Whinfell. And that had spurred Paul on. He had guessed that Leslie had been between twenty-five and thirty when his son was born and it hadn't taken too much delving to find and then obtain a copy of Leslie Quaile Woods' birth certificate. And to his delight he found that Leslie's father had been called Henry Quaile Whinfell. He could find no other Whinfell sons. The marriage certificate that he had applied for and received just a few weeks earlier showed that Henry had married late in life, in Bristol. Henry's age was on his marriage lines. It just remained to get Henry Quaile Whinfell's birth certificate, which Paul was now looking at. And there it was. Not conclusive proof by any means. That would be very hard to get. But surely anyone with any common sense could assume that Cecil Quaile Woods was the father of the illegitimate child born to his servant in his vicarage and called by his name.

So now he really did have something to say to Jenny. He opened the door and called her, but there was no answer. He realized that the washing machine was silent for once and that there were no baby Joseph noises in the house. It was dark and silent.

'Jenny?' Her coat was gone from the pegs in the hall and the buggy wasn't in the porch. She had gone out without telling him where.

Paul knew that he should be disturbed when his wife didn't even acknowledge his presence. But he was beyond worrying about all that, because he had something even bigger to think about. He, Paul Whinfell, had inherited Quaile Woods' musical ability and deep-rooted spirituality. He was back in Fellside, brought here by the will of God. He too could be a key person in a religious revival, like Quaile Woods, as Jenny had suggested.

There was something Paul could do straight away in his great-grandfather's memory, but with a modern touch. He'd already made a start. It would mean some more planning, plotting even, but he thought Jenny would approve if only he could confide in her. And what better way to win her back than by doing something which would go straight to her heart.

* * *

'So how was *The Dream of Gerontius*?'

Robert smiled at Edwin and Alex over the generous glasses of cold fizzy white wine he had poured them. The atmosphere could have been as cold as the drink, but Suzy had made sure it wasn't. She had been just as keen as Robert to invite Alex and Edwin round for supper and get everything on a normal footing.

So, she told herself, what if Robert had slept with Alex? Well, in the world of media these things happened all the time. She remembered wryly how she had had to meet Nigel's lovers even when their marriage was supposedly working! She left them all to talk while she banged about in the kitchen. She decided to serve some tomato bruschetta as an appetizer, but one tray had already been knocked off the coffee table on to the floor by Molly; all the fuss of picking up broken baguette and slippery tomato, wiping the table, sponging the carpet and relegating the food to the bin had bizarrely broken the ice. Suzy had gone through the rigmarole with her usual good humour.

'Welcome to The Briars, also known as Fawlty Towers. Except you're not paying! Or you'd want your money back.'

When she disappeared to get some more bruschetta, it was the first time since the guests had arrived that there'd been a hiatus in the chatter. Hence the small talk about Elgar.

'It was really good,' Alex said. 'I enjoyed it.'

And it *had* been really good. Edwin had called at the bungalow to pick her up as arranged. They had set off straight away. Edwin had said nothing about her second identity until he was clear of the village and on the A69.

'So you're also Sandy McFay. That's incredible! Robert told me.'

'Yes. I asked him to. I was rather embarrassed about it myself, and he owed me a favour.' She had glanced at Edwin, who'd looked straight ahead at the road. 'Did he tell you everything?'

'I assume so.'

'I'm afraid I've changed a lot since then. Mentally for the better, at last. But looks-wise for the worse.'

'Really? Don't fish!'

Alex laughed. 'Were you very surprised?'

'Gobsmacked, as they say, at first. But it made sense. You were a bit of a woman of mystery, you know!'

'Not anymore!' Alex had laughed. She pushed aside the thought that, where women of mystery were concerned, he still hadn't come clean about the Marilyn Frost story. Things he'd said about her kept popping back into Alex's mind. But this isn't the moment to ask, she'd thought.

Once Edwin and Alex had arrived in Newcastle, the atmosphere between them had changed. Alex found it easier to be her new 'old self', talking knowledgeably and fitting in with the metropolitan crowd. She had lost enough weight to wear a new smart size sixteen suit, and she felt stately rather than elephantine. The *Dream of Gerontius* was excellent. They both knew it and they both enjoyed Cardinal Newman's high-flown Victorian poetry about the soul's journey through death.

'He started the Oxford Movement, didn't he?'

'Yes, with Pusey, Keble and others. But Pusey stayed an Anglican when Newman defected to Rome. It's partly thanks to Pusey that we have anything like a real parish church music tradition outside cathedrals.'

'But what about the old West End gallery choirs in villages? The lovable locals playing in the church band in Thomas Hardy's *Under the Greenwood Tree* and all that?'

Edwin was impressed. 'That was rurally based. In the huge new city churches they had to create a tradition. And that's what people like Pusey did. And Quaile Woods when he went to Uplands.'

In the interval, Edwin had spoken more freely than he could remember about the frustrations of his work — how he felt at a creative standstill, but was working on the Psalms. He feels more at ease with me, Alex had thought, because he knows I've hit the creative buffers too. It's as if we're kindred spirits. They'd had supper afterwards in an Italian restaurant. It was after midnight when he'd dropped her off. He'd got out of his car and kissed her lightly and competently on the lips. It had been a seal of camaraderie rather than passion but it made Alex tremble.

'I'll come and pick you up to go to The Briars tomorrow,' he'd said. They had not discussed the invitation to supper with Robert and Suzy. Suzy had phoned each of them individually but had made it clear she was inviting them both.

'Thanks. A lift would be good. Changing buses in this weather tends to ruin your hairdo!' Alex had answered, but said nothing more. She knew the ball had to be in his court. He was the one who had been wrong-footed by her, the frump who had turned out to be a famous author and lover of his close colleague. He was just as friendly as before and even more talkative, but the conversation was on a more general level. He was treading carefully now.

The next evening, on the drive over to Tarnfield, they were both of them tense and unusually quiet. Edwin was worried about seeing Alex and Robert together; Alex was both curious and repelled by the thought of visiting Robert's marital home. But when they arrived at The Briars, the moment took over. Molly was in her pyjamas stretched out in front of the telly, eating forbidden sweets and determined not to go upstairs until the visitors arrived. By the time the bruschetta debacle was over and she had been banished to bed, and then the cat had been extricated from under the sofa where it had hurtled in mock terror, a knockabout atmosphere had taken over and there wasn't time for embarrassment.

At the table Suzy calmed down and took a big gulp of red wine. 'Mmm, that's better. Sorry about all the commotion. We've got Parmesan salad for starters and then two sorts of lasagne. It's a bit basic but I'm still not a virtuoso on the Aga!'

'Great!'

'Thanks!'

She waited for the murmurs of routine appreciation to die down and for the meal to be served. Then she said, 'Listen, there's something that's been on my mind a lot recently. And I don't mean the revelations about Alex alias Sandy, though that's been pretty exciting! It's something else.' They looked at her expectantly.

'I want to talk to you guys about it, because it's bothering me. Do you think the Frosts are really guilty of Morris Little's murder? Because I don't.'

32

O Lord, thou hast searched me out and known me;
thou knowest my down-sitting and mine up-rising;
thou understandest my thoughts long before.
Psalm 139:1

At the same time, Lynn and Neil Clifford were having Saturday supper at the rectory with their daughter. It was a rare occurrence. Neil was frequently at weekend meetings which went on into Saturday evening, and when he wasn't on scheduled business there were often unexpected visits from parishioners who were either distraught or disorganized.

Lynn had always had a full social circle of her own with lots of friends, but she felt that other people, especially women of her own age, were always aware she was the priest's wife. But that wasn't true of Suzy Spencer. Lynn had grabbed a coffee with Suzy earlier in the week and had seen at once that Suzy was much happier and more relaxed. Suzy had said that Edwin and Alex would be coming to The Briars for supper on Saturday to renew old acquaintances. Lynn had talked to her brother and he had told her, very tentatively, of his new friendship with Alex. Like all good sisters, Lynn had said nothing and had made the right noises. But she was glad to get more information from Suzy.

'Alex Gibson is actually an author and an old friend of Robert's, but she had a breakdown and they lost touch years ago. She's Sandy McFay, writer of kids' books. I bet Chloe used to read them.'

'Oh yes! We had them all!' Lynn had looked momentarily sad at the thought of her daughter's rumbustious adolescence. She forced herself to cheer up and concentrate on what Suzy was saying. It was rather exciting! But she was shrewd enough to realize there was a subtext in all this, and that perhaps in time either Suzy or Edwin would tell her more. And she was pleased when Suzy added that when the ice was broken she would have a bigger party.

'With Edwin and Alex, and you and Neil, and maybe Ollie's parents and Wanda Wisley and Freddie, and even that couple up at Fellside Fellowship, though she always glares at me. She's very stand-offish! Oh, and Mark Wilson of course!'

'Paul and Jenny are perhaps a little troubled,' Lynn supplied quietly. 'I know Jenny can be very off-putting, but she's a bright woman. She's a couple of years older than Paul and I think she was rather in the lead, until the baby came. I think she might be finding it hard playing second fiddle now.'

Lynn paused for a moment to think about Paul Whinfell. He was one of the people who had come to see Neil unexpectedly, right in the middle of a mealtime, earlier in the week. He had seemed both disturbed and excited, keyed up in some way. Neil had not mentioned the visit to her after Paul had left. Lynn didn't mind. You expected to be excluded occasionally, as a priest's partner, she thought. Sometimes things cropped up which needed to be sorted out there and then, and domestic life must work around that and ask no questions.

But on Saturday night the Cliffords were just *en famille*. Chloe emerged from her room to help Lynn set the table. Lynn had noticed that Chloe suddenly seemed keen on helping with the housework. It was uncharacteristic and, though at first Lynn welcomed it as a bonding thing, she soon realized that it didn't lead to more conversation. Chloe would take on big messy tasks like mopping the floor or cleaning the windows or washing the dishes with a sort of passive thoroughness, head down, wearing her annoying little headscarf and an apron over shapeless clothes. Lynn found herself thinking cynically once or twice that Chloe was making rather a meal of it, especially as they had a dishwasher. But she told herself she should be grateful Chloe was at home, safe, being helpful. A lot of mothers would give their eye teeth for that.

She brought the casserole to the table and Neil said grace. It was a tradition they only maintained when they were all together; it reminded her of when Chloe was a little girl, and it made her eyes water. As her daughter reached out to take a baked potato, Lynn noticed a ring on her wedding finger.

'Good heavens, Chloe, what's that?'

'That — oh nothing. Just a ring.'

'But it's got lettering on, hasn't it?'

'S'pose so. It's a virginity ring. A lot of people are wearing them now. It means that you don't believe in sex before marriage.'

'Really? Well, that's a good thing, isn't it?' Neil said, biting into his potato.

Lynn wasn't sure what to say. She had always assumed that her daughter was still a virgin, principally because her boyfriends had all been immature local boys whom Lynn knew. She was pretty sure they'd had few opportunities. In any case, none of Chloe's relationships had shown evidence of heaving hormonal passion; they'd been more about power. And in Leeds, of course, Chloe had been unsuccessful with boys altogether.

But her mother had thought that, like other girls, Chloe would eventually latch on to some youth and they would have sex, taking the right precautions of course. It had never occurred to her that Chloe might embrace the values of an earlier generation, and she felt vaguely suspicious about the ring. Then Lynn told herself not to be silly: no Christian should feel twitchy because her daughter wanted to be a virgin on her wedding night, should she?

'It's an interesting idea,' said Neil in his slightly academic way. He loved his daughter, but he was cross with her for leaving university and didn't know how to approach her. Before, he had indulged in a sort of lighthearted joshing with her which was totally inappropriate now.

'Where did you get it?' Lynn asked anxiously. She knew why she felt uncomfortable. The ring was too much of a declaration.

'Aha, never you mind, big nose!' For a second, Chloe's face assumed that cheeky, half-humorous, half-rebellious expression that had been her trademark until recently. Then the moment passed and she was back to being impassive again. Lynn was astonished how much she missed her daughter's insolence.

'OK,' she said, as always scared to provoke her only child. 'Are you going to come with us to church tomorrow?'

'Well, not if you don't mind, Mum,' Chloe said. Then she added as an afterthought: 'I'd rather go up to Fellside Fellowship. I like it there, and I can talk to Jenny.'

It was a cruel thing to have said and Lynn felt as if she had been slapped. But she merely asked, 'More stew, sweetheart?' and again the moment passed.

* * *

At The Briars, Edwin and Alex had exchanged an unmistakable look of complicity when Suzy mentioned Morris Little's death.

'So you think so too? That there's something odd about it?'

'Yes.' Edwin tucked into his pasta.

'But what? Why is everyone so coy? I don't know much about it, but I do know that Norma Little told Robert she didn't think it was the Frosts. I didn't like Morris and it's my guess he enraged a lot of people. And the Frosts are blamed for everything round here.'

'That's certainly true,' said Robert cautiously. 'There have been a lot of other incidents, too. Freddie and David Johnstone have both had odd accidents. The Chorus is getting depleted.'

'Actually . . .' Alex paused. 'David Johnstone was injured at the convent too, like Freddie.'

'What?' Suzy and Robert both leant forward.

'He fell into a hole that had been dug there. Pat Johnstone saw it all and told my sister. She wanted to know if I'd noticed anyone digging up the garden at the convent, but I hadn't.'

'So how come he had a road accident?'

'Pat thinks someone dug a pit, trapped him in it, and then decanted his body into the car and sent it rolling down the hill to that tree.'

'What?' Suzy raised her eyebrows.

'But if Pat was there why didn't she rescue him?' Robert asked.

Alex said, 'She'd followed him to try and smoke out his fancy woman. One of the many. She was more interested in who dug the pit than in David's accident.'

'Sounds like a nice woman,' Suzy said drily.

'She comes over as the dutiful wife, a bit silly and thick, but she's sharp underneath. All this is in total confidence, by the way. Pat told my sister, who's a bit of an innocent, and it was easy for me to worm it all out of Christine.'

'But it seems ludicrous!' Suzy said.

'And there's another element in this, equally ludicrous,' said Edwin. He told Robert and Suzy about the psalter with the torn-out first page.

'So I was right!' Suzy said triumphantly when he'd finished. 'There is something very odd going on. Funny how those Psalms keep cropping up. The missing psalter, and the Fellowship's winter course on the Psalms . . .'

'And your research, Edwin,' said Alex. 'Edwin's been looking into the work of a Victorian clergyman, Cecil Quaile Woods. He was rector at Uplands and wrote settings for the Psalms.'

'Yes.' Edwin nodded. 'His music for the psalms of praise was published. But no one knows what happened to his settings for the psalms of lament. I've been trying to recreate his chants in a minor key but it hasn't been too successful.'

'So the Psalms are all over this case!'

'Yes. How weird!' Edwin spoke quietly. 'How did Morris die? His teeth were battered in. I think that's in Psalm 58. And Freddie? We laughed about it, but the great bulls of Basan are in Psalm 22. And the word you used was a give-away, Alex. The pit David Johnstone fell into. The pit comes in more than once. Psalms 28 and 30, for instance. And 55. Is this a coincidence?'

Then Alex interrupted. 'Hey, don't let's get carried away. There are other elements to all this. Morris was black-mailing people, after all.'

'Including me.' Edwin spoke quietly. 'Morris emailed me saying that if I applied for the head of department's job he'd tell people I slept with my pupils.'

'And did you?' Suzy asked, her TV researcher persona to the fore.

Edwin took it in good part. 'No! Certainly not. I went out with Marilyn Frost. We were virtually engaged. She was over eighteen.'

'Which all goes to show that Morris Little was an evil bastard,' Suzy said. 'If he was blackmailing you, Edwin, with so little to go on, what else was he up to? Half of Norbridge probably wanted to smack him in the mouth. Those poor old Frost kids are just scapegoats. You agree, don't you Robert? After all, you've been writing about it . . .'

Robert was almost apologetic. 'Well, I wouldn't call it writing. I've been trying to cobble together some sort of idea for a novel for my creative writing course. I chose Morris Little's murder and was trying to write one of those "factional" things but it hasn't been going too well. Shall I get my notes?'

'Yes!' Suzy grabbed his plate. 'I'll put this back in the oven.' She disappeared towards the kitchen while Robert went upstairs to the spare room they still called his office, though now the floor was piled high with Suzy's detritus.

Alex and Edwin were left alone. 'Is this just a dinner party game?' Alex leant forward. 'Or do they really think something bad happened?'

'I don't think they'd play around with something like this. A few years ago they were on the fringe of a couple of nasty murders in Tarnfield. They know how serious it can get.'

* * *

In the small dark cottage on the outskirts of Uplands, Freddie Fabrikant was sitting by the fire, his legs in plaster propped on a stool, and a CD blaring out. In frustration he clicked at the control, and silence dulled the room.

'Wanda?'

'Just a minute, for God's sake.' There was a groaning noise. Freddie grimaced.

'Have you got your head in the toilet again?'

'Yes. Must be something I've eaten.'

Freddie was irritable. He was supposed to be the sick one, but Wanda had some sort of tummy bug and he was terrified of touching her in case he got infected. It was bad enough, he thought, when your legs were working, having to lumber up and down the narrow stairs which went from the tiny landing to the corner of the living room, cottage style. The skin was itching in the plaster casing and he felt fat and even more bulky than usual. What was more, he just couldn't sing sitting down. There was no reverberation.

The concert was traditionally held on Palm Sunday. But that morning he had received a letter from the hospital telling him his casts would not be removed until the Monday, the day after. He knew he wasn't going to be ready. But *The Crucifixion* had to be sung before Easter! If they could postpone the concert, to Good Friday, say, just those extra few days would make all the difference. And now David Johnstone was in hospital there'd be no fuss from the sponsor.

'Get me the telephone, Wanda!' he shouted. He would call Edwin Armstrong and leave a message, asking if the concert could be put off. There was no doubt some of the parts were a bit thin. Freddie liked *Sturm und Drang* not prissy churchy singing. He tried to work out how many rehearsals he'd been to since the beginning of January. The answer was, not enough. The best one had been the week when he'd forgotten his wallet and gone back to the Abbey — and heard that funny remark about virgins.

The thought gave Freddie an idea. Or to be fair, the extension of an idea he'd already had. 'And Wanda,' he roared, 'get me the laptop too.' It wouldn't hurt to put out a few feelers, he thought. And it would be much more interesting than sitting here vegetating.

When a whey-faced Wanda appeared from upstairs she was surprised to find that Freddie was laughing to himself. For a minute he looked as if he was going to pull her towards him, but at the smell of vomit on her breath he remembered the bug.

'*Mensch*, Wanda!' he said and pushed her away. 'Disgusting!'

33

Teach me to do the thing that pleaseth thee, for thou art my God; let thy loving spirit lead me forth into the land of righteousness.
Psalm 143:10

Robert came back to the supper table, a sheaf of papers in his hand; Suzy reappeared with apple pie and cream, and his warmed-up dinner on a tray. The middle-class dinner party atmosphere had dissolved and been replaced with an air of almost anxious enquiry.

'What have you put on paper, Robert?' Suzy asked.

'Well, my feelings were that the Frosts were drugged and would confess to anything. I think they were responsible for the power cut because that's the sort of pointless vandalism they would be up for. But someone else could easily have socked Morris in the face and the Frosts could have found the piece of wood.'

'Yes!' Alex was alert with interest now. 'I found Tom Firth with the body at least five minutes after the power cut. Five minutes in the dark is a hell of a long time, believe me. You almost get used to it. And I know for certain that Morris had an old psalter in his hand. But I also know, and don't ask me how, that a page was missing. I think it was the front page. Tom Firth said the same thing.'

'Now we're getting somewhere. Someone wanted the title page destroyed. We have that as a fact and it doesn't sound like the Frosts.'

'And you should know,' Alex said drily.

'OK — so I was in a relationship with Marilyn Frost.' Edwin shrugged. 'But that's not why I'm interested in all this. I'm involved because someone very violent was near to you, Alex, literally, and that worries me. You could have been hurt yourself.'

Mollified, Alex leant back in her chair. 'Why don't we look at everything, however tangential, which impinges on this business? That was the way I used to write my books, when I had the confidence. I'd note all the things that interested me and look for a thread. Do it in an arbitrary way. I guess you've already got a list, Robert. Let's just add to it. Everyone should say anything they think might be relevant. Rob can write them down and see where we get. I'll start the ball rolling — the Frost clan.' She glanced sideways at Edwin.

'The Psalms,' Robert offered.

'And the convent,' said Suzy.

'Tom Firth and the body.' That was Alex's second contribution.

'Chloe Clifford and her breakdown,' Suzy jumped in.

'Freddie Fabrikant's accident,' Robert added.

'David Johnstone and his whole property empire,' Edwin said quickly.

'Local history,' Alex finished up.

'Local history?' Robert turned to her, surprised.

'Ask yourself, what were Morris's interests? Choral singing. Local history. And blackmailing people — not for money but for power and pleasure. And in order to blackmail people, you have to know things. What did Morris know most about? Local history! Maybe recent history, in Edwin's case. But he was a mine of information about Norbridge.'

'And genealogy,' Edwin added. 'He was into that too.'

'Was he?' Alex turned to him. 'What makes you say that?'

'The favourites on his computer were ancestry.co.uk and findmypast.co.uk. And your books, Alex. They're all about families, aren't they? That's the common thread there. *The Wizard of Workhaven* — that's based on St Ragnhild's chapel on the coast and a local boy who discovers his father is the big landowner. And *The West Coast Pirate* — a local man who's dispossessed and then finds that he's really the lord of the manor . . .'

'OK, so my plots are a bit samey.'

'No! I'm not getting at you! I'm just saying that Morris loved that stuff. They were the only books in his room.'

'So let's add genealogy. I think we should each take an area of this mystery and research it. I'll take genealogy.' Alex felt more motivated than she had for years.

'I'll talk to the Johnstones,' Edwin contributed. 'I should visit David in hospital as secretary of the Chorus. I can talk to Wanda as well. You should know that she was going to meet Morris that evening; that's why he was in the college!'

'Aha!' Robert chimed in. 'I'd wondered about that. So that's why he was there! That's a good lead. For my part, I'd like to research the convent.'

'No,' Edwin said quickly. 'I'll do that. I've got a solicitor chum who'll help. Why don't you do the Johnstones instead of me? And you should talk to Norma again. That's plenty. What about you, Suzy?'

'I'd like to talk to the people at Fellside Fellowship.' And to Mark Wilson, she thought to herself. Not that her motives were anything other than pure research. 'What started me on this was that I remembered Morris boring me about trying to save the Fellside convent building. He sounded really nasty.' She thought about the women she had seen from Rachel's roof garden. 'Maybe I could do nuns too!'

'Nuns?' Edwin looked at her sharply. 'I think that comes under my remit, Suzy. Someone must own that convent and there must be an order listed somewhere which used the building.'

'So we've all got something to do,' Robert said. 'When shall we meet up?'

'It's Shrove Tuesday next week,' Suzy said. 'I'll do the kids' pancakes while you're at the Abbey Chorus, but I'll save some batter and why don't you both come here afterwards and have some? It gives us a few days. If we get nowhere, we can drop it and go into Lent suitably chastened. But if any of us finds anything significant, then we can dedicate the next forty days in the wilderness to finding out what really happened.'

'I like it!' Alex said. 'Let's go for it.'

* * *

On Pancake Day, Suzy was hard at work in the kitchen. She had always liked Shrove Tuesday. She'd altered her shifts to make sure she was at home, and she had bought all the ingredients for the pancakes in advance. As she beat the batter, with Molly's help, she went over the new facts they had discovered about Morris's murder. As Rachel had suggested, getting involved in the Little murder case was like trying the murky water of crime a toe at a time. So far, she felt fine about it — it was stimulating, an intellectual exercise which might help the much-maligned Frost boys, interesting but not really scary. Her confidence was coming back.

She liked Alex and Edwin, too. Edwin had opened up in a way she wouldn't have thought possible. And though she and Alex were very different, they shared a sense of humour. Later on Saturday night Alex had talked about her research for her books. Her dogged attention to detail, her isolated work, locked into her computer or the library, was all totally unlike Suzy's gregariousness. I need other people, Suzy thought, whereas Alex is self-contained. Alex had gone into the depths of despair alone whereas I was much more likely to scream for help!

And Robert had responded to that scream, literally, nearly two years ago. But that didn't mean he had any less respect for her. They had talked for hours after she came back from Rachel's. She loved him more than ever now she knew he had feet of clay.

'So you were never the perfect husband?'

'No, obviously, though I did work at it.'

'Well, don't ever work at it with me. It's tough enough having to work when you need to earn a living! We don't need that sort of strain. Just love me!'

'I do!'

'And I love you too! Very much.'

But that did not prevent her from appreciating the gorgeous Mr Wilson. On Sunday afternoon, as agreed, she had taken Jake up to the Fellowship and hung around until Mark came to talk to her.

'Awful about David Johnstone's car crash,' she'd said.

'Yes, I called in to see Pat earlier today. She's going away to her son's in Croydon for a few days, but David's having another operation next week so she's coming back for that. He's not doing very well.'

'Fellside seems accident prone at the moment. David, Freddie. It must put a lot of strain on you.'

'Yes.' Mark had leant forward confidentially, his large clear eyes looking into hers. He is quite scrumptious, Suzy thought. 'Things haven't been running so smoothly here, as you've probably gathered. I must apologize. The rehearsals have been quite chaotic lately.'

'Yes, I suppose they have.' Suzy wasn't aware that it was any worse than before, but then she would hardly have known.

'To be honest,' Mark had said quietly, 'it's been more difficult for Paul lately. He's very fraught. Please don't be impatient with him. Three crises in two months . . .'

'Three? David, Freddie, and who else?' She had been aware of sounding unusually nosy.

'Morris Little. That was the first and it added hugely to his stress levels. Paul and Morris were in contact, you know. Paul was due to meet Morris that evening. Of course it never happened, but it must have shaken Paul quite a bit.'

'Absolutely.' Suzy's eyes had widened.

Mark was saying, 'Don't say anything to anyone about Paul having a rough time. I'm quite worried about him.'

'And Jenny?'

'She's wonderful. Absolutely wonderful. But the baby's very demanding.'

'Tell me about it! Kids can be awfully hard work.'

'Yes, I'm sure they can. Especially if you're a single parent!'

Mark had looked at her in a way which would have made her melt if she hadn't taken a grip on herself.

Perhaps because of that, she hadn't answered him, and he had moved off to get back to the band causing musical mayhem on the stage. It was only afterwards that she wondered to whom he was referring when he mentioned single parents. And then she realized that he'd meant her, Suzy Spencer. She had felt a tingle of guilt. She ought to make it clear that she and Robert were very much an item.

But then again, there was no harm in a bit of flirting, was there? It was really rather exciting to think Mark Wilson might find her attractive! And he certainly trusted her. She had felt privileged that he had spoken to her in that confidential way. Mark was a caring person, worried about his friend, and he had talked to her. And anyway, she had told Robert all about it when she got home, and they had laughed about it.

It was when she was lost in thought, the batter dripping off the whisk and Molly shouting 'Mummee!' that she remembered one of her earlier conversations with Mark. They had been talking about inheriting musical talent and family stuff. And he had said that Paul Whinfell was mad on genealogy. And so was Morris. Could that be the link? Although almost everyone was into family history these days. But even so . . . She made a mental note to mention it to Alex.

* * *

Alex had spent all day Sunday at the computer. Edwin had given her all Morris Little's emails in hard copy, and the print-outs of his articles. There were reams of it. She had tidied it all into folders — work on Norbridge, music, sent emails, draft emails, a list of the last fifty sites Morris had visited. She wanted to find a threatening email which matched with something Morris had dug up through one of his hobbies. If he really did have the information to needle someone seriously, might that person resort to violence?

She followed his genealogy trail, tracing the Little family. He had constructed a half-hearted family tree, using ancestry.co.uk, findmypast.com, genesreunited.co.uk, and a few others. The Little family was transparent. Morris's father and grandfather had owned the shop, and before that they had been blacksmiths. His mother had worked in the store and his grandmother and great-grandmother had been in service. On the face of it, there was nothing there. Morris seemed to have become bored with it. But if he was uninterested in his own family after a few generations, why had he visited the genealogy sites so assiduously? Who was he looking up?

Edwin had reluctantly let her have the blackmail emails. They were all ugly and trite. Nothing Morris threatened to reveal was very terrible, Alex thought. They were silly, embarrassing misdemeanours like her own. The worst was the threat to expose a councillor for *being up yourself having posh dinners with that barrow boy David Johnstone who everyone knows is dealing in the hard stuff*, which might have been drugs. She shrugged. She suspected that in every town in the world, someone in the business community was part of the drug-dealing network, hard or soft. It wouldn't surprise her if Johnstone was on the fringes of that, although he did not strike her as either ruthless or psychotic enough to be a major player. But Johnstone was a crook. She was intuitively sure of that.

She found Morris's work on old Norbridge fascinating. How sad, she thought, that such a talented man should have gone to waste like this, nursing his resentments and hating anyone who was lucky enough to have an education. She imagined him slowly realizing from boyhood onwards that the shop was to be his life, whatever talents he had. It must have been like a slow, growing prison. No wonder he was uninterested in his own family history. But she told herself not to get sentimental. There was a nasty streak in Morris which wasn't just the product of his disappointment. Look what he had done to Edwin!

She took her glasses off and rubbed her eyes. She had been reading Morris's material for over four hours. It made a change to think about Edwin.

He had been seriously affected by Morris's email. But just what had Morris threatened to do? Morris had said he would reveal 'where Marilyn Frost is now'. But why would that be a scandal? Was Marilyn a prostitute? Or in prison? Would it matter if she was, and it became widely known? In fact, wouldn't something like that be common knowledge anyway? Her notorious family would surely have no problem with it. And if it was something as straightforward if unpleasant, why didn't Edwin tell me? Alex thought. Why was Edwin so protective of Marilyn that he threw up the chance of being head of department just because of some sort of chivalrous idea of keeping her secret?

Wherever Marilyn was, surely her dysfunctional family would know? There was the mother, and also her uncles and stepfather. Edwin had mentioned them all. And Jason and Wayne, of course. And hadn't Edwin said something about sisters? That was strange. No one else ever mentioned any Frost girls. How very odd, Alex thought. Where was she now?

34

Deliver me not over into the will of mine adversaries, for there are
false witnesses risen up against me, and such as speak wrong.
Psalm 27:14

Robert hadn't been lucky in his research. Norma Little was working hard in the shop, but she agreed to see him as soon as she could — probably the next week. He said he wanted to talk about a memorial to Morris in the concert programme, which was true. He also said he knew Edwin had looked into Morris's work and that he'd been impressed, and he would be working with Edwin to try and make something of it.

'Something for the *Cumberland News* mebbe?' Norma asked hopefully.

'Well, possibly.' Robert sighed. He understood her longing to see Morris praised in print, and the local paper was what mattered most to her. It would be good for business too! He hoped that Edwin would be able to come up with something from Morris's paperwork that was worth publishing. So much of it seemed to be collations of other people's work or half-formulated, slightly mad theories.

And there was the spite, of course. Robert had been distressed by the cruel emails, and was relieved never to have received one. And, like Edwin, he felt some guilt and sadness too. Perhaps they shouldn't have been so quick to dismiss Morris as an old bore. Maybe that evening, if he had gone for a drink with Morris, then Morris would not have gone to the college and met his attacker.

But Morris hadn't acted as if he'd had an important meeting to go to. He had indicated that Tom Firth should join him for a drink. But maybe Morris was being clever. Taunting Tom would ensure the boy went his own way and, looking back, Robert realized Morris had said nothing to his fellow basses about going to the pub. Clearly, Morris had not wanted to advertise his meeting at the college. Edwin would surely find out more about that when he talked to Wanda Wisley.

In the meantime, Robert arranged to go and see David Johnstone in hospital on his way home on Monday evening. Robert didn't like to admit it, but he didn't want to spend Sunday at David Johnstone's bedside when he could be at home with Suzy. Their relationship had resumed its old warmth even if there was still a sense of its being unresolved.

He waited for Suzy to get home from dropping Jake at the practice at Fellside Fellowship. And Molly was out at her best friend's house. They would have The Briars to themselves, and this time he wasn't going to retire to his study.

* * *

Edwin had telephoned Wanda Wisley on Sunday morning. She had sounded distinctly ill, and his first thought was that she had a hangover.

'I've got a tummy bug,' she said grumpily. 'I feel like shit.'

'I'm sorry to bother you, but there's something I'd like to discuss with you. It's rather important. If you're unable to come out, would you be able to see me at your cottage for half an hour?'

'Is this department business?'

'Yes.' Well, in a sense it was.

'Oh God, if you must.' Wanda sounded world-weary but slightly less snappy than usual.

Since discovering that she had failed to tell the police about her abandoned meeting with Morris, Edwin had let his anger with her slowly grow. But he hadn't been sure how to approach her. Now he was involved with the other three in what Suzy called their 'research', he felt more aggressive. At the back of his mind he rebuked himself for not having the balls earlier to try and do something for Marilyn's brothers. He had believed that the Frost boys were capable of murder. But not this murder. It made no sense.

When he arrived at her cottage, Wanda was waiting for him, dressed in old jeans and a massive sweatshirt which he guessed belonged to Freddie. She looked very pale without her make-up and her nose was red and shiny.

'Come in. I don't know what it was that wouldn't wait.'

'I need to talk to you about Morris Little.'

'The old bore who got himself murdered?'

'Yes. Is Freddie about?'

'He's upstairs, and believe me when he's up there with his legs in plaster I'm not bringing him down, if I don't have to. He's watching DVDs in the bedroom.' She looked around shiftily. Edwin thought, she doesn't want Freddie to hear this.

They sat down in the funny cramped sitting room which took up the whole ground floor, with the big fireplace, and stairs in the corner making a fake inglenook.

'Wanda, I know Morris had arranged to meet you the night he died.'

'Oh, fuck. How did you find out?'

'Morris's wife asked me to clear out his emails. You need to know that there are several of us who think the Frost kids are innocent. We want to go to the police with more evidence. It's important. Was Morris definitely coming to see you?'

'Well, we'd spoken on the phone and I'd said perhaps I'd be there . . .' She reddened. 'I didn't think of it as a real commitment.'

249

'So what did Morris say? Did he say he'd come over at a certain time? Was he coming alone? Did he mention bringing someone else?'

Wanda thought carefully. 'He said he'd got an interesting document. Something to do with one of those stodgy Victorians he was obsessed with.'

'Cecil Quaile Woods?'

'That's the guy!' Now that she realized Edwin wasn't going to cart her off to the police station, or threaten to tell the Principal, Wanda was more co-operative. 'Actually, you know, he did say it would be handy to meet me around six o'clock, because he had some other people to see.'

'Other people?'

'Yes. I remember that because when it got to three o'clock I thought, oh bugger this, I'm going shopping.' She wasn't going to confess that she had completely forgotten about meeting Morris. 'I wasn't going to hang around until six o'clock. I called Freddie and said we'd meet outside McCrea's.'

'So you were out with Freddie all afternoon?'

'Yes, I certainly was! Do you think it was me who hit that old fart over the head with a plank? Not that I'd have stopped myself, if he bored me anymore than he had done already. But no, I'm not your villain. I was out all afternoon in various stores, and even when Freddie left me hanging about for half an hour the Principal saw me — so there!'

'Where was Freddie for that half-hour?' Edwin asked suddenly.

'God, I don't know. In McCrea's some of the time buying a disgusting waistcoat for himself and a tatty red velvet scarf for me. He didn't come back till after six o'clock. He was probably chatting up the waitress in Figaro's. You know what he's like.' Wanda laughed. She's so relieved that she's not implicated, Edwin thought, that she hasn't realized she's exposed Freddie.

There was movement at the top of the staircase.

'Wanda,' Freddie said, his voice booming gruffer than ever, 'you never told me we had a visitor.'

He hung on to the landing banisters which made a sort of gallery over the sitting room and smiled at Edwin, but — whether it was the pain in his legs or something else — his grin was more of a grimace. Wanda might not have realized that she'd dropped Freddie in it, Edwin thought, but Freddie had heard exactly what she'd said. And he knew just what it meant. She had an alibi, but he didn't.

* * *

At the hospital on Monday night, Robert looked at a much-reduced David Johnstone. He was asleep, breathing noisily, tubes attached to his nostrils. Robert had had no idea that he was so ill. He looked very yellow.

Pat Johnstone was there, fidgeting. She laughed her usual cackle when she saw Robert.

'Nice of you to come. It's so boring here!' She laughed again, as if Robert had come to see her rather than David. 'I'm off to my son and daughter-in-law's tomorrow for a break, but I've got to be back at the end of the week. *He'* — she shrugged towards the immobile figure on the bed — 'has had another op but they say he needs more tests. Funny colour, isn't he?' She sounded annoyed.

'How is he?'

'Not recovering as well as they'd hoped. That's why they're doing tests on him. Obviously.'

'I'm sorry to hear that.'

'Yes, it's a real nuisance.'

She and Robert looked at each other across the bed. What can I say? Robert thought. I've no idea how to make small talk with Pat Johnstone.

'Is David's business coping without him?'

'Seems to be. The branch offices are anyway. Of course he always had other schemes on the go.' She cackled. 'Don't know what's going to happen about them.'

Her eyes glinted, and Robert remembered what Alex had told them. Pat needed to get her hands on David's

251

money. She must live in fear of him leaving her for one of his girlfriends, and taking the money with him.

'Property schemes?' Robert asked, innocently.

'Usually.' Pat's eyes narrowed. 'He had a lot of interests.' She talked in the past tense.

Robert searched for something to say to fill the silence. Fishing, he asked, 'D'you mean hobbies? Was he interested in family history? That's the new craze, isn't it?'

Pat cackled even more than usual. 'Hobbies? David? You must be joking. And the less we know about his family the better. No, the only family history David would be interested in was who owned what! Now, that would get him going. Like that other chap who came a cropper.' There was a sort of malevolence in Pat's face that Robert hadn't seen before.

'Who? Freddie Fabrikant?'

'Nah. He's just a big windbag. I meant that chap David couldn't stand. Morris Little from Uplands store. They were allus arguing about buildings. Now they're both out of it.' Pat seemed pleased.

Robert thought: What's this all about? David had behaved like Morris's greatest fan. The idea that David and Morris were at odds was news. He looked down at the sick man, still in his drugged sleep. 'I'll come back when he's awake,' Robert said. 'Tell him that the Abbey Chorus is thinking of him.'

'I bet,' said Pat nastily, and cackled again.

* * *

On Tuesday night at nine o'clock, Suzy, Robert, Edwin and Alex sat around the big kitchen table at The Briars, eating pancakes.

'So what've we got?' said Suzy, with her mouth full.

'Nothing of interest in Morris's family tree, but he was clearly investigating someone. He was into all the ancestry sites,' said Alex. 'But not his own, unless his wife can enlighten us.'

252

'I've got nothing from Norma Little. I can't see her till next week at least,' Robert said. 'However, Pat Johnstone is interesting. She said that Morris and David were at each other's throats over something to do with buildings. Property deals maybe?'

'That's new,' said Alex. 'Johnstone was always saying that Morris was a great bloke, lying obviously. And the property angle is interesting. Maybe my bungalow is part of that. What have you got, Edwin?'

'Wanda admits that she abandoned a meeting she had planned with Morris where he was going to show her some documents. Maybe one of them was the psalter.'

'And I heard from Mark Wilson' — Suzy blushed slightly — 'that Paul was due to meet Morris the night he died.'

'So a lot of people could have met Morris that night. And are we all agreed that the Psalms come into this somehow? Or is that just fanciful?' Robert asked.

'I don't think so,' said Edwin. 'There's the question of the missing psalter. That's fact.'

'So what hypothesis would fit all this random evidence?' Suzy asked.

Alex Gibson thought hard. Plotting was surely her bag. But it was different when you couldn't start from scratch. Finding a thread between real clues was much harder. Edwin suddenly put his hand on her arm and she felt it like an electric shock.

'Could it be that the psalter held some sort of evidence which the attacker didn't want Morris to reveal?' he asked.

'Like what?' Suzy said. 'A controversial new chant, for example? I don't think so, Edwin. Not in the twenty-first century. Unless it was written for Britney.'

'OK, I take your point.' Edwin smiled, surprisingly relaxed these days. 'Anyway,' he went on, 'you must agree, Suzy, the book is crucial to all this. And Alex says it was the beginning that was missing. What usually goes at the beginning of books?'

'The dedication! So maybe it was the dedication which was the point,' Alex rushed in.

'Yes. Someone didn't want the front page of a unique old book to be seen. A book that would be a curiosity perhaps, but not necessarily terribly valuable. The idea of a dedication does fit,' said Edwin.

Robert had been writing on the back of his notes. 'I think we're looking at this wrongly. Instead of trying to get a crime to fit, let's look at the people in the frame. We're all agreed the Frosts are not necessarily the murderers, aren't we? So who do we know could have met Morris? OK, half of Norbridge of course, but he was in the Music Department on the quietest afternoon of the year, and he was being discreet about the meeting. So whoever met him either had to have an arrangement to meet him, or to know he was there, or to bump into him.'

'So there's Wanda Wisley, though she says the Principal saw her in the shopping mall. And by extension, Freddie Fabrikant,' Edwin said. 'And you should have seen his face when he realized that Wanda had put him in the frame.'

'But why would Freddie kill Morris? Anyway, Freddie was injured himself later.'

'No, Suzy, don't ask about motives. Just list those people who knew he would be at the college, and who had the opportunity,' Robert said. 'So far there's Freddie, and Wanda — unless we check out her alibi with the Principal. And the Frosts — we can't count them out.'

'And Rev Paul,' Alex said unhappily. 'I don't want it to be him, but he was supposed to be meeting Morris.'

'And he's mad on genealogy,' added Suzy.

'Not to mention the Psalms,' Edwin said grimly.

'Do you think we're really on to something?' Suzy said suddenly. 'Or is it that we're just bleeding heart liberals who want the Frosts in the clear?'

'Some of us might have other motives,' said Alex, looking at Edwin.

'You mean Marilyn?' Edwin said. 'Yes, that is part of it for me. I know Marilyn's brothers were horrible, and capable of violence. But I don't want them to be Morris's murderers.'

'So why isn't Marilyn involved in trying to exonerate them?' Suzy voiced the question Alex had been desperate to ask.

'Yes,' Alex added. 'Shouldn't we talk to Marilyn? After all, this is more her bag than ours, isn't it?'

Edwin's face darkened, giving him once again the cold saturnine look which Suzy found so off-putting. He looked down, failing to meet their eyes.

'All right,' he said. 'If you think it's so important, I'll ask Marilyn to meet us.'

Alex felt a fleeting moment of triumph, followed quickly by fear. What will this do to our friendship? she thought. Oh God, what have I done?

35

Man goeth forth to his work, and to his labour, until the evening.
Psalm 104:23

Tom Firth couldn't sleep. It was a Wednesday morning and
he was due at college at ten o'clock for a class. But he felt both
excited and frustrated. It would be weeks before he saw Poppy
again. He needed to get the cash together for a trip to Newcastle,
and anyway he couldn't stand the thought of his dad finding
out he was going to see a girl, and taking the piss. The only
thing worse would be his mother's delight which would be
quickly followed by silly questions. Parents! So irritating.

Though maybe that wasn't entirely fair. His mam especially had always been on his side, in her own nosy way. And
from what Poppy said about her parents, they'd been all for
her going to uni, and they'd helped her out with money. It
wasn't that parents were bad, necessarily. They were just . . .
irritating. And stupid too, a lot of the time.

But Chloe Clifford's parents weren't stupid. For a priest,
Neil Clifford was OK. He had come to see Tom again after
Christmas and had said sensible things.

Tom had asked him: 'About Morris's body. It keeps
coming back to me.'

'Don't try and put it out of your mind. Think about it. Talk about it to people. People who won't fuss. Me. Your counsellor. Perhaps Alex Gibson? There's a fine line between repressing the memory and dwelling on it too much. You are the only person who will know the difference. It's not that easy. But I think you're bright enough to understand what I'm saying, aren't you?'

Tom had nodded. That was exactly it. He had been asking himself: when did thinking about it get morbid?

'Anyway,' Neil had added, 'at your age lots of new things happen. Be open to them. Something else will crowd out that memory soon.'

He had been so right. Getting off with Poppy had been brilliant. And it took up all his thoughts. Except . . . there was still Chloe. Neil seemed such a good bloke — but his own daughter was all over the place. Chloe's mum was nice, too. He remembered going round to the rectory in the summer holidays when she'd been listening to Bach's Magnificat in the kitchen. He'd commented and she'd smiled. She hadn't gasped and said, 'Fancy you knowing that!' or raised her eyebrows or made questioning noises or started talking about effing exams. Mrs Clifford was all right.

So why was Chloe all wrong? What was going on with her? Tom thought about when he and Poppy had tried following her. That had been a miserable failure. Chloe had got off the bus in Fellside and disappeared.

Tom tossed about in bed, his long scrawny body winding the thin duvet all round him, till he threw it off in annoyance and got up to pad through the cold room and stand by the radiator under the window. It was early. From his house he could see over the other terraces' roofs to where the fells started like a dirty smear on the horizon.

He got dressed quickly without bothering with a shower. He left the tangled bed, grabbed his hat — it would be cold out there and anyway Poppy wasn't around — and pulled on his parka, picked up his bag and flung the strap over his shoulder. His dad was away and his mam and little brother

257

were asleep. He crept down the stairs and into the kitchen. He took some scrap paper out of his bag and scribbled a note saying he had gone to college early. That would surprise them, but there would be no questions till tea-time and he'd think of something to tell them by then.

He shut the front door behind him quietly, left the gate of the tiny front garden swinging, and strode down the street. The air was cool. If he walked briskly he could be at the Uplands crossroads in ten minutes and pick up the bus to Fellside. Then he would walk up and down the high street until he could work out exactly where Chloe Clifford had disappeared to.

There had to be some turn-off he'd missed, unless she'd gone into someone's house. But surely she'd have had to stand on the step for a minute, and they'd have seen her — unless she'd had a key, but even then she'd have had to get that key out and open the door. Anyway the houses on that end of the street were either converted to council offices, or small shops, or lived in by a few old people. And she had literally disappeared in seconds.

Had someone been holding the door open, ready? But if that was what had happened, wouldn't they have seen her walk up the street towards the residential end? It didn't make sense. Even if she'd turned straight into the Co-op, they'd have seen her come out or caught up with her when they went in themselves.

But she must have gone somewhere, mustn't she? And if he could work out where, he could message Poppy all about it, on-line. Because despite everything, he could tell that Poppy was worried about her friend. And it was catching. Now he was worried, too.

* * *

'Ash Wednesday.' Robert had got out of bed and opened the curtains. 'But it still looks wintry out there. I'm coming back to bed for five minutes.' He snuggled down beside Suzy, whose nose was almost the only bit of her showing.

'Brrrrr . . .' she shivered. 'And to think, a few weeks ago I thought spring was here.' She lifted her head up just high enough for Robert to slip his arm underneath. 'That's better.' She cuddled into him. 'What have you given up for Lent?'

'Not that!'

'I hope not! No, seriously?'

'I thought about alcohol but nowadays we've got such a lot to celebrate I don't want to do it! Jake and Molly doing well at school — and Nigel seems to be leaving you in peace . . .'

'Is that all?' Suzy said, pinching him.

'Ouch! Well, there's also the fact that we're friends again.'

'Too right! I never want to go through an ice age like that again. Thank goodness we've sorted things out.' Not totally, she thought. But it wasn't bad.

They lay there enjoying the warmth of each other. A few minutes later she said: 'Are you going to church tonight? If you are, we'll need a babysitter. I'm working late and missing the Bible study.'

'I might go to the Abbey at lunchtime then. The one here at All Saints is in the evening.'

'Is that where you get ashes smeared on your forehead?'

'No! That's a very High Church idea. I think it's rather nice in a symbolic way but it's straight out of Roman Catholicism. Some Anglicans do it, but they're more likely to be in city churches with High Church traditions rather than round here. I don't think anyone in the Norbridge area goes in for that.'

Suzy glanced at the clock on the bedside cabinet. 'Seven fifteen. Time to get up. At least we're ahead of the radio news coming on and setting a note of doom for the day!' The alarm was set for seven thirty, but that always meant a mad scurrying around the house to get Jake on the school bus and Molly ready for the current car rota.

She put her toes out of bed and swung the rest of her body to follow them. It wasn't so bad once you made yourself do it. The Briars was an old house with high ceilings and big rooms. The bedroom had an unused fireplace which Suzy had encouraged Robert to open up. It had a pretty Victorian surround which looked great, but the draught was noticeable. That's typical of me, Suzy thought. The visuals are everything so we all have to freeze because it looks nice.

That reminded her. 'Mary's rug cleaned up well. Did you notice it was back in Molly's room?'

'It's not Mary's rug, Suzy. It's our rug. That's all in the past.'

'OK, OK. So you're fine and living in the present. But do you think the same is true of Edwin?' Suzy was on her way to the bathroom, but stopped to hear his answer.

'I wonder. His affair with Marilyn was the talk of the town, you know, and it must have been horrendous for him when it ended. Mary was taken ill at about the same time, so I don't remember much about it.'

'This Marilyn seems a bit of an oddity. Or is it just Edwin's usual dark manner?'

'No.' Robert was out of bed too, but he sat on the edge, thinking. 'Nobody ever mentions her. And it is strange that Marilyn's not more involved with her brothers. But then again, her family isn't exactly the Waltons, is it? I mean, she might just want to put as much space between her and them as possible.'

'Do you think Edwin really will get in touch with her? Will she meet with us, d'you think?'

'I don't know. And that might be hard for Alex.'

'What? Meeting her new boyfriend's former lover?'

'Exactly.' He paused. 'Oh . . .'

'Well, I did meet your former lover, Robert. And we survived. But you and I have had two years and a lot of drama together.'

'And Alex is a bit less easy-going than you are.'

'You should know.' Suzy made for the door, but Robert caught her by the arm.

'You're the only one for me, Suzy. I really love you.'

'I know,' she answered. 'But I just hope it works out as well for our friends. Having Marilyn Frost bursting onto the scene might alter everything.'

* * *

Tom had caught the bus to Uplands and was astonished to find it was half full. As a student he was rarely out before nine o'clock and that seemed early to him. He'd imagined that only a few strange mole types would be poking their noses out of their holes to get to work in the morning before eight o'clock. He was surprised to find two of the Fellside Co-op assistants were on the bus, plus a couple of the council workers whose head office was up there, and a smattering of builders' labourers and farm workers. His breath steamed up the window and he was suddenly blinded by the rising sun as the bus swung a dramatic turn eastwards and dropped into the village. In the west behind him was the still-dark coast, sloping down the steel draining board of the wintry shore. Ahead were the fells.

The bus stopped a few yards downhill of the Co-op. Tom leapt off the bus first and then watched where the people went. The two women made for the shop. Two builders started to mooch down to the council estate — probably doing more improvements to the council houses, Tom thought. The farm labourers walked straight off down Scafell Street.

Weird, Tom thought. He wasn't sure which way to turn. For the sake of it, he walked downhill, passing the car park for Fellside Fellowship at the side of the old St Luke's. It was a completely ring-fenced gravel semicircle which would hold about ten cars. The chapel was closed, the windows grey and blind. Nothing was happening there this morning and there was no reason to think anything had been happening there the previous Saturday when he and Poppy had followed Chloe.

The village petered out, with the turn-off to the twenty or so council houses to Tom's left. He turned around and walked back up the village, past the Co-op and to the end of the street. Then he turned again and started to walk down to the bus stop, past the council offices.

It was then he realized he hadn't seen the council workers since getting off the bus. The council offices had taken over a section of the terraced houses. The houses had gated passageways between them leading to the back yards. Suddenly Tom understood: now the houses were offices, there was one narrow public passage between them, leading to the rear of the buildings.

Feeling self-conscious, he turned sharp right, down the passageway, as if he knew where he was going. Behind the council offices, the old back gardens had been concreted over and a couple of cars were parked there. The rear garden walls had been knocked down to allow the cars in, and the yard opened out onto a parallel road.

Tom crossed the yard and found himself virtually in open country. He could see the old convent, over the fields to his left, and to his right a lane seemed to sink deeper down into the hillside. He followed the lane downhill, past a Gothic-shaped door cut into the opposite wall, and then saw he was traipsing further into farmland. The lane seemed to wind away from Fellside; then it turned at ninety degrees towards Workhaven and the coast. Tom had heard about David Johnstone's road accident, and he wondered if this was the spot. The car would have careered straight on, missed the turn, and hit a big tree which was there on the corner.

So had Chloe sneaked between the houses into the council office yard and out here? But why? There was nothing doing here. There was no point in going further into the countryside. Tom could see that there were no buildings ahead, not even a byre or barn. He turned around once again and walked up the hill back towards the village, his calves feeling the pull. He walked straight through the council offices' car park and out through the narrow passage between the strips of terraced houses, into Fellside's main street. So much for his detecting ability. He still had no idea where Chloe could have gone that Saturday.

And then he saw her. For a moment he thought he had imagined it, but it was her. She was walking down the hill in front of him to the bus stop. He could hardly believe it, but it was definitely Chloe in that silly headscarf, wearing a long shapeless coat and clumpy shoes. No one else in the neighbourhood looked like that.

His first instinct was to follow her, hanging back to see where she went. But that was ridiculous. She was obviously going to the bus stop. And where else could he be going? He had to think of something to say if he bumped into her, and to gain time he went into the Co-op. Maybe the bus would come when he was in there and he could avoid her.

The two women on the till stared at him. There was no one else in the shop and he felt stupid. He couldn't hang around in there for ages waiting for the bus to come and go. He would look like a plonker. He scanned the newspaper rack and saw one tatty copy of the previous week's *Cumberland News*. Great, he thought. I'll buy this. If Chloe asks me what I'm doing here I'll say I've been looking everywhere for this newspaper for a project I'm doing — and the last one left was in Fellside.

He paid for his paper and leafed through it. There was a feature on Sandy McFay's books, one of his favourite authors. That was OK, then. He could say he wanted to get a copy of this article.

He walked out of the Co-op to the bus stop. Chloe Clifford was the only person there. For a minute she looked as if she wished she hadn't seen him, but it was too late.

'Hey, Tom! What are you doing here?' She sounded like her old bossy self. Trust her to ask the questions, he thought, though she kept her face ahead looking for the bus.

'Er, I've come up here to get this last copy of the *Cumberland News* for last week, still on sale in Fellside. Bit behind *The Times* here, you know!' He laughed noisily at his own joke, hoping Chloe wouldn't rumble him. 'And what are you doing up here yourself?' he asked, trying to sound nonchalant and take the initiative.

'Oh, me? I just came to see someone. If you see my dad, don't mention it. You know what a fuss they make. *Sooo* irritating.'

'Yeah, totally.'

Tom moved from foot to foot. He was really cold now. Chloe hadn't actually looked at him. She stared forwards, tensely waiting for the bus, which came into view and bounced down the hill to pull up abruptly. He followed her into it and plonked himself down beside her. Chloe gazed out of the window. Suddenly annoyed and demeaned, Tom poked her on the arm.

'Have you been in touch with Poppy? She really needs to talk to you.'

'Don't tell me what my friends need!' As if suddenly unguarded, the old Chloe turned angrily to face him.

To his surprise, Tom noticed a big grey smear across her forehead.

36

Sing unto the Lord a new song; sing praises lustily unto
Him with good courage.
Psalm 33:3

Paul at the Fellowship didn't hold an Ash Wednesday service. That sort of thing was for bigger and more traditional parishes, he argued. But this year Jenny had challenged him.

'You should take a communion service for the start of Lent,' she had said. 'I'm sure Mark agrees. He would help at it.'

'But we've got Bible study tonight. The start of the real Lent course. That's enough.'

These days, every time Mark was mentioned Paul felt uncomfortable. He was aware of Mark's popularity and his easy intellectual processes. Mark could argue for anything and make it sound right. But am I just jealous? Paul asked himself. I'm such a poor fish, Lord, he would pray. Sometimes it seemed incredible that he had come as far as this, and then he had to acknowledge that much of his success had been because of Jenny. She was the one whose faith was solid and whose support had brought him through his own crises, time and again.

But now that support wasn't there. Jenny was still tired, still distant, and she increasingly looked at him as if he had crawled from under a rock rather being one. He was spending ever more time at the computer, trying to find out more about Quaile Woods and the Whinfells, as if that would give him the foundation he needed.

And it was so interesting! He'd started to delve into the whole system of church patronage in the nineteenth century. He'd been fascinated to find that Uplands, the mother church, had been in the gift of the Cleaverthorpes. Then the father of the current Lord Cleaverthorpe had transferred his rights as patron to the Bishop. But he'd insisted that the family should still be consulted when a new incumbent was appointed. It was archaic, and a million miles from the straightforward suburban churches in Bristol and Manchester where Paul had served his probation as a curate.

But it harked straight back to the man Paul believed was his ancestor. Quaile Woods had come to the north after a childhood in Middlesex and an education at Oxford where he'd met the elderly Pusey. According to Henry Quaile Whinfell's biography of Quaile Woods, he'd also met and befriended Cleaverthorpe's son, which is how he had got the living. He must have come north aged thirty in 1860, brimming with almost missionary enthusiasm — but from a High Church perspective.

Paul, on the other hand, had qualified as a teacher after doing his first degree in geography. That's how he'd met Jenny; her uncle was a vicar and he had helped them navigate through the system. But during the three years of his training for the ministry, Paul had never been anything other than a straightforward evangelical. One of his great strengths had been the geographer's ability to assess the information on the ground and get on with it!

Despite their faith, there seemed little relationship between him and his putative great-great-grandfather. It was like reading about another world. He had been fascinated to find that Quaile Woods had been chaplain to the convent in

Fellside. These women's orders had sprung up like mushrooms in the nineteenth century. They supposedly accommodated the surplus single upper-middle-class women. Their male equivalents had been following the flag to the outreaches of Empire. Paul had done some research. At one point there had been over twenty thousand Anglican nuns in Britain. The Whinfell book referred to the order at Fellside as the Fellside Holy Sisters. Like most of them, it was a completely independent, local order. This one was fuelled by the passion of Sister Clementina, a Cleaverthorpe daughter who had dedicated herself to prayer and good works. Interestingly, in his biographical book Whinfell referred to the order as 'Quaile Woods' Order' as if the vicar had somehow owned it. But all female orders needed a male priest — without one they couldn't have the sacraments.

Paul looked at his watch. It was midday. He was still in his pyjamas and he'd forgotten his Bible study for the morning, which he did instead of reading the daily office. He had no idea where his wife was. He still hadn't told her about the notion which was bumping around in his head like an unmoored boat.

He pulled his dressing gown round him and bumbled into the hall, feeling as if he had been in another world. 'Jenny!' he shouted. She was in the kitchen. He could almost sense her fury, although she didn't answer him. She was bent over the high chair, feeding the baby.

'Jenny, we have to talk. I want to tell you about an idea I've had.'

Jenny turned on him. 'You want to discuss ideas with me, do you? Well, that's new. You've spent three hours this morning in that study of yours without even getting dressed. What's happened to you, Paul? Are you having some sort of breakdown?'

'No.' But even as he said it he wondered. He had spent the whole morning in the nineteenth century. 'No! Listen to me, Jenny.'

'Why should I listen to you? When was the last time you listened to me? Joseph is completely overtired and not eating properly. When was the last time you played with your own son? You're too busy playing with your computer. I'm going to take him out in the buggy. He needs fresh air.'

She hauled the still-howling baby out of the high chair. She would change him later and anyway he smelt OK. She strapped him into the buggy, aware that Paul was hovering over her uselessly, trying to say something.

'I'm going out,' she snapped. She hurtled out of the house and into the street, head down. For a moment she had no idea where she was going.

And then the buggy almost ran over somebody's large feet. A man's. Dressed in dark clothes, he was big enough to hide the sun for the moment when she saw him. Looking into the light, it took her a moment to focus.

'Oh,' she said, suddenly calmed. 'It's you. What are you doing here?'

* * *

Edwin saw Tom loping ahead of him in the corridor later that day. 'Tom!' he called.

The boy turned, his fresh face open, but it crowded into a frown when he saw Edwin. 'Yeah?'

'Have you got a second?'

Tom looked around suspiciously, but none of his mates was in the corridor so he followed Edwin through the doors into the Music Department, head down and face pulled into a grimace. What was Mr Armstrong after? Was he in trouble for something? For a minute he wondered if Edwin knew he had told Chloe about the psalter. But what harm could that do? Even so, these things weren't rational. Tom had learnt from his father after his lacklustre performance at school that it was always best to expect a bollocking and to meet it with either aggression or dumb insolence.

Edward was unlocking the office door. 'Step in,' he said. He was rather embarrassed about what he had to offer Tom, so he seemed more saturnine than usual — with the result that Tom hung back looking truculent. The moment of hysteria over Morris's death which had brought them together was long over.

'I've got a proposition for you,' Edwin said, looking very serious.

Tom wasn't sure what he meant, but thought the word sounded a bit like punishment.

'A what?'

'A proposition. A suggestion. You may feel it's a bit over the top. I mean, you don't have to say yes, and you can think about it if you want. It's quite a serious matter.'

Tom was now both wary and confused. 'Yeah? What is it?'

'Sit down, Tom.'

Tom huddled into the chair under the window, looking round as if for a quick escape route.

Edwin stayed standing. 'You've been really regular attending the Stainer rehearsals. I assume you've listened to a CD of the piece?'

Tom wondered what to say and decided on the truth. 'Nah. I haven't downloaded it and I'm a bit skint at the moment.'

'So do you know how the piece goes?'

'Oh, yeah, course. I've got the score, haven't I? I've had a good look at that. I can read music, you know. It's all a bit dated but not bad.'

Edwin breathed a sigh of relief. 'We need two soloists, a bass and a tenor. The committee has asked Freddie Fabrikant to sing bass.'

So? What's this got to do with me? The question was written all over Tom's face.

He looks totally uninterested, Edwin thought. This might be a mistake. 'And we'd like you to sing the tenor.'

Tom went on looking at the bookcase. Then his face shifted, and he brought his eyes round to Edwin's. 'What?' he said.

Edwin sighed, and repeated: 'The committee would like to ask you to sing the tenor solos. It's hard work of course and if you feel you can't cope . . .'

'Me? *Me?* Do you mean me?'

'Yes, of course I do. Why else d'you think I'm talking about it?'

'But what about the others? The adults?'

'You've got the best tenor voice in the choir, Tom, and you're a quick learner. And Robin the musical director will help you. So will I. We've still got five weeks. You can do it. I suggest you and I and Robin meet an hour before the others each week and practise. I'm sure you'll be good.'

Tom was gobsmacked, truly gobsmacked. That was the best way to describe his feelings, although chuffed-to-bits came a close second. He examined his feelings from the outside — a technique he'd learnt from his counsellor after Morris's death — and was surprised to find that the one thing he didn't feel was nervous. This wasn't an exam or horrible homework or a presentation to the class. This was music and he could do it. It needed work, of course, but he liked doing that. It was his meat and drink.

'When's the concert, again?' he asked.

'Palm Sunday. The week before Easter.' Oh dear, Edwin thought, was that the only comment Tom could make?

'Oh.' Tom looked crestfallen. Poppy wasn't coming back until Maundy Thursday, the Thursday before the Easter weekend. 'My girlfriend . . .' The words sounded so strange, he had to stop and listen to them bounce around the room. He swallowed. 'My girlfriend won't be home from uni for it.'

'So are you saying no?' Edwin asked, on the verge of irritation.

'No! I'm saying yes!' Tom stared at him. Plonker! What idiots adults were. Would he turn this down? As if!

'Good!' Edwin breathed out, astonished at how relieved he was. 'Look, the committee will also offer you a very small fee for this. It's an unusual move but we recognize that there'd be expenses for you — buying a suit perhaps and maybe getting a CD player of some sort of your own. It's not much but we're offering you some money out of the funds. Is that all right?'

Tom gazed at him while he took it all in. 'All right.'

'That's that then, Tom. I'll see you at five-ish next Tuesday. And I'll lend you my CD in the meantime. Here it is.'

'Thanks.' It was all starting to sink in and Tom felt rather wonderful. It was truly great that Mr Armstrong had asked him. And one good turn deserved another.

'Mr Armstrong?'

'Edwin.'

'OK, Edwin. You know Chloe, your niece?'

'Yes. What about her?'

'She's gone really weird. I've seen her twice up at Fellside, once a week ago on Saturday and then again today, and I don't know what she's doing there. Someone should tell her parents. I don't know what's going on — but something is. Poppy says she's seeing some man.'

'Chloe? But she looks terrible these days. Those clothes she's wearing!'

'Exactly. And when I saw her today she had a dirty great mark on her forehead. She's really going downhill. Anyway, I just thought you should know.'

'Yes. Well, thank you, Tom. I'll mention it to her mother.' But he knew he wouldn't. He couldn't bear to see Lynn's pain. But he would try to speak to Chloe himself.

'So, Tom, see you next week.'

'And Mr Armstrong, something else. When that fat woman, Miss Gibson, found me and the body, you know, with the book, the psalter, I told you there was a front page missing, didn't I? I could tell, because it'd been torn out, but in a neat way.'

'Yes. Alex said so too.'

'Well, I've been thinking. At first I thought someone had taken the page out of the book once Morris was dead. But there wasn't time. And anyway, why not take the whole book rather than just one page? Someone did that in the end, didn't they, so why would they rip out one page first!'

It was a good point. 'So what are you suggesting, Tom?'

'Well, just say Mr Little brought the book into college with the front page missing in the first place? I mean, say Morris was the one who took the page out? Maybe the page is at his house. And if someone found it there, that would prove there was definitely a psalter, wouldn't it? So then the police wouldn't think me and Miss Gibson were plonkers, would they?'

* * *

Paul Whinfell had dressed in casual clothes and gone back to his computer. He had a lot to think about. So far the only progress he had made with his idea was to prevent anyone else from getting in the way of it. He wanted to talk to Jenny without the fear of Mark's involvement. He put his head down and worked for about two hours until the room felt cold. Then he remembered Jenny hadn't come back.

He got up to make a cup of coffee, wondering what he should do, when he heard the back door open and the unmistakable sound of the buggy being dragged into the kitchen. 'Jenny,' he said, 'where've you been?'

'Oh, just out for a walk. I needed the space and Joseph went straight off so I walked around just to keep him sleeping. He's awake now, but calm.'

So she was talking to him. This was a good sign. She even smiled. Her walk had done her good.

'That's great. And it's the Bible study group tonight so we need to eat early. What's for tea?' he asked, but tentatively. That was the sort of question which might make Jenny explode.

But she said gently, 'I'm making a shepherd's pie. I've got some mince in the freezer.'

Shepherd's pie! That was good. His wife hadn't peeled a potato for weeks and their menus had been increasingly erratic.

'Who's coming to the Bible study group?' she asked.

'Oh, the usual suspects,' Paul said.

Jenny actually laughed. Then she said, 'I've got something to say.'

'What's that?' Paul felt a moment of terror.

'I'm sorry. Really sorry, Paul. I've been walking and thinking for hours. I've been full of my own resentment lately. I've been selfish. You're the priest and you've got a lot of responsibility; I should respect that.'

'Oh, Jenny.' He was weak with relief. He moved towards her and hugged her awkwardly as she unstrapped the now smelly baby from the buggy. This time she didn't wince or squirm away from her husband.

'He needs changing,' she laughed. 'I guess having Joseph has taught me that some of my ideas about equality are a bit impractical. This is the role I've chosen, after all. I'm going to try harder at being your wife, Paul. You deserve it.'

'That's a lovely thing to say,' her husband breathed back at her. He felt almost tearful.

'Go and get on with your work. I'll look after Joseph and then make us a cup of tea,' Jenny said softly.

A few minutes later, as he bent over his keyboard, she came into his office with a mug of hot tea and a biscuit. 'There you are,' she said, smiling.

Paul had a moment of uncertainty. This wasn't the feisty, argumentative Jenny he had fallen in love with. But it made for a more peaceful life. Whatever had made the change in her, it was wonderful. She actually looked really pretty again, he thought.

And he even liked the little headscarf she was wearing!

37

*For a man walketh in a vain shadow and disquieteth
himself in vain; he heapeth up riches and cannot tell
who shall gather them.*
Psalm 39:7

Two days later, Alex Gibson was on the phone to Suzy
Spencer. 'Pat Johnstone's back from her trip down to
Croydon to see her son. She's phoned my sister and asked us
round for drinks and nibbles this evening. It's not just social,
believe me. Pat may well be a friend of Chris's but she's not
a friend of mine. I wonder what she's after?'

'Well, you must go. The Johnstones are deeply into this
business, don't you think?'

'It depends what you mean by "this business".'

'Good point. I don't really know myself. But it'll be
interesting. Are you and Edwin coming over after the Chorus
practice again next week?'

'I don't know . . .' Alex's voice drifted away a little. She
had no idea what would happen with Edwin. He had dropped
her off at home on Shrove Tuesday night without mention-
ing meeting again, and this time there had been no kiss. They
had chatted animatedly about the evening, and about what

they hoped to discover about the murder, but Alex felt as if Marilyn Frost was somehow sitting in the back of the car. She wasn't going to mention her again, but Edwin seemed to be self-consciously avoiding saying Marilyn's name.

On Ash Wednesday Alex had gone to the Fellside Fellowship Bible study course. Suzy hadn't been there. But as if in compensation, Mark Wilson had come over to chat to Alex, saying how much better she looked.

'I'm getting over it now. I had flu really badly over New Year.'

'No wonder, after everything that happened! You must have been run down. I didn't realize it was you who found poor Morris Little,' Mark had said sympathetically. 'If I'd known, I'd have come to see you. It must have been awful. Paul never told me. I can't understand why he didn't visit you.'

'Perhaps it's because he thought Neil Clifford was my vicar?' Alex suggested.

'Seems a bit odd to me. But there again, Paul has been a bit touchy on the subject of Morris's death. He's had a lot of worries since Christmas.'

'Well, he seems happier now.'

'Yes, thank goodness.' Mark smiled.

Alex had looked across at where Paul and Jenny were talking to each other, in the centre of an admiring group which included Lynn and Chloe Clifford and Pat Johnstone. Jenny was listening to her husband with an air of near reverence and Paul was basking in it. Jenny had had her hair cropped, making her look elfin and pretty.

Chloe's putting on weight, Alex had thought. She looked lumpy now, in a heavy skirt and the inevitable headscarf, tied back so her ears stuck out. There seemed something wrong with her, but Alex thought it would be cruel to say so to Lynn who seemed so pathetically grateful that her daughter was there at all.

The next evening, after her telephone conversation with Suzy, Alex was picked up by Christine Prout to go for the drinks and nibbles at Pat Johnstone's imposing house.

'I'm not sure what this is about,' Christine said nervously, her plump chins wobbling. 'I do like Pat, but she's a bit of a cold fish. Look at the way she left David after he fell into that hole up at the convent.'

'Well, there's no harm in discovering what she wants,' Alex said.

Pat Johnstone opened the door to them wearing an expensive-looking silky top and tight black trousers, with a lot of very bright jewellery. Christine was wearing a dark tweedy skirt and a lambswool sweater, while Alex had managed to get into jeans for the first time in years. She was glad she'd put her latest designer shirt on top because Pat looked as if she was about to give a party.

'Come in! It's lovely to see you.' Pat had the air of the hostess-with-the-mostest, and Alex wondered if she'd already been at the vodka tonics. 'Do sit down. Drinkies?'

'Oh yes,' Chris breathed gratefully, 'but I'm driving, so just a little one.'

'And I'm on the wagon,' Alex said.

'Are you? That's probably why you've lost so much weight. D'you smoke? Oh, well, I hope you don't mind if I do. It is my house after all.' She cackled as if the thought was a novelty. 'I'm taking advantage of David being in hospital to spoil myself a bit. Have one of these . . .'

She pushed a lavish pile of superior supermarket party food at them and then sashayed in and out of the kitchen with ice, bottles, different types of fruit juice and a cut glass dish of lemon. She's certainly pushing the boat out, Alex thought, enjoying her freedom.

'How is David?' she asked.

'In a bad way, really. He's a bit of a funny colour and he vomited blood yesterday. Yuk. They say his liver isn't in very good nick. Well, I could have told them that, the way he used to drink.'

Then all of a sudden, with a new intensity, Pat turned to Alex and said, 'Look, there's no point beating about the bush. I bet Christine told you that David's accident really happened up at the convent . . .' Christine started to protest, but Pat waved at her imperiously. 'I knew you would talk to your sister, Chris, when I thought about it. You leak like a bucket, but your heart's in the right place. It doesn't matter. It helps, actually.' She patted Chris's hand to reassure her that she wasn't too angry. 'And that made me decide,' Pat went on emphatically. 'All this cloak and dagger stuff that Dave went in for, it's bollocks.' She cackled again. 'We're all girls together, aren't we? Follow me into his den.'

Pat walked across the parquet hallway and flung open the door to David's office. 'He'd go ballistic if he could see us!' She picked up a pile of papers from David's desk and walked back to the living room where she dumped them on the coffee table.

'Get a load of this,' she said. 'Here's masses of stuff including—' she looked triumphantly at Alex '—an estimate for buying your bungalow!'

'I can see that,' Alex said. She was momentarily staggered by the size of the offer.

'Yes!' Pat cackled. 'So listen. Now David is in hospital and can't get on with this, I want to do it myself. So that when he gets better I'm in on the act. Or if he doesn't get better — well, I can follow on with whatever he was planning. Once I've worked out what it was!' She beamed at them.

'That's a bit, well, calculating isn't it?' Christine said nervously.

'Exactly!' said Pat proudly. 'And how about it, Alex? Can we do a deal on that dump of yours? I'll give you a really high price. I've just discovered from the bank that David put loads of money in my name in case he went bankrupt. It changes everything. For a start, I don't have to give a toss about his other woman. My lawyer says that even if David left the house to his slapper, they couldn't throw me out of my own home. And there's all this cash now. I'm going to forget about tracing her through her tatty scarf,' she said to Chris.

'So you're not interested?' Alex asked.

'That tart? Nah, I'm going to pretend she doesn't exist. I've got bigger fish to fry.' She cackled. 'You see, if David dies, I don't know what's in his will. But this money in the bank account is mine. David can't take the money back while he's ill—' then her face clouded '—but if he gets better he'll get it back off me somehow.'

She was still scared of David while he was alive; Alex could see that. But dead, he was an asset. What a couple! She and her husband were as bad as each other, Alex thought. Pat was still explaining . . .

'If I buy the bungalow I'm covered, even if he gets better. I'll tell him you suddenly decided to sell and I had to act fast. But I'll make sure the property is in my name. It would be the only thing I've got of my own. It'll be much harder to get a house off me than a bank account. Crafty, eh? I've got the bugger!'

Alex swallowed the urge to say: I'm not sure about that. And anyway this sick man is your husband, the father of your kids — but she reckoned Pat was well beyond that sort of appeal. She was unsure what to answer.

'Well, I'll certainly think about selling up,' she said. She looked down at David's papers. A photocopy of something which seemed rather familiar peeped out at her from under the lists, property details and plans. 'What's this, Pat?' Alex thought back to that drunken conversation with Pat at the Workhaven Motel. 'Is this the photocopy from the old book you talked about?'

'Oh, that? With the big Q on it? God knows. David collected all sorts of stuff.'

'Could I borrow it?' Pat's eyes narrowed. 'It's just because I'm interested in calligraphy,' Alex lied. 'You know, old writing. It's only a photocopy, after all. I'll let you have it back at the Chorus on Tuesday.'

Pat was clearly wondering whether a refusal would discourage Alex from selling the bungalow to her. And she was finding it hard to work out where an old page of a book might come into it. David did sometimes just pick up a load of junk — and she needed Alex on side.

'Oh, all right then,' she said. 'Take it. I'm having another drink.' She tottered towards the kitchen to get more ice from the fridge. She said over her shoulder, 'I can't see what it's got to do with anything anyway!'

But I can, Alex thought, feeling cold in Pat's overheated lounge. Suddenly she was absolutely sure it was at the very core of things, because she was convinced it was a photocopy of the front page of Morris Little's psalter.

* * *

When Alex reached home a few hours later, having been dropped off by a rather shocked and quiet Christine Prout, she put the photocopy on her kitchen table before even taking off her red coat. Why was she so sure?

But she was absolutely certain. The photocopy was exactly the same dimensions as the book she had seen in Morris's hand. The print typeface seemed familiar, too. It wasn't a brilliant facsimile because some of the ink was smudged and she guessed it had been copied on an old fax machine — odd, because surely David would have had access to a really good copier at his office. But it was the wording which fascinated her.

The Psalms of Lament, it said in beautiful illuminated Latin script. And underneath, *Chants by Cecil Quaile Woods*. And under that, in a smaller but equally beautiful typeface, she read, *Dedicated to my friend John Stainer*. And there was something else. In inked handwriting was added *and to my son Henry Whinfell*, with a flourishing signature alongside. Fascinating. Hadn't Edwin said that Quaile Woods was the local Victorian hero? A churchman who lived for his flock? Yet he had signed a copy of his psalter for his son. So much for the saintly celibate priest!

And from Edwin's perspective, as Morris Little had indicated, there really was a strong connection between the famous

Victorian composer Sir John Stainer and the Cumbrian clergyman. Here was the evidence of their friendship.

But who was this Henry Whinfell whom the priest acknowledged in handwriting as his child? And why wasn't he called Henry Quaile Woods if he was the man's son? On a whim, she sat down at her computer and went into Google. And there he was — Henry Whinfell, the biographer of Cecil Quaile Woods as listed just in passing by the Norbridge Local History Society of which Morris Little had been a leading light. Had the son written the biography of the famous but secret father?

I must tell Edwin about this, she thought. Never mind Marilyn Frost and her mysterious hold over him, and his famous reticence. They would have to talk again — soon. This was just too good to keep to herself.

She rang Edwin's number and was elated to sense the delight in his voice in response. But you ain't heard nothing yet, she thought!

38

Teach me thy way, O Lord, and I will walk in thy truth;
O knit my heart unto thee, that I may fear thy name.
Psalm 86:11

'Chloe!'

Edwin nearly walked past his niece in Norbridge town centre, but caught sight of her just as she was turning a corner. He had been thinking about Alex and her amazing find: the dedication to Quaile Woods' book of psalm settings! Even a photocopy was amazing. He could hardly wait to see it. As a result he had almost missed Chloe. He had gone into Norbridge to collect some cleaning on Saturday morning and suddenly realized that it was Chloe coming out of Tesco's. She looked so different these days. And his head was spinning.

On top of everything else, he'd finally managed to speak to Freddie Fabrikant, who had sounded very cagey but had eventually admitted that his leg plaster wasn't coming off until Easter Week. Could the Stainer concert be postponed? It was a big decision, but Freddie was the only possible bass soloist at this stage. It was a huge nuisance. And Freddie had sounded peculiarly tetchy, as if he was on the verge of saying something else but felt uncharacteristically inhibited. It was odd. Edwin thought about Freddie's missing hour on the day Morris had died, but put it out of his mind because there was something else more urgent to think about.

When would he meet Alex? He desperately wanted to see the missing psalter page, but whatever he did next would set the tone for their whole relationship, and it was another big decision. But here he was to pick up a clean jacket. Funny how the practical things were the real deciders: if he wasn't thinking about taking her out to dinner, why was he rushing into town for the dry cleaning?

'Hi!' he said to his niece, after she had turned round in surprise. He saw that she had a heavy bag of groceries. That was odd, too, he thought. Lynn was into Fair Trade and fresh vegetables, but Chloe's bag was bulging with packet food.

'Oh, hello,' Chloe said in a dull sort of way.

'How are you?'

'Fine.'

'Would you like a lift?'

'No thanks, Uncle Edwin. I'm getting the bus.' She stood awkwardly looking at him, saying nothing more, as if waiting for his permission to go.

'We haven't had a chat for ages,' he said. 'Not since Christmas.'

'No, well, you were too busy solving murders then, weren't you? All of you,' she said with a sudden flash of her old spirit.

'Actually, if we were doing that I think we made a mistake.' Edwin laughed ruefully.

'What d'you mean?' Chloe looked suddenly curious. It was the first spark of interest he had seen in her in months.

'Oh, just that a few of us think that Morris Little's murder isn't as straightforward as it seems. Why don't you come to Figaro's with me and I'll tell you all about it?'

That might give me a chance to talk to her and to find out what's wrong, he thought. There was a sort of griminess about Chloe he couldn't pin down. He thought that maybe everything about her was just a little bit less than squeaky clean. Her hair was cut short and stuck out of the inevitable scarf in an unkempt way; her clothes looked dusty. He felt a moment of unease about using the murder to keep her interested — after all, hadn't he told Tom Firth not to mention the psalter to anyone? But what harm could there be in talking to Chloe?

Most importantly, she was his niece, and looking at her standing in the car park, a caricature of her old self, he realized how much he loved her. He had known her since before she was born. This wasn't how Chloe was supposed to be. He suddenly thought that he should try anything to rebuild their old bond.

Chloe certainly looked more engaged. 'All right,' she said.

She trundled ahead of him to Figaro's, which was less crowded than usual. It was the first time he had seen tables outside, even though the shopping precinct was sheltered and covered. But it was still too cold for them to sit out. Inside the steamy coffee shop, he and Chloe found a squashy sofa and she sank into it.

'What would you like?' he asked.

'Peppermint tea, please.'

'Are you sure? You used to like hot chocolate?' He could see that Chloe was fatter but she didn't look particularly healthy. He was surprised that Lynn was letting her eat ready meals. Typical of the young, he thought — pre-packaged dinners and detox tea drinking! Totally inconsistent.

'No, just the tea,' she said firmly.

He picked an espresso for himself and a mug of tea for Chloe, and rejoined her on the sofa.

'So what d'you mean, you were wrong about Morris Little and the Frosts?' she asked bluntly. Her face was more alert than it had been for ages. He had seen her once a week at the Abbey Chorus practices when she drifted in and out, and he had tried to talk to her once at Lynn's, where she had been on her knees scrubbing the kitchen floor. He'd received no response other than a dutiful grunt.

But this time she even gave him eye contact as he told her about how he and Alex, with Robert and Suzy, had banded together to discuss what had happened. He kept it light and made it sound as if they were four cheerful chums driven by curiosity.

'It was Suzy and Alex who got us going on this,' he said.

Chloe nodded sagely. 'Female intuition,' she said.

Six months earlier, such a remark would have been said with rolling eyes and an air of taking the mickey, but now Chloe was deadpan and deadly serious. He glanced at her. She was thinking hard, he could tell. He went on to tell her about the psalter and the way the accidents seemed to have a link to the Psalms, without breaking any confidences about David Johnstone and his fall. Even without that, it was the sort of colourful rendition he thought she'd enjoy.

'Well, there you go,' he said. 'One thing's for sure. A psalter in Morris's hand went missing. And Freddie Fabrikant was attacked by the bulls of Basan. You can't square that with the Frosts. We think someone else was lurking in the college that night. Interesting, isn't it?'

Chloe nodded and put her nose into her cup. He seemed to have caught her attention. And it's even more interesting now, Edwin thought to himself, if Alex really has found a photocopy of the psalter's front page. When Alex had called him late the previous evening, excitement in her voice, he had loved the warm sound of her, no longer tense and defensive. But he was careful not to suggest to his niece that his relationship with Alex was anything other than friendly, and, for reasons he couldn't explain, he said nothing about the photocopy of the psalter which Alex had found. Perhaps that was her territory, until he saw it for himself.

Chloe had said nothing, and he suddenly knew he had lost her. He tried to regain her attention. 'And what about you, Chloe? Are you thinking about going back to university?'

She looked at him as if he had started to speak a foreign language. 'What? Of course not! Don't be ridiculous.' She laughed in a rather harsh way. 'No,' she said firmly. 'My work is here.'

The pompous phrase sounded rather ludicrous. He reminded himself that Chloe was only eighteen and had always been young for her age, despite being noisy and self-opinionated. Eighteen is nothing, he thought . . . she's a child.

Yet Marilyn had only been eighteen when they met and twenty-two when they parted, and she had been totally in command of herself. How different two people could be.

And what the hell was he going to do about Marilyn?

While he was distracted, Chloe had stood up, clutching her groceries. 'Thanks for the tea, Uncle Edwin. I've got to go.'

'Really?'

She was already on her way. He watched her traipse out of the coffee shop, and his heart sank. His attempts to reach her had been useless.

* * *

Robert and Suzy were having soup for lunch in the kitchen at The Briars. Jake had gone to Newcastle for the day with Ollie to buy some musical stuff and Molly was at her new best friend's.

'I've been wondering,' Robert said. 'With all this talk about property — you know, Johnstone and Alex's bungalow and so on — what do you think The Briars would be worth?'

'I've no idea. More than I got for my house in Tarn Acres, certainly.'

'And you've still got your half of that money in the bank, haven't you?'

'Robert, if this about me living here rent free . . .'

'Of course it isn't! And you more than pay your way with the bills and the groceries. Anyway, we all knew this was a short-term emergency thing. No, I was thinking more about whether we should consider buying something else. Together.'

Suzy's minestrone slipped off the spoon and splashed back in the dish.

The Briars had once belonged to Mary's family, but they had sold it years before and Robert had struggled to buy it back for her. He and Mary had lived in it for twenty-five years, but they hadn't been able to afford to do much with it and now the strain was beginning to show. The Briars wasn't just untidy these days, it was becoming a bit dilapidated.

'Well, Robert, somewhere in the far distant future I supposed something like that might happen. But to be honest . . .'

'Just getting life for the children back on an even keel has taken up all your energy, hasn't it?'

'Yes. It's only since I talked to Rachel that I realized it. But I also realize we do have to think about the practical side of things. Whatever happens,' Suzy took a deep breath, 'I need to get a divorce. Nigel doesn't really want me. I'm just a handy stopgap until the next supermodel comes along. Or to be realistic, the next available bit of totty. He isn't going to change.'

'And the children?'

'They love their dad, but he was never really a family man. Children were accessories for him, the sort of thing you acquired at a certain life stage, a justification for the detached four-bedroomed house and 4x4 car. He'll be wonderful when they're older and want to go Christmas shopping in Rome or New York. As long as Molly stays pretty of course.'

'She will, if she's like you!'

'Smarmy!'

'But seriously, Suzy, we should think about getting somewhere new, together.'

She stood up to put the dishes in the sink. 'It's a thought. Thank you, Robert.' She crept up behind him and kissed him.

* * *

The phone rang in Alex's bungalow. She dropped the property section of the local paper, which she had been reading with new interest, and grabbed the phone. She was desperate for it to be Edwin.

'Hi!' he said with a sort of strained nonchalance. 'Sorry I didn't ring earlier. I met Chloe in Norbridge.'

'How is she?'

'Awful. I tried hard to get her to talk. I even told her about our discussion on the murder and about Morris holding a psalter, to try and generate some interest. I hope you don't mind?'

'Why should I mind? It was you who wanted us to be discreet.'

'True. And talking of the psalter, I really want to see the page you found last night.'

'You didn't mind me ringing you so late?'

'No. Not at all. It's exciting. Would you like to meet for supper? Should I pick you up? Sevenish?'

'Oh yes!' Alex could not keep the relief and excitement out of her voice. 'That would be lovely.' And it would give her the afternoon to do some research. She had been too excited the night before to concentrate, and this morning she had found herself waiting for Edwin to call, but now her mind could engage.

Whinfell was a most unusual name. So, Quaile Woods had a son called Whinfell, acknowledged in his own handwriting on the dedication of his psalter. And the current vicar of Fellside, nearly a hundred and fifty years later, was also a Whinfell — Paul Whinfell. Alex quickly Googled Paul and found all his details on the Uplands Team Ministry website. Paul Whinfell had been born in Bristol, hundreds of miles away from Cumbria. But there were so few Whinfells that it was quite possible to believe that Rev Paul had Cumbrian antecedents. And who could say what homing instinct, or even half-remembered family chatter and buried memories, had led him to want to come back up north? There had to be a connection.

When you knew your stuff it wasn't too hard, and Alex had retained her subscription to several genealogy websites. She logged into ancestry.co.uk and clicked on the 1861 census. The Reverend Cecil Quaile Woods came up as resident in Cumbria. Of course. He had started his ministry here in 1860 — hadn't Edwin told her that? But there was no Henry Whinfell. Nor was Henry there in 1871. There were a smattering of other Whinfells though — a dock worker in Workhaven and his wife, and their daughter, a child called Harriet. But as Alex tapped on, she found that in the census of 1881 a Henry Whinfell was listed in the parish of Uplands, the only person with that name.

Alex took a deep breath. Going into the records, she found that Henry Whinfell had been a baby in 1881, and was listed as son to the woman named Harriet Whinfell. He had been living at Uplands Rectory and his mother Harriet was named as a spinster and servant, unmarried. So he was definitely an illegitimate child. Her fingers skipped over the keyboard. By the 1891 census the Whinfells had gone from the rectory, but Henry was living with an elderly couple in Workhaven and was named in his relationship to the head of the household as grandson. His mother, Harriet Whinfell, had disappeared. Presumably she had married and was listed somewhere under another name, leaving her illegitimate child with her parents.

What about the census of 1901? Alex clicked on it, keyed the name Whinfell into the search and clicked again. Up came the answer. The old couple must have been dead by then because there was only one Whinfell listed in the whole of England. He was twenty years old, and now using his full name of Henry Quaile Whinfell. He was listed as living in Bristol with a couple called Fortune, Harriet and Fred. His relationship to Fred Fortune was listed as stepson. So quite clearly, Henry had left Cumbria to live with his natural mother when his grandparents died. And if there was only one Whinfell in Bristol in 1901 it was highly probable that he was the ancestor of Paul Whinfell, also from Bristol.

Alex sat back, drained. There was no need to carry on clicking, though there would be lots more work to do to take the lineage further forward. It had taken a few hours and it was in no way conclusive, but it looked at the very least as if Paul Whinfell of Fellside Fellowship had a long-term family connection with Cecil Quaile Woods, whose book of psalm chants dedicated by hand to his bastard son had been in Morris Little's possession the night he died.

But there was one missing link. How had the photocopy of the dedication ended up in David Johnstone's possession? There was no evidence that Johnstone knew about the Whinfell and Quaile Woods relationship. But Morris was into genealogy. He probably guessed that Paul was the descendant of Quaile Woods. And what had Mark told Suzy about Paul? That he had been wanting to meet Morris . . .

Alex's thoughts were heading in one direction. Paul Whinfell had been planning to see Morris. Paul Whinfell was into genealogy. And Paul Whinfell seemed to have something to hide. So for some unknown reason, was it Paul who had beaten Morris to death?

39

Shall thy jealousy burn like fire for ever?
Psalm 79:5

'But why would Paul kill Morris?' Edwin asked as they paused after their main course at the beautiful country restaurant he had chosen. He had perused the photocopy of the psalter's dedication and was unsure whether to be more excited about Quaile Woods' acknowledgement of his illegitimate child, or the connection between the Cumbrian composer of church music and the famous organist of St Paul's Cathedral, Sir John Stainer.

Around them the sandstone walls glowed. There was a high barn-style roof and a huge fire, despite the spring daffodils and irises piled in massive glass vases on the bar. There were candles on the table and a piano playing, and they had already enjoyed the best part of a bottle of wine. I ought to stop, Edwin thought, or we'll have to abandon the car and get a taxi.

'I don't know. But remember what Robert said. Look for who could have done it, not who might have done it.'

'And what about Freddie's accident? And David and the pit? And the Psalms connection?'

'I told you, Edwin, I don't know. But I do believe that Paul Whinfell is Cecil Quaile Woods' great-great-grandson. It's not that hard to discover, and Paul's supposed to be interested in genealogy. He must know himself. Maybe there's a reason why he's keeping it secret? Maybe he killed Morris rather than let it come out? It would certainly tarnish Quaile Woods' image!'

'But it's only conjecture, Alex. Harriet Whinfell could have got pregnant by anyone, and called the baby Henry Quaile out of respect for the vicar!'

'Then how do you explain the handwritten dedication? It says *to my son Henry Whinfell*. It's a declaration!'

Edwin looked at her. She was animated, and her beautiful skin glowed. Her hair was long and dark auburn, glossy and catching the light from the log fire. But the most important thing was the empathy he felt with her. She's like me, he thought, a dark horse. We're both intense, and we understand each other.

With Marilyn he had been like a moth attracted to the light. He could see her in his mind's eye, running towards him with the sun behind her, her long Titian red hair flowing like toffee, with all the different lights in its curls, and her white skin and eyes like sapphires. She had been such a beautiful girl, and so open to the joy of the world around her. Whereas Alex had experienced the pain of disappointment. He had once heard someone say there was no depression without false expectations. He never wanted false expectation again.

She said, 'What are you thinking about? Marilyn?'

So she had guessed. 'Yes, I am. I spoke to her today. She phoned me this afternoon.'

Alex felt a knot round her ribs. It was the stifling scum of thick ropey jealousy, just as she had felt it for Sam's new wife and child. The wine came back sourly into her throat and she knew her lips were tightening in a downward scowl.

'That must have been nice for you!' How petty it sounded.

'Yes.' Edwin smiled sweetly, unaware of the bitterness in her voice. 'She sounded well. And the good news is, she's going to come and meet us all.'

'Oh, great!'

'What's wrong?' Edwin had been looking into the fire with a happy smile. Then he glanced back at Alex and saw the darkness on her face.

'Oh, you know, Marilyn this and Marilyn that . . . I'm fed up with all this mystery, actually. So in a way I'm glad she's going to show up and we can all get the measure of her.' It was snide, and it wasn't true. Alex suddenly realized that the last thing she wanted was to meet the beautiful and enigmatic Marilyn Frost.

'Alex . . .' Edwin slipped his hand across the table and took hers. It felt cool and silky, and her long pale brown fingers looked like the smooth sandstone in the boulders in the wall behind her. Her nails were beautiful, long and almond-shaped, a perfect dark pink. 'If you think I'm in love with Marilyn you're wrong. That's all over. It has to be. But I promised her I wouldn't talk about her after she went. To anyone. And I've kept my promise.'

'So she must be pretty special.'

'Believe me, she is!'

The intensity in his voice made the knot in Alex's stomach tighten to an unbearable degree. I can't bear to go through all this again, she thought. 'D'you mind if we go home, Edwin? Could you get the bill? I don't feel very well. It's a while since I've drunk so much.'

She really did look paler. As he looked at her, she got up and walked towards the ladies' toilet. She was there for a while, leaning with her head over the sink. The world was spinning round again, but she didn't know whether it was wine or shock. Or apprehension. They had had such a lovely evening, talking so closely about their work and the past, with no constraints, until Marilyn had been mentioned. Alex shook her head, trying to displace the awful memories that crowded in like triumphant demons from Hieronymus

Bosch, each prodding her with a pitchfork. She saw herself screaming outside Sam's new home at one o'clock in the morning, and then scratching him on the face in a black moment of rage. And she saw the car wreck when she could have been killed. Or worse, killed someone else.

I could do murder, she thought suddenly. Suzy couldn't. Robert certainly couldn't. But I could. And Edwin could too. That was one of the things binding them. But I don't want this, she thought. I don't want this intensity. I really don't want to sink back into jealousy and hate. It's better not to love than to love to distraction.

She washed her hands carefully, and made a decision that would banish the demons. There was no point in trying to have a relationship of any sort with Edwin. She was falling in love with him, and love for her meant passion and drama and a switchback ride of highs and lows. The companionship she saw in Robert and Suzy, the easy family atmosphere they had created from the least likely ingredients, was not for her.

She held her head up when she went back to the table. Edwin saw someone almost magisterial in her calm. She's beautiful, he thought.

'Shall we go?' she said. 'I can settle up with you in the car.'

'No really, it's my treat. I've been looking forward to this all day. Did I tell you,' he said, trying to lighten the atmosphere, 'that I spoke to Freddie this afternoon? He wants the concert postponed until he's had his plaster casts removed. I talked to the Dean and we're thinking about doing it on Good Friday instead. I know sacred oratorios are traditionally done on Palm Sunday but for *The Crucifixion* it fits because Stainer wrote it for St Marylebone Church in London and they do it every Good Friday.'

'But if we do that we'll lose some singers who are going away for Easter. I know the Dixons are off to Spain.'

'They're no great loss, to be honest. I think one of the other sopranos is away too, which is a bit more worrying as the top line is quite weak. I could do with three more good sopranos, but I've no idea where I could get them. Thank goodness for you. It's been much better since you joined.'

Alex smiled at him gratefully. Instead of making a scene, provoking her as Sam had done, drunk on his own selfish happiness, Edwin was calming her and keeping her with him. He held her coat for her.

'That's a nice thing to say.'

'And Tom's girlfriend will be back from university by Good Friday. He was delighted when I said we'd postpone it till then. It suits everyone.' They left the warmth and scent of the restaurant and walked out, down shallow stone steps and through the garden to the car park.

'Are you feeling better now we're outside?' he asked.

The night closed around them. It was peaceful and Edwin was bending towards her, solicitously. For a few seconds Alex thought: it's all right, yes, I can hack this. But that was just an invitation to the demons over her shoulder to shout taunts from the playgrounds of hell: 'Hey, what about Marilyn. She's really special. He said so!'

In the car Edwin said, 'When will you be able to get your licence back?'

'It isn't so much my licence that I need to get back, as my nerve. I could have started driving again a few years ago, I think. But to be honest I haven't thought about it. I haven't got a car so it doesn't matter.'

'But it would help so much, living around here.'

'Yes, if I stay here.'

Without speaking, Edwin pulled up at the side of the road. 'You wouldn't move away from here, would you?'

'Why not? Pat Johnstone might be a greedy old crone, but on the other hand I could get a lot of money for the bungalow from her, or someone else. Even splitting it with my sister would leave me well enough off to buy something decent.' But not in London, she thought. Where the hell would I go?

'Don't go away,' Edwin said. 'Look, I know my relationship with Marilyn is hard for anyone to understand.

People think I'm weird, and that if a man has a normal sex drive, it has to be satisfied. They accept that it's OK to turn to anything — porn, prostitution, infidelity, all the rotten things you can think of — rather than just stop having sex. But it isn't really like that. Lots of men are like me, hurt in some way. And then they just withdraw from the whole tacky business.'

'So has there been no one since Marilyn?'

'I've had two holiday affairs. And there was a married woman in the north-east for a while.'

'So there was no one to replace her?'

'No,' he said. 'Not till now.' He was looking ahead, not touching her. Then he turned to her. 'Alex, I know I'm going hopelessly slowly. But please, please bear with me. Give this a chance. It doesn't have to be a rollercoaster, you know. Between the two of us, we're both old enough and young enough not to have to rush things.'

Alex felt her spine tingle. 'But you don't really know me. I was mad, literally mad, with jealousy of Sam's woman and her child. I know I'm capable of really deeply bad feelings. I can feel them starting now, towards Marilyn. I'm really not sure if I can cope.'

Edwin said, 'It will be all right, Alex. When you see Marilyn, you'll understand.'

I doubt it, Alex thought.

* * *

On Tuesday, after the Chorus practice, Robert and Suzy sat in the kitchen at The Briars with Alex and Edwin, and they talked through the new facts again. The photocopy of the dedication at the front of Cecil Quaile Woods' psalter was in front of them.

'So you're pretty sure that Paul from Fellside is a descendant of Quaile Woods on the wrong side of the blanket. Which is interesting, but surely not important?' Robert asked.

'It is if Paul had arranged a meeting with Morris. We know that from Mark, who says the meeting was cancelled. Maybe Paul lied to Mark and actually met Morris.'

'But where does David Johnstone come into it? How did he get the photocopy?'

'That's been worrying me,' Alex confessed. She moved to get her coffee and accidentally nudged the photocopy, which was on light, curly fax paper. It slid off the kitchen table and floated gracefully to the floor, falling face down.

'I hope it's all right,' Suzy said anxiously as Robert scrambled for it. 'The floor needs a bit of a wash. It's rather greasy.'

Robert laughed. 'It's fine. There's just a blob on the corner.' He put the photocopy back on the table. There was a tiny grease stain now on the top left-hand corner. Idly, Alex picked it up again, and turned it over.

'Hey,' she said, 'there are pencil marks up here I didn't notice before. The grease from your floor makes them stand out, Suzy.'

'There's no need to be quite so loud about it!'

'No, seriously. Look.'

Alex had put the photocopy face down on the table. They could all see two letters in the top right-hand corner. They were an M and an L.

Edwin said, 'I recognize that hand — even just those letters. That's Morris Little's writing.'

'So the photocopy was originally Morris's? That makes no sense. Why did it end up with David Johnstone? He and Morris hated each other.'

'But that doesn't mean that they couldn't meet. Maybe Morris gave this to Johnstone in return for something. Or to prove that there was a Stainer link with Quaile Woods. Or for any number of reasons . . .'

They sat looking at the greasy, smudged photocopy of the dedication page to Quaile Woods' psalter. 'Well, I know that short of a miracle we'll never find another copy of this,' Edwin said slowly. 'Or the rest of the psalter either. I've been searching for Quaile Woods' version of the psalms of lament for about a year now. Nothing has ever turned up.'

'But don't you see?' Robert said excitedly. 'Morris must have had the original to photocopy it! If you look closely at this photocopy, you can see that it's the copy of a sheet that has been carefully torn out of the book. Look . . .' They peered with him at the faintly ragged edge which ran down the inside of the printed sheet.

'You're right!' Edwin said. 'And when I was talking to Tom Firth last week he made a really good point about Morris having removed the page himself!'

'So the originals might well be somewhere in Morris's house.'

'But I searched the place for interesting material,' Edwin said. 'And Norma gave me access to everything. There were no old documents there. Believe me, I'd give my eyeteeth for anything that proves a link between Quaile Woods and Stainer!'

'But you said yourself that Morris's filing system was idiosyncratic at best,' Alex said.

'I'm going to see Norma sometime soon,' said Robert. 'I could have another look for the originals, Edwin. It would be a very exciting find.'

'But we still get back to asking how come the photocopy ended up with David Johnstone? Was Morris trying to convince him of something? Was there money in it?'

'We could always ask Johnstone,' Suzy said sensibly.

Robert shook his head. 'Last time I saw Johnstone he didn't seem capable of a friendly chat. He's in a bad way. Whoever lugged him into his car and set it off down that back road might end up as guilty of murder as the person who brained Morris Little.'

'And then knocked his teeth in, psalmist style!'

Suzy rose to make more coffee. 'You know,' she said, 'this is all very well but we're not really getting anywhere. The Frosts are still banged up on remand and no one seems to care. Did you get anywhere with their sister, Edwin?'

Edwin nodded slowly. He was embarrassed, Alex thought. He was almost growling when he said: 'Actually, she'd like to meet you all. It would be great if you could invite Marilyn here, to The Briars. She can only come on Mothering Sunday, two weeks on Sunday. I could pick her up from the station and bring her over. Would that be OK?'

40

O how amiable are thy dwellings, thou Lord of hosts!
Psalm 84:1

February and March are in some ways the hardest months
to bear in the North Country. Winter can be cruel but you
know where you are. In this no man's land of the seasons, the
crisp frosts and even the occasional drama of snow are over,
followed by endless grey rain.

There was mud all over The Briars. Even when Jake and
Molly left their shoes by the front door they seemed to walk
damp and mire through the hall. The carpet, which had been
there for many years, was now an indeterminate shade of
porridge colour with suspicious blobs on it. The back door,
which led into the kitchen, seemed perpetually surrounded
by discarded boots and children's coats, some of which ended
up on the floor and impeded anyone getting in. Mary's once-
bright copper pans hanging on the wall were now dingy, and
Suzy's attempts to come to terms with the stove had led to
smoky patches up the walls. Robert was competent at basic
DIY, but he could hardly be described as keen, nor would
he be rushed by anyone. After a howling draught threatened
to give them pneumonia, he finally got round to mending

the smashed window pane in the cold little downstairs lavatory. It had been broken by Jake's football. In fairness, one Saturday Robert painted the walls in Molly's room a ghastly fuchsia pink which thrilled her and which Suzy thought was way above the call of duty, though she spotted that he hadn't moved the wardrobe but just left that corner magnolia. Molly didn't notice — she thought it was 'supercool'.

Suzy was working extra shifts now as the production schedule for *Geordies in Space* hotted up. She had tentatively suggested to Robert that they get a cleaner for a while, knowing that Mary had always done all the housework herself. To her surprise Robert agreed, and even put an enquiry email out at the college, which resulted in Wanda Wisley's 'daily' fitting them in for a couple of weeks.

'I'm pretty busy at their place,' she said. 'That gadgee's a pain, with his legs in plaster. He keeps roaring at me not to touch things, and then roaring at me when I leave 'em alone. And she's pretty peaky all the time. Tummy bug, or so she says.'

This season is truly dreary, Suzy thought. We shouldn't have to give up things for Lent — Lent gives up on us! A few days after their last meeting with Edwin and Alex, there was a bout of particularly nasty weather, with wind howling down from the fells and lashing rain. Robert discovered that the storm had beaten down the door on the old garage at the side of the house, and he asked Edwin to come over at the weekend and help him and Jake board it up. Alex came with him and, while the two men and the boy struggled with chipboard and hammers, unlikely workmen, Alex and Suzy made coffee.

'Have you thought any more about the murder?' Suzy asked.

'Not really. I don't suppose there's much we can do. It will be up to Marilyn, I suppose, to try and get the thing looked into.'

'How do you feel about meeting her?'

'Strange. I'm trying not to think about it. Last Friday, Edwin and I went to hear the *St Matthew Passion* in Keswick and on Friday we're going over to Newcastle again. We get on very well. But I guess everything's on hold until the famous Marilyn has been and gone.'

'Odd that she can only come on Mothering Sunday. Is she seeing her family?'

'The whole business of Marilyn is odd, if you ask me. I get the impression from Edwin that she has nothing to do with her mother anymore, so why this Mother's Day visit is so vital I don't know!'

'And you can't ask?'

'Absolutely not. Edwin seems to have made some sort of promise he won't break. Talking about Marilyn is strictly off the agenda.'

On the Wednesday of the following week, Suzy met Lynn Clifford at McCrea's.

'How's Chloe?' she asked.

'Oh, much the same,' said Lynn brightly. But there was a tic at the corner of her eye, and her smile was strained. Suzy took a deep breath.

'Look, Lynn, I've no idea myself about teenage girls. Not yet. But I've seen Chloe in town and she's not dressing like the other girls. She looks rather, well, odd. And she's very keen on the Bible study course.'

Lynn smiled softly. 'Well, that's a good thing, isn't it?'

'Oh, I'm not knocking what you and Neil do. But isn't Chloe, well, a bit extreme? She's very intense about it, isn't she? I mean, aren't you just the tiniest bit worried?'

To Suzy's horror Lynn's face crumpled as if she was going to burst into tears, but she recovered herself. 'Suzy, I have faith in God. Neil and I realize that Chloe is going through an odd phase. But we believe that if we pray about it, we'll be given understanding.'

'Yes, well, I often think that if God had meant us just to pray about things he wouldn't have given us legs!'

Lynn laughed. 'But in this case, Suzy, I don't know what else we can do! I'm just grateful that Chloe came home and didn't go through all this in Leeds, away from us. And I'm there a lot more for her. She may not realize it, but I'm ready when she is. She'll come round, I know she will.'

I hope so, Suzy thought.

At what was now officially the Lent Course at Fellside Fellowship the next evening, Suzy sat with Lynn and Alex, while Chloe was in the front row looking devotedly at Paul and Jenny. Suzy noticed that, this week, Jenny had a prettier version of Chloe's shapeless headscarf. Jenny's cropped wavy hair poked out from under it in short pretty curls, and she had chosen a striking blue colour. These scarves must be a new fashion, Suzy thought. She made a mental note to catch up with the latest celebrity trends. Maybe we're all supposed to be into Soviet chic, she thought.

She found that she was looking round the room, rather than concentrating on Jenny's analysis of Psalm 71. It was tedious stuff, but Jenny actually smiled once or twice and glanced adoringly at her husband. The only other new development was that Mark Wilson was off on a Norbridge Council away-day, and Freddie Fabrikant had been brought to the meeting by Wanda, who had pushed his wheelchair in, taken one look at the assembled company, and disappeared faster than you could say Dimitri Shostakovich.

Could Freddie have been involved in Morris's murder? He was certainly big enough to smack somebody effectively, and he might not know his own strength. But wasn't Paul a more likely candidate? There was something rather neurotic about him, Suzy thought, though she knew that these days she was always suspicious of clergymen. She thought they were all inclined to be excessive and egotistical, while she expected women priests to show common sense and under-standing. It was irrational, Suzy knew, but not entirely. The few women priests she had known had all been sensible, kindly and inclusive, whereas the men . . . Although she had to concede that Neil Clifford seemed OK.

But what about women murderers? It could have been a lucky blow which finished off Morris. Jenny certainly seemed passionate enough to take things to extremes. She was coldly distant with Suzy and had a resentful manner when dealing with other women. Maybe she disliked her husband being wrapped up in genealogical research and had taken this out on Morris. Unlikely, though. Pat Johnstone was at the Bible study meeting, too and, from what Alex had said, Pat was calculating enough to have a go at anyone who stood in her way. Even Alex could have done the murder. She was strong enough and she had no alibi either. She had mentioned how much she disliked Morris Little for his nasty remarks about her drinking.

'And now for our final prayer,' Paul said, and Suzy snapped back from her imaginings.

Then they filtered out into the night, and she drove home to find that some of the work Robert had done on the garage door had collapsed. There was muck all over the hall floor, which he had walked in after going outside to do emergency repairs.

The Briars seemed rather sad, she thought. One of the light bulbs had gone in the hall and the old mahogany staircase looked shadowy and gloomy as a result. The living room, where they'd had so many lovely fires in the depths of winter, now had a blind black dusty socket where the glowing flames should be, and smelt of cold ash. She noticed how grey the paintwork looked. And the cat had trodden dirty little pawprints over the cream easy chair, one of the few nice things she had brought from her own home.

Poor house! she thought. The Briars was a lovely place but it certainly needed some attention. She thought again about Robert's suggestion that they should find something of their own. If they were going to sell it they would need to do some work. And it made sense. But somehow she didn't feel the enthusiasm for the idea that she would have expected.

Robert was in the kitchen putting his tools away. 'Bloody door!' he said.

Suzy laughed. It was nice to hear Robert getting cross, something he usually left to her. She went over to him and gave him a hug.

* * *

A few evenings later, Alex couldn't sleep. She got up at one o'clock in the morning and pushed her feet into her slippers. She pattered next door into her kitchen which, like her bedroom, had a view over the fell to where it drooped into the quarry.

She made a cup of tea and stood looking out of the window. The back of the house was bleak. There was nothing between it and Norbridge. The bungalow stood alone on the ridge.

As Alex watched, she saw something which at first she couldn't place and then she realized it was only a light, on the hill to her left. Was it poachers? she wondered. Or a car? But there was only one source and it wasn't moving. She blinked, and then it had gone. Funny, she thought. It looked as if it was coming from the old convent. But then again, it might have been her imagination. Or a spaceship coming to turn them all into aliens. Alex was getting tired of constant speculation. The Little murder just went round and round in circles in her head. Like the others, she felt the Frosts might have been wrongly accused, but Alex had a tougher attitude. The boys had done little to help themselves and by confessing, at least to start with, they had given the police every reason to haul them in.

The Frosts were typical of a lot of families, she thought. A teenage unmarried mother from a bad background has one child and then teams up with a series of other men to produce a drug-ridden brood. Except that there was some confusion about how many siblings the lovely Marilyn actually had. She and Edwin had an unspoken moratorium on discussing the matter in detail, and, though she picked up the odd detail, she still hadn't quite worked out who Marilyn's sisters were.

Though she didn't want to do so, she found herself thinking about it again. It was odd that Marilyn hadn't visited her brothers earlier. What had Edwin said? — that she hadn't been allowed to. But that was nonsense, wasn't it? The Frost boys weren't in solitary confinement!

And why was Marilyn so loath to come back to Norbridge? If *my* sister were remanded in custody you wouldn't be able to keep me away, Alex thought, but then the very idea of fifty-year-old Chris being in trouble with the police was really quite funny. Unless you knew Pat Johnstone. Now there was an older woman who was capable of crime. Alex shuddered.

She left the window and the cold dark stretch of countryside beyond, and went back to the snugness of her bedroom. She tried reading for a while, but all her thoughts and fears about Marilyn Frost went round in her head.

And then a thought dropped into her brain from nowhere. She lay stock still. No, don't be ridiculous, she told herself. She shut her eyes and willed herself to sleep.

* * *

Edwin usually found this part of the year unbearable. He was deeply frustrated about not being able to find out more about Quaile Woods' music, but agreed with Alex that they had to wait. If the police started investigating again, maybe more information about Morris's research would come out. Or maybe Robert would find out more from Norma.

The weather was windy and wet, but he and Alex went to a few really good concerts. And one day they both sneaked away and had a wonderful walk around Derwentwater, with tea at Watendlath.

He spent extra evenings practising with Tom Firth, whose voice was developing a rich powerful timbre despite his age. Tom, so gauche and non-committal in speech, was gifted in song.

And he visited Freddie several times. Each time, he got the impression that Freddie wanted to unburden himself about something. And he was also aware of the big man's pent-up power. Wanda would open the front door and look at Edwin as if he had emerged from under a stone; then she would take herself off upstairs from where he could hear the sound of her computer keyboard clacking. He knew she was working on some learned article.

He also found time to visit his solicitor friend and ask him about the convent. 'Oh, that's a well-known local mess,' his friend said genially. 'The nuns were a one-off order, totally independent. There were quite a few like that in the nineteenth century, most of them in the south of England. This order lasted longer than most because they mainly recruited local women and concentrated their efforts on the slums in Norbridge and the Fellside quarry workers and miners.'

'That's quite a geographical spread!'

'Before they had a car, they had a house in Chapterhouse where they would stay overnight, and put up the fallen women they rescued. But that was a little terraced place which was sold about twenty years ago. They had the deeds to that one. But they never had any deeds to the big convent. They claimed old Cleaverthorpe had given it to his daughter, but there's no record of it.'

'What do the Cleaverthorpes say?'

'Not much. Old Cleaverthorpe isn't very interested. Rumour has it that the Cleaverthorpes gave it to someone who held it on the nuns' behalf anyway. There was no need for title deeds because it was built by Cleaverthorpe on Cleaverthorpe land. On top of that, women weren't considered to be up to property owning, especially if they were supposed to be praying and doing good works!' The solicitor laughed. 'I wish my wife would try it instead of shopping. Anyway, the convent isn't worth much, especially if the local history people push for it to be listed and what-have-you, though I gather that's off the boil now. It would be much more desirable to developers if it could be demolished or rebuilt.'

'What would it take for that to happen?'

'Oh, if the neighbours found it was a hazard to them. Broken drains or falling masonry, that sort of thing. But there aren't any neighbours if I remember rightly. Oh, yes, that tatty bungalow on the hill. But I don't know who lives there.'

I do, Edwin thought. So that was David Johnstone's end game. Hadn't Alex said that Reg and Christine Prout had talked about a possible leisure development? It wasn't the bungalow David was after. That was just a sprat to catch a mackerel. He had really been after the convent.

'Thanks a lot,' Edwin said.

'No bother,' said his friend. 'And by the way, whatever happened to that lovely girlfriend of yours? Marilyn, wasn't it?'

'Don't ask,' Edwin said, and he meant it.

41

Such knowledge is too wonderful and excellent for me;
I cannot attain unto it.
Psalm 139:5

In the week before Mother's Day the weather did one of those sudden reverses which characterize early spring. Icy showers of hailstones swept into Norbridge like advancing Border reivers. In Tarnfield a sudden flurry of tiny snowflakes settled for an hour on the few hardy daffodils which were poking their heads above the earth.

For some reason Suzy felt she had to do a big clean-up at The Briars for Marilyn Frost's visit. She started the day before. As usual she had sent her mother a bouquet, and she tried to ignore Molly's messy attempts to paint her own card as a surprise, but Mother's Day was on her mind.

It should really be named Mothering Sunday, she thought, as Edwin had called it. It was the traditional break in Lent, when visits home were allowed for apprentices who were indentured away from their families. In some areas the mothers had baked large spicy Simnel cakes, with heavy marzipan icing and eleven marzipan balls around the edge, representing Jesus's disciples — without Judas, the baddie who betrayed Him. They hadn't been common in Manchester, but Suzy had seen them with delight in bakers in Carlisle and Norbridge.

'I don't know why I'm bothering!' she shouted to Robert as she hoovered round him. 'I'm treating Marilyn's visit like royalty!'

In Uplands Parish the children were always given tiny bouquets at church for Mothering Sunday. There were nearly a hundred children, and making up the little posies was time-consuming. Lynn usually did it along with one or two of the other mothers in the parish, but this year Chloe insisted on helping, torturing the flower stems and heaving sighs of quickly suppressed irritation when the flower heads fell off. Really, Lynn thought, it would have been quicker and more economical to do it herself! She had hoped that several hours spent together on the task would make Chloe chattier. There were times when she felt they almost got there. After Chloe had spoilt her fourth posy, there was a moment when Lynn felt her daughter would suddenly explode, but instead Chloe put her head down and started again, not with real commitment but with a sort of melodramatic meekness.

On Sunday morning, Edwin phoned his mother and then went to communion at the Abbey. His religious faith was so bound up in music and tradition that he was sometimes unsure if it was really there. Alex, he knew, was into church history and singing, but had no belief in God. That didn't matter, he thought. We all get there in our own time. Or God's time, anyway. And some of us were much, much faster than others.

He ate lunch by himself in a pub in Carlisle and then went to meet Marilyn from the train. For once it was early, and she was standing outside the station in the wintry sunshine. She was a little bit plumper, but she still looked very much as she had done the last time he had seen her. His heart didn't lurch, and though he felt slightly nervous of her, he couldn't have felt less romantic. Marilyn had a new, more confident, slightly earthy timbre to her voice and had acquired a flatter Midlands accent. She was oblivious of the stares she got, and strode over to meet him.

'Hi, Edwin,' she said, and kissed him on the cheek. 'The train got in ten minutes before time. Astonishing.'

She got into his car, and smiled at him. 'I'm staying in Keswick tonight and going to see the boys tomorrow morning. It's going to be a shock on both sides, I'm afraid. What time are we meeting your friends?'

'Three o'clock.'

'Oh, then can we go on a little tour on the way? I'd love you to drive through Chapterhouse. And could we go via Fellside? It would be great to see the place again. It's good to be back!'

He drove her over to Norbridge, hearing her exclaim at long forgotten landmarks. In the town, Marilyn even saw one or two people she thought she remembered — an elderly man walking a dog who was perhaps once her teacher, and a woman who looked like a neighbour. Marilyn was easy to talk to, Edwin thought, but not easy to reach. He suddenly missed the closer, more human contact that he had with Alex, with all her doubts and fears. They drove through the town, taking in the Chapterhouse estate, and then headed west to Fellside. The industrial village looked almost pretty in the clear sunshine, with the fells frosted with snow on the tops, and the occasional burst of daffodils. As they drove down the main street, he saw Rev Paul and Mark Wilson walking ahead of them with a group of kids and parishioners, on their way to St Luke's. He remembered Suzy saying there was a rock band practice that afternoon.

'Who are those people?' Marilyn asked.

'The trendy vicar at Fellside Fellowship and his coterie. Why d'you ask?'

'I thought I recognized someone, but I can't put my finger on it.'

The mind plays tricks on you when you revisit a place, Edwin thought. As they grew nearer to Tarnfield, Marilyn became chattier. She's bracing herself for this, Edwin thought. It can't be easy.

He bumped down the dirt lane towards The Briars and pulled up in front of the house. Marilyn opened the car door, sweeping up her long skirts.

'You don't need to help me out of the car,' she said. 'I'm getting used to it.'

Suzy heard the car as she came into the front room of The Briars.

'They're here, Rob,' she called. 'Will you open the door?'

Alex was already in the front room, her hand stretched to take the coffee that Suzy was offering. But Suzy had stopped, with the tray on a dangerous slant. She was looking out of the window at the visitors, transfixed.

'What is it?' Alex asked.

But Suzy just turned back to her, eyes huge with astonishment. They heard Robert, for once fazed, say, 'Oh! Well . . . er . . . do come in. I'll take your coat, Edwin. Go straight into the front room, er . . .'

Alex knew then that her mad idea had been right. She took a deep breath and got up to greet the famous Marilyn Frost. She knew she was the only one of them who was prepared for this.

'Hello, Sister,' she said.

* * *

Later that night, Suzy snuggled up to Robert. Their guests had stayed till late because there had been so much to discuss. And after they'd left, Jake had come home after a long rehearsal session, demanding to talk about the band. They were practising something special and exciting for Easter Sunday; Robert and Suzy would have to be there. Suzy caught Robert's glance. After what they had been discussing that afternoon, Jake's involvement with Fellside Fellowship was worrying.

'So what did you make of our new friend the nun?' Suzy asked Robert once they were alone in bed. 'Were you surprised?'

'Astonished! I would never have recognized her. Of course she was still beautiful, but with her hair under that veil, and having put on some weight, she looked very different.'

'She's not a full nun, is she?'

'No. She told us about that when you were making tea. She said she felt called when she was in her early twenties after Edwin started taking her to church. But these days the average age for postulants is about forty. Marilyn had to work for a further six or seven years before they'd even discuss it with her.'

'And what stage is she at now?'

'She's a novice. She wears the habit but she's not been accepted for life yet. They'll make her stay a novice for a few years because she's so young, relatively speaking, though she must be about thirty now. But she knows that this is her vocation.'

'How did she get into it?'

'The old Anglican sisters from Fellside had a mission in Chapterhouse. She'd known them all her life. Her mother was drifting into drugs and alcohol, and the nuns were her stability. She was always attracted to that life, but like most people she just wanted to be ordinary in her teens.'

'Poor Edwin.'

'Oh, I don't know. The Marilyn he loved was this ethereal, romantic creature he plucked from the depths of Chapterhouse. But the real woman is practical and oozes common sense. I really liked her.'

'Yes, she was certainly down to earth.' Suzy sighed. Marilyn had listened to their theories about the murder with a highly sceptical air. Her work in the convent in Derbyshire involved prison visiting and dealing with crim- inals, particularly those who had committed crimes against women. Though not alarmed by the conclusions that Robert, Suzy, Edwin and Alex had come to, she had asked searching questions.

So had Suzy. 'Why has it taken you so long to come back?' she'd asked.

'My family told me they wanted nothing to do with me. I'm a major embarrassment to them. They despise me for what I've done — you should hear my latest stepfather on the subject. He actually practically threatened me with grievous bodily harm if I came back to Norbridge! That's why Edwin has kept my secret.' She laughed. 'And it's also because if the boys thought there was any money to be got out of the order they'd be down there hanging round. It would be terrible.'

'But even so, why didn't you come back as soon as they were charged? Wouldn't that have been the Christian thing to do?'

'The order isn't like that,' Marilyn had said. 'We give ourselves up to a life of prayer and good works in the discipline of a Rule. Our Mother has to decide what I can and can't do, with input from me of course. If every sister buzzed off whenever there was an individual family crisis, there would be no order. Mothering Sunday is a good time to come because it's the break in our Lent observance. And anyway,' she added practically, 'I had no idea that the boys even wanted to see me. It could have been totally counterproductive.'

'So have we given you anything to go on now?' Alex had asked.

'Yes and no. I can't really buy into this theory about the Psalms. That's very far-fetched. And I know what the law would say about the missing psalter — that you're highly emotional people who are interested in music and you imagined it.'

'But Tom and I both saw it!' Alex had said.

'I'm sure you did, but there's no evidence. It's easy to have false memories. I've had a few today myself, thinking I recognized people in Norbridge. That won't wash, I'm afraid!'

'So what makes you think there's a case for the boys' innocence?' Robert had asked.

'The fact that Morris Little had a meeting arranged with Wanda Wisley, and she told you that he was planning to meet other people too. The prosecution service needs to know all that. Thank you.'

Put like that, it seemed that they had done everything they could. Suzy felt rather flat, although she enjoyed talking to Marilyn later about the order and the social work they did, especially in the prisons. Even before joining the convent Marilyn had done some amazing work, dealing with men who had deep psychological problems with females. But underneath the chat Suzy still wanted to talk about the murder. She was surprised by the strength of her own feeling. Wasn't she the one who was supposed to be traumatized by that series of deaths in Tarnfield? Unable to move on? Not anymore. She was drawn towards this and, despite everything, she was sure that the Psalms were involved. The bullocks and the pit and Morris's smashed teeth kept coming back to her. I feel it has to do with a chorister, she told herself. Someone who knows about singing and church music. A chorister at the Abbey.

'I'm still intrigued by the music connection,' Suzy said in bed to Robert's armpit. 'And the genealogy stuff. And Freddie and David having accidents at the convent.' He laughed and wriggled round towards her.

'Can't you sleep, Suzy? I'm shattered. Look, maybe if the police drop the case against the Frosts, they'll investigate further and it will become clear.'

'But how did Edwin feel about it all, do you think?'

'A bit disappointed, I suspect. I think that he'd been hoping the case would unearth something more substantial that would help in his work on Quaile Woods. But we should leave it to the legal system now. Let's forget it, Suzy.' He switched off the light and spooned into her. Soon she could hear his even breathing.

But she felt deeply unsatisfied.

* * *

At the bungalow, Alex sat at the kitchen table with a cup of hot milk and looked at the sleeping pill she had placed next to it. She had asked the doctor for just a few more tablets, in case. She felt she needed one tonight or she would never

314

sleep. Meeting Marilyn had been an amazing experience. This practical, pleasant woman with her brisk attitude was so far from the romantic creature of her imagination that she mocked herself for her own stupidity. Even when she had half-guessed that Marilyn might be in a religious order, she had imagined her as a sexual rival, a sort of Cumbrian Audrey Hepburn. Alex laughed at herself.

She hadn't spoken to Edwin since he left The Briars to take Marilyn to the sisters' house in Keswick, where she was staying. But she knew he would phone her. She felt as if she had been through some huge but understated crisis, a little valley of the shadow of death.

Because jealousy was like death. It killed feeling. You became evil and dead to reason. But in a moment of clarity Alex thought: it was nearly always a two-way thing. Sam and his girlfriend had contributed. She had been goaded by their smug self-righteousness and their flaunting of their luck. In a flash, she understood that her husband had needed the excitement. He had ended up stuck with a small child in a little house, aged fifty, with a drab woman he didn't love. But there had always been the drama of Sandy and her Bad Behaviour to bind them.

Edwin had been different. He had never used the issue of Marilyn to provoke. And he had persuaded Marilyn to come to Tarnfield so that Alex could see for herself. He could easily have turned her into a romantic mystery to keep Alex at bay, using Marilyn to protect himself. But he had introduced them as soon as possible. And Alex had seen that Marilyn was really a very normal woman, with no interest in preventing Edwin from living life to the full. Marilyn might be a saintly person, Alex thought, but Edwin is a good man too.

And I'm not jealous. She tried the feeling again. She even attempted to work herself up into loathing of Marilyn. But she really couldn't. It was a wonderful, heady, warm release from the black side of her own personality. She was tempted to say, Thank you, God, but of course she was an agnostic.

She sipped her milk, and stood up to put the sleeping pill down the sink. And through the window she saw that light again, up the hill on the left, at the convent. Forget it, she told herself. It's in someone else's hands now. All that is over. I can put Morris Little and the psalms of lament, the Johnstones and the convent, all out of my mind — and get on with my life.

42

Draw me out of the net that they have laid privily for me,
for thou art my strength.
Psalm 31:5

A few days later Edwin met Robert by chance in the canteen at the college. 'Any developments with the Frosts?' Robert asked.

'I don't know. Marilyn can't get to the phone all the time and from what I know of the order they'll want her to get her head down, doing what she's supposed to do. We are the World, you know, which is what she repudiates.'

'You don't look too repudiated!' Robert said. Edwin had that indefinable look of a happy person.

'Oh, I've been seeing a lot of Alex. We're going to another concert tonight, actually. And to be honest, I'm glad we're doing the Stainer on Good Friday. It gives us four extra days and it fits really well; Freddie will be a big hit, not to mention Tom, who's marvellous.'

'And what about your work?'

'Well, I'm still intrigued by the Quaile Woods psalms. It's infuriating to think some arbitrary thief might have taken the psalter with no idea of its importance to church musicians. And Morris could have put the original of the front page anywhere. You know what his filing system was like. It's probably under Z for Zany Church Music!'

'Well, I'm still going to see Norma as I said I would. I promised her I'd try and write something about Morris. So I'll have one last look.'

Robert had arranged to go and see Norma Little on Wednesday evening and, even though the impetus had gone, he was as good as his word. She let him into the hallway at the side of the shop, a dark little entrance smelling of crisps and groceries and some indefinable cleaning fluids. It was a big shop, so it had a large stockroom at the back full of all sorts of things from cases of wines and spirits to large packets of washing powder and toilet rolls.

He followed her upstairs to the crowded sitting room above the shop.

'How far have you got with Morris's research?' she asked anxiously. 'If we don't get something in the paper at around the time of this concert, everyone will forget him.'

'No, they won't,' Robert said reassuringly. 'But I'll try. Look, Norma, we think he might have been on to something really very interesting. But to prove it we need to find the page of a book — a long narrow book.' He outlined for her with his hands the traditional landscape shape of a psalter.

'Nah, never seen anything like that,' Norma said. 'Mind you, he kept things all over the place. He put his will in with the cigarettes.'

'What?'

'Yes, one of Morris's jokes. You know, Wills — used to be big cigarette manufacturers in Bristol. Morris was always having a bit of fun. We got some horror mags once and he stored them with the lacquer and conditioner. You know, hair-raising.'

Robert sighed. It sounded just like Morris, taking the mickey and being a nuisance, proving how clever he was even after death. He remembered Morris punning the last time they had spoken: '*Sax and drugs and rock and roll.*' If that was how Morris filed things, the original frontispiece of the psalter could be anywhere in the house.

He asked Norma to show him into the office again, and he spent an hour searching but with no luck. On the way out he promised her he would write something about Morris's theories on church music and send it to the *Cumberland News* as soon as possible.

'You will keep your eyes open, Norma?'

'Yes, I will. If I find any old book stuff I'll let you know.'

'One more thing. Can you think of any reason why Morris might have shared his research with David Johnstone, the estate agent?

Norma said firmly, 'None whatsoever. Morris couldn't stand the man. He said he was a greedy parasite.'

And that seemed conclusive enough, Robert thought as he drove home. They would never know how Johnstone got the photocopy of the frontispiece — unless he recovered and told them, which seemed increasingly unlikely. Robert would try to write something complimentary about Morris for the paper, including Stainer's connection with Quaile Woods, and also the lost psalter. It would be an adequate article, though essentially a rehash of old stuff. But at least it would be something in Morris's memory. For all the nasty things he had done, Morris had been a notable local historian. The Chorus owed it to him.

* * *

Towards the end of the week Edwin met the Principal of the college at a reception for a new Head of the Engineering Department. After the usual chit-chat, Edwin decided to take a risk.

'I wondered, do you remember seeing Dr Wisley just before Christmas? In the shopping mall in town? You were with your wife.'

'Why do you ask?'

Wanda had been off work a lot in the past few weeks. Edwin had been standing in for her and she'd been grateful in a reluctant way. She seemed to be constantly ill but she had been rather more approachable and Edwin had started to like her. He thought that he should try to get her alibi for the evening of Morris's death corroborated, especially if her planned meeting with Morris was going to be important to Marilyn's case and she was questioned officially.

'Oh,' Edwin tried to think of a plausible reason, 'Wanda thinks she mislaid some scores we'd been working on. They weren't important. She said she probably dropped them in the mall. But she can't remember which day it was, though she does remember seeing you.'

The Principal stroked his chin. 'Goodness, Edwin, that's three months ago. But I do remember because it was a very busy day. We saw Wanda near Figaro's on the Friday before Christmas. My wife had insisted on my coming out to help her choose a present for my mother. I wasn't too pleased about it because I had to dash back to the college for an important meeting.'

'So it would have been around six o'clock?'

'Oh, yes. I know that because I had to get back to see poor David Johnstone. We were meeting to discuss selling the sports fields, and he was the best estate agent in the county. Oh look, there's the Deputy Head of E-learning. Do excuse me . . .'

Edwin sipped his wine slowly. So David Johnstone, too, had been at the college that evening. That was certainly something new.

He met Robert, Suzy and Alex at The Briars after Chorus practice the Tuesday before Holy Week. When Edwin told them the latest development, Suzy stood up in irritation and grabbed the wine bottle she had opened earlier.

'Oh, this is getting too complicated. Have a drink, everybody.' She had worked an extra day shift at Tynedale TV and had come home frazzled. Once Molly was in bed she'd poured herself a generous glass of Merlot and was feeling uninhibited. 'I mean, what this boils down to is that

320

every man and his dog could have been at the college to meet Morris. Tom Firth, you, Alex—'

'I'm not a dog. Not anymore!'

'No, be serious. Paul Whinfell is supposed to have had a meeting with him, and no one knows where Freddie Fabrikant was. Now there's David Johnstone. All of them were choristers or musicians and might have been interested in a psalter. Why don't we go mad and suggest that Mark Wilson was there to do the accounts, and Chloe Clifford was enrolling for Hindustani night classes? Or perhaps Jenny Whinfell was there to give student counselling because she's so nice, ha ha. Or Neil Clifford was holding a seminar on devil worship? We're supposed to be refining this down, not expanding our theories to encompass all of Norbridge!'

'The Frosts' defence lawyers should check up on everyone in the college that night. Surely the security guards have a list of visitors?' Robert suggested.

'Apparently not,' said Edwin. 'The swipe card system had failed. It might have been one of the Frosts' preliminary acts of vandalism. The guard was just letting anyone in. He shouldn't have, of course, but it frequently happens.'

Suzy said, 'I still think it's weird. The Psalms are the clue. It's someone who's a singer, a chorister who knows the greatest songs in the Bible. The Psalms seem to have been written for choirs, for goodness' sake. Look at all those weird instructions. You know what I mean. *O clap your hands, tune up the trumpets*, that sort of rigmarole.' Suzy was waving her glass about dangerously. 'I've always said it was about religion.'

'Well, we can do nothing but wait, I suppose,' Robert said. 'And you never know, Norma Little might unearth something from under the bottles of bleach in the storeroom.'

'What, filed under whitewash, or down the pan?'

Robert laughed. 'I know it's frustrating, Suzy. But we really can't do anything.'

'Until something else happens to prove my point. This might not be over, you know.'

The others looked at her. The idea of another 'accident' had never occurred to them.

* * *

Pat Johnstone had downed four vodka tonics. The latest call from the hospital staff had said that David was comfortable but they needed to chat with her. She told them she would go over there the next day. She hadn't been for the last few nights. Her elder son had come up at the weekend to see his father and had had long, man-to-man conversations with the consultant which had left her feeling excluded. If they wanted her they could wait.

She had got things as organized as possible, for any eventuality. She had left a message on Alex Gibson's phone suggesting they talk soon about a price for the bungalow. The woman never seemed to be in these days. She'd also called the Prouts. Reg Prout was rattled, she knew that, because he worked for the council. He would know what David had planned. She chortled as it occurred to her that Prouty was probably in David's clutches, somehow or other. No wonder he was scared.

But not for long. David looked to be on his last legs. She wondered again about his will. She had no guarantee at all that he would have left her anything and she hugged herself in relief that she had found out about the bulging bank account in her name. If David snuffed it, she would get the cash, so there would be no need to press ahead with buying the bungalow.

Then again, David was clever. If he was on to something, she still wanted to be part of it. The bungalow was a step in the right direction. If David aimed to buy it, it had to be worth having for some reason.

She tried to watch telly but her favourite soaps seemed more boring than her own life. She had one more drink but felt stone cold sober. She thought about her new car. She had already taken advantage of David's illness in one little way. Seeing that he never treated her, she could spoil herself, couldn't she? A week ago she had traded in her family saloon for a deposit on a nippy little coupé. The trouble was that she had nowhere to go in it.

'I'm going out for a drive,' she said to the television. She changed into loose, dark trousers and flat shoes, and found a quilted jacket. She went outside to test the air. It wasn't too cold. She fetched her torch from the cupboard under the stairs, in case she needed to get out of the car; then she paused. It would do no harm to take the cocktail shaker with a nice mix of vodka tonic. The other drinks had hardly hit the sides. She filled up the shaker, adding a little bit of ice and lemon as a nice touch. Lovely!

She drove towards Fellside without thinking why. She didn't mind David shagging some old slag from the council estate there. She could even have used the information to get a nice comfy divorce settlement. The idea of his infidelity left her cold. But if he was onto something about property, she wanted to know. And that bungalow was part of it. Not to mention the convent, and that pit . . .

She drove aimlessly around the silent village where no one was venturing out. After ten o'clock the place was dead. For the sake of something to do, she parked by the derelict convent and smoked a couple of fags.

Then she saw a light. It was inside the building. It was dim, and she could only just make it out between the slats of the boarded-up windows. She took a gulp from the hip flask. The door of the new car opened so smoothly there was hardly any noise; she got out and stood up. The door clicked quietly closed. It was even nicer to smoke outside. The air was soft, and warmer than it had been for months. She took another swig and finished another ciggie. Then she saw the light in the convent again.

I've got my torch, she thought. I'll be all right. I know to avoid any holes in the ground! Perhaps I'm as smart as David — smarter even! She switched on the torch and started to walk towards the building when she saw there was a newly defined path round to the back. She followed it, slightly nervous about leaving the road behind but also rather excited. If people were working on the place out of hours, it would mean they'd stolen a march on David and she wanted to know what was going on.

As she moved towards the building, she tripped slightly. There was something catching around her ankle. She moved her other foot forward, but that was also fixed in something soft but catching. Nothing to worry about, she thought. Just a stumble. No pit! But then her feet wouldn't move. I'm tangled, she thought, as if I'm in a net. She tried to kick it away, but if anything the net tightened. She screamed and kicked, but her feet became even more constricted. Then she stumbled, her hands scrabbling in the earth. The torch had rolled away and she felt something jerk her knees from under her so that her face fell into the dried mud and gravel of the path. She couldn't scream for the dirt in her mouth. And then the blow from behind on the back of her head cut her cackling for ever.

43

I was glad when they said unto me:
We will go into the house of the Lord.
Psalm 122:1

Holy Week is a normal working week for most people in Britain until the bank holiday of Good Friday. But Maundy Thursday is also a religious day, as the anniversary of the Last Supper where Jesus commanded that His followers should eat bread and drink wine in remembrance of Him. 'Maundy' is a corruption of the Latin *mandatum* — a command. Jesus commanded that we should love one another.

Not much of that around, Suzy thought as she pored over the internet to find out more. In a tradition centuries old, the sovereign of England gave money on Maundy Thursday to male and female subjects, members of each sex both equal in number to the monarch's age. Kings in the past had washed the feet of the poor, and touched people to cure them of King's Evil or scrofula. It was also the day when the altars were stripped of the Lenten array and churches left bare, with crosses enshrouded in black or purple for Good Friday. Quite creepy, Suzy thought.

'I've never heard of anyone having scrofula these days,' Robert said when he came back from the last Chorus practice before the concert. Suzy had been at home, working on the computer, and had looked up Holy Week out of interest. 'Maybe it was just eczema. Anyway, I bet it would take more than the Queen's touch to cure it. Bring on the antibiotics, I say.'

'You sound cheerful. How was your practice?'

'Excellent. Freddie is huge in every way and Tom is absolutely superb. It's the top line which has problems. Two of the sopranos have gone away on holiday, though the Dixons cancelled their trip to stay and sing. It was good of them, but Millie hardly makes any difference. It's a good job we've got Alex. She's excellent.'

'So will I enjoy the concert, heathen that I am?'

'I think so.' Robert came over and kissed her. 'Any messages?'

'Oh yes, Norma Little phoned. You know what a gruff voice she's got. Something about a case of wine. She said you could pick it up on Thursday when she closes at eight o'clock. I didn't know you'd ordered any wine.'

'No, I didn't. Maybe it's a gift.' Robert's article, in truncated form, was due to be published in that week's *Cumberland News*. He had phoned Norma, who was thrilled.

'I got another funny message, though,' Suzy said. 'Look. You'll never guess who it's from — Jenny Whinfell!' She showed him a printed email. It was a short note addressed to *Hi, Suzy!* in a very chatty way, inviting her to *a new and totally innovative Anglican Women's Group* which was having its inaugural meeting on Thursday night. The message went on, *We really need people like you who have a different, exciting approach.*

'I don't know what's come over her,' Suzy said. 'Alex says she's been much pleasanter lately. And I'm rather flattered.'

'Even if her husband's a murderer?'

'Robert, we don't know that. You're the one who said we should stop thinking about it. Anyway, if he is, Jenny will need all the support she can get.'

'Who else has been invited?'

'Well, Lynn hasn't, which really surprised me. I phoned her earlier and probed a bit without giving too much away. I didn't want to be tactless. But then again, she's happy with being an ordinary Anglican woman, so she wouldn't need this!'

'What about Alex?'

'I can't get her. She was at the Chorus practice, and now she's probably gone out somewhere glamorous with Edwin.'

'Are you going to go?'

'Might as well. I'm all for women's things. Can you pour me a drink?'

Robert opened some wine and settled down beside her. 'I'm looking forward to Easter,' he said. 'First the concert on Good Friday, then we could have lunch out somewhere on Saturday. And we could go to the Lakes on Easter Sunday and come back for Jake's big band session!'

Suzy snuggled up to him full length on the sofa. 'Sounds good. Sort of normal. You know, maybe I was wrong about the Morris Little thing. Shades of the Tarnfield murders influencing my judgement, I expect.' She lapped her wine at a dangerous angle. Lying on the sofa, she could see a nasty crack in the ceiling.

'By the way,' she said, 'never mind Easter; this is really the time of the great Do-It-Yourself festival. Just watch the TV ads. They're even more frantic at the moment because the shops fear that DIY is dying out.'

'It certainly is in this house!'

'But The Briars is looking really sad. Do you think we should try and do something? Or is there no point if you want to sell?'

'I don't know.' Robert sipped his wine. 'I can't face the thought of getting the toolbox out after my abortive attempts on the garage door.'

Suzy laughed. Then the phone rang and, groaning, she staggered upright to answer it. 'Hi,' she said.

There was a long and tense pause. Her voice faltered. 'Oh, no . . .' She sank against the wall.

'What is it?' Robert said.

'It's Alex. She says Pat Johnstone has been found dead. In the quarry at Fellside. It looked like she was drunk and wandered over the edge. But Alex's sister says they found traces of something round her feet. Something like netting.'

* * *

On Wednesday night, Alex, Edwin, Suzy and Robert met more soberly at The Briars. The Bible study course had been cancelled because of Pat Johnstone's death.

'The police are treating this one as suspicious,' Alex told them. 'My sister Chris is devastated. She says it looked as if Pat had stumbled over the edge. She'd been there for days. But the net round her feet made them wonder.'

'But it's the Psalms again!' Suzy said. 'Robert looked in the Concordance and there are six references to catching people in nets in the Psalms. It's not the nice New Testament fishers-of-men nets thing. It's about snaring people like animals. We must tell someone.'

Edwin said, 'We have. I've given Marilyn all the information. I phoned tonight and insisted on talking to her. I think Pat was snooping around Fellside because David Johnstone was after Alex's bungalow, so that he could buy it and become a neighbour of the convent. Then he could complain that the old place was a danger to his property. That way he could force the ownership issue and get a quick sale before anyone could slap a preservation order on it. It was the convent he was after. But that deal's dead in the water now he's stuck in hospital and Pat's dead.'

'We've done all we can, Suzy,' Alex said, and put her hand over her friend's.

'But we must be able to do more!'

'Like what?' Robert asked.

'Oh, I don't know.' Suzy got up to make more coffee. 'I'm being silly, I expect. But it's so frustrating! By the way, Robert, have you spoken to Norma Little?'

'No, but I'll go and see her tomorrow if you and Alex are going to this new Anglican Women's thing. Are you?'

'Yes. I think we're both astonished at discovering that Jenny Whinfell is our new best friend.' Alex laughed.

'Has anyone else been invited?' Robert asked.

'I only know of Alex and me so far,' Suzy said. 'But there must be others. We've been asked to go to the vicarage at Fellside, though goodness knows how she'll fit us all in.'

Alex said, 'Life goes on. Look, I think we need to lighten up a bit tonight. Whatever happened to Pat may turn out to be an accident. She may have caught her feet in some agricultural garbage and tripped. It's awful, but it doesn't have to be so sinister. And there's nothing we can do about it. Let's have a glass of wine. And we can look forward to the Stainer concert on Friday and to Jake's performance at Fellside on Sunday as well!'

'Yes.' Suzy smiled for the first time that evening. 'My son the rock star!'

* * *

The following evening, Suzy drove to Fellside and parked at Alex's bungalow. They'd decided to meet in advance for moral support and walk down to the council estate together.

'I wonder what Jenny really wants. It will probably be the same old stuff. The church usually wants you to embroider hassocks or butter bridge rolls,' Suzy said.

'Or embroider bridge rolls and butter hassocks. That *would* be innovative.' Alex laughed.

'Any more news on Pat's death?' Suzy asked.

'No, although I gather David is very ill. Liver failure. My sister talked to his son. He says David must have been in a bad way before the accident. They tested him routinely for spleen rupture and found that his liver was already pretty far gone. A transplant's the only answer and quite honestly there probably won't be enough time. They've told him about Pat, which hasn't helped, but he had to know.'

329

They walked on together in silence. Fellside was deserted. A dog barked somewhere out on the hills. Suzy shivered. 'This might all be rather stupid. I like to go to church but I don't really know what I believe. I don't want to get too involved. Maybe we should turn back.'

'I'm an agnostic myself. But I like church too. And how often do you get the chance to meet innovative women round here?'

'True. OK. Let's keep on walking, then,' Suzy said half-heartedly.

'It could be interesting.'

'Or maybe provide material for a TV show, *Anglicans in Space*!'

Alex laughed. 'We only need to stay a few minutes, to be polite. Then we can go back to my place and have a drink.'

Suzy was about to agree, as they turned into the cul-de-sac where the Whinfells' vicarage was. But a small figure in droopy clothes hailed them before they could open the gate.

'Great! You've come,' said Chloe Clifford. 'We've got a much better venue now. Follow me!'

* * *

Robert and Edwin had decided to go and see Norma Little together. 'We can pick up the wine, say nice things about Morris, have a pint, and get home to find out what the innovative Anglican Women's Group was all about,' Robert said.

'Good thinking,' Edwin answered. He had volunteered to drive them over in case Norma insisted that Robert try the wine there and then. It was a bit of a mystery about why she'd decided to give him a present like that. She would obviously be pleased about the article in the *Cumberland News*, but her attitude previously had been that it was really Morris's due.

But Norma was delighted to see them both. 'Come in, come in,' she growled. 'Glad you got the message. Come upstairs; it's up there.'

Robert looked at Edwin and shrugged. But if Norma wanted to lug a case of wine upstairs, for them to lug it down again, that was up to her.

'Do you want a coffee while you look at it?' she said.

'Look at what?' Robert asked. 'I thought we were picking up some wine?'

'Wine? No! It's what I found . . .' Norma glanced at him strangely. 'Well, I thought you'd be more chuffed. Here it is anyway.' She pushed an old plastic carrier bag at Robert. He looked at her questioningly.

She said crossly, 'I don't know what you mean about wine! I phoned you to tell you I'd found what it was what you wanted me to search for! Old paper. There's loads of stuff in there. Photocopies! You were right thinking Morris had stored it somewhere funny. I found it under the last case of German white. I think it's because it's stuff from the old convent.'

'German white? Do you mean wine? Blue Nun?' Edwin couldn't keep the amusement out of his voice.

'Yes, well, that was Morris's joke,' Norma said defensively. 'And it's funny that you should be the one to pick it up, Mr Armstrong. What with your girlfriend and all . . .'

'What do you mean?'

'Well, Morris knew all about Marilyn Frost being a nun. He went round to her step-dad to complain about the boys' thieving. Of course he got no joy on that but he stayed talking, and found out about her. There wasn't much Morris couldn't get out of people with the help of a few cases of free beer!'

'Oh,' Edwin said quietly. 'But it doesn't matter now. I don't think Marilyn's vocation is a secret any more. She's been back to Norbridge recently to see her brothers.' So that's how Morris found out where Marilyn was. That's another link in the chain, he thought. Did Norma know her husband used his knowledge to be a low-grade blackmailer? Probably not, he thought. Poor, spiteful, petty-minded Morris. And anyway, all that was over now. There were bigger things to think about. Robert was pushing the bag of papers at him, saying nothing.

Edwin took one look at them, and then he needed to sit down. In his hand he held a bag full of what he suspected was historical dynamite.

* * *

'Just follow me,' Chloe said. 'It's only a short walk away.' Her voice had changed. It was charged with excitement.

'But where are we going, Chloe?' Suzy said sharply.

'It's all right. The others arrived earlier. Mum's already there. And Jenny. It's going to be good. Look, we turn down here, round the back of the council offices, and across the road and in through this gate.'

'I thought Lynn wasn't involved,' Suzy said.

'Oh yes,' said Chloe. 'She's really keen. Jenny contacted her at the last minute.'

Suzy and Alex exchanged glances. Then Suzy shrugged. If Lynn was there, the meeting might be conventional but it would certainly be properly organized.

'This is the back door to the convent,' Alex said. 'It must be.'

'That's right!' Chloe said. 'You'd think everyone would know about it. Come in!'

She smiled, with a sort of innocent enthusiasm that transformed her face. 'It's OK,' she said. 'The group's been working on this for a few weeks. It's all fine. We've got the Bishop's approval and everything.'

She opened the door, which was cut into the wall. Instead of leading up into the garden as they expected, it went straight underneath the grounds. Ahead of them, a strip of neon lighting illuminated a bright, white, cellar-like room with stairs at the end. Alex looked at Suzy.

'I'm not sure this is for me,' she said. 'I'm a bit claustrophobic.'

'Oh please!' Chloe said. 'Everyone will be so disappointed if you two don't come.'

She smiled again, and Suzy thought: she's really only a child. This is likely to be silly, but if it helps, I'll go in. Maybe official work really had started on repairing the convent. She stepped forward. I'm a mum too, she thought, and I'd do anything to help bring Lynn and her daughter closer. Maybe being an Innovative Anglican Woman would do it for Chloe.

Alex waited a second, took a deep breath and followed her.

'Great!' Chloe said again, and shut the door behind them. 'Follow me. It's lovely upstairs.' She almost skipped ahead of them.

'Go on,' Alex said. Suzy followed Chloe up to the main building.

She was right: the convent was beautiful. The hall was large and square with a lavish mosaic floor and a big oak staircase rising up under a domed ceiling with a fine stained glass lantern. How could anyone want to demolish this? Alex thought. David Johnstone must have been mad. Or so greedy he couldn't see how fabulous it was. However weird the meeting would turn out to be, it was a privilege to be inside the convent.

'Look at this,' she whispered to Suzy. 'Gorgeous, isn't it!'

Suzy nodded. She had already smelt the faint acrid smell of incense. Chloe was behind them now, urging them towards a wide polished oak door.

'In there,' she said, and for an awful moment Suzy thought she heard a note of glee in the girl's voice.

* * *

Edwin had to blow his nose. I think he might be going to cry, Robert thought.

'Look at it!' he said. 'It's wonderful!'

'But it will fade, Edwin. These photocopies made on flimsy fax paper always do.'

They had made their excuses and left Norma's as quickly as possible. Edwin had wanted to look at the photocopies at his cottage, where he had Anglepoise lamps, a keyboard and a better quality photocopier. His copies of copies would have to be reductions but they'd be better than nothing.

In the carrier bag there were letters, documents and scraps of music. All had been copied on curly paper on Morris's old fax machine. They were already starting to fade slightly.

Now at his desk, Edwin was overwhelmed by the find. There was another copy of the original of the front page of Quaile Woods' psalter. There were letters from John Stainer, pieces of music the two men had worked on together, and more correspondence. But there was no full psalter.

While Edwin pored over the musical stuff, Robert looked at the letters. There was one which transfixed him. It was nothing to do with Stainer or music. It was a short note to Quaile Woods from Lord Cleaverthorpe. And it referred to his gift of the convent to Quaile Woods on behalf of the sisters of Fellside.

Rustling through the other documents, Robert found what looked like a rough draft of a will. In it, Cecil Quaile Woods had left all his worldly goods to his son, who was unnamed.

So that was it, Robert thought. Morris had found proof that the old convent had been given to the sisters' chaplain, presumably on their behalf. And then in his old age Cecil Quaile Woods had acknowledged that he had a son in his will. But the only evidence of the son's identity was that handwritten extra dedication on the title page of his psalter. He had written in his copperplate writing *and my son Henry Whinfell*. It was as if the priest had gone so far towards confessing — and then pulled back. Maybe in the full will he had been more explicit. But without that, it was only the psalter dedication that provided the missing link.

And if Quaile Woods had left everything to his son, and his son was Henry Whinfell, then would Whinfell's descendants be entitled to the convent? Is that what Morris had been about to tell people? Using his tatty photocopies?

At the back of his mind Robert had been wondering why a dedicated local historian like Morris would tear out a page from an original Victorian book. But now he understood. Morris used the fax copier because it would take long documents; these were the wrong shape to reproduce exactly on a modern compact machine that would only take A4 paper. But if he had wanted to photocopy the psalter's title page in a hurry, the only way to feed it into his machine would have been to remove it. Robert was willing to bet that Morris had intended to restore the page lovingly to the psalter once he had used the photocopy to prove his point. Maybe he had felt that taking the original of the title page over to the college was too great a risk.

So how had David Johnstone got hold of it? And where were the originals now? In fact, where were the originals of all these documents?

'Look at this, Edwin . . .'

But Edwin was absorbed by a scrap of paper with a particularly interesting setting of the Nunc Dimittis scrawled on it. Was it by Stainer or by Quaile Woods? If the two worked together that closely, was it possible that Quaile Woods had even contributed to *The Crucifixion*? Stainer had condemned his own work later as too populist. Was it possible that Quaile Woods, with his simple faith and his terrible remorse over an illegitimate child, was the real inspiration behind the moving, accessible oratorio? Edwin's head was spinning. But he needed the originals.

Robert put the documents carefully to one side while he went on probing in the bag to make sure there was nothing they'd missed. Loose at the bottom was a set of big unwieldy keys. To the convent? he wondered. Morris must have got them from the nuns, or Lord Cleaverthorpe, perhaps in his role of local historian. He must have been able to come and go pretty freely in order to find all this stuff.

Then the phone rang.

'Bugger,' said Edwin. 'Just when we don't want to be interrupted.' He reached for it and Robert heard him say, 'What?' Edwin put his hand over the mouthpiece and turned to him. 'It's Neil. He says David Johnstone died this afternoon. And Neil wants to talk to us tonight. He says it doesn't matter how late it is — he'll be a while getting back from the hospital.'

'We should go over there and see him,' Robert said. 'But look at this . . .'

Robert was just starting to tell him about the documents when there was a tremendous banging at Edwin's door. Edwin got up and went downstairs. He opened the front door of the cottage and looked at the hooded creature in front of him.

44

*Yea, even mine own familiar friend, whom I trusted,
who did also eat of my bread, hath laid great wait for me.*
Psalm 42:9

Alex and Suzy went in through the oak doors; they both gasped. They were in the convent's original chapel. It was rectangular with a few oak pews, and ahead of them was a cast iron grille with a door beyond to the left. The altar was behind the grille. The walls were covered with beautiful linenfold panelling and the floor yet again was in mosaics of all different colours. Above them, a vaulted ceiling was painted blue with golden stars and silver moons.

'Sit down,' Chloe said, shutting the oak doors behind her.

'It's fabulous,' Alex breathed.

'Yes,' said Suzy. 'But there's no one else here. Where's Lynn, Chloe?' Suzy knew her voice sounded slightly shrill. This wasn't right.

'Just a little white lie, like about the Bishop,' Chloe said softly. 'Mum isn't here. But Jenny is. Look!'

Suddenly, music from a CD player filled the chapel. It was some sort of plainsong, and after a moment Suzy recognized it as Psalm 22, traditionally sung on Maundy Thursday while the altar was stripped. Now it was sung in a girlish voice. I bet that's a recording of Chloe, she thought. And then from the left, a small figure in a long white vestment came from the left-hand door. She was followed by a much larger figure, hooded and in white, who immediately turned to the altar.

'Oh God,' said Alex. 'This is downright creepy.'

'Shush,' said Chloe. She went past them to the side aisle where she too slipped a white hooded cassock alb over her head.

'Who's the man?' Suzy said.

'It's Paul. It must be, because the woman is Jenny Whinfell.'

The three people, the large one flanked by the two smaller ones, genuflected, and the two women turned to face Alex and Suzy.

* * *

'What is it, Tom?'

The boy stood there in his fleecy parka jacket, hood still up, swaying slightly, and looking awkward. 'I feel like a right plonker now.'

'That doesn't matter. What do you want to tell us? Look, Mr Clark and I are really busy. Is this important?'

'I don't know!' Tom growled.

'Tom,' Robert said, 'sit down, just here on the sofa. Would you like a cup of tea or coffee?'

'Nah. I'm OK.'

'So tell us why you're here. You've got a big day tomorrow with the concert. You should be practising and resting, surely!'

'But that's it!' Tom spluttered. 'I couldn't rest. I'm all on edge. This concert is the biggest thing that's ever happened to me. Almost . . .' he added, in loyalty to Poppy.

'So why did you come to see Mr Armstrong? Is it a problem with the music?'

'Nah!' Tom said, contemptuously. 'Of course not! No, it's Chloe. She's my girlfriend's best mate and I promised Pops that I'd keep an eye on her. When I couldn't settle tonight — that's excitement, *not* nerves—' he said sternly to Edwin, 'I decided to go up to Fellside. You see, it's Maundy Thursday.'

'Yes, Tom, we know that,' said Robert patiently.

'Well, it's obvious.' Tom was resuming his usual pitying tone to adults. 'Chloe was at Fellside on Ash Wednesday with a big dirty smear on her head. Ash! I looked it up on the internet. They do that sometimes at communion services, but not round here. So I thought there must be something funny going on. And then I thought, maybe she'd be lurking around Fellside tonight too, Maundy Thursday, because there might be more weird services going on up there. And I was right.'

'What do you mean, Tom?' Robert said softly.

'I saw Chloe coming in and out of the convent by a door down on the Workhaven Road. A couple of other people went in. One was that nice woman.'

'Which nice woman?'

'You know! Miss Gibson. And another woman. I couldn't see properly who it was. They went in after Chloe. And then someone came round and locked that door after them. A man . . .'

Edwin looked at Robert. 'The Anglican Innovative Women's Group!'

'But at the convent?'

'Yes!' Tom was shouting now. 'I'm telling you there's something funny going on there!'

'But it's all boarded up,' Edwin said. 'We can't get in.'

In answer, Robert held up the keys from the bottom of Morris Little's carrier bag.

'I think we can,' he said.

* * *

'Welcome,' the man said sonorously. The plainsong chant filled the chapel and the smell of incense wafted towards them. Alex was looking faint. Claustrophobia, Suzy thought. She tried to make her voice sound normal, conversational, which was hard against the wailing plainsong. But this crazy pseudo-churchy environment was all wrong. She stood up.

'Turn that music off!' she called. 'This isn't a service. What on earth is going on here?' She heard Chloe's horrified gasp, which gave her more confidence. 'Are we supposed to be having communion? Do you really have permission to be here?'

'You should be seated,' the man in the robes said in his chanting voice, his arms raised, facing the altar.

Suzy fought the atmosphere. 'This is a travesty. What are you doing?'

Jenny Whinfell came down to stand at her side. 'You're supposed to be reverent,' she hissed. 'We're the New Puseyites for the twenty-first century. Now is the time for a new discipline and an end to the decadence of the Western world. We're starting a new religious order. It's a brilliant idea. It's for women to be both in the world and under the Rule. We identified you both as unhappy and unfulfilled women. We were too, Chloe and I. Now we have something to live for. I will be a good wife, and Chloe will be a virgin bride!'

'That's right,' Chloe said. 'It's wonderful.'

'And how long have you been involved in this, Chloe? Doing up the convent?'

'Three months,' Chloe said. 'Since December.'

So that explained it, Suzy thought. She felt anger like a red tide. This man was a religious maniac. He must be obsessed. Religion was so often the spur to madness; she had seen it before. But in his case it was also linked to greed. This man was taking advantage of women at their weakest. But she wasn't going to be one of them. She wondered what was in the chalice he had placed on the altar? Just alcohol? Or something designed to help lull their responses?

Still standing, Suzy said calmly, 'This is all rubbish, Jenny and Chloe. I can see the attraction. But you're wrong. A religious order isn't a place to hide. Quite the opposite. Real orders are much tougher than this nonsense.'

She thought of Marilyn and her down-to-earth practical help for the needy from all classes of society. Those sisters were women who knew the world as well as anyone who was living in it, swamped by the day-to-day. They had the faith which meant they were prepared to face the worst criminals and hate the sin not the sinner. Jenny and Chloe's dressing-up act seemed pathetic by comparison.

Suzy felt her brain gearing up. She needed time to think but she also needed to act. Somewhere in all this, she suddenly knew that Marilyn had the key. Marilyn had said she had seen someone she remembered in Fellside, someone she couldn't quite place. And Marilyn worked with men who had committed crimes against women. Not just rape, but men who robbed old ladies or took advantage of teenagers. And where was she based? Derby. In the Midlands. Who else had told Suzy he was from the Midlands?

'I know who you are,' Suzy said to the big man in the hood. 'And you're a shabby con man.'

Jenny Whinfell made a noise between a scream and a shout of outrage.

* * *

Robert hurried towards the car, with Edwin and Tom behind him. 'Just what did you see, Tom?'

'I told you. Chloe came across the road with two women. One was Miss Gibson. Chloe opened the door to the convent cellars with a key. I could see beyond her to where the underground rooms were, all painted up white. They went in and then a man in a hooded jacket came.'

'Where did he go then?'

'He went in after them and slammed the door.'

'But it's just an old building, Tom. He might simply have been closing the door after them. Why were you so spooked?'

'You don't understand. He was all dressed in black with a red scarf round his face and a hood. I heard him locking the door from the inside. It's the only way into the convent, and the door creaked and I heard the bolts thud. It was like a horror film. And now they're in there with him.'

'Were there any other people?'

'Chloe and this man. And Miss Gibson and the other woman. They were the only ones I saw . . .'

'It doesn't sound like a normal church group meeting,' Robert said. 'I think we should call Neil Clifford and ask him to meet us there. He can tell us about David Johnstone later. But right now I think we might need the services of a real priest to find out what this is all about.'

'Bloody right,' said Edwin, and started to accelerate through the darkness of the deep-set country lanes towards Fellside.

* * *

'Are we supposed to fall at your feet and take part in some ludicrous pseudo-service?' Suzy was shouting.

Chloe looked edgy. Her eyes flickered from Suzy to the man in the hood.

'So that's it, is it?' she called out. 'For goodness' sake, Chloe, how stupid do you think we are?'

Pretty stupid was the answer, she thought. She and Alex had been marked out. The pathetically grateful single parent and the middle-aged drunk, along with the confused teenager and the mother suffering post-natal depression.

'Jenny, listen to me,' she shouted. 'Jesus died to take away our sins, not our brains! Religious orders are a good thing. But not for adolescents, and women just months after childbirth. You were at your most vulnerable. Think about it! You might wish to be weak, but we don't. You've picked the wrong people. We're going now,' she said.

'No! Don't go!' Chloe sounded desperate. 'You must take communion!'

Suzy felt a new reserve of courage. She wasn't going to let this cheap crook make fools of herself and her friend any longer. Or Chloe. Or even Jenny. He was sick, she was sure, and dangerous too, but she wouldn't let him win.

'How much money have you given him, Jenny? Where's your student loan been going, Chloe?'

'He's our chaplain,' Chloe said.

'Oh, bollocks. He's not even ordained,' Suzy said. 'I know who he is.'

Suzy walked towards the altar; then she stopped. She needed to get the man away from his position of power at the east end of the chapel. He needed to be brought into the body of the church and made to talk.

'Face me!' she yelled at the hooded figure. 'Face me, Mark!'

Mark Wilson spun round and his hood tumbled off.

'Oh God!' Alex said, gasping and wheezing for breath. 'I need to get out. Suzy, I can't take this.' She began to stumble towards the door.

Wilson calmly watched her. 'It's all right,' he said. 'She can't leave. The cellar door is locked and bolted.'

'What's this all really about, Mark?' Suzy shouted, keeping a row of pews between her and Mark Wilson's robed figure. She noticed that his cassock was crudely stitched, Chloe's handiwork no doubt, and that his stole was a red velvet scarf. 'How many people have you attacked to keep this crazy scam to yourself? Morris Little? Freddie Fabrikant? David Johnstone? Pat?'

For the first time, Wilson looked at her properly. 'Not Morris,' he said in his normal voice. 'Just the others.'

Jenny Whinfell gasped. 'Mark!' she said in horror.

Almost casually, Wilson lashed out with his left hand and caught her on the side of the face. He didn't even look at her. Then as she staggered, he kicked her expertly several times with a flick of his foot and she went sprawling into the nave, where she lay still. Chloe watched him, her face blank at first but then registering confusion. She still thinks he's right, Suzy thought. Chloe has been brainwashed. But she has to realize . . .

Casually, Mark Wilson strolled towards Suzy.

'Seeing you want to spoil our Maundy Thursday service and go straight to the homily, I'll tell you. I didn't kill Morris Little. But I knew he was going to spill the beans about who could inherit the convent. He called the Fellowship before Christmas to ask Paul to meet him. I took the message. He told me it was about this place. I already had my eye on it, so I went to the meeting instead of Paul, easy-peasy. Paul had told me all about his genealogical searches. He couldn't talk to his stupid wife. She was too wrapped up in herself, until I got to her and made her see the light, selfish bitch!'

He kicked Jenny again, in passing. Chloe gasped. Now crouching on the floor, Jenny Whinfell whimpered.

'So who killed Morris?'

Wilson laughed. 'Not me! Someone else. I bet you'd like to know who! He met Morris first in the corridor. No one else was there and Morris told him all about how he'd discovered who really owned the convent. Morris showed him a photocopy of something. He said it proved Quaile Woods had a son and that his descendant should be the rightful owner! Your murderer asked if Morris had told anyone else and the fool sniggered and said, no, not yet. Your man went berserk. I saw him thwack Morris on the head with a handy bit of timber before taking the photocopy and legging it. Then I came out of the Music Department office and gave Morris an extra smash in the teeth — Psalm 58 — for his interference, and took the psalter just in case.'

'Who was it, Mark? Who killed Morris?'

'Wouldn't you like to know? I needed to get rid of him too, of course. But God took care of that for me. I just bided my time and he came to me. Psalm 55. And the other nosy bastard too. Psalm 22 again — a good 'un. Bingo!'

'So what are you going to do now, Mark?' Suzy said almost conversationally. In the corner of her eye she could see, as Mark confidently walked down the nave to talk to her, that Chloe was behind him.

'Oh, that's easy!' Wilson suddenly thrust out his left hand and took a burning candle from a tall candlestick at the side. 'I'm going to deal with you and your tubby mate for a start. I know you've been onto me . . .'

Oh God, Alex thought as she gasped for breath by the locked door. Of course, Edwin had told Chloe all about their research and Chloe must have told Mark.

Wilson said, 'You should know your Psalms, Mrs Spencer. Oops, sorry — Ms, isn't it? Such a pity a lonely old cow like you didn't join the order. It would have done you the world of good! We might even have had a little one-to-one study! Now listen. Do you know this one? Psalm 39: *My heart was hot within me and while I was thus musing, the fire kindled* . . . Good one, eh? When the chapel burns down, and you lot in it, I'll be the man who nearly, but not quite, got you out. I'll be a hero round here and made for life. You'll burn — and all this stuff too.'

From the deep pockets of his robe Wilson took out a sheaf of documents. Suzy could see letters, pieces of music, and the Quaile Woods psalter, plus a loose leaf which was the original title page and dedication.

'They were all here, locked in a drawer upstairs. They'll all be purified in the fire.' Wilson laughed. He waved the candle madly.

Suzy took a deep breath. And she found herself praying with a pure, deep, desperate fierceness she had never experienced before. Dear God, she said, please, please let Chloe give me eye contact. She could be my own child. Please save her. Anyone could be used and abused by a man like Wilson. Just let me have one glance from Chloe . . .

She looked at Chloe and the girl looked back. And Suzy nodded.

With one movement Chloe brought the candlestick down into Wilson's shoulders and he fell to the floor.

45

Therefore shall every good man sing of thy praise without ceasing;
O my God, I will give thanks unto thee for ever.
Psalm 30:13

The front door of the convent opened and the night air rushed in, cold on the clothes of the men. Alex was bent double by the door, desperate for breath, but as the clear atmosphere filled the chapel she felt herself straighten.

'Edwin,' she said, and he held her closely to him.

Suzy staggered to the front pew and put her arms round Chloe. 'You were wonderful, Chloe. It's over now.' Chloe looked up and her face cleared. Suzy let her go and she ran towards the back of the chapel.

'Dad!' she called, and Neil Clifford held out his arms to her.

'Is he OK?' Alex came over and looked at the supine Wilson.

'I think so. She got him between the shoulder blades, but the real damage was done when he hit his head on the front pew. Edwin should tie up his hands with that red velvet scarf thing.'

'He seemed to be using them as stoles. Trophies as part of the vestments. Ugh!'

'Every woman in the district had one of those things from McCrea's,' Suzy said. She walked over to Robert, who was helping Jenny Whinfell.

'He's told us a lot, Robert,' she said. 'But not everything. The psalter is here. Plus other documents, the originals. Is Jenny OK?'

Alex and Robert were supporting her. Jenny Whinfell looked wild-eyed and bruised. 'Where's Paul?' she asked, before she passed out.

* * *

Good Friday dawned, the penultimate day of Lent. Suzy and Chloe had spent much of the night at the police station before being allowed home. Then Chloe was taken off by her parents. Jenny Whinfell was in hospital.

Wilson, though that was not his real name, was in custody, but the police hinted to Suzy that he might be unfit to plead. His criminal record included robbing and attacking elderly women and at one stage seriously assaulting a Roman Catholic priest. He had been a Catholic altar boy in his youth. He wasn't an accountant, and he had been in prison for fraud and deception, where his religious obsession had developed — along with his housebreaking skills. He had been on prescription drugs for depression, some of which he had been feeding to his two female followers in their 'communion wine'.

From the police hints, and from Neil and Lynn who spent hours overnight talking to their daughter, Robert and Suzy pieced together the jigsaw. When David Johnstone knew he was dying he had wanted to confess, openly. He told Neil and the police that he had attacked Morris in a fit of rage at the college. They had met by chance in the corridor and Morris had taunted him, flapping his photocopy of Quaile

347

Woods' handwritten dedication, saying he knew who the real owner of the convent might be, and that it would soon be out of his clutches. The taunting was enough to make the alcoholic and irascible Johnstone see red.

And all the time Wilson had been listening round the corner in the Music Department, where Morris had planned to meet Paul — on his way to what he hoped would be a conclusive encounter with Wanda Wisley, music expert. She would, Morris believed, confirm that the psalter was genuine and that Quaile Woods was an important musician.

Wilson was maddened to think that the convent, which appealed to him on some deep subconscious level, might go to the man he already thought of as a rival — Paul Whinfell. That would ruin the scam he already had in mind. But only Morris could supply the missing link between Quaile Woods and Paul Whinfell, through the dedication and the draft will! Once Morris was dead, Mark thought he was safe from any claim of Paul's. He still had to deal with other people who were after the convent like David Johnstone and Freddie. But once they were out of the way, he hoped that he could run a real religious order, centred on himself. There seemed an endless supply of silly, needy women in the world.

By chance, he had been carrying a CD of carols after a Fellside Fellowship Christmas lunch, and had put it on a computer in the empty office. Then he had set about beating Morris's jaw with the length of wood to fit in with his own mad idea of righteousness as he interpreted Psalm 58. When the Frosts coincidentally fused the lights, Mark had waited, and watched Alex and Tom find the body. When they had gone, he had stolen the psalter just in case there was any other evidence in it, and left through the Music Department entrance, flinging the wood where the Frosts found it.

At some point during one of his many visits to the convent, Mark Wilson had found the original documents which Morris had photocopied. Morris, with the respect of the local historian, had taken his photocopies and replaced the originals in the locked drawer of the vestment wardrobe where they had been left by Quaile Woods over a century earlier. Poor Quaile Woods had obviously never summoned the courage to give the psalter to his son!

Later, Wilson had let the bullocks out of a shed to chase Freddie when he started to snoop around, after Freddie had betrayed that he had overheard Mark and Chloe in the Abbey talking of virgins. The attack on Freddie had been unplanned, but prompted by Jenny's explanation of Psalm 22. But that had given Wilson more ideas. He had trapped both David and Pat Johnstone with the defences based on the Psalms, which he boasted about creating around the convent.

Suzy and Robert arrived home in the early hours of Good Friday morning; then they stayed up talking all night with Edwin and Alex. Between them, they found things slowly fitted into place.

'And the Stainer concert?' Suzy had asked as dawn rose.

'It goes ahead,' Edwin said firmly. 'There is no way I'm scrapping the concert or missing being there, after all this work.'

'Hey! That's great!' Alex touched him on the arm, and he turned and kissed her.

* * *

On Good Friday evening, weak from lack of sleep, Suzy sat in the congregation at the Abbey. Above her the vaulted ceiling soared, and in front of her the stark wooden altar symbolized the bleakness of a world which for three days believed God to be dead. But I don't, Suzy thought to herself. Not anymore. When she had felt that only she herself could bring about the triumph of good over evil, she had prayed with a desperation she didn't know was possible. And she knew that something had happened in reply. Alex, and Robert, and even Chloe, might think it was her own strength of character which had made Chloe meet her eyes. But Suzy knew it was something more.

She waited for the organist to come in and the choir to take their seats. Edwin was on a high, she knew. But he was still worried about his soprano line.

And then as the choir filed in she saw them. Three very buxom, large, fair-haired women aged forty-plus, taking their places on the front row. They were ushered to their seats by a tottering but walking Freddie Fabrikant.

Die Jungfrauen, Suzy realized. So that was what Freddie had been so pent up about! He had brought his backing group to sing *The Crucifixion*!

The music swelled with Tom's amazingly confident yet poignant tenor solo leading to Freddie's answering bass, and then the melodic chorus where Freddie's Virgins took up the words with pure, strong voices. *Jesu, Lord Jesu, bowed in bitter anguish and bearing all the evil we have done . . .*

Suzy felt the tears of relief prickle behind her eyes. Despite everything, the concert was beautiful. And as it progressed, it seemed to be completely uplifting. When the choir reached the famous *God so loved the world*, Suzy felt an overwhelming sense of peace. Surely she too could face the world now, with more strength than ever? Last night, her actions had saved other people — with help from some agency beyond mere humanity.

She would never think of herself as vulnerable again. At last, she had moved on.

46

Let everything that hath breath praise the Lord.
Psalm 150:6

On Easter Saturday, Paul Whinfell got his little boy out of the cot and played with him before changing and dressing him. It was true, as Jenny had said, that it was something he hadn't done too much of. But she hadn't given him much chance. Jenny herself had become completely proprietorial about Joseph after deciding to give up work. It was as if she had to prove she was the perfect mother, just as she had proved she was a great teacher and a potentially able deputy head.

Paul had spent much of the night in turmoil. Jenny was still in hospital with severe shock, plus bruising and lacerations from Wilson's kicking. But as well as that, Paul now realized that his wife had been suffering from serious post-natal depression. He should have guessed. Success as a career woman meant nothing when it came to having a baby, except perhaps that you tortured yourself with impossible standards. And became very lonely. That was why Wilson had been able to get to her.

And Paul was still shocked about that himself. How could he have been so stupid and blind? He consoled himself with the fact that the police had said to him several times that Wilson was an accomplished con man with a predilection for the Church.

But what did this mean for his faith? Paul had prayed in the night with a new urgency. He wanted Jenny to be well again and Joseph to be OK. He wanted it to be like it had been, before Mark had come along and wormed his way into their lives.

'Come on, son, eat it up,' he said, spooning slushy cereal into Joseph's tight little mouth. The baby spat it out and said something which sounded to Paul like 'Mummy'. This was going to be tough, he thought. But his Big Idea was still there. And in the night, his prayers had told him that he was still Rev Paul of Fellside Fellowship, and he had to go on.

But a phrase Jenny had used came back to him: 'the beauty of holiness'. Wilson was mad of course, but a germ of his thinking had taken root somewhere in Jenny's mind and she was a very intelligent woman. Maybe there was room for more than one way of worship at Fellside? Maybe the St Luke's side should reassert itself again? Perhaps he could start services with a few more traditional elements. Matins maybe, and evensong. Jenny could take those services, because you didn't need to be ordained. That was the brilliant thing about the Church of England. With just a little bit of effort you could suit everyone.

And it all fitted with the big idea. He had wanted to persuade Jenny to become a reader or a deacon first, and then ultimately a priest. There was no reason at all why Fellside Fellowship at St Luke's shouldn't be a job-share. He would need to persuade the Bishop and it would take time. But it was worth a try. After all, his useless obsession with genealogy had meant he was practically doing that with the charlatan Wilson. How much better to do it with his own wife!

And he would forget the Whinfells and Quaile Woods and the past. He had learnt the hard way that it was *now* that mattered.

* * *

Lynn and Neil Clifford had a sleepless night too, the second on the run. Chloe had been questioned by the police at length, but when Wilson had been examined it was clear that his principal injury had come from hitting his head on the pew. And Suzy Spencer and Alex Gibson had both explained that Wilson was threatening to set them alight before Chloe took action.

'You were so brave!' Lynn said.

'I was so *stupid*!' Chloe replied angrily. 'But no one told me that people who go to church and do all the right things could be con men like that. What was I supposed to think? Neither of you were that bothered anyway . . .'

'That's not true, Chloe,' Lynn said. 'We had no idea either. Mark Wilson was utterly plausible.'

'You're supposed to be my *parents*!' Chloe said accusingly.

'Take one of these tablets, sweetheart. You need to rest. It will all seem better when you wake up.'

Like a child, Chloe had allowed herself to be put to bed and had slowly drifted into sleep. The doctor called again while she was dead to the world, and looked down at her. 'They're terrifically resilient at that age,' he said. 'And Chloe has come out of this with her self-respect restored, if what I hear is true. She averted a major tragedy.'

Thanks to Suzy Spencer, Lynn thought gratefully. When the doctor had gone, Lynn sat by her daughter's bed. Since the nightmare of Maundy Thursday, she had not had a single hot flush. Could a major horror drive out a minor one? Would they come back? Or was the misery of the menopause finally over?

She leant forward and stroked her daughter's head.

'It's hard for me, Chloe,' she whispered. 'I never had a mother and sometimes I thought I was the only person in the world who felt such extreme devotion. I would have cut my arms and legs off for you. Yet at the same time you could drive me mad. But I guess everyone is like that. I just didn't know and I was frightened of it. But I love you so much, Chloe. And from now on, I know that mother love means standing up *to* you as well as standing up *for* you. But we'll sort things out as we go along.'

Her daughter's eyes shot open.

'Bloody right we will,' she said grumpily. But she grasped her mother's hand. The old Chloe was back.

* * *

On Easter Saturday, Robert and Suzy had their last meeting with Alex and Edwin to discuss the case.

'So it's wrapped up,' Edwin said, drinking his coffee at the kitchen table at The Briars. 'But there are a couple of other things we've got to report on!'

'Wait till you hear this,' Alex added.

'Wanda Wisley called me this morning,' Edwin went on.

'To congratulate you on last night's Stainer concert and to thank you for making Freddie a local star?' Suzy asked.

'Wanda? You must be joking. No, she was far more involved with her own situation.' Edwin laughed. 'Actually, it looks as if I might be head of department after all, for a little while anyway. Wanda's tummy bug has turned out to be rather long-term. She's pregnant!'

'And Freddie's now striding round like a prize stallion,' Alex added. 'His legs are better as if by magic! We called on them on the way here.'

'Hey! Let's open a bottle of champagne!' Robert said.

'And there's more,' Edwin went on. 'One of my mates from Durham University was in the audience last night and he thinks Tom might be able to get in there to read music next year. It means changing his courses and taking extra tuition, but I think his dad might see the light now, after the concert. Tom really was wonderful. And he'll be near Poppy in Newcastle.'

'And,' Suzy said, raising her glass, 'it's two years to the day since I met the gorgeous widower Robert Clark. I have to say, it's been the most incredible two years of my life!'

* * *

On Easter Sunday, Suzy went to church with Robert. She wanted to say thank you and to rest her body and soul in the familiar words and music. As she was leaving the church the vicar, Linda Finch, stopped her.

'How are you, Suzy? I heard about it all . . .'

'I'm fine, Linda. Quite a dramatic week, though. Look, I'd like to talk to you sometime soon. I think I'd like to get a bit more involved at All Saints.'

'That would be great. Call me!'

Suzy and Robert walked slowly back to The Briars. Molly ran ahead of them with her friend. It was a soft, blue April morning. In the pure fresh sunlight, the sandstone of the house glowed, but as they walked up the lane, Suzy could see the peeling paint and the sad splits in the woodwork.

'The old house certainly needs a makeover,' Robert said.

He made mugs of coffee for them both and they sat outside on the garden bench. The daffodils were all out, and a few tulips lolled at the edge of the flower beds. Jake had been in bed when they left but he was up now, wearing disreputable jeans and a horribly scruffy shirt. He came into the garden carrying a screaming Molly upside down, the racket ruining the peace.

'Can we get our Easter eggs now?' he said truculently. He was half aware of what had been happening over the last few days but, like Chloe, he was entering that phase when his real interest focused on himself. He would be sixteen this year, Suzy thought with a slight shock. He was half child, half man, and suddenly the child was uppermost, racing round the garden, pushing Molly over on the damp grass so Suzy knew there would be green marks all over her daughter's new mauve jeans. They searched frantically for the eggs.

'Found it!' Jake said in a voice that still astonished her by its depth. 'Thanks.'

He stood awkwardly in front of them. 'I've heard from Dad,' he said. 'He's not coming for us next week.'

'Oh,' said Suzy neutrally.

'I think he's got a new girlfriend.'

'Well, that's Dad for you.' Her hand found Robert's. 'That will be fun for him.'

'You are coming tonight, aren't you?' Jake asked, with just a trace of anxiety.

'To the surprise session of the Fellside Big Band? Yes, of course, if Paul's still doing it!' Suzy said.

'It's still going ahead. Definitely. Mark Wilson wasn't that good, and a lot of work has gone into it. And there are guest stars . . .'

'This wouldn't be Freddie Fabrikant and *Die Jungfrauen* by any chance?' Robert asked.

'How did you know?' Jake looked impressed. 'But you will be there, Mum, won't you? And I know it's not your thing, but you'll come too, won't you, Robert?' Molly had come to stand by her brother, aware of the minor drama. Robert looked at the expectant faces of his family.

'Of course I'll be there, Jake.'

The boy grinned and lolloped away, his sister behind him squawking about her Easter eggs.

'Thanks,' Suzy said, putting her head on his shoulder. 'I know it means a lot to him.'

She looked round the big, untidy garden. 'Robert, this is the children's home now. It's not just an emergency measure anymore. I want to stay at The Briars. And we could use my money to do it up. Properly, I mean. Make it ours. And theirs.' She nodded at the two figures walking up the path, one tall and ungainly, the other skipping and waving her arms.

'Are you sure, Suzy? I once said I would go wherever you wanted to go!'

'I want to be here. With you.' She paused. 'Robert, will you marry me?'

He stared at her, deadpan. 'So it's all right if you ask me, is it?' he said. 'I'm not sure.' She looked back at him for a moment of exquisite doubt, and then he started to laugh.

'I'll give you a whole night to persuade me!'

EPILOGUE

Six months later, an old but impressive Land Rover stopped outside the Whinfells' cramped vicarage. A small, bespectacled, elderly man in the front passenger seat got out to reveal a worn waxed jacket and green wellies. He walked up to the house, flourishing a sturdy walking stick, and rang the doorbell.

Jenny answered.

'Is the Reverend Paul Whinfell at home? It's Lord Cleaverthorpe.'

Astonished, Jenny ushered him in. He sat in their living room, refused a coffee, chucked Joseph under the chin and said, 'It's this business of the convent. It's always been a bugger, y'know. I gave that local history chap the keys but I never realized what he'd found out. I've looked at all the documents and so have my lawyers. And it's a mess.'

'Well, I've put it out of my mind.' Paul smiled, at ease. 'One or two people said I might have a claim but we decided it wasn't worth pursuing.'

'Yes, well, even so, something's got to be done with the damn place. No one really knows what's going on with it. My ancestor certainly gave it to this Quaile Woods fella, but it's clear that it was intended for the order. The last nuns handed it over to the diocese although technically it wasn't theirs to dispose of. But anyway, I went to see the Bishop about it, a few days ago, and we came to an arrangement. If it suits you . . .'

'Me?'

'Yes. We came to a decision between us. You can have the place, as long as you agree to open the chapel. It's not that big, y'know. Make a good house for children on the ground floor, and you can have rooms or a retreat or what-have-you upstairs. You talk to the Bishop about that. The council are filling in the quarry to make a lake, so it'll be quite pretty out there, and I'm prepared to put some money into doing the place up, seeing as you're family.'

Paul gulped. Then he shook his head. 'But you're mistaken. I'm not family. There's no conclusive evidence that I'm descended from Quaile Woods. And even if I were, that doesn't make me a Cleaverthorpe.'

The old man laughed. 'Genealogy? Load of bunkum. If you were a real North Country lad you'd know you can't trust birth certificates. You never know which dogs got over the wall. But family secrets, now then, that's different!'

'I'm sorry?'

'Never mind your dirty Victorian vicars. You should have taken a closer look at the women.'

'The women?'

'The only sure breeding line. We in the aristocracy know all about that. You have to keep tabs on your women!' He sniggered. 'You were too obsessed with the male line! You should have listened to the locals, sonny. It's a well-known Fellside fact that your great-great-great-granny was the by-blow of the first, greatest Lord Cleaverthorpe. You won't find it on any websites, but it's true. Believe me.

'You're family all right. Nothing to do with Quaile Woods. You've got your great-great-great-grandmama Harriet Whinfell to thank for it. Or Harriet Cleaverthorpe, as she would have been known if the old goat had only played fair and married her mother! So the convent's yours, if you want it!'

THE END

NOTES

The Psalms

The Book of Psalms is a collection of religious poetry from ancient Israel, forming part of the Hebrew Bible (to Christians, the Old Testament). The collection of 150 psalms was compiled over many centuries, bringing together several earlier collections, and reaching its present form probably between 400 and 300 BC. Psalms were composed to be sung to music, though we can have no idea what that music sounded like.

They are sometimes called the Psalms of David. King David was ruling Israel about 1000 BC. He was a noted singer and musician, and no doubt contributed psalms to the collection, but many refer to events after his time. For example, some psalms glorify the temple at Jerusalem (Zion) which was built by David's son Solomon. Others were written during the exile from Judah to Babylon in the 6th century BC — *By the waters of Babylon, there we sat down and wept when we remembered Zion* (Psalm 137:1). About half the psalms have headings which attribute them to David, often linking them to events in his life as recorded in the Bible in the books of Samuel, but these headings were probably added by a later hand. 'A psalm of David' could mean that it is about him, or about later kings in the dynasty he founded, or written in his style — or that David himself might have written it.

Most psalms can be put into one of two categories: happy and sad. In the Hebrew Bible the whole collection is called 'The Book of Praises'. The happy psalms extol God for his work in creation and in the history of Israel. Some of them glory in Mount Zion, God's holy dwelling-place in Jerusalem, and in the divinely appointed kings who have been endowed by God with the ability to govern with god-like righteousness. Some give thanks for God's blessings on individuals as well as on the community as a whole.

But about a third of the collection are psalms of lament for the plight of the individual. Many seem to have been written for specific problems, especially cases of illness, injustice and persecution. The heading of Psalm 102 sums up many of them: *A prayer of the afflicted, when he is faint and pours out his complaint before the Lord.*

These psalms often follow a consistent pattern. First, there is an invocation to the Lord: *Give ear to my words, O Lord; give heed to my groaning* (5:1). Then there is a description of the distress, sometimes questioning God's apparent inaction: *O Lord, heal me, for my bones are troubled* (6:3); *Why dost thou stand afar off, O Lord?* (10:1). Sometimes there is a protestation of innocence, or a confession: *I walk in faithfulness. I do not sit with false men* (26:3–4); *For I know my transgressions, and my sin is ever before me* (51:3). Then comes a petition to God for deliverance, and sometimes for vengeance on enemies: *Turn, O Lord, save my life* (6:4); *As they have waited for my life, so recompense them for their crime* (56:6–7). The typical lament closes with an expression of confidence, and a vow to praise God: *The Lord has heard my supplication; the Lord accepts my prayer* (6:9).

Many of these psalms seem to have been composed for use by the sick, containing much about specific physical maladies. Medical resources in ancient Israel were primitive. The only course of action was to seek healing from God; indeed, other methods would have been regarded with suspicion. A sick person would be seen by others as having been singled out for God's special punishment, so friends would blame and ostracize the individual.

In all psalms about sickness, the subject's enemies are never out of his mind. Psalm 41 seems to be spoken from the sickbed, but the speaker's main preoccupation is not with the illness itself but with the reactions of three groups of people: his old enemies look forward maliciously to his death; curious visitors go away and spread stories to blacken his reputation; and even *my bosom friend in whom I trusted* just walks out. The threat from enemies features in about thirty-six psalms. The victim feels alone and impotent, making no effort at self-defence.

The people of ancient Israel understood the whole of life, in all its detail, as being directed and controlled by God. If he is to be praised for His blessings, then it is hard to avoid blaming Him for life's evils. In the modern world, the poetry of the Psalms still gives expression to the despair and bewilderment of people trying to make sense of a confusing and hostile world.

* * *

Quotations from the Psalms in *The Chorister at the Abbey* are taken from the Book of Common Prayer. This version is still widely used in worship and so is the most familiar one for many Anglicans and Episcopalians. The translation was made by Miles Coverdale, who had been commissioned in the reign of Henry VIII to translate the whole Bible into English. Coverdale's was a 'second-hand' translation, based not on documents in the original Hebrew (for the Old Testament) and Greek (New Testament), but on available Latin and German translations.

His first Bible was printed in 1535. It was later nick-named the Bugs Bible because of Psalm *91:5: Thou shalt not nede to be afrayde for eny bugges by night* . . . Coverdale produced a revised version for the Great Bible published in 1539, correcting 'bugs' to 'terror'. This was the Bible placed in all English churches. The Psalms from the Great Bible are the version still in the Prayer Book. Later translations, whether in the Authorized Version ('King James') or modern editions of the Bible, have been based on the original Hebrew, and show that Coverdale's work was occasionally inaccurate and inconsistent. Verse numbering is sometimes slightly different: there was no division into verses in his first translation.

(Quotations in these notes are from The Revised Standard Version of the Bible.)

Sir John Stainer (1840–1901)

Stainer was brought up in Southwark, south London, son of a schoolmaster who taught him to play the organ. He was a chorister at St Paul's Cathedral from 1847 to 1855 and was allowed to play the magnificent organ there; he sang at the Duke of Wellington's funeral. In 1856 he was appointed organist at Tenbury College in Worcestershire. In 1860, Stainer went to Magdalen College, Oxford, as organist; the University had already awarded him the degree of Bachelor of Music before he became a student there. At Oxford, he met and married Eliza Cecil in 1865. The following year, he became a University examiner in music.

He returned to St Paul's Cathedral in 1872 as organist, and remained there for sixteen years. This was a period when, partly because of the influence of the Oxford Movement (the 'Puseyites'), there was a lot of interest in improving the standard of worship in the Church of England. The music was a major aspect of this movement. During his time at St Paul's, Stainer worked hard to raise the standard of music in the Cathedral. He also became a government inspector with the job of improving the standard of musical education throughout the country, especially in training colleges, and he examined thousands of students.

Stainer suffered from deteriorating eyesight, and this led him to resign from St Paul's in 1888, the year he was knighted. The next year, with his eyesight improving, he went back to Oxford as Professor of Music. He was a regular worshipper at St Cross Church, where he became a church-warden. In 1901, he and his wife were on holiday in Italy when he was suddenly taken ill, and died. He was buried at St Cross Church.

Sir John Stainer was a prolific composer of church music: anthems, cantatas, hymn tunes and settings of services. His hymn tunes — over 150 of them — include 'Love divine, all loves excelling', 'Gracious Spirit, Holy Ghost' and 'Lord Jesus think on me'. Two of his best-known tunes — 'Come thou long expected Jesus' and 'All for Jesus' — are included in *The Crucifixion*, which is today the piece for which Stainer is best known. He composed it while at St Paul's; it was first performed in February 1887 at St Marylebone Church, London. Part of its attraction is that it suits a parish church choir and organ, with the congregation joining in the hymns.

Though Stainer travelled around the country, raising musical standards and examining students, he had no special connection with north-west England or any clergyman in that area. Cecil Quaile Woods is an entirely fictional character.

ACKNOWLEDGEMENTS

I would like to thank my friend Lesley Beames for reading the manuscript in its initial stages, and my friend Victoria Kingston for her advice. As with everyone who helped me and whom I mention in these acknowledgements, they bear no responsibility for any errors, which must all be ascribed to me.

Peter Elman was a fount of knowledge on family history and internet genealogy, and I am indebted to him not only for his support and interest, but for checking on the procedures covered in the book and with help in making the plot work.

I found Susan Mumm's book *Stolen Daughters, Virgin Mothers: Anglican Sisterhoods in Victorian Britain*, published by Leicester University Press, extremely useful and also a very good read which I can highly recommend. Sister Margaret of the Convent of the Holy Name in Derby gave invaluable assistance on the life of an Anglican sister.

My knowledge and enjoyment of choral music has been boosted by all my friends in Bart's Choir, including Dr Caroline Evans who patiently answered questions about fractured skulls and liver failure while we practised Berlioz and Rachmaninov. Thank you!

The Reverend Michael Learmouth and his wife Bridget of St Andrew's Church, Thornhill Square, Islington provided their support as always. Errors in the portrayal of Anglican procedure in this book are solely mine, though I hope they are few and far between.

Clare Scott of Orton Grange Farm Shop and café not only provided me with a Cumbrian venue to launch my first book in the series, *The Flower Arranger at All Saints*, but she also helped me on some agricultural details.

Roland Jones, solicitor of our parish, helped on the intricacies of property ownership.

I would like to thank my daughter Alex for her patience and interest, and her fiancé Peter Brooks for at least initially inspiring me to write about a young man — though Tom Firth turned out to be a very different character from Pete, as always happens in books!

Finally I would like to thank Richard for all his encouragement and support. Now a churchwarden, he still found time to help me with *The Chorister at the Abbey*, and to sing bass with Bart's Choir, and to guide me through the Psalms of David. But Morris Little, who also sang bass and knew his psalms in this book, is certainly not based on Richard who is so good, you couldn't make him up!

FREE KINDLE BOOKS

DO YOU LOVE FREE AND BARGAIN BOOKS?

Do you love mysteries, historical fiction and romance? Join thousands of readers enjoying great books through our mailing list. You'll get new releases and great deals every week from one of the UK's leading independent publishers.

Join today, and you'll get your first bargain book this month!

Click here to start getting lovely book deals!

Follow us on Facebook, Twitter and Instagram

@joffebooks

Thank you for reading this book.

If you enjoyed it please leave feedback on Amazon or Goodreads, and if there is anything we missed or you have a question about, then please get in touch. The author and publishing team appreciate your feedback and time reading this book.

We're very grateful to eagle-eyed readers who take the time to contact us. Please send any errors you find to corrections@joffebooks.com. We'll get them fixed ASAP.

Printed in Great Britain
by Amazon